THE
BLOOD
ROYAL

Also by Barbara Cleverly

The Joe Sandilands murder mysteries

The Last Kashmiri Rose
Ragtime in Simla
The Damascened Blade
The Palace Tiger
The Bee's Kiss
Tug of War
Folly du Jour
Strange Images of Death

The Laetitia Talbot mysteries

The Tomb of Zeus
Bright Hair about the Bone
A Darker God

THE BLOOD ROYAL

A Joe Sandilands Murder Mystery

BARBARA CLEVERLY

Constable • London

Constable & Robinson Ltd
55–56 Russell Square
London WC1B 4HP
www.constablerobinson.com

First published in the UK by Constable,
an imprint of Constable & Robinson, 2011

First US edition published by SohoConstable,
an imprint of Soho Press, 2011

Soho Press, Inc.
853 Broadway
New York, NY 10003
www.sohopress.com

A copy of the British Library Cataloguing in Publication
Data is available from the British Library

UK ISBN: 978-1-84901-996-5

US ISBN: 978-1-5694-7987-2
US Library of Congress number: 2011018007

Printed and bound in the UK

1 3 5 7 9 10 8 6 4 2

MIX
Paper from
responsible sources
FSC® C018575

For Steve

Prologue

London, 1920

'Are you sure this is the place, cabby? It looks rather grand . . .'

'St Katharine's Square, number one, guv'nor, just like you said. They're all grand in this neck of the woods. This *is* a Royal Borough, sir. But if you don't fancy it, we can always move on.'

'No. Wait here. I'm in no hurry.'

The passenger in naval uniform peered again through the gloom of an October evening, taking in the magnificence of the four-storey mansion.

'Well *I* may be in a hurry,' the cab driver objected. 'Fog's coming up.'

'A pea-souper, eh? I've been away for years. I've forgotten what they look like.'

'Pea-souper nothing! This one's going to be a brown Windsor, judging by the smell of it. Straight up off the river. It's to be hoped they've got the acetylene flares alight round Trafalgar Square or I'll never get you back to the station, guv.'

The Navy man was barely listening, all his attention on the stuccoed, balconied façade. Electric lights penetrated the growing darkness, offering a welcoming orange glow behind drawn curtains. In the upper floors, lamps or candles were moving between rooms as staff came off or went on duty.

1

'Well at least there's someone at home,' he said, awkwardly throwing a conversational pebble into the silence ponding between him and the young woman by his side.

She made no reply.

He took her hand and gave it a brief encouraging squeeze. 'Nearly there, Miss Petrovna. Three thousand miles and three years – but you've made it!' He spoke with a cheerfulness he couldn't feel.

Sensitive as he'd become to his companion's moods, the captain interpreted the barely audible response as a mew of distress and his resolve began to crack. He had avoided saying farewell – he was embarrassed by emotional leave-takings, especially those made in public – and there was nothing more to add.

Even so, he launched into one last speech. 'Look, Miss ... um, Anna ... there's still time to change your mind. You don't have to do this yet. Come home with me.' After the slightest pause, he resumed: 'My wife would make you very welcome. Joan is a fine woman – she'd care for you. Get you properly on your feet. Our family doctor is no slouch and he'd rally round, I know. It needn't be for long. Just as long as you choose.'

She turned reproachful eyes on him and shook her head in regret.

The captain realized with a shock that he'd experienced the same devastating rejection years before. How many? Well over twenty ... He'd been no more than a boy in short trousers. He'd been tramping the moors with his father when they'd come across an injured otter. A very young female. His indulgent old pa had allowed him to carry the animal home in his jacket. He'd cared for her, fed her, watched her grow strong and mischievous. And always closing his ears to the concerned parental advice: 'Wild creatures, otters. Never think you can house-train 'em. Taking little things, of course, but you shouldn't get fond of 'em.'

The day came when she escaped from her pen and wrecked his mother's kitchen.

He hadn't waited for his parents to tell him his duty. It was clear. He'd taken her back into the wild himself, choosing a spot where he knew the fishing was good and there was a thriving otter colony. On the river bank he whispered goodbye, never really thinking she would leave him.

Pain had gathered and lodged in his young throat like a ball of india-rubber, threatening to suffocate him, as he watched her leap with delight into the water, dive, surface, dive again, swimming away from him. He'd turned, swiping at the tears in his eyes with the sleeve of his rough sweater, and begun to blunder back home across the meadow.

A piercing chirp had made him stop and turn and there she was behind him, on the bank again, wet fur comically spiked, staring at him with intelligent black eyes. Black eyes he could have sworn were asking where on earth he thought *he* was sloping off to. The moment he started back towards her, calling her name, she turned, yipped in satisfaction and dived into the water.

He never saw her again.

In a busy and danger-filled life, he'd scarcely thought about her until this moment of parting raised the same choking pain.

'Very well. Message received, cabby! Look, wait here with the young lady, will you, while I go and announce us. I'll be a few minutes.'

The door was opened by a butler as he approached.

'Captain Swinburne? Good evening, sir. Her Highness is expecting you. Will you come up to the drawing room?'

He followed the butler down the spacious hallway and up the stairs. They made towards an open door through which filtered smoky, autumnal music – a Chopin nocturne, he thought. When they entered, the pianist abandoned her piece and came smiling to greet him. A striking-looking Russian woman in her fifties, dark hair streaked with grey, she made a reassuring impression on him: friendly and . . .

3

yes, he would have said – motherly. Somehow, he hadn't expected motherly. Or small.

Sherry was offered and politely refused. He declined to take a seat by the fire. Facing him across the rug in front of the fireplace, the princess came straight to the point. 'You have her, Captain? Our Anna?'

'Miss Petrovna is waiting in the taxi, Your Highness, and eager to see you. I wanted to have a word with you in private before I leave her in your hands.'

She listened intently as he moved through his account. He confirmed that the girl had been found close to death on the doorstep of the British consul in Murmansk in northern Russia. On recovering sufficiently, she had begged to be given a passage to Britain where she knew members of her family were living. The consul had wired Swinburne aboard his ship, which was patrolling the Arctic waters, and he'd agreed to take her on board and bring her back to Portsmouth where he was due to call in for a refit in the autumn.

He was quite certain that none of this was fresh news to the Russian lady but she listened intently to every word, seeming to value his first-hand report.

He told her how pleased the ship's doctor had been with the patient's progress. The best food the galley could provide, fresh air, exercise and the stimulation of a late summer's cruise along the coast of Norway had almost restored her to full physical health. The captain was careful to explain that the ship had been conveying back home a consular family who had gladly lent one of their maids as nurse cum chaperone so all the proprieties had been observed.

The Russian acknowledged this with a tilt of the head and an understanding smile.

But it was the girl's mental state that he needed to lay out for her future guardian. 'She has suffered unbelievable hardship ... torture would not be too strong a word ... and three years of unremitting squalor. Anyone less strong

4

and tenacious of life would not have survived. But it will be some time before she's fully recovered. It's possible that the services of an alienist might be called upon with advantage.' A radical suggestion, but the princess seemed not to be offended. She even nodded in acceptance and Swinburne felt emboldened to press his point. 'There are physicians in London with certain skills acquired in the war . . . Anna's condition is in some ways similar to what I have witnessed in men experiencing the prolonged terrors of the battlefield. And, survivor that she is, she deserves the appropriate treatment. I would like you to be aware of this. I will not leave her in any situation that I do not judge to be capable of responding to her condition.'

He knew he was going too far. His stewardship was officially at an end; he had to recognize the superior authority of the noble lady to whom he was daring to dish out advice and demands. But Captain Swinburne was not a man to retreat from a position he'd taken up, whether his feet were on the deck of a gunboat or on a silken rug in a douce London drawing room.

She looked up at him sharply, scanning his weather-beaten features and standing firm before the challenge in his very English blue eyes. He steeled himself to receive the set-down he'd merited.

But the princess's response when it came was thoughtful. 'Captain, it occurs to me that losing *your* support could constitute yet another blow to Anna's well-being.'

'I did what I could. Believe me, ma'am, it was her choice to break the bond we have established.' The words stretched between them, vibrating with a resentment he had not intended. He hurried to add: 'But an encouraging sign, I'm sure you'll agree. She's ready to move forward. She recognizes now that she has a future and I do believe she is making plans for it.' He broke off, unwilling to say more, and indicated that he was ready to bring her in.

As he turned to leave the room, Swinburne's attention was caught by a photograph, the one at the forefront of a cluster of silver-framed portraits arranged on the grand piano. He exclaimed and went to examine more closely a group of five or six earnest-looking young women dressed in nurse's uniform, a flutter of angels gathered in a semi-formal pose around a bed in a hospital ward. The wounded soldier at the centre of their attention looked suitably overawed.

'There she is! That's Anna! Good Lord. She actually *was* a nurse. So much she didn't tell me . . .' Responding to the invitation in the Russian's expression, he smiled, his eyes returning to the photograph. 'One of my crew was careless enough to cut his leg to the bone on a day when our doctor was ashore in Trondheim. They brought him to me, dripping blood and swooning, and Anna, who was with me on deck, snapped out of her torpid state and had the chap sedated, stitched up and bandaged with all the skill of a medic in no time. Saved the leg, I reckon.'

The princess chuckled. 'She was always a fine needle-woman. But none of these girls was truly a nurse, you know. Amateurs all, some more capable than others. Some with decorative merit only. You're looking, Captain, at the contents of the topmost drawer of the Russian aristocracy doing their bit in wartime for their country. The Empress Alexandra herself led by example and floated through the wards in cape and wimple dispensing comfort. Though I ought not to disparage their efforts – they meant well, and, in Anna's case, acquired a genuine skill, they say. But, Captain . . . you do well to pick her out amongst so many beauties, all wearing an unflattering starched headdress . . . ?'

The question was lightly put but Swinburne picked up an underlying tension. Was he being quizzed in some way? Had the photograph, prominently placed as it was, been set there deliberately as some kind of test? The captain was a straightforward man, who couldn't be doing with traps and subtleties. His reply came at once.

'Be assured ma'am, I'd know her face anywhere. It's the line of the nose, like a Greek statue, and the dark eyebrows – they have the sweep of a gull's wing. She's the one on the far left. I'd no idea this was her world.'

The princess, who had been tugging at the pearls at her throat in some suspense, sighed with relief at his identification and stopped her fidgeting. She came to stand at his side, looking at the photograph with him, relaxed now and companionable. Whatever test she'd just administered, he seemed to have passed it. 'Yes, Captain, that is indeed our Anna. My poor cousin Peter's daughter. I held her in my arms the day she was born.'

He was pleased to note in her voice the tremble of an emotion she could no longer hold back, the tears gathering in her eyes, the furtive hunting in her sleeve for a handkerchief. She accepted the crisp square of linen he offered and put it to use with grace and murmured thanks. After a moment, she spoke again more brightly. 'As a child, Anna spent many summers with us in the Crimea . . . she will feel at home here with me now. But I share your dismay at a world so abruptly and tragically torn from us. Anna would have made a good marriage. She could have had her pick of the finest young men of Europe. Probably not royalty but a count at the very least . . . a duke perhaps? Sadly now all dead or dispersed and she herself ruined beyond any hope of—'

She suppressed the alarming thought and her tone became crisp. 'But that is all past, and we must look, as you say, to her future. You may leave her with us in total confidence. I have heard your words and understood the deeper concerns on which you are tactfully silent. I say again – I will provide the care she needs.'

Swinburne had heard the same tone from admirals and generals. There was only one acceptable answer: 'Yes, sir. Of course, sir.' This tiny, decisive woman he had no knowledge of and no reason to trust had, unaccountably, got under his defences. He nodded his superfluous agreement. 'Yes, ma'am. Of course, ma'am,' he said, and he smiled as he spoke.

Swinburne bowed and made to leave.

'Wait, Captain!' She hesitated for a moment, then picked up the photograph and handed it to him. 'If you will keep it for your eyes alone you may have this – some slight reward for your care. But be discreet. We aristocrats all have a price on our heads still and are pursued. London is full of ruthless men, not a few of them our enemies.'

As he took it from her, murmuring his thanks, he caught a flash of indulgence and pity in her eyes. She'd guessed his secret in minutes. Time he was gone.

The two women ran into each other's arms, exclaiming softly in delighted recognition. Swinburne skirted silently round them in the hallway, glad enough to hear:

'Aunt Tizzi!'

'Anna, my dear girl! At last! We have you safe.'

In the outburst of tears and sobs that followed, they didn't hear him leaving.

He was blameless. As innocent as the obliging bird that gobbles down the inky, sweet berry of the deadly nightshade and then flies off unwittingly to disperse the seed, Captain Swinburne had just dropped off a deadly cargo in a fertile corner of London.

He prepared to move on.

'We're finished here, cabby. Back to Piccadilly while you can still see the road.'

He shouldn't have looked back.

A last glance through the window showed him Anna. She'd come outside again and was standing motionless, neither waving away nor beckoning back, watching him leave. The fog was coming down and he couldn't make out her face but, in his imagination, he saw her dark otter's eyes following him as the taxi drew away.

Chapter One

Joe Sandilands had grown out of the habit of packing. In India, his many journeys had been eased by the silent and efficient attentions of a bearer. And now, six weeks after his return, he was ashamed to find he'd almost lost the knack.

In irritation, he left his suitcase in the middle of the living-room floor, gaping open in readiness for the inevitable afterthoughts. These swiftly followed as he cruised about his room, his eye lighting on things without which he couldn't possibly survive a long weekend in the country. As he passed his bookshelves he tweaked from the ranks the Wodehouse he hadn't had time to read since his return. He threw it in. A packet of Fribourg & Treyer cigarettes followed. There would be boxes full of Turkish or Virginian available to guests on every gleaming table at the great house he was about to visit but he never liked to be seen helping himself. He paused and considered. Could it be interpreted as an insult to one's host – taking one's own supplies?

The ludicrous question betrayed the level of his anxiety concerning this jaunt. He defiantly chucked in another packet. He followed it with a bag of mint humbugs.

Glad to be distracted by a peremptory hoot from the river, he went to stand at the window, looking down on the restless surface of the Thames and listened while the bells of Chelsea Old Church struck the hour. Six o'clock.

9

Cocktail time. His sister Lydia, a stickler for punctuality, would be getting back from her shopping expedition at any moment. Time to go down and help her with her bags. There would be bags! And the hand-operated mechanism of the lift he knew terrified her, though, independent girl that she was, she would never summon help. Joe started guiltily as he heard her upstairs already and letting herself into the flat.

She called out a greeting and dropped a cascade of packages and hat boxes on to the sofa. Responding to Joe's raised eyebrows, she said, 'Just a few things. The rest are being delivered to Surrey.' She kicked off her shoes and, cursing gently about the traffic in Sloane Street, came to join him at the window. Joe poured out a gin and tonic and handed it to her. They listened for a moment in companionable silence to the swash and rustle of a tugboat towing a flotilla of barges upstream into the glare of the westering sun.

'I love this time of day,' Joe said, sipping his dry sherry.

His sister looked at him in disbelief. 'Isn't it time you found somewhere better than this? Tiny rooms you can only get up to in a dangerous, wheezing old lift? An attack of vertigo every time you look through the window? Lots Road power station on one side, smoky tugs going up and down the river all day – and night too, as far as I can see . . . Joe, you're living in a coal hole!'

'It suits me,' Joe said defensively. 'I like the river from this distance. Nobody knows where I am. I can get a bit of peace and quiet. And anyway, this place seems to suit *you* well enough too – handy for Harrods and always a spare room to be had when the sales are on. What more could a girl want?'

'A little less of the bachelor austerity, is what.' Lydia put down her glass and moved around the room switching on lamps and plumping up cushions. 'Your Mrs Jago only cleans this place for you – you can't expect her to add any decorative touches. Why don't you let me . . . Ah! Getting ahead with your packing, I see?' She made for the open suitcase. 'I'll help you.'

Always a mistake to let an older sister help you with your packing.

Joe reckoned that the damage had been done, the precedent set, when he was a boy and going off to school for the first time. At that moment of uncertainty he'd been grateful for a bossy girl counting handkerchiefs, refolding his shirts and confiscating his cache of marbles. Today the twenty-nine-year-old, six-foot commander at Scotland Yard that he had become resented the attention. He decided to do a bit of commanding.

'Do leave off, Lydia. I'm only going away for a weekend in the country.'

Lydia wasn't listening. Up to the elbows stirring about amongst his things, she'd pounced on an alien element. 'A Cerebos Salt tin? What's this doing hiding amongst your dress shirts, Joe?' She held it away from her and shook it. It rattled. Lydia stared at the familiar blue and white container with distaste. 'What have you got in this rusty old thing? Not still smuggling marbles, are you? Or is this your stash of spare bullets for your big bad Browning?'

Joe snatched it from her and twisted off the lid, revealing the innocent contents. 'Toothbrush, paste, shaving things. Happy with that?'

'No. Not a bit. Think, Joe! You're off to stay at the country seat of an earl, trying to make a good impression on your elders and betters . . . what's his lordship going to think? More to the point, what's his *footman* going to think when he unpacks for you? You'll be a laughing stock below stairs. I'll pop out to Bond Street tomorrow, first thing, and get you a decent wash bag.'

'You'll do no such thing! I've always used a Cerebos Salt tin and I see no reason to stop.'

'But it's disgusting – it's rusting away.'

'What do you expect? It's travelled across oceans and

11

halfway round India. It made an appearance at a far grander establishment than Gratton Court.'

'India? Oh, no! You're telling me you took this insanitary object with you when you stayed with the Maharajah What's his name?'

'I did. A humble salt tin stood on a marble bathroom shelf in the Palace of Ranipur, batting for England amongst the crystal, the jade and the gold accessories, placed there – without comment – by the bearer who unpacked my things.'

'I'm surprised someone didn't remove it.'

'Someone did. When I unpacked on my return to Simla I noted that my faithful old receptacle had been taken away and replaced ... with a brand new Cerebos Salt tin! This very one.'

Lydia chuckled. 'Now that's style.'

'That's Indian good manners – and humour,' Joe agreed quietly. 'Can't tell you how glad I am to be home, but ... I miss the laughter, Lyd. And the colour. In sober old London.' He saw dismay dawning in her eyes and hurried to add: 'But I've done with serious travelling for now. Got a career to relaunch!'

A sudden understanding of the tin's significance silenced her. Schoolboys, soldiers and now, apparently, strapping great police commanders – they all needed a reminder of home in strange or threatening situations. Lydia put it back in the suitcase. 'You can always claim then that it was a gift from a maharajah – should anyone ask,' she said comfortably. 'But I suppose they must be used to eccentricities at Gratton Court – the old Prince of Wales was a constant guest there in the good old days.' She gave a mock shudder. 'Now I shouldn't have liked to view the contents of *his* salt tin!'

Joe responded to his sister's unexpressed anxiety. 'I'll be fine, Lyd. Don't worry about me. Big boy these days. And it's not as though it's an interview I've been called up for. There's nothing much riding on this, you know. I've already got the job – had it for two years now. They just want to check I can drink my soup without slurping and get through dinner with a selection of rabid old fire-eaters without poking one in the eye with a fish knife. I shall keep smiling, tell a few tall stories, sing baritone in the after-dinner choruses round the grand piano and shoot a commendable but not showy number of birds.'

'What are you using for guns?'

'Pa's old pair. I've sent them ahead. Respectable but nothing flashy. Now if we were going for real game, I could have impressed them with the Holland & Holland Royal I used in India. Sir George insisted on giving it to me. Not many charging buffalo offering themselves as targets on Exmoor, though.'

'You *used* it in India? Joe, you don't like shooting animals.'

'True. But the animals in question were tiger. Man-eaters both. With hundreds of deaths on their rap sheets!'

'Both?'

'I shot two of them, in as many minutes. One male, one female. They were hunting as a pair.'

Lydia laughed. 'You're having me on. Sounds like the beginning of a good yarn, though, for when the port starts to circulate.'

'Oh, if I were vandal enough, I could carve two grooves on the glossy French walnut stock of the Royal. It saved my life. But I prefer to carry my grooves concealed.' With a sister-baiting grin of mischief, Joe pushed up his right sleeve to show her two raking claw marks, well healed by now. He enjoyed her squeal of horror. 'I had the luck to be treated by an English doctor who'd studied ancient Indian medicine. Lord only knows what he poured into the wound but it worked a treat. Wounds can go rotten faster in India than they did in Flanders.'

Lydia shuddered. 'Well, watch your back, little brother. I've sneaked a look at the guest list you've popped behind the clock on the mantelpiece. Impressive and surprising.

13

Something's brewing. And I think I can guess what – I read the papers! And I get Marcus to repeat the political gossip he comes by at his club. He can't always make sense of it but he's worth hearing. England's not been standing still while you've been living it up in India, you know – it's started rolling downhill. Joe, the men you're meeting are not only running the country – they're a ruthless, manipulative bunch.'

'Oo, er . . . I shall think of them as the Gratton Gang.'

Lydia was not to be diverted. 'These men aren't going to be the slightest bit interested in your table manners and your small talk. In fact, I do rather wonder what exactly they might be wanting from a minnow like you.'

She squashed the suggestions he was about to make. 'Well, you're getting a reputation for defusing a crisis, Marcus says. "Defusing" – in my dictionary that spells danger. Don't let these grandees use you for a cat's paw while they skulk in safety behind the barricades, Joe. You know what you're like for leading the charge.'

Sensing a sisterly assessment of his character about to be fired in his direction, Joe employed a diversionary tactic. 'Lyd, why don't you open up one of those boxes – you know you're dying to. Pop on one of your new hats and I'll take you out to dinner.'

Chapter Two

In his office on the third floor, Joe was putting the finishing touches to a frantic hour of desk work before leaving to catch his train to the west country. He picked up a fountain pen and signed the six letters remaining on his desk. The signature was in black ink, and unaccompanied by any flourish. He gathered the typed pages together into a neat pile, replaced them in a folder and ran a satisfied eye over the shining and – at last – clear surface of his desk.

He rang for his secretary.

'Ah, Miss Jameson. All done. It just remains for me to apologize for the last-minute bustle, thank you for your stalwart assistance and say – I'll see you again on Tuesday.'

'Not *quite* all done, sir. You'd forgotten this. The latest assassination attempt.'

With an arch smile, she placed a file in front of him. 'They've just sent it up. It's the one you requested from Special Branch. I had to ask for it three times . . . they *would* keep trying to tell me it wasn't for *our* eyes.' Miss Jameson raised elegant brows to convey her disbelief at such lack of respect. 'I have to say, Commander, I don't much care to do business with those *gentlemen*.' Her voice frosted the word lightly with distaste. 'They are not the most congenial of people to deal with.'

'I rather think that's the whole point of them,' Sandilands said drily. 'Thugs – I quite agree. Upper-class thugs, but thugs all the same. And a law unto themselves, they'd like us to believe. So very well done to have wrung it out of them.' He opened the file and began to flip through the pages, frowning, instantly absorbed by what he read.

'I had to threaten to go down there and fetch it myself,' she persisted.

Joe sensed that he hadn't sufficiently acknowledged her tenacity. He looked up and gave her a questioning smile. 'Down there, Miss Jameson? Bold of you to plan a frontal assault! You're not meant to know the location of their HQ.'

'Oh, sir! Everyone knows they're holed up in that little wooden hut on the island in St James's Park. Duck Island, I believe they call it. It's just beyond Horse Guards – a minute or two away. I'd have gained access if I'd had to swim across their moat!'

He believed her.

For a moment he savoured the vision of Miss Jameson arising from the water, clad in white samite, mystic, wonderful – and crowned in duck weed – ready to challenge the doughty lads of the anti-terrorist squad and he smiled. He glanced across at the confident woman who thought nothing of taking on, single-handed, the Special Irish Branch. Should he tell her that her target had relocated some years ago? That 'the Branch' had moved into Whitehall and were even now beavering away not so very far from where she sat at her typewriter? No. She was happy with the folk story. And the élite squad were fanatical about preserving their anonymity. An anonymity that, in his recently acquired covert role at the Met, the commander was honour-bound to respect.

'Just keep an eye on them for us, will you, Sandilands?' He'd been briefed almost as an afterthought by a superior. And he'd realized, with a sinking heart, that he'd been handed a poisoned chalice. In addition to the CID role that went with his job, he'd been landed, since his return, with an ill-defined responsibility for this other clandestine and self-reliant branch of the British police force. Deliberately ill defined? Joe suspected as much.

'They won't give *you* the runaround, young man! Still full of beans and raring to go, I observe.' This compliment, from a survivor of the Boer War with yellowing moustache and matching teeth, was never likely to turn Joe's head. 'Try to understand them,' the advice flowed on, 'with your background of skulduggery that shouldn't be too hard. Takes one to handle one, eh, what? Make it your business to find out what these boys are up to. They're on our side, of course – and we thank God for that mercy! – but an occasional reminder that they report ultimately to the Police Commissioner at the Yard mightn't come amiss. They will try to ignore that.'

Sandilands had shrugged and smiled his acquiescence. His sister was right – he was never able to turn down a challenge. With the reins of the CID in one hand and the Branch in the other, however, he'd found himself in charge of a spirited and ill-matched pair. Steady hands, though. So far he'd avoided landing arsy-tarsy in the ditch. But his secretary would have been disturbed to know of the chain of command that ran from the political branch down below right up to his own desk. Chain? Thread would be more accurate, Sandilands thought. A fragile thread he'd already had to put a knot in twice since his appointment.

He rewarded his secretary with the response she best appreciated: a grin and 'Attaboy, Jameson!'

A mistake.

Under cover of his approval, she was encouraged to slide in a supplementary question or two. 'The latest attack in the West End, I take it? That's what this is all about?' She pointed to the file. 'The shooting? Poor General Lansing. He's a very old friend of Daddy's. I do hope he wasn't badly hurt?'

'Lansing? No. Hide as tough as a cavalryman's derrière. Er . . . bullets bounce off him, I should say.'

Four years of war, followed by three of intensive training for the Metropolitan Police and a further year on secondment to the Calcutta Police, had left Joe accustomed to an exclusively male working environment. He didn't always manage to tailor his language for a female audience. Amalthea Jameson graciously affected not to notice his lapses.

The announcement that he was to be granted, on taking up his post again after his return from India, the services of a full-time personal secretary had been surprising. The two other officers of his rank, uniformed and in the later years of their service, were accorded no such privilege. Even more surprising was the failure of these fellow officers to take offence at the blatant preferment of the young upstart. A knowing smirk and a pitying shake of the head spoke volumes to Joe. They didn't envy him.

'I visited the general yesterday in St George's. He's doing well,' he offered in reassurance.

'I'm glad to hear it. I've been following events in the press. With no file available in our office, one gets one's information where one may . . .' She gave an apologetic smile, but her eyes accused him of secrecy.

'Depressing stuff, Jameson, in the papers, and usually exaggerated. Believe them and you'd be running into a Russian Bolshevik or a Latvian anarchist round every corner. You'd never venture out,' he reassured her lightly.

'But that's *three* attempted murders now in as many days, I gather. Three attacks on three military gentlemen,' she persisted. 'And each with – I wonder if it had occurred to you, sir? – a different *modus operandi*. Puzzling, that. Don't you agree? The first, I understand, was no more than an assault with a blunt instrument – a cosh? – the second with a knife and this last with a pistol. And all unsuccessful!' She gave a scoffing laugh. 'How much practice can a self-respecting perpetrator need? What a bungler is at work, one might conclude.'

'Not, perhaps, if a fourth attempt were to come off tomorrow, Miss Jameson. Even I can detect a certain escalation in the level of violence used. And the one vital feature the victims have in common. But thank you for your observation.'

His reprimands usually bounced off the shield of her smiling compliance but on this occasion she did not hurry to agree with him. In a tone which signalled sorrow rather than anger she said simply: 'They're here, aren't they? Here with their bombs and their bullets. Spreading terror among us.'

'There were over one hundred reported violent incidents in the Metropolitan area over the last week, Miss Jameson. Three of the victims happen to be known to you personally and you draw a dramatic conclusion from this slight evidence.' He paused for a second before admitting: 'But I have to say, I happen to agree with you. The editors of our daily newspapers don't share your social connections and inside knowledge and they haven't yet put two and two together. I'd ... we'd ... prefer that they didn't. Keep it under your hat, will you? With the present undermanning in the force, I doubt we could contain the effects of an anti-Irish backlash tearing through London. Open warfare on the streets? It's not inconceivable.'

She nodded. 'Understood, sir. I'll put this into your in-tray to await your return.' She made to scoop the file on his desk.

'No, I'll keep it. I note they've only entrusted us with the flimsies.'

'Third copies I'd say, sir. A calculated insult. But I can make them out. Would you like me to ... ?'

'Thank you, Jameson, I'll manage.' He peered at the faint blue letters. 'There's nothing here I can't take away to work on. I'll slip it into my briefcase to read on the train. I like to have something to set the pulses racing when I'm travelling.'

'Not taking your diary along for the journey, then, sir?'

It was a moment before he realized his secretary had attempted a joke.

'I'm no Oscar Wilde, Miss Jameson,' he said repressively. 'However, if I were compelled to review the passage of my life between here and Devon, I would agree with Oscar that "each day is like a year. A year whose days are long".'

He hoped he'd not been too squashing.

'And the nights? Each one an eternity . . .' She lowered her gaze to her immaculate calfskin shoes, sighed, and shook her head gently, hinting at some deep sorrow.

'Ah! Insomniac are you? It's these hot nights . . . we all suffer. I may have the answer for your condition. Wincarnis, Jameson! The Mysterious Restorative. I recommend a slug before retiring. Ten thousand doctors and my mother swear by it, and my mother's never wrong.' He glanced at his wristwatch and, alarmed by what he saw, shot to his feet.

'The Cornish Riviera Express leaves at ten thirty. Do be sure to take one of the slip carriages for Taunton, won't you? No need to worry – you have a good forty minutes, sir.' The voice, quite unabashed, dripped honeyed reassurance. It had the irrational effect of irritating the commander beyond reason. 'I hope you don't mind, sir, but anticipating that you'd be running late I took the liberty of ordering up a squad car and driver for you. You'll find it sitting panting down below on the Embankment.'

Joe did mind. He toyed with the notion of making use of the dreaded word 'austerity' and wagging a reproving finger at her, but he hadn't the time. He let the moment pass and here she was, smoothing down the already smooth chignon at the nape of her neck and dimpling.

'Ten minutes to Paddington as long as you're not held up in Park Lane . . . you'll have time for a cup of tea. You have your ticket, sir? Clean handkerchief?'

Joe suppressed a schoolboy urge to present his freshly washed hands, front and back, and bare his faultless teeth in a ritual snarl for Matron's nightly inspection. A spurt of mischief pushed him to pat his inside wallet pocket in a theatrical manner. Impervious to teasing, she tilted her head in acknowledgement of his gesture and nodded her approval. The woman was turning herself into his nanny.

If your taste inclined to the statuesque – and Joe's did – Amalthea Jameson was undeniably attractive. She was a tall, well-shaped blonde from a good military family, a product of Cheltenham Ladies' College and Oxford. She had had her training with a recently retired deputy commissioner and was eagerly sought after by his colleagues. Sandilands had to agree with them that he was an ungrateful bastard who didn't deserve her. Sly approaches suggesting her transfer to the department of a more appreciative boss had been made to him. Quite out of order, he thought. Miss Jameson was not a commodity to be traded, and as she seemed happy – suspiciously happy – to serve the office of commander in spite of the apparent demotion, there was little he could do but grind his teeth and try to appreciate her undoubted qualities.

Ah, well . . . perhaps she would find some poor soul, marry him and leave? And then he could put in for a male secretary who wouldn't sigh in his ear and concern himself with the state of his handkerchief. Trivialities! Joe reproved himself for being distracted by them. Time he followed his guns to the country.

He was under no illusion as to the style of entertainment on offer: an all-male gathering, the other guests being stars from the government and the military. A general flown in from Ireland, an admiral snatched from his battlecruiser, the flamboyant head of the Secret Service lured from the Savoy Grill and a press baron: all these featured on the list Commissioner Horwood had himself written out for him in pencil. It had concluded with the name of the head of the diplomatic service. And perhaps this outspoken mob would be needing the active services of a diplomatist before the weekend was out. The presence of Max Beaverbrook, leader of what he himself called 'the Press Gang',

21

promised to be somewhat inflammatory when another name on the list was that of Winston Churchill, the man he had seriously annoyed with his articles in the *Daily Express*. Joe expected a clash of antlers at worst, point-scoring at best. They'd been promised a soothing after-dinner performance from the exiled Russian bass, Chaliapin, accompanied by Rubinstein on the piano and, according to the pencilled note, a soprano called *Olga?/Vera?* would be released from Covent Garden to put in an appearance on the second night. Nothing but the best on offer for the Gratton Gang, evidently. But his sharp sister had it right, Joe reckoned. 'Minnow' had been a little derogatory, perhaps, but all the same . . . he did wonder what on earth a not-very-exalted policeman could be expected to contribute to the occasion.

He would have been glad of the reassuring presence of his mentor and friend, Sir George Jardine, at his side. It had been some time, in the turbulence of Calcutta, before Joe realized that the deceptively suave governor of Bengal was the eyes and ears of his Britannic majesty in India, the *éminence grise* behind the viceroy. The man who oiled the wheels of empire. But he was by no means a sinister presence in company. Whenever the affable and approachable Sir George entered a room, the mood lightened, the chatter speeded up and laughter broke out. And George had been quick to see, in the new Scotland Yard detective seconded to his police force, a sociable and clever young aide. Together, the two of them, with mutual understanding, made up a tongue-in-cheek charm department that eased the social levers. Joe sighed and comforted himself with the thought that at least the Commissioner, as his present boss, might possibly be in his corner.

A working weekend and Sandilands, if anyone noticed him, would be on trial of some sort. The Commissioner had said as much in his forthright, old soldier's way: 'Don't be shy, Sandilands. Sing for your supper. I'm sorry I can't promise any young ladies for you to fascinate but at least you'll be able to concentrate on the matters in hand.' The ironic gleam in the brigadier's eye told Joe that unofficial reports of his encounters in India had followed him home. 'We'll see what your year's apprenticeship with George Jardine has done for you,' the brigadier chuntered on. 'I hear very good things from my old friend. He rather curses me for enticing you back to London. He had expectations that you might be persuaded to stay on in India and train up in the dark arts of . . . er . . . dynamic diplomacy. Would that adequately convey the flavour of the strong-arm shenanigans and double-dealing you and George go in for? Help him keep the Raj on the rails is what he meant.'

Joe had politely disclaimed any talent for diplomacy, dynamic or otherwise.

'Well, you turned down what could have been a spectacular career, young man. I'm sure you had your reasons.'

By his silence and downcast eyes, Joe indicated that he was unwilling to share them and the brigadier hurried on: 'Still – you survived a year with George. Takes some doing! It must have left you supremely placed to undertake the very particular demands we're about to make on you. You thought India was a serpents' nest of intrigue and violence? Just wait until you get your briefing on the capital. Some silly oafs tried to bomb Westminster while you were away pig-sticking and sinking the chota-pegs. And they were a whisker away from blowing up Scotland Yard. And now we're getting these attacks on military gents. In broad daylight and on the street! Work to be done, my boy! And not much time.'

Joe was uncomfortably aware that he could be absenting himself from London at an inconvenient moment. He'd calculated that on these last long days of a long hot summer the regular villains would be cooling their toes in the sea at Southend, but the tug of war between his impatience to be off and his feelings of guilt at a fancied dereliction of duty was making him uneasy. No one would blame him.

23

The Special Branch wouldn't even notice his absence. And the CID superintendents he'd be leaving in charge would heave a sigh of relief. The granite features of that Yorkshireman he was beginning to trust . . . Superintendent Hopkirk . . . loomed into his mind. Yes – Joe was both annoyed and reassured by the thought – Hopkirk and his team of inspectors would be glad to be getting him off their backs for a bit.

On a whim, against all protocol, he'd nipped into the inspectors' room without being announced the other day. Just to keep them on the hop and remind them of who he was. He'd remembered and put a name to most of the faces through the thick fug of cigarette smoke, faces that glowered back at him with suspicion. The resentment hadn't lasted longer than the few seconds it had taken him to dive with his usual military authority straight into a discussion.

The moment had been a good one – the men appeared to have been sunk, not in the usual seditious talk, but in a serious discussion of police business when he burst in, and they hadn't felt caught on the back foot. The impromptu meeting ended with good-humoured quips on both sides. He'd felt easy enough in their company to announce that he might be off the scene for a few days and to demand reassurances that they wouldn't go about the place getting into trouble while he was away. He'd been pleased to provoke the traditional response delivered with ponderous irony: 'Won't do anything *you* wouldn't do, sir – you can bet on that much!'

Predictable but, at least – less stiff . . . more accepting.

And yet the relief at his news, though silent, was perceptible. He harried the troops. He knew that. He had no intention of letting up.

And now – decision time: to go or to make his apologies? He toyed for a moment with the notion that he had a choice in the matter and tried out one or two of the dozen convincing excuses available to him. He selected one.

24

Correctly reading his uncertainty, Miss Jameson sighed in understanding.

It was the sigh that triggered his decision. The undemanding open moorland beckoned. And, after all, he wasn't going quite to the ends of the earth. Hopkirk could always send a telegram to summon him back if anything blew up. Oh, Lord! *There* was a thought that could have been better expressed. He grimaced.

The company gathering for the weekend party promised to be intimidating but they might well be congenial – if the birds were flying well and the right mood was struck. Joe enjoyed shooting and lively conversation. And the food at the grand house would be good; he thought he could count on that. There would be wine – perhaps with a bit of luck tankards of foaming Exmoor ale would accompany Cook's game pie?

Joe grabbed the old army trenchcoat he kept by him winter and summer from the branched hatstand by the door and threw it over his arm; he tweaked his bowler hat from the topmost twig. The daily reminder of his slavery to the city, the hat was a hated object and, in a gesture of defiance, decision and mischief, he lobbed it across the room at Miss Jameson.

She caught it in flight with the swift reaction of a lacrosse player and clutched it dramatically to her bosom: a lady accepting her knight's gage of honour. The size seven and a half bowler was barely equal to the task of encircling her left breast, he noted, and looked away, disturbed by the image. It was his guess that she would take the opportunity of having the wretched headgear cleaned and re-blocked during his absence. Well, let her get on with it. He'd decided to replace it with a soft stalker's hat from the gents' outfitters in Taunton High Street.

It usually poured with rain when he was in Devon but the promise of being back in the country, at peace under a dripping tweed brim, the scent of wet earth and heather filling his nostrils, made him quiver with anticipation. He was eager for the undemanding company of two or three tail-wagging, slobbering spaniels at his heels. In imagination he scratched their throats, turning his head this way and that to avoid their blasts of pungent breath. With a jaunty wave he dashed off to clatter down the stairs and out to the waiting motor car.

A day or two of freedom and comradeship on the moors stretched before him, walking, riding and tracking wild creatures instead of predatory humans. And no Miss Jameson! Bliss!

Chapter Three

'Cupper tea, constable? You've got ten minutes before the Bristol Flyer gets in. Naw! Go on! Put your tuppence back in your pocket, love – it's on the house. Drop of milk, one sugar was that?'

'Thank you, Stan. I'd love one. But I'm paying all the same. Rules are rules.' The insistence could have sounded prim but Woman Police Constable Lilian Wentworth softened her words with a broad smile. In any case, Stan the tea man was not about to take offence. Not from Miss Wentworth. From his stall on the platform he saw everything that happened on the station and he was always ready to oblige the boys – and the women – in blue with his impeccable information and advice. Especially the honest ones who did a good job.

He nodded his approval, accepted her pennies and handed over a mug of tarry tea. 'Some of your blokes aren't so particular!' he commented. 'In fact where's that PC who's supposed to be escorting you today? Useless great lummox. He'll be in the back of the refreshment room, I expect, refreshing himself.'

He didn't add 'with a pint of brown ale'. Police Constable Halliday, six foot burly beat bobby, married, five children, a betting man, was always on the scrounge.

'You've got that wrong, Stan. *I'm* escorting *him*. I'm

27

responsible for my partner, they tell me. I may have to carry him home at the end of the day.'

Stan grinned at the thought. Lily Wentworth's height was at the lower limit for acceptance on the force, he would have guessed. And, as far as anyone could judge, under all those layers of blue serge uniform, she was as slender as a whippet.

'On Waifs and Strays patrol all week, then, miss? Looking out for runaways?'

'That's right. Makes a nice change from last week's duty – Hyde Park! Six days on the trot from four in the afternoon till eleven in the evening.' Lily Wentworth rolled her eyes to convey the horror. 'On Public Order and Lewd Behaviour Prevention patrol.'

Stan grimaced in sympathy. 'They give you women all the worst jobs. Did you catch anyone in ... flag ... in flag—' Stan cut short his unthinking burst of curiosity.

'*Flagrante delicto*? With his trousers down, you mean? I'll say! I've seen more male posteriors in action than an army doctor. All shapes and sizes.'

Stan's face creased with embarrassment at the answer he'd provoked. The women police were noted for their frank way of speaking. He'd never allow a daughter of *his* to join their ranks. Even if they'd take her. Mixing with rough, foul-mouthed coppers every day – that was no occupation for a girl. Some of the language they used flummoxed *him*, army veteran though he was. They didn't swear – oh, no, far too ladylike for that. But they knew all the right words for all the wrong things. Things that, as unmarried ladies, they didn't oughter know. And they didn't scruple to use them. Sometimes they even expressed the inexpressible in Latin. Educated girls, the lot of them. Had to be. They stood up in open court, bold as brass, and delivered evidence that made the magistrates' hair curl. The beaks sometimes had to clear the general public out of the courtroom before a woman policeman was allowed to open her mouth and give testimony.

'We got a good bag. We netted a member of parliament, a duke's valet and a lawyer – a King's Counsel, no less! – and several professional gentlemen. They spent the rest of the night closeted together in a cell in the Vine Street nick!' Lily's laugh was suggestive of mischievous thoughts. 'Can you imagine, Stan, how the conversation went?' She put on a pompous Music Hall voice: '"I say, you chaps – regular customers at this establishment, are you? Well, I'm in a position to offer you sinners a little useful advice . . ." I blame the spring weather, Stan. It brings out the worst in men. Seasonal urges? If *I* were Commissioner, come March the twenty-first, I'd double the park patrols.'

Stan liked to listen to this girl. She didn't have the pursed lips and strained vowels of other ladies he'd heard talking – the ones who sounded as though they were sucking on an ice cube. Her voice rushed along, reminding the Yorkshireman of one of his native moorland becks, going somewhere and carrying you along with it, frothing with good humour. He asked her a question to prolong the conversation. 'Did they get away with it?'

'Course they did. A clear case of collusion whilst in custody. The accused all denied the charges of lewd conduct. They claimed to be members of the Hyde Park Ornithological Society.'

'Bird fanciers?' Stan wheezed with the effort of suppressing a laugh. 'That's a new one!'

'They told the magistrate how they were skulking in the shrubbery by the Serpentine – as you do when you're innocently studying the antics of the golden-crested wren. Or was it the great crested grebe? One or two were a little under-rehearsed. Though one of them – impressively – managed to come up with *Podiceps cristatus* which earned him an approving nod from the magistrate. Abruptly, their peaceful activities were curtailed by the arrival of a pair of over-officious officers of the law (that's me and Halliday). "Aha!" says his honour knowingly, "*Custos officiosus*! Dark blue plumage? Yes . . . Thick as sparrows on the ground, these days." They all fell about laughing at his little joke and were out on the street again by noon. Not even a five quid fine. Waste of police time.'

The constable sighed and then added, her tone brightening: 'But better than the arrests, we made at least ten interventions. Always better to *prevent* an attack than arrest someone for it afterwards, don't you think, Stan? If there's anything more satisfying than catching and thumping a rapist, it's decking one before he's had a chance to hoist his mainsail.'

Stan pretended not to hear. Chattering . . . pent-up . . . mind elsewhere, he decided indulgently. Expecting trouble. He'd noticed that while she sipped her tea, smiled and talked, her eyes never stopped moving, surveying the crowd gathering along the platform on to which the incoming train would spill its west-country passengers. And she'd positioned herself behind the tea urn out of sight of anyone coming on to the platform from outside. She was using him as cover. He didn't mind.

The young woman seemed to have her own unorthodox tactics for crime-fighting. The male constables spent their time swaggering up and down on the platform. At the sight of the uniform, the pickpockets, con-artists and pimps melted away into the shadows, only to drift back unscathed the moment the tall helmet disappeared from view. WPC 1555 wasn't walking about, flushing out her prey and sending it scattering before her. She was lying in wait. In her calculating watchfulness Stan saw something that reminded him of native hunters he'd seen in India in his army days. The village tiger trackers could sit for hours, days even, up a tree watching over the lure of a tied-up, bleating goat. When the moment came they would be instantly alert and firing. Stan's tea urn was her tree and he was pretty sure he knew where she'd find her goat.

Smart girl, this one. And careful.

Stan looked surreptitiously at the slight form swamped by the heavy uniform and wondered how she managed with her unimpressive height and weight to convey such determination. The military cut of the jacket with its official Metropolitan Women Police Patrol badge was intimidating but it did not allow of easy movement. The high collar, Stan noted with a stab of sympathy, was, on this warm day, chafing her slender neck and raising a nasty red mark. The hat, which was held in place by a chin-strap, was a wide-brimmed dome like a riding helmet. It sat heavily on her head almost snuffing out the pretty face below.

Stan sensed that it was a pretty face. He was not at all certain that he'd be able to identify number 1555 if he ever saw her out of her uniform. Grey eyes? Green? He'd have guessed grey eyes but – her hair? No idea. He lowered his gaze, embarrassed to be caught staring, and turned his eyes to her boots. They couldn't be comfortable. Knee-high, laced and made of a heavy leather, they could have been designed for Charlie Chaplin. And yet he'd seen these women take off and fly in them in pursuit of a villain. They'd trip up, kick out, stamp and do their ju-jitsu – anything to get a man down and incapacitated.

'You have a good view of the platform here, Stan?'

'I keep an eye open. I watch for kids getting off the train without an adult. They're always easy to spot. They don't know which way to turn. Up from the country – most of them can't read so the signs mean nothing to them. If it looks like there's going to be real trouble I scoop 'em up and take 'em along to the stationmaster's office. Good bloke! Family man himself. He calls in Dr Barnardo's or the NSPCC or the Sisters of the Night. I was a runaway myself, miss,' he confided. 'From the north. Years ago. I know the signs. And I can spot the vultures gathering . . . Like now . . .' Stan's voice rasped with dread. 'Here they come.'

The words struck chill. Wentworth waited anxiously to hear more. But Stan just nodded, absorbed by the crowd beginning to gather to greet the train. Most of them were clutching a platform ticket in their hands.

31

'What do you make of that lot, then?' he asked.

Unresentful at being challenged by the old soldier, she murmured her way through the individuals and groups. 'Reading from the left . . . if they'll just keep still a minute and let me clock them . . . Two girls. Under twenty. Maids' day out clothes. Excited. They're so alike they must be sisters. Probably here to welcome a third and younger sister up from the country to take up her position as between-stairs maid . . . Of course, they *could* be alumnae of the local house of ill repute on a recruitment drive. Aphrodite's on Park Lane? No, I don't think so.

'Moving along we have two ladies. Uniformed nanny and her well-dressed employer. Judging by the small bicycle that the nanny's holding – a shining brand new one – I'd say they're waiting for the lady's seven-year-old son who's taking a break from his prep school . . . Sick leave? But a bicycle like that – it's bait that could lure any child into trouble. In the hands of the wrong adult. How am I getting on, Stan?'

He smiled and nodded his approval of her reasoning.

'Next along. Young man. Smartly turned out. Straw boater. And spats. Spats in summer? Trying too hard, would you say? He must be waiting for his lady-friend. Yes, look – he's clutching a bunch of florist-bought flowers in one hand. Hothouse roses. Expensive. And in the other he's got what would seem to be a grotesquely coiffed poodle on a lead. He's brought the dog along to meet its mistress. It clearly doesn't belong to the young gent. It rather hates him, do you see?

'And then, just arrived, a very well-groomed middle-aged man. Sleek dark hair. What do you bet he smells of Trumper's best hair oil? Foreign-looking. I think we have a valet waiting for his gentleman. Possibly lives in Mayfair and he's strolled on to the station at the last moment, every hair in place, to take charge of the hand luggage.

'And at the end there's a young man with a clipboard. Military bearing. Bored. Commissionaire's uniform is that?

A flunky of some sort, anyway. He's been sent out by a London club – the Army and Navy? – to scoop up some doddery old duffer and steer him safely to St James's.'

And, after a moment: 'They all seem to have come to collect someone in particular. I can't say any one of them strikes me as a vulture, Stan.'

'Not vulture. No, I got that wrong. Those birds hang about in noisy mobs, don't they? What we've got circling today is one silent professional. A sparrowhawk.' Stan shuddered and glowered at the crowd. 'That's what they call them. Miss, you ought to watch out for the—'

His words were cut off by the screech of the approaching train's whistle, the swoosh of steam and the protest of huge wheels grinding to a halt. Doors slammed, greetings were called out, passengers jumped down from the train. The platform ticket holders surged forward hallooing with varying degrees of eagerness, claiming their people.

Lily ticked them off in her head as they made contact. 'Well, I got three out of five right, Stan,' she muttered.

The two maids were suddenly three – peas in a pod, twittering with excitement.

A podgy seven-year-old squealed in delight at the sight of his bicycle and shook off the attentions of his mother and his nanny.

A heavily moustached survivor of some ancient war was helped out of a first-class compartment by two porters. He placed himself with a harrumph of greeting into the hands of the flunky with the clipboard.

But she'd been wrong about the dark-haired 'valet'. To Lily's surprise, an elegant young lady teetered up on high heels and flung herself into his arms, instantly elevating him from a role of subservience into a matinee idol. Lily watched their embrace for a moment, enthralled, with a mixture of wonder and envy.

The young man in spats, scanning the platform anxiously, had yet to make contact.

It was Stan who spotted them first.

33

He pointed and mimed a message above the din. Two children were getting hesitantly out of a third-class carriage. The older one, a girl of about eleven with badly plaited pigtails hanging down her back, turned and helped her brother to jump down on to the platform. Lily noticed, with a stab of pity, that the girl was smiling, trying to make a game of it for the little boy. The pair stood for a moment, reeling back from the assault of the noise, sniffing the warm sooty air like wild creatures. They were poorly dressed: the girl was wearing a grey cardigan with holes in the elbows over a drooping cotton frock, while the boy's clothes were a size too big for him. Their shoes were fastened with baler twine and worn down to nothing at the heels. They were both very skinny. They were also by themselves.

Lily watched as they tried with a pathetic sense of duty to slam shut the heavy door behind them and failed to move it. They gave up, looked about them to see if their shortcoming had been noted and braced themselves to face a new and probably hostile world. Hand in hand, they stood, each clutching a small parcel done up with string.

They began to shuffle forward with the crowd and the girl suddenly pointed, seeing the sign for the exit and mouthing the word. They moved towards it.

The Sparrowhawk was watching them as closely as Lily. He let them take a dozen paces from the train, checking that no adult was following on behind.

Satisfied that they were alone, he made his move.

He strolled over and spoke to them, doffed his boater to the little girl and bent down to their level, his face wreathed in pleasant smiles. The poodle, trained in its responses, Lily was quite certain, licked the children's hands and fussed about, wagging its stumpy tail.

Their new friend was in no hurry. He talked, he listened and he did a lot of laughing. He didn't make the mistake of alarming them by offering to take their precious parcels from them. Finally, he handed the dog's lead to the little girl and himself took the boy by one hand, his flowers still clutched in the other. A charming group, they set off for the exit.

Clumsy with excitement and dread, Stan grabbed his crutch and came round from behind his stall, growling a warning. 'There they go. Never seen that one before but he's a wrong 'un if ever I saw one. A real professional. Are you going to do something? Where's that useless nincompoop of a police constable?'

He started to hobble forward himself but Lily grabbed his arm and held him back. 'No! Wait! We have to let them get as far as the barrier. Otherwise, he'll get off with some excuse about escorting them to the lavatory or the refreshment room. Rules, Stan! Stay back!'

She padded quietly after the little group, allowing them to move along four paces ahead of her. They passed the lavatory. They passed the refreshment room. In his total confidence the Hawk didn't bother to look back. With a display of a jolly young uncle's concern, he checked that the children had their tickets in hand to present at the barrier.

When he was a few yards from the exit and clearly committed to leaving, Lily launched her attack. She dashed forward, scattering the children and the dog, and hurled herself at the man's knees from behind, turning her head to avoid his thrashing heels. He crashed on to his front, flowers flying everywhere, banging his chin on the paved floor.

'What the hell!' he roared.

'Police! You're under arrest!' Lily shouted, and before he could struggle free she threw herself down firmly, bottom first, on the man's neck. She took her police whistle from her tunic and gave three blasts. Where *was* PC Halliday? With no powers of arrest herself, she could do little without Halliday's authority. His curses smothered by voluminous layers of Harrod's tailoring, her prisoner was writhing like a spade-sliced worm. His body bucked strongly, all his senses alert now, muscles working to shift the incapacitating weight without breaking his own neck.

'Halliday!' More blasts of the whistle sent the crowd hurrying off in all directions in their eagerness not to become involved in police business.

She heard Stan scream a warning as he lurched forward: 'Watch it! Knife!'

There was a gleam of metal as the man reached behind and pulled a flick knife from his back pocket. His right thumb worked the switch and an evil length of steel shot out, with the swift flicker of a snake's tongue.

The sudden descent of a polished half-brogue Oxford on to the man's knife hand produced a muffled scream. A second application of a leather heel with thirteen stone of well-muscled Englishman behind it elicited more yells and oaths. The crushed fingers spread, their grasp on the knife broken.

Lily's eyes followed the immaculate shoe upwards along an elegantly trousered leg to a dark tweed Norfolk jacket. A hand reached down holding a handkerchief and the knife was taken up delicately by the tip of the blade.

'You'll be wanting to preserve the prints in evidence, officer,' suggested a voice whose assurance echoed the quality of the tailoring. 'This weapon may well have been used in previous crimes.' The stranger laid the knife at her feet and straightened. Lily noticed that he kept his brogue firmly on the Sparrowhawk's hand.

She was aware of a hatless head of well-barbered black hair, a brown face, clean shaven and confident to the point of unconcern. With an outpouring of relief she began to gabble her thanks. 'Oh, well done, sir! Lucky for us you were passing. Always a member of the public ready to come up in support, thank God,' she heard herself say. 'The Commissioner should hear of this.'

'I'm sure he will, Miss ... er, Officer 1555. One way or another.' He seemed amused. 'Ah! And here, a little late, and buttoning up his unmentionables, comes your valiant escort. Let's hope he has at least remembered his handcuffs.'

The stranger's voice took on a military tone as Halliday panted up. 'Constable! Glad you could join us. You nearly missed the party. Arrest this recumbent person on a charge of attempted kidnap of minors, intent to wound a female officer of the law, uttering obscenities in a public place and littering the environs of the station. And anything else that occurs to you.'

He stepped aside and retrieved an untrampled white rose stem from the floor, broke off the bloom and stuck it with a flourish into the band of Lily's hat, which had remained firmly in place throughout the proceedings. 'Oh, and let's be sure not to forget proxenetism,' he added. 'I'm sure a little research will confirm: proxenetism. Cuff the villain and take him to the local nick. You may give my name as a witness of events.'

'Sir! Yes, sir!' Halliday grunted, hauling the prisoner's arms behind his back and clicking on the cuffs. 'At once, sir!'

'Dash it. I may have missed my train,' grumbled the military man and, snapping off a gracious salute to Lily, he picked up his overcoat and briefcase and marched off at the double. Lily watched him go, mortified that she hadn't thought to return his salute. Still, with her right hand firmly entangled in the Hawk's greasy hair in the prescribed controlling hold, the other clutching her whistle, perhaps the gentleman wouldn't have expected it.

Halliday turned his attention to Lily. 'Proxy what was that?' he said. 'What was he on about?'

'He meant procuring. Getting hold of young children and exploiting them for felonious purposes. It's from the Latin word for pimping. We've collared ourselves a predator, Halliday. A sparrowhawk. But that chap – the country gent with the nifty footwork and the nice smile – what did he say? Use his name? I didn't hear him give one. Should we—'

'He doesn't need to give it. Everybody knows *him*! Commander Have-a-go-Joe Sandilands,' Halliday groaned. 'That's who you were showing off for. Interfering sod! Nice smile? Huh! And you're trying to tell me you didn't know him? Pull the other one!'

'No, honest, Halliday, I didn't.'

'Well, you can get up now, 1555 – the prisoner can't breathe. And your audience has slung its hook. Take that silly bloody flower out of your hat! What *do* you think you look like? Gawd! I was only in the gents for a minute,' he protested. 'He got my number. I saw him looking. That's my police career over.' He glowered at Lily. 'But I'll tell you something, Miss Showoff, if I go down, I'll take you with me. There's things they ought to know about you.'

Lily wasn't going to allow his threats to dampen her triumph. 'He got my number too,' she said. 'I don't think that was a man who misses much. But first things first – never mind this villain . . .' She gave one last triumphant bounce on the Hawk's head before she struggled to her feet. 'And never mind the commander. Where are those children?'

'It's all right, I've got 'em safe,' said Stan, appearing with a child firmly in each hand. 'While the PC's organizing that piece of filth's accommodation I'll just give these two nippers a glass of milk and a cheese sandwich. They look as though they haven't eaten for a week.' And, turning to the wide-eyed pair: 'Welcome to London, kids. I think that's enough excitement for one day. Come along o' me and this lady policeman. Naw – don't you fret about the dog. We'll see he's all right. You're all going to be all right.'

Chapter Four

September 1922

In the warm intimacy of the rear seat of a London cab, Admiral Lord Dedham stretched out his long legs and adjusted the scabbard of his dress sword so as to be sure not to snag the trailing chiffon gown of the woman by his side. It had been a long, hot evening filled with far too many blood-stirring speeches – the most incendiary of them coming from his own lips, he readily admitted. He'd received a standing ovation and that sort of thing always went to the head however tight one's grip on reality; he'd taken on board too much adulation and too many drinks for comfort. He was longing for the moment, soon approaching, when he could relieve his chest of its cargo of medals and slip out of his much-bedecked dress uniform.

But until that blissful moment arrived, he was more than content with the present one. Even at his time of life – which he thought of as 'vigorous middle age' – the admiral still found that the capsule of darkness to be found in the back of a taxi, lightly scented with gardenia, good cigars and leather, sliding secretly through the roistering crowds of central London, had its enlivening effect. It had been even more invigorating in the swaying hansom cabs of his youth but his ageing bones could never regret all that bouncing about over cobbles. He reached out and seized the white-gloved hand left invitingly close to his on the banquette and lifted it to his lips with practised gallantry, a wary eye on the driver.

The observant cabby's eyes gleamed in the rear-viewing mirror, his shoulders shook perceptibly and he launched into a cheery offering from *Chu Chin Chow*.

Lord Dedham had seen the musical extravaganza three times. It was his favourite musical comedy. He recognized the sumptuously romantic duet 'Any Time's Kissing Time'.

Cheeky blighter, Dedham thought, with an indulgent grin. Typical London cabby. Ought to be keeping his eyes on the road, not spying on his passengers. He wondered if his companion would take offence. Many women would.

His companion responded to the effrontery by leaning mischievously towards the admiral and biting his ear, her aim, in the dark, surprisingly sure. Then she joined in with the song, timing her entrance perfectly, weaving her clear soprano voice into the chorus to sing along with the cabby.

'Nearly there, my love,' growled Dedham. 'Did you ask Peterson to wait up?'

'As though he'd agree to do otherwise, Oliver! He'll be there waiting with your eggnog at the ready. But I dismissed your valet. I'll help you out of that clanking regalia myself.' And, as though the promise of eggnog and wifely ministrations was not enough to stiffen the sinews, she squeezed his arm as they turned from the hurly-burly of Buckingham Palace Road into the quiet opulence of the streets approaching Melton Square. 'Oh, it's *so* good to have you home again, darling, and I shall go on saying that until you beg me to stop. And when we arrive, you will remember to do as Joe told you, won't you?'

'Dash it all, Cassandra, we're in Belgravia not Belfast!' he objected.

Lady Dedham quelled her husband's predictable splutterings by her usual method of putting a finger firmly over his mouth. 'And thank God for that! But your young friend at the Yard is worth hearing. It's a very simple arrangement. It makes complete sense. We must prepare ourselves to observe this routine until all the unpleasantness blows over or you and that fire-eater Churchill stop making sabre-rattling speeches, darling, whichever is the sooner. *You* it was who insisted on dismissing the police protection squad Joe kindly set up for you, and now you must perform your part of the bargain.'

'Protection squad!' The admiral spat out his derision.

'He didn't have to do that, you know – over and above his duty. You're an ungrateful piggy-wig, Oliver. You listen to no one. I can't think why you objected. Those Branch men he sent round were terribly discreet . . . really, you'd no idea they were there. And the young one was incredibly handsome! I was so enjoying having him about the place. He cheered us all up.' She weathered his splutter of outrage and sailed on. 'But you agreed to the commander's alternative proposals and I for one shall hold you to your promise. I have a part too, you know, and I fully intend to play it. I expect nothing less from you. Now – tell the driver what you want him to do. And don't cut it short – I shall be listening!'

The taxi pulled up in front of a late Georgian house on the northern side of the park-like boulevard that was Melton Square. Heavily porticoed balconies and densely planted patches of garden gave these houses an air of discreet dignity. Dedham looked about him with satisfaction at the solid grandeur, the sedate Englishness, the well-lit pavements, of what he considered to be the heart of London. Nothing truly stirring had happened, in public at least, here in the Five Fields since the Earl of Harrington's cook had been set upon and beaten to death by highwaymen a century before. Since the arrival of the gas-lamps, the only crimes hereabouts were committed behind closed doors by the inhabitants themselves and went unrecorded unless, chiming with the spirit of the times, they gave rise to an ennoblement of some sort for the perpetrator. There were more rich, influential villains per square yard here in

41

this genteel quarter than in Westminster, the admiral always reckoned.

He frowned to see one of these approaching. A gent in evening dress, opera cape about his shoulders, top hat at a louche angle over his forehead, was weaving his way uncertainly along the pavement.

'I say, Cassie.' He drew his wife's attention to the staggering figure. 'Who's this? Do we know him? He looks familiar.'

'He *is* familiar! Look away at once, Oliver!' Cassandra put up a hand, seized his chin and turned his head from the window. 'I forget you scarcely know your own neighbours. But that's ghastly old Chepstow. Drunk as a lord again!'

'If that's Chepstow he *is* a lord,' objected Dedham, trying to turn for a better view. 'He's entitled, you might say.'

'It's no joke, Oliver! Stay still and give him time to move off. He'll recognize you. And you're the one man in London everyone – drunk or sober – wants to talk to and shake hands with. You really have no idea, have you? You're twice a hero now, you know. He'd expect to be invited in for a nightcap. Darling, you've been away from me for six months! I've no intention of sharing you with any old toper.' She pulled his head down into an enthusiastic kiss. 'Ah . . . there he goes . . . Now, Oliver – the cabby's waiting. Get on with the briefing.'

The driver had been grinning in understanding throughout the conversation. He seemed to have a sense of humour and Dedham prepared himself for a sarcastic response to the guff he was about to spout. However, the man accepted his fare and the generous tip he usually enjoyed from the denizens of these fifteen square acres and listened, head tilted in an attitude of exaggerated attention, to the request that came with it. He nodded when the briefing was over and returned a simple 'Understood, sir' in response to the crisp naval tones.

As instructed, he hooted twice and waited for thirty seconds before winking his headlights three times. He even managed to keep a straight face throughout the proceedings. 'There we are, sir. Signal acknowledged. Light's come on in the vestibule,' he said, enjoying the game. 'And the front door's opening. Here we go! Time for the lady to make her sortie.'

With a snort of amusement Lord Dedham understood that the man had been listening as his wife rehearsed him in his exit tactics.

'Road's clear and well lit, sir, no suspicious persons or obstacles in sight, but I'll get out, take a quick recce and then launch the lady.' The driver had suddenly about him the briskness and wariness of an old soldier. 'Just in case. You never know who's lurking in the shrubbery these days.'

He got out and walked up the path, peering into the bushes. He kicked out at an innocent laurel or two before returning to the rear of his motor to open up for Lady Dedham.

'Fire Torpedo One!' she said with a grin for the cabby and, clutching her evening bag tightly in her right hand, she walked off quickly towards the front door the butler was holding wide in welcome. She turned on the doorstep and gave a merry wave.

Before the driver could fire his second charge, a slight form dashed across the street and accosted him. 'A taxi! What luck. In fact, the first stroke of luck I've had tonight. Park Lane please, cabby. Pink's Hotel – do you know it? And fast if you wouldn't mind.' The stranger fiddled around, tugging open with nervous fingers the velvet evening bag she carried dangling from one wrist. She exclaimed with frustration as a handful of coins fell clinking to the ground, and her thanks to the cabby, who scrambled on his knees to retrieve them in the dark, were embarrassed and voluble. Her discomfort increased when she caught sight of Lord Dedham's legs reaching for the pavement. 'Oh, frightfully sorry! Cabby – you already have a fare?'

'Don't worry, miss!' Dedham's reassuring voice boomed out. 'Leaving, not entering. It takes a while to get my two old legs working in concert. You may drive straight on, cabby. As soon as I've disembarked my old carcass.'

'But you told me just now to wait until—'

Lord Dedham cut him off. 'Nonsense! The lady's in a hurry. Take her where she wants to go.'

He accepted an arm in support from the grateful young girl and struggled out, shaking down his uniform and straightening his sword. Very pretty, he thought, with a sideways glance at the slender figure under its satin evening coat and the pure profile set off by the head-hugging feathered hat. He wondered with amused speculation from which of his well-to-do neighbours she could be running away. Not a difficult question: it must be that bounder Ingleby Mountfitchet at number 39. She'd appeared from that direction and was casting anxious glances back towards his house. Dedham followed her gaze with chivalrous challenge. It wouldn't be the first time a girl had fled screeching in the night from that cad's clutches. If rumour was right he'd been kicked out of his regiment. And it would seem that in civvie street his conduct continued to be unbecoming of a gentleman. High time someone took him by the scruff of his scrawny neck and told him that sort of behaviour would not be tolerated in this part of town. Dedham resolved that neighbourly questions would be asked. By him. In the morning.

He walked the few yards to his door, smiling, eager to share his piece of salty gossip with his wife.

He reached the doorstep and greeted his butler with an affectionate bellow. 'There you are, Peterson. All's well with us, you see. We've survived the evening. Though it was touch and go at one point – her ladyship nearly died of boredom. During one of my own speeches!' The expected joking sally was the last intelligible pronouncement the admiral uttered.

Two dark-clad figures crept from the laurel bushes. One called out the admiral's name. When he spun round, identifying himself, they took up position with professional stealth, a man on each side of the doorstep. Both men fired at the same time.

'Service Webleys,' the admiral had time to note before, caught in the cross-fire, he was struck by two bullets in the chest.

An onlooker would have concluded, from the victim's reaction, that the shots had missed their target. Oblivious of his wounds, he strode back outside with a roar of outrage and drew his sword from its scabbard.

The man who had commanded the fire-power of a dozen twelve-inch guns and a crew of seven hundred aboard a battlecruiser in the North Sea now found himself fighting for his life with a dress sword, alone on his own doorstep, but he laid about him with no less relish, attacking by instinct first the larger, more menacing of the pair. He caught him a slicing blow to the cheek. A combat sword in fine fettle would have split the man's face in two, but, despite the blunt edge, the admiral was encouraged to see he'd drawn blood. Delighted by the howl of pain he'd provoked, he went for the smaller man, chopping at his gun hand.

A third bullet hit Dedham in the heart.

His sword clattered to the paving and he folded at the knees, collapsing sideways into the arms of his wife. Unconcerned for her own safety, Cassandra had run back to her husband and knelt by his side, supporting him with her left arm. He opened his lips to whisper 'Kiss me, Cassie' as he'd often joked that he would in a playful tribute to his hero, Lord Nelson, should he be laid low and preparing for death. But no words would come. He couldn't seem to draw breath. And Cassandra's attention was elsewhere. With a croak of astonishment, the admiral blinked to see his wife freeing her right hand from her bag. Unaccountably, the hand he'd so recently fondled in the taxi now held a small pistol which she fired off, shot after purposeful shot, at the fleeing pair. Her scream of encouragement to the butler rang in his ears: 'After them! Stop the ruffian scum, Peterson!'

Lord Dedham smiled admiringly up at her and his eyes closed on the sight of his wife taking careful aim down the barrel of her Beretta.

The two gunmen raced to the taxi, firing backwards over their shoulders at Peterson who chased after them armed with nothing but fury and his bare hands. They bundled themselves into the back seat next to the shrieking woman in the feathered hat. Unsurprisingly, she rapidly made space for them and their guns on the back seat.

Hit in the shoulder and leg and bleeding on to the pavement, the butler raised his head and watched as the motor erupted into a three-point turn. In his agitation, the driver seemed to clash his gears and the car ground to a juddering halt, its rear licence plate clearly in view in the light of the lamp. Peterson focused, stared and repeated the number to himself.

In the distance a police whistle sounded and the boots of the beat bobby pounded along the pavement. Peterson called out faintly.

At last, the taxi screeched off with a great deal of revving but little forward momentum.

The turbulence in the back seat threw up a stink of sweat, the iron odour of blood and a reek of cordite. This noxious cocktail was accompanied by a gabbling argument in a language the driver could not understand. But rage soon expressed itself in plain English. 'Stop farting about, you bastard! Drive!' the larger of the two men snarled. 'To Paddington station. Fast. Miss one more gear and you get it in the neck yourself. Like this.' He pulled back his gun to point it ahead through the open window at the beat bobby who had placed himself squarely in the road in front of the taxi, one hand holding a whistle to his mouth, the other raised in the traffic-stopping gesture. This calm Colossus held his position as the taxi came on, impregnable in his authority.

Two shots sent the imposing figure crashing on to the road.

The cabby swerved violently and deftly mounted the pavement to avoid running over the body.

'Leave it to me, sir,' he said, apparently unperturbed by the hot gun-barrel now boring into his flesh. 'I know these streets like the back of my hand. We'll go the quickest way.' And, light but reassuring: 'Don't you worry, sir – I'll get you to the station all right.'

Chapter Five

Joe looked up from his notes and ran a hand over his bristly chin. He blinked and focused wearily on his secretary across the desk. 'Who did you say, Jameson? Constable Wentworth? Oh, Lord! My nine o'clock interview. Didn't I say she was to be intercepted and her appointment deferred?'

'Well, she's sitting out there now in the corridor, sir, large as life. I've no idea how she managed to sneak past them at Reception. I did tell them.' Miss Jameson dabbed at her eyes with a damp handkerchief. 'Today of all days!' She gulped and sniffed in distress. 'We've got quite enough on our plate. She's only been summoned to hear her dismissal. I'll tell her to go away and come back later. A week here or there can't signify.'

'No. Wait a moment.' He pulled towards him a file bearing the constable's name and number. It also sported an ominous red tag.

Discharge.

Notice of termination of employment with His Majesty's Metropolitan Police. Announcing that an officer was surplus to requirements was always a difficult duty when not deserved and, as far as Joe was aware, none of the women did deserve dismissal. Mostly, they left with relief to get married or because their ankles swelled. When the austerity cuts demanded it, he had chosen to break the news to the men himself, rather than expose them to the abrupt, acerbic style of the Assistant Commissioner whose job it normally was, but had left the women to be dealt with by a high-ranking female officer like his cousin Margery Stewart, better acquainted with the subject and better equipped by nature with a comforting shoulder to cry on.

The young woman waiting outside was a special case, however. And time was running short.

The decisions arrived at in last month's Gratton Court conference Joe now saw had been right and timely. With a grim irony, it had been Admiral Dedham himself who had argued against them and, outvoted at the time, had immediately set about dismantling the sensible schemes. After last night's tragedy, it fell now to Joe to reinvigorate the plans without delay, before worse occurred. Before *much* worse occurred. His deadline was a week on Saturday. Not long enough.

'Bring her in, Miss Jameson. I do need to see her. Might as well get it over and done with.'

While Miss Jameson's back was turned, he slipped the red marker off the file, considered throwing it away in the bin, then put it in his pocket. The outcome of this interview was by no means certain. And, whatever the result, he had an unpleasant task ahead of him, a task imposed upon him by a pincer movement from above. At Gratton he'd found the courage to make his views clear and they'd heard him out but in the end, as the youngest and least experienced of the assembled strategists, he'd been overruled. Politely, he'd been made aware that his role was one of ... what had Churchill said? ... *implementation*, not grand design.

'Cat's paw.' Lydia had it right, as ever. If all went well, they would take the credit. If disaster followed, Sandilands would carry the can.

Joe screwed his eyes closed and conjured up without too much difficulty the face that went with the number on the file. It had made quite an impression on him. The station platform. Smoke and noise. And in the middle of the mêlée, a pretty girl grinning in triumph. Under her bottom one of the West End's nastiest specimens and in her hat a jaunty rose. Joe smiled as he remembered the scene. He recalled watching the tiger-like silence of the stalk, the swift pounce, the fearless attack. He hadn't forgotten the eager rush of gratitude for his intervention, delivered in an attractive, low voice. The constable could well be the best England had to offer in the way of womanhood, he thought with a rush of sentimental pride.

And that was something he would have to eradicate from his thinking in this job: Edwardian gallantry. There could be no place for the finer feelings in this ghastly modern world. Chivalry itself had fallen victim to bloody-handed assassins, if he read the situation aright.

Yes, this had to be the right girl. If he were minded to preachify, he might even say that Fate had delivered her into his hands that day at Paddington.

And the next day down in Devon, he had delivered her into the hands of three of the most ruthless men in the land.

'Look no further, gentlemen,' he'd said, after a second glass of port. 'If this is really what you are prepared to do, I think I may I have the very girl for you.' He'd even announced her name and number. Satisfyingly, eyebrows had been raised, grunts and nods of encouragement had broken out. Warmed by the general approval, he'd undertaken to haul her aboard.

Joe shuddered. He'd saved her from a knifing at Paddington but had probably exposed her to a worse fate.

He'd have to play his cards carefully. He could take nothing and no one for granted. This wasn't the army where orders were given, received and blindly obeyed. The woman was perfectly free to reject his overtures and scoff at his suggestions. And foul up some well-laid plans.

Lily Wentworth followed Miss Jameson into the room and looked about her. Astutely anticipating a dismissal committee, he guessed. Her eyes rested briefly on him, widened in surprise, narrowed again in distaste and slid down to her boots. Well, if she'd been expecting to see the knight-errant from Paddington, all smiles and panache, she was going to be disappointed this morning; what she'd got was a Sandilands sore and seething with rage. He realized that in his dark-jowled state he presented an unappetizing sight. With not a minute to dash to his Chelsea flat and change, he'd resorted to a quick cold splash in the gents' washbasins an hour ago. He'd stared back in dismay at his image in the mirror: black stubble, red eyes, and a dark tan looking unhealthily dirty in the morning light, as well as throwing sinister emphasis on the silver tracery of an old shrapnel wound across his forehead. If he'd encountered that face in Seven Dials, he'd have clapped the cuffs on and searched the owner's pockets for a stiletto.

The cold wash hadn't gone far towards dispelling the night's build-up of fatigue and filth. He glanced down at his blood-stained tie and cuffs. His attempts to dab them clean had not been entirely successful. Whose blood? It could have been from any or all of the four victims. Ah, well . . . she'd probably seen worse down the Mile End Road at chucking-out time on a Saturday night. No need to draw attention to it. He rose to his feet and came round his desk to greet her.

'That will be all, thank you, Miss Jameson,' he said genially enough. 'Go and get yourself a cup of tea or something. You look as though you could do with one. Oh, and while you're at it, remind PC Jones I haven't had mine yet. Tell him to bring a tray. Two cups. Milk and sugar. Biscuits too – gypsy creams would be good – not that dog kibble he brought me yesterday.'

The door closed and they were left staring at each other.

'Sir, I arrived early for my appointment . . .'

'Did you now?'

'I did knock.'

'Good. Good. Thought I heard something.'

Disconcerted by the fresh-faced, soap-scented presence, Joe went to open another window. That done, he began to pace about in a distracted manner.

51

'Sorry to have kept you waiting, Miss Wentworth. We're running a bit late today. Look here . . . I'll get straight to it.' He began to speak in her general direction. 'You may have heard . . . no, how could you? Anyway – there was something of a bloodbath last night in the West End. Admiral shot to death on his doorstep, butler wounded, beat bobby left for dead like a dog in the road, London cabby fighting for his life in hospital,' he confided in a rush. 'Carnage on the streets, I'm afraid. You'll read all about it in the papers, no doubt. It's just what those hyenas have been waiting for. I've been . . . um . . .' he glanced at the telephone sitting in the middle of his desk, 'involving myself. Rather emphatically. Hard to stand back when one of the victims was a man I counted as my friend. And a friend avowedly under my protection at the time.'

He stopped his pacing and added bitterly: 'There will be many to ascribe responsibility for the whole shambles to me. Not least myself.'

His flood of alarming information seemed to have rendered the girl speechless. Well, how else might he expect a young policewoman to respond to a throbbing monologue from her superior but with a wise silence? Finally she managed to say softly: 'I'm so sorry you've lost your friend, sir. You must be very distressed. And you must want to be left alone to get on. Would you like me to go away for now? I can come back some other time.' She took a step back towards the door.

He held up a staying hand. 'No, don't go. I shall mourn the admiral later and in my own way. Which is to say with targeted vigour.' He shot a glance of such deadly intent in her direction that Lily looked aside. 'Now you're here, come on over and let's renew our acquaintance.'

She approached the desk, ignored the chair set in front of it and stood to attention as she'd been trained. Feet a precise eighteen inches apart, straight back, shoulders down, palms to the rear. All very correct. To salute or not to salute? Joe realized she was questioning the protocol.

She hesitated for a moment, then, apparently deciding he merited the gesture, gave him a perfect salute.

He managed a grin. 'Returning mine of the fourteenth, I take it? Thank you. Do sit down and we'll start again.'

Puzzlingly, the girl stayed on her feet.

Wrong footed by her silence and rigid stance, Joe relaunched the conversation in a welcoming and very English prattle.

'Looks as though it's going to be hot again today.'

'We've had the hottest summer for twenty-seven years, I understand, sir.'

'Yes . . . When will it end? Pigs keeling over with heat stroke at the county show . . .' he offered with a bland smile.

'Reckless swimmers getting into difficulties in the Serpentine.'

'But there's *some* good news. We have our Prince of Wales back home safe and sound at last.'

Her voice was tight with strain as she returned yet another answer in this tedious sequence. 'After eight months touring India, he will be acclimatized to this heat.'

'Well, that'll do for our review of the papers,' Joe said, and fell silent.

In pursuit of his brief he began to pace about the room again, noting for the record, in what he hoped was an unobtrusive fashion, her height, weight and general deportment. He was relieved to see he'd remembered correctly the trim figure, the modest height. He couldn't be sure about the face. With the downcast eyes and the large-brimmed hat, she could have been anybody.

A closer inspection was now essential. He went to perch on the front edge of his desk, eyes on a level with hers, improperly close. This overbearing male behaviour was calculated to disturb, to test the subject's mettle. It was a crude ploy he'd had much success with in the interrogation of male prisoners, military and civilian. The scar skewed his face and Joe had learned to use the sardonic twist with its suggestion of pain survived to intimidate his subjects. He'd noticed that even the tough nuts were unable to hold his eye. Their gaze faltered and slid to one side. They began to fidget and tell him their lies with less confidence.

If the girl ran whimpering from the room or kicked him in the shins at this point, he wouldn't blame her but that would have to be the end of it.

She responded by staring calmly at a spot on his tie, a slight twist of disdain on her lips.

Perfect.

'Now then, Miss Wentworth . . . er, Lilian? That your given name?'

'I'm usually called just Lily, sir. By those who know me. "Constable" by those who don't.'

His scrutiny had been over close and over long. And perhaps it was unfair to expose her to blood-spatter and bristle at this hour of the morning. When she caught him inspecting her feet he muttered: 'Those boots are a disgrace. Not your fault. Poor quality leather. Won't take a polish. The men wouldn't put up with them for two minutes. I'll have a word in the right ear.'

'It will go straight out through the left, I'm sure, but thank you for the thought, sir.'

Was the tone rebellious? Joe frowned. Not yet. Just this side of acceptable. He'd push her further. He peered playfully under her brim, questioning. She went on looking straight ahead, impassive.

'Why don't you sit down? I don't want to conduct this interview standing. We may be here some time.'

She sank uneasily on to a chair.

'You're smaller than I remembered,' he remarked.

'Tall enough to satisfy the height requirement.'

Joe picked up a pencil and scratched a note for himself: 5'6"?

'And younger.'

'I lied about my age. Sir.'

A swift glance into the unblinking, innocent eyes told him she was certainly lying now. Personal details of recruits were meticulously checked. Joe knew when he was being needled. He wrote again, taking his time: *26, could pass for 18. Insubordinate?*

'And your weight, miss? You would appear to be . . . er . . . not exactly well covered in the flesh department.'

He'd clearly touched a nerve at last. The nostrils flared and her voice when she replied was glacial: 'After eight years of privation, sir, are we surprised? There's been a war on.'

He scribbled: *Skinny. Insubordinate!* 'Look – remove your hat, will you?'

She took off her hat and placed it on her lap.

Joe stared at her hair in surprise. 'Always interesting to see what you're hiding under those domes. Glad to see it's just a dolly-mop of hair and not a bomb.' He glanced again at her thick bob and scribbled a note on a pad. 'Tell me – again for the record – how would you describe the colour of your hair? Blonde?'

'Say straw, sir. If it could possibly be of any interest to anyone.'

Joe thought Miss Wentworth's shining flaxen hair would interest any man. He busied himself for an annoying moment or two, unconvincingly jotting a further note: *Hair – fair, fashionably cut. Brows and lashes darker. Green? eyes. V. pretty* . . . and cut himself short.

He was making a pig's ear of this.

Should he have delegated the unwelcome task to his super? To his Branch man? Joe reassured himself by remembering both men's lack of experience with the fair sex and their declared antagonism to the Working Woman. No, neither officer could have gone one round with this sample. He was becoming increasingly certain his choice was a good one. He just had to make the right approaches.

He settled back in his chair, trying for friendly and approachable. 'Now, before I tell you why you're here . . .'

he indicated the file with her number on the cover, 'I'd like to congratulate you on your prompt and decisive action at the station. I've entered a commendation on your file. Would you like me to read it out for you?'

'Thank you. Very good of you, sir. I'll take it as read.' And, sweetly: 'I'm sure my commanding officer could have passed that on and saved you the trouble.'

And, of course, she was right. A man of his rank didn't concern himself with the actions, however creditable, of a lowly policewoman.

'Quite. But I did have, you will recall, a personal interest in the episode. And I'm the chap, for the moment, in charge of hiring, firing and redeployment, not your CO. Redeployment, Wentworth. Which brings me to the second reason for calling you in.'

She startled him by leaping to her feet, triggered, Joe thought, by the word 'redeployment'. With automatic good manners he rose also, registering surprise.

'I know what you're up to. Before you proceed with this, sir, I have to tell you that I will not accept redeployment. I will not be sent to some northern city with the likes of Constable Halliday.' Her eyes narrowed to a glare. 'Nor will I stand here and be sacked.'

Joe listened in astonishment as she forged on: 'This would seem to be a bad moment for both of us. I'm leaving now to go away and write out my resignation from the force. It will be on your desk within the hour. It will make mention of the impossibility of suffering any longer the prejudice and arrogance the women are confronted with at every turn. To say nothing of the low pay and the long hours. And the questionable company of tarts, drug fiends and corrupt coppers.'

She must have been aware that her words sounded undignified. Pre-prepared words, he guessed, that she'd been mulling over and getting together while she'd been sitting in the corridor expecting dismissal. Well, the girl showed some spirit and he wasn't looking for a doormat. He decided to take her insubordination on the chin.

She hurried to finish, eager to be away. 'I'm sorry, sir . . . not the Ciceronian speech I'd planned. A bit light on concessive clauses and qualifying phrases.'

'And possibly charm, Constable?' he teased.

'It'll have to do. You must excuse me. Good day to you, Commander. I'll leave you to your sorrows and . . . more demanding concerns.'

Petulant, foot-stamping stuff. Good girl. But it was decidedly inconvenient for him. Joe began to think he'd mishandled the whole thing. He'd allowed her to provoke him. He'd certainly raised her hackles and now they risked losing her. In what looked very like a rush of light-headed recklessness, she turned without waiting for his dismissal and made for the door.

His voice, lazily enquiring, snaked after her, catching her by the ankle, staying her step. 'Don't you want to hear what became of the children in the case?'

It seemed he'd come up with the one formula that would have stopped her from leaving the room. She hesitated.

'And the villain whose head you sat on? Were you aware you broke his nose? Resume your seat and hear me out. That's better,' he said as she settled on the edge of the seat. 'Ah! Here's our tea. Put it on the desk, will you, Jones? Thank you, that'll be all.' He heaved a layer of files and boxes on to the floor to accommodate the tea tray, then he took up the pot and filled two cups. 'Drop of milk, one sugar, I understand? You always pay for it. And these are your favourite biscuits. Do have one.'

He relished her astonishment for a moment. 'I'm a detective by inclination. I still poke about, making enquiries. Military Intelligence during the war. It leaves its mark, don't you know. Once a busybody, always a busybody. I took time to speak to old Stan on my way back through Paddington. He was very happy to talk about you. And I was more than happy to hear his eulogies. I'm going to confess to you, Miss Wentworth, that, though I rather relish the influence my rank brings me, I've been promoted out of step with my interest . . . if you follow me. I find there's a sight too much form-filling, committee-sitting and politicking in it to please me.'

He accompanied his speech with a rueful smile. It seemed to alarm rather than reassure the girl he was directing it at but he pressed on anyway. 'However – we're not here to talk about *my* career. I want to propose a change of direction for you, Miss Wentworth. I don't know where this nonsense about redeployment to the north comes from. You are in no way bracketed with that reprobate Halliday.' He leafed through the file and found the sheet he wanted. 'Halliday . . . Yes, here we are. He has indeed been sent north – to Yorkshire for re-training – and no one's expecting to see him back in the metropolis again.'

Joe read on for a while, absorbed. 'Your ex-partner had some pretty unkind things to say about you, I'm afraid.' Silently, he scanned the vindictive phrases meticulously recorded by his superintendent, flinched, and decided not to reveal them. *Common as cat shit and twice as nasty . . . Gift of the gab . . . Looks like the bleeding fairy on the Christmas tree – but don't turn your back on her or you'll find out what her wand's for . . .*

'You must be awfully glad he's gone, Miss Wentworth. Not quite sure what they'll make of him in Yorkshire – more of a man, one would hope. No – I propose to deploy you in a different area, though still within the city of London. I have in mind a different role for you. And a different partner.'

He waited until, intrigued, she turned her eyes back to him before announcing with a mock bow and a broad smile: 'Myself. Now – two exhibits.' He shuffled his files again and produced a photograph. 'What do you make of that?'

She seemed stunned but she took the photograph with a shaking hand and studied it. It provoked a spontaneous reply. 'It's a posed group photograph. Centre front I see an elderly and distinguished gentleman in the uniform of a high-ranking police official . . .'

'He's Chief Constable of the Lancashire Constabulary,' Sandilands supplied. 'Philip Lane. Fine fellow. Go on.'

'And the lucky man has surrounded himself with a retinue of twenty or so pretty women. All young. Under thirty? I'd have said women policemen if they weren't in mufti. Silk stockings, smart shoes, lovely frocks . . .' She paused for a moment, appreciating what she was seeing. 'And they all look very pleased with themselves.' She must have caught the flash of humour in his eye and dared to add: 'Especially the Chief!'

'Oh, Lane's having a happy time. He dislikes the women's uniform as much as I do. And there's something else we agree on – those women are indeed in the police though they are not being used, as they are here in the Met, in a social service role. Escorting schoolchildren across the road, prising illicit couples apart with a crowbar in the park, sitting on sparrowhawks . . . that would seem to be the limit of our expectations of the women's patrols, Miss Wentworth. Tedious, degrading stuff. No, my friend Lane employs his girls as part of the detective force. Look at their faces. Sharp as a pin, every last one of them! You could send any of those women in like a terrier down a foxhole and she'd flush out her prey.'

'They're *detectives*, these women?' Incredulity and envy were blended in her tone.

'Yes, indeed.' He looked at her sharply, pleased with her reaction. He thought he was beginning to understand what made this girl tick. And her interest chimed with his own. He would have no problem in fostering it. 'You're impressed by these young ladies?'

'I'll say! Detectives! I hadn't realized it was possible. Lucky women!'

Joe smiled in quiet triumph to hear the longing in her voice. He was seeing his way through to his goal at last.

'I believe, along with Philip, that the talents of you and others like you are being under-used in the force,' he confided. 'But the Geddes Axe has swung over the police service as much as other public services – we have a four-year war effort to pay for, after all, and we musn't grumble, Wentworth, must we? But your numbers have been halved – you're reduced to fifty now, I believe, and the ultimate target is a mere twenty. And that doesn't please some of us. I, for one, am determined to hang on to the core of exceptional women remaining to us and pray that Nancy Astor can work her magic in Parliament to get the women's contingent reinstated.'

Daring and undisciplined. A view contrary to that of the Commissioner himself. That would make her think and wonder.

He gave her a glance across the desk, the calculation in the eyes meant to be offset by the smiling lips. Joe thought grimly that he was probably recreating the effect, in his present state of dark dishevelment, of an ancient Greek reveller he'd seen decorating a vase in the British Museum. Bearded, knowing, conniving and with the same winsome smile, the Attic figure had been leading a garlanded heifer. With one reassuring hand he caressed the silken flank, with the other he tugged on the rope, urging the animal forward up the Sacred Way. If you walked round and inspected the far side of the vase, you could see that they were only steps away from an altar where they were confidently awaited by the priest who stood at the ready, sacrificial knife raised.

'Your name, Miss Wentworth . . .' the smiler with the butcher's knife administered a further calming pat, leaning confidingly towards her though there was no one else in the room, 'has come to the top of the dismissals list, as I would imagine you've calculated, perceptive girl that you are. And that's exactly what I ought to be doing this morning – handing you your cards and showing you the door. You were aware of this, of course?'

He waited for her nod before going on. 'But it's my opinion that you would be a loss to the force and I'm suggesting a way of circumventing the necessity to terminate your contract. I propose a scheme which, rather than striking your name from the roll, will put it in brackets and move it sideways, so to speak . . . something on those lines,' he finished vaguely. A slashing hand mimed the expunging of her name and was followed by a demonstration of the bracketing: two cupped hands moving with the care of a cricketer's to draw aside and bring to safety.

Lily's eyes followed them, mesmerized. Large, brown and capable hands. The message they were conveying was easily understood. In the small space between them lay her career. It could be dropped or held firm and she was powerless to decide the outcome.

She made no comment and he pushed on. 'But further, I think there should be a change in the character of your employment. I've chosen you, Miss Wentworth, to help me out. In a rather unusual duty. It's all a bit hush-hush. Got a dainty summer frock, have you? Well, I want you to mothball that ugly blue outfit you're wearing, get into mufti and do a bit of undercover work for me.'

'What? Like a spy, you mean? Like Mata Hari?'

Joe managed not to smile at her innocent remark but his reply was light and teasing: 'Something like that, perhaps. But I don't envisage you making an appearance, like that unfortunate lady, before a firing squad. And seducing generals would be an entirely optional activity. No – I simply want you to blend in with the surroundings I'm going to pop you into. I want you to help me sort out a little problem I find I have.'

'Why me, sir?'

'Because I've seen for myself that you have pluck and initiative. From your file – and from the admiring Stan – I gather that you are utterly reliable. And – a rather essential element in my schemes – you're a girl who doesn't mind getting her hands dirty. The task I have in mind is hardly one for a lady . . .'

Her glare told him he'd made a faux pas. Unaccustomed to making social gaffes, Joe was flustered. 'Er . . . don't misunderstand me. I intended no insult, Wentworth. And you *will* understand that when you embark on the very particular task I'm about to set you. I was merely trying to convey that I have no use for idle flibbertigibbets who spend their mornings in Asprey and their evenings in Ciro's.'

'Horses for courses?' she suggested.

'Exactly! You know where you are with horses,' he said, grinning. 'You read me right – I'm not looking for a thoroughbred so nervy you have to clap blinkers over its swivelling eyes to stop it dancing sideways.'

'If you're seeking a plodding percheron, I can't help you, sir.'

'Quite! I'd be looking at you a long time before a cart horse came to mind, miss! No – what I've got my sights on is a hunter. Light bay with an intelligent eye. Shows courage over fences. Ideally one that doesn't bite your hand off down to the arm-pit when you offer it a sugar lump.'

At last she'd smiled at him. He returned her smile and forged on. 'Now – a further test. The lout you sat upon at Paddington . . . the Sparrowhawk. Had you been in charge of the case instead of Inspector Proudfoot, how would you have proceeded with him?'

She nodded and sat forward in her chair, understanding that her interview had, at last, got under way. She spoke up with confidence. 'I'd have located his headquarters and raided it.'

'Easily said – but if he refused to reveal its whereabouts? And I have to tell you – he *did* refuse. Rather forcefully. Hard man under that foppish exterior.'

'I would have assumed so. But there were other indications. The flowers were freshly bought and the florist

whose wrapper was still around them might have something to tell. But, for speed, I'd have consulted the one
reliable witness we already had at the scene. The witness
who would have led us straight to his base of operations.
I'd have just followed the dog, sir. Let it lead me to its
home, which would most probably have been a shortish
distance away – I'm guessing somewhere north of the park,
along the Bayswater Road. Then I'd have mounted a raid.'

'Good. Good.' He nodded. 'Proudfoot – and the dog –
got there in the end.'

'And the little girl and her brother?'

'Are safely lodged with the aunt they'd set out to find in
London. She lives out east in one of those streets between
Petticoat Lane and Spitalfields . . . they'd never have found
her under their own steam. The poor woman! She'd no
idea they even existed, so it must have been quite a shock
when the NSPCC knocked on her door. But she rallied
round quite admirably, they report, and took them in. And
what a Dickensian scene I imagine *that* to have been! They
were runaways from a particularly distressing situation in
their home village. Brave little pair. They'll come through.'
Something in her expression made him add: 'And yes, I
shall be checking on their well-being.'

He slid a file across his desk at her. She'd passed the first
two of his four tests. Physically: perfect. Under nine stone,
less than five foot seven and attractive. Intellectually:
astute. But what sort of a strategist was she? He needed a
girl who could think for herself, and fast. He'd decided
which fence to put her at.

'And now we come to it . . . the reason I summoned you
here. Your first case, Wentworth. Disturbing, urgent and of
national importance. I want you to acquaint yourself with
the contents of this file, which must not leave my office.
When you've read it—'

She interrupted him. 'Sir, excuse me but I'm meant to go
on Park patrol in half an hour.'

Joe wasn't pleased to be distracted by routine. 'Park patrol? Forget it. Don't concern yourself with regulations. Consider yourself removed from whatever were your daily duties. I'll have a word with your commanding officer. Tell me – to whom do you report?'

'To Inspector Margery Stewart, sir.'

'Ah! There's a piece of luck. The Honourable Margery, eh? A distant cousin of mine. I'll square it with her. Leave all the boring operational stuff to me. Now – this file . . .'

The telephone rang and he snatched up the earpiece at once.

'Speaking. Ah, yes. The matter is in hand. In fact I have her here in the room with me right now.' Sandilands glanced across the desk at Lily, who was politely scrambling to her feet to leave the room. He flapped a hand to indicate that she should remain seated. 'No. I won't be pushed on this. You interrupt my interview. Yes, yes . . . entirely suitable. And I'm sure I can say ready and able . . . Not fully briefed yet, of course.' He paused to flash a placatory smile at Lily. 'Understood . . . I'll work to that.'

He replaced the earpiece, deep in thought, then exclaimed, made a pantomime of shaking the fatigue from his head, and picked up the phone again. When the switchboard answered, he asked, 'Can you reconnect me please with that last number? It was extension 371.'

'You've got Sandilands back. I forgot to say – don't try to get me here at my desk until at least tea time. I shall be out at the scene.' A burble of protest at the other end was audible even to Lily and set Joe frowning. 'It's my back yard. My concern. My responsibility. You'll just have to await further instructions.'

His broadside delivered, he hung up, grinned at Lily and picked up his conversation where he'd left off. 'When you've read it – and assuming the telephone doesn't ring in the meantime to announce that the Home Secretary has decided to accept the resignation I put on his desk first

64

thing this morning – we'll proceed to St George's hospital with a notebook and a bunch or two of flowers. Now—'

'Hang on a minute! You've turned over two pages at once there. *Your* resignation? Blimey! Sir!' Astonishment stripped away the veneer of cool accent, revealing something more earthy and emotional below. 'You're never giving up. Over this business of the admiral? Go on with you. You shouldn't do that, sir.'

He bit his lip. Fatigue. He'd said too much. But what the hell! It had provoked a spontaneous but sympathetic reaction. Joe decided to follow up his unexpected advantage. 'Least I could do in the circumstances. You and me both – in the same boat. And if *I'm* scuppered, so are you. Your career and mine are hanging by a thread this morning. And, I'll tell you, it's the same thread. With gross unfairness I carry on as though nothing has happened . . . I offer you a new partner one moment only to have you discover the next that he is compromised. Professionally speaking, of course.' He peered at her suspiciously, realizing that her composure was unusual. 'Some girls would have been wailing at me by now . . . or weeping . . . Don't you care?'

'I'm still trying to absorb your news, sir. And its implications.' She leaned towards him, fixing him with eyes which he could have sworn held a certain understanding and – at last – approval. 'And of course I care. It would seem to me that a great injustice is about to be done. It's not my place to say it, but – don't go chucking in the towel. Surely there's something you could do?'

He sighed and leaned back in his chair, looking away to glower moodily into the middle distance. And then, with the brittle firmness of a man who has just come uncertainly to a decision: 'It seems to me we have three choices: we can combine our strengths – such as they are – to plot a rearguard action and go down fighting; we can accept our fate and hear each other rehearsing our farewell speeches in the taxi; or we can simply jump ship. Leave this mess behind us. Climb aboard the next boat train and be in the casino

65

in Monte Carlo by tomorrow evening, glass of champagne in hand.' Joe fell silent, caught out by a sudden heady vision of eyes full of mischief holding his over the rim of something chilled and fragrant. The champagne bubbling between them was Pol Roger 1911. The eyes were dark and deceitful, and after all these months they still had the power to ambush his thoughts.

He saw Lily's very different eyes flare in surprise and fix at once on the notes in front of her. All three of his suggestions were alarming and ought never to have been uttered, fuelled as they were by a cocktail of exhaustion, tension and guilt, and triggered by the lethal touch of female sympathy. Always his Achilles heel. Joe sensed, too late, that he was losing control, teetering on the crest of an emotional wave and threatening to drag this innocent down with him. What must she have thought?

She seemed aware of the danger and, when he might have expected a hissing intake of breath and an offended drawing away of skirts at his desperate third suggestion, she replied calmly, 'I don't agree. There is a fourth. And I suspect it's a course you've already decided on. We simply carry on doing our jobs for a bit longer. I've got a week to work out. That's the routine. Not sure how long you have – it's probably different for the upper ranks. I would suggest carrying on normally while awaiting further developments. See what the Home Secretary has to say and then think again.'

He nodded glumly, regretting his outburst and avoiding her eye.

'And then, sir, when you know the worst, I'll join you in whichever of the above schemes seems most attractive. With a preference for the last.'

He looked at her in sharp astonishment, scanning her face for signs of flirtation.

'But may I substitute Nice as our destination? I hear it's much more agreeable than Monte Carlo in high summer.

And they have palm trees along the promenade. I've never seen a palm tree.'

Her manner, relaxed and completely un-coquettish, let him off the hook. There was no hint in her tone that she had interpreted his suggestions as in any way salacious. The potential dynamite of his careless third proposition had, in a cool way, been acknowledged and playfully rendered harmless. Joe responded with a surprised stare and a cough, and was back in control again. 'Point taken, constable. Nice it is, then. We'll agree on that much. Though perhaps we shouldn't dismiss Biarritz too readily . . . Now, finish up those biscuits. You won't be getting any lunch today. I'm going to leave you here to absorb that lot while I dash to my rooms and change and then set out for Jermyn Street for a shave. There's a man at Trumper's who can make a down-and-out look like Douglas Fairbanks in ten minutes flat. He may well be able to work his magic for me. Can't be seen going about London looking like a ruffian. To think that today of all days I chose to wear a slouch hat!'

He grabbed a black felt hat from the hat stand and put it on, pulling it down exaggeratedly low over his forehead and leering. 'There! What do you think? Shall I be taken for a Bolshevist, do you suppose?'

Lily responded to his flash of good humour with a chuckle. 'Well, it's certainly a *look*, sir. It goes with the red eyes and the purple bags under them. Cosmopolitan roué – would that be what you're aiming for? It may pass in Piccadilly but I wouldn't try it out in Eaton Square. They'll string you up from the nearest lamp post.' She turned back to the notes he'd passed her, eager to make a start.

'And don't think of making a run for it,' he said, before he left. 'I shall alert my secretary on my way out and tell her she's to have you detained if you so much as put your nose round the door. She's just across the corridor and she has a button to the desk downstairs. Oh . . . er, should you need to . . . um . . . Miss Jameson will show you the way.'

Oh, Lord! That was another thing. Facilities: females for the use of . . . Could they provide? He assumed there were such things in the Yard as Miss Jameson would have complained otherwise. And it was likely to be the least of the problems this wretched scheme threatened to lumber him with. Joe glanced over his shoulder at the earnest young face already totally absorbed by the distracting bone he'd thrown her way.

Bloody orders! This was a good officer. She deserved better.

Chapter Six

Left alone, Lily sat for a few minutes trying to make sense of the hastily assembled file. This was decidedly 'works in progress'. A pile of papers had been scraped together from various sources: scene of crime notes, press cuttings and even letters on headed writing paper. This bird's nest was destined, she expected, after passing through Miss Jameson's typing machine, to be the building blocks of the final case file. After reviewing all the material and admiring the quality of the scene of crime work carried out by torchlight through the night, Lily managed to put it all into chronological order.

A devastating tale was beginning to emerge. From the earliest documents, she understood that Sandilands had, last month, set up a protection force from the ranks of the Special Branch for Lord Dedham, along with one or two other prominent military gents. Evidence had led him to suppose that they were likely targets for the Irish gunmen of Sinn Fein. Three distinguished men, including General Lansing, had been attacked in varying and – Lily judged – amateurish fashion the month before on the streets of London. There had been an attempted cudgelling, a knifing and – most seriously – a shooting where the bullet, mis-aimed in the struggle, had passed harmlessly through the general's upper arm. All the victims had defended themselves with spirit and none had been seriously hurt. None of the assailants had been apprehended.

'Thuggery on the streets of the West End,' had been the deduction of two of the victims. But the third, Lansing, had sought out the receptive ear of Sandilands to express a different, more thoughtful, view. He'd exchanged words as well as blows with his two assailants and had been intrigued to receive a torrent of abuse delivered with an Irish accent. A southern Irish accent, he'd said firmly. His family had property near Dublin and he knew what he was talking about. Apart from Lansing's certitude, there didn't appear to be an obvious Irish connection and no one had claimed responsibility for the outrages, but someone – Sandilands? – had taken the pattern as a warning of worse to come as the situation in Ireland grew ever more inflamed.

Every day Irish desperadoes were setting their own cities ablaze, shooting and blowing up their countrymen, with no regard for age or sex, it seemed. Lily had cringed at the reports of families bombed to bits in the middle of the night, of men kidnapped, tortured and executed, of bodies left in the gutter. Only the day before, a little girl had answered a knock on the door and been shot in the stomach. With a shiver, Lily remembered reading the press speculation that the daily murders and explosions being suffered by that country could easily be exported to England.

Beaverbrook's journals had thundered on for weeks about the dangers. It was just a matter of time and opportunity, they asserted. Significantly, the words 'desperado' and 'hooligan' had been replaced by the more alarming 'terrorist'. There was a large population of Irish settlers in London, many with military training in the British army. They would have easy access to the arms and ammunition which lingered on in anonymous dumps in discreet places after the war and they would have the will and the skill to use them. In a city crowded with immigrants from many nations, the Irish blended in better than most, being indistinguishable in appearance from the native Englishmen. And unless they cared to engage you in conversation, revealing their accents, or announce to you at gunpoint that they were Irish, you would never know who was about to blow your brains out.

Sandilands seemed to have been handed a list of endangered politicians and public figures. Police squads had been allocated to these gentlemen. But before his plans could be put into action, the patrols had been stood down at the request of the potential victims themselves. Copies of their letters to Sandilands had been kept. *Dear Commander . . . frightfully grateful and all that . . . military man myself . . . not in my own capital . . . no necessity . . . must therefore decline . . .*

With the protection withdrawn and the admiral shot dead, questions would be asked in the press and in Parliament – to say nothing of every public bar in the land. 'And where were our policemen in this?' was likely to be the most politely phrased enquiry. Resignations would be expected. Sandilands was quite right to have fallen on his sword – Lily feared that his position was, indeed, untenable. Until she turned up a note he had carefully kept. The note authorized – indeed, demanded – the instant suppression of the police guard on the gentlemen concerned, who had no wish for it to continue. It was judged an expensive manoeuvre and an unnecessary one. The note was signed by the Home Secretary himself.

Lily put it conspicuously at the front of the file.

The investigating CID officer at the scene of the assassination of Dedham, a Superintendent Hopkirk, had been there in minutes and seemed to have done a thorough job in the short time that had elapsed. She noted and admired the neat handwriting, the succinct phrasing. The officer must have been miffed to find a deeply involved, guilt-ridden and angry commander on site and breathing down his neck, she guessed. With the map of London she always carried with her and the pencilled sketch on squared paper provided by the inspector, she was able to pull together the outline of the atrocity. And Lily was left, after absorbing all

71

the dimensions, bullet counts, and initial witness interviews, with a feeling of sorrow for the dead man. And for his wife, who had reacted to the outrage with incredible courage, throwing herself into a firefight with the retreating gunmen. A formidable pair, the Dedhams.

Everyone in the land knew of Lord Dedham. Naval man turned politician, speechmaker extraordinaire, rather in the simple style of Mr Churchill, he told the truth as he perceived it with a clarity that appealed to everyone.

When it came to political speeches the admiral used the tactics of the bare-knuckle fighter: get the first blow in and make it a cruncher. His views on the unrest which had preceded and accompanied the signing of the Anglo-Irish Treaty had been delivered with the gloves off very recently in Dublin. He'd accused the prime minister himself, Lloyd George, of working with the king's enemies and had gone so far as to condemn him for having 'shaken the bloody hands of murderers'. Dedham was a clear enemy of Sinn Fein and denouncer of the bombs and bullets that organization used instead of words.

The admiral had been sure of many things, but after his years of service in the Navy he was most certain that 'if we bale out and leave Ireland, Britain is faced across the sea with an enemy that blocks its trade routes. And that is to say – the end of the British Empire. Shall all the gallant sacrifices made fighting the German foe to the east count for nothing, set at nought by a treacherous stab in the back from our neighbour to the west?'

Sandilands had inserted a news cutting reporting this speech, delivered to an enthusiastic audience on 24 May – Empire Day. The occasion had been a memorial supper to mariners lost at sea and Lord Dedham had further stoked the fires of patriotism by finishing with a quotation from Rudyard Kipling:

> *The tumult and the shouting dies;*
> *The Captains and the Kings depart:*

72

Still stands Thine ancient sacrifice,
An humble and a contrite heart.
Lord God of Hosts, be with us yet,
Lest we forget – lest we forget!

'Ouch!' Lily muttered as she leafed through the details. 'Bet there wasn't a dry eye in the house.'

They were dealing with a national hero but also a victim who had enemies running into the hundreds if not thousands. Enemies with powerful, armed and ruthless forces behind them to do their bidding. 'A crazed and driven foe' might have been Kipling's verdict.

It had been Dedham's first day back in London when he'd been ambushed. A crucial moment of imbalance, well judged by the assassins, Lily thought. And yet something had gone disastrously wrong for them. The gunmen, both Irish by birth, it was surmised, had been caught almost immediately after the killing. They'd been arrested and interrogated initially in the Gerard Street police station only two streets away from the admiral's doorstep.

Rustling her way through the sheets Lily began to pull together a story of remarkable courage. The cabby whose taxi the killers had commandeered had driven off in the direction of Paddington station but had almost immediately taken a turn off the main road into Gerard Street. There he'd swerved at the last minute and driven his vehicle at speed in through the gates of the police station, hooting his horn. The duty sergeant at the gates had instantly slammed them shut, trapping the taxi and its occupants in the courtyard. A squad of coppers just coming off duty in the West End had surged out and arrested everyone.

Their bag consisted of four persons: two gunmen, both injured. At the moment of arrest, one had a slash across the left cheek and a .22 bullet embedded in the muscle of his back, the other had a broken wrist.

A young lady passenger, hysterical but otherwise unhurt. She'd given her name and a Mayfair address and, after interview, had been released from custody, insisting on a police escort back to Park Lane. Lily had a clear impression from Superintendent Hopkirk's dry phrasing that they'd been only too glad to lay on a squad car and driver to take her home. Anything to get her out of their hair.

Lastly, the taxi driver. Discovered slumped over his wheel unconscious and at first thought to be dead. Revealed by his licence to be a Mr Percy Jenner, ex-London Rifle Brigade, he'd been hit over the head with a blunt instrument, probably the butt of a gun. He'd been conveyed to St George's hospital where his condition had been stabilized. A constable with a notebook was at his bedside.

The bodies of the admiral and the beat bobby who died trying to stop the taxi had been taken to the morgue and post mortems were under way. The work was top priority and in the hands of Dr Bernard Spilsbury himself. Report awaited.

Lily looked up from her task, stretched her back and considered. It seemed straightforward enough: successful assassination, bungled getaway, capture of culprits. But there were details that left her with an unease, a need to know more – and more precisely. She began to write a list of questions in her notebook. She was finishing her reading of the file with the last of the exhibits – a cutting from the previous week's *Times* newspaper quoting the whole of Admiral Dedham's rip-roaring speech in Dublin, a clear incitement to murder – when she remembered there was one important thing she had to do before Sandilands returned.

Lily looked at the clock. He'd been gone for almost two hours. Where were his rooms? How long did it take for a shave? He'd said ten minutes. Allowing for brisk walking time there and back to somewhere close by . . . Albany? . . . she'd probably left it too late, she judged. She listened. All on the third floor was silent. She crept to the heavy door and opened it an inch. She was reasonably certain that she would now have early warning of anyone approaching down the corridor, or the door of Miss Jameson's office opening. Lily returned to the desk.

She sat for a few moments staring at the telephone and wondering if she dared. With the hurdle of her decision to resign successfully jumped, what had she to lose? She found the courage to lift the earpiece.

The operator at the switchboard answered in her precise but strangulated tone. They were all graduates, these telephonist girls, and renowned for the way they could torture the English language. Lily had applied for such a post with a laundry in Clapham advertised in the newspaper over a year ago but had given up at the first hurdle when she discovered that of the other eight hundred applicants for the position, many had a degree from a university and most had a cultured, upper-class voice.

'An internal number please, miss,' Lily said firmly. 'Could you put me through to extension 371?'

A few mechanical noises were followed by a gruff male voice. 'Yes?'

'Hello. This is switchboard again,' Lily announced in a fair copy of the telephonist's voice. '*Do* tell me I'm through to Catering Supplies?' She managed to insert a touch of uncertainty.

'I can't. You're not.' The voice was military. Uncommunicative.

'Oh, no! I've done it again! Most frightfully sorry, sir!' she gushed. 'I do hope I've not disturbed you. Please forgive me. It's my first day going solo, you see. I'm on test. I *so* hope you won't tell? I think I've just inserted my toggle into the wrong slot and made a bad connection . . .'

A guffaw greeted this. 'We've all done that, darlin',' said the fruity baritone, unbending suddenly. 'Think nothing of it. Your secrets are safe with me. Well, they would be, wouldn't they – this is the War Office here. Ho, ho!' He seemed to find his remark hilarious but stopped slapping his thigh long enough to add: 'And when you do finally plug into Supplies, tell them to change the tea. That Darjeeling they're using this month is as weak as gnat's pee.'

'Assam? Shall I suggest Assam, sir?'

'Yes. That the dark brown stuff? That should do it. Well – good luck with the test, Iris! This *is* Iris, isn't it?'

'I didn't give my name, sir. That would be against the rules.' Lily summoned up exactly the right touch of scandalized rebuke. 'Goodbye, sir.'

She replaced the receiver, stunned by what she'd heard.

War Office? What had Sandilands and, it seemed, herself, by association of some not-yet-defined form, to do with the War Office? For what exactly did they need to know that she was 'ready and able'? Why did they have a presence in the Scotland Yard building? The questions lined up to ambush her. The answers did not immediately present themselves. There were rumours in the force that a shadowy enforcement arm of some sort had a toehold in the Whitehall warren. Everyone had heard of 'C' and his department of patriotic scoundrels. MI1b? Or was it MI1c? Had Lily stumbled upon an organization of that nature? Not such a formidably secret department, she concluded, if an interloper like herself could ring them up and discuss tea supplies.

This flippant thought was supplanted by a more chilling one. She had done nothing to bring her own name to their attention. And yet their earlier conversation with Sandilands showed that they knew of her. Indeed, seemed to have plans for her. Plans on which she had not been consulted. What had he said? 'Not fully briefed yet . . .'

'Mata Hari?' Lily had suggested half-jokingly, taking a stab at a description of the work he had in mind for her. A female spy, Dutch by birth, Miss Hari had used her allure to get information from both sides of the recent conflict. It was rumoured that, at the time of her arrest in a Paris hotel, the exotic dancer turned courtesan counted, amongst her many lovers, the German crown prince and the chief of the French anti-espionage bureau and that crucial information had passed from head to head to head on the pillow. All too unregulated. No one could be quite certain to whom the wretched woman really owed allegiance. As an agent, she had been turned and turned again. Done to a crisp, was the final decision, and she had been removed from the scene. A put-up job by the French it was generally thought, with the compliance of the British. The affair was considered significant enough to have her put on trial and executed by a firing squad in 1917.

If it was a woman with skills of this dubious nature they were seeking, they would have to look elsewhere. Their choice was laughable. Lily's sense of proportion kicked in. She was confident that she failed to fill the bill on two vital counts. Her most exotic dance was the tango she'd learned at the Stretton Academy of Terpsichore on Saturday mornings and she had never had a lover, civilian or military. Really – she'd had enough of this shambolic crew, playing at war games and juggling with careers.

Lily reached into Sandilands' paper tray and took out a sheet of writing paper. It was entirely suitable that it should be headed *Scotland Yard, Whitehall.* She wrote down her name, rank and number at the top and followed this with a brief statement of her resignation from the force, *For reasons made clear to you this morning,* she summarized. *With immediate effect,* she added, dating it. Nothing further. He had heard her views. She folded it, wrote his name on the outside flap and put it away in her pocket. It gave her the reassurance of a lifebelt tucked under her shoulders. She owed him nothing. He could ask nothing of her.

And yet she was disconcerted to find her mind returning to the possibilities he had distractingly opened up. No woman would be made such a tantalizing offer, out of the blue, without the most demanding payback being extracted, she reasoned. What had his proposition amounted to? No less than an instant elevation to detective officer working alongside the commander. Could that be right? That was no opening position with a laundry in Clapham.

She tried to remember what Sandilands had said in his doubtless manufactured confession. That he'd been in Military Intelligence during the war years ... that much she was prepared to believe. Had he ever given up his role or was his present position a screen for other, murkier activities? Perhaps he was still at war and fighting on fronts other than crime? And why would he suppose that he was automatically entitled to count on her assistance with his schemes?

She was trying to recall all the wars in which England was involved from Afghanistan to Zululand and had got stuck on Ireland when she heard Sandilands stamping back down the corridor.

Chapter Seven

Sandilands went straight to Miss Jameson's room across the corridor and stayed there for a few minutes before returning to his own office, where he found Lily closing the file and laying down her pencil.

She looked up and gave him a friendly smile. He swept off his hat, offered a clean-cut profile and asked: 'Well, what do you think of Raoul's handiwork?'

'Raoul is an artist, sir. He could find a position with the finest embalming parlour in the land.'

He grinned. He decided he could get along with her cheerful lack of deference. 'Well, how's it going with the Dedham affair? Reached any conclusions?'

'It's a bit early for conclusions, sir. There's a lot of evidence still to come in. But I have one or two thoughts.'

'Go on.'

'There's something not quite right with all this. Someone at the centre of it is telling you naughty lies.'

Joe had decided as much himself in the early hours. 'You think so? But it's perfectly straightforward, isn't it? A shooting occurred and the killers were apprehended, guns still smoking in their hands. And we have a confession from both of them.'

Lily produced Hopkirk's sketch. 'Where exactly had these men concealed themselves to lie in ambush? They must have been laid up there for ages. No one could have predicted to the minute – or even the hour – when the Dedhams would fetch up home at the end of their evening.

I don't suppose they knew themselves. And these thugs weren't just passing by. This was not their territory. They wouldn't have been comfortable here.'

'And regular police patrols would have picked up – at the very least recorded – any doubtful strangers,' Sandilands confirmed.

'According to Lady Dedham the cab driver checked the shrubs nearest the house before she alighted and gave her the all clear. She had her wits about her but tells us that she too saw nothing of concern near the house. And yet, less than a minute later the gunmen emerged from these very bushes . . .' She pointed with the end of her pencil. 'Did the cabby look properly? Was he mistaken? Or was he lying and leading them into a trap?'

'What a pity he's unable to speak for himself.'

'Is it known, sir, how they engaged his services? How they came to be riding in that particular cab?'

Joe noted her foresight. 'Yes. I asked Lady Dedham. All above board. The cabs were lined up outside the hall when the meeting turned out and the Dedhams took the next in line. They weren't the first and they weren't the last out. Luck of the draw.'

'Look – what do you think of the possibility of distraction, sir? Deliberate or accidental?' Her pencil moved south to the opposite side of the road. 'There's a sort of little green area over here . . . it's hard to envisage what's on offer from a map . . .'

'Shrubs,' Joe supplied. 'I skulked around in there myself. You could hide a couple of quiet men in there for hours.'

'Righto. Let's picture them hiding here while the cabby does his reconnaissance and safely unloads Lady Dedham. Then we imagine him walking back to the taxi to assist the admiral . . . it's at *that* moment that the men run across the road and hide in the bushes near the doorstep. A diversion could well have been staged then, don't you agree? Though the circumstances are not yet perfectly clear.'

'Yes. The arrival of the next fare. The young lady who barged in to commandeer the cab.'

Lily read from her notes: 'Miss Harriet Hampshire, giving an address in Park Lane.' She paused, her brow furrowed in thought. 'It rings a bell with me . . . Is this one of the houses near Pinks Hotel, sir?'

Joe nodded.

'And Miss Hampshire claims to have been in Melton Square, visiting a friend. At least that's what she told Superintendent Hopkirk.'

'I saw her,' he said. 'Briefly before they drove her home. Stunner! She'd certainly have diverted the admiral's and the driver's attention. Yes, two dark-clad men, profiting from a distraction, could have got across the road to the forward cover position without being spotted. And they were wearing rubber-soled shoes. In any case, any sound would have been masked by the noise of the taxi engine, which had been left running.' He heaved a sigh. 'The admiral dismissed the cabby, and strolled down to his front door. The moment he stood on the doorstep, off guard and backlit by the hall lights, they struck.'

'I'm wondering why the cabby didn't set off at once, sir?'

'Waiting – as he'd said he would – to make sure all was well?' Sandilands suggested. 'Some sort of argy-bargy with the girl? Checking directions?'

He broke off and then said, with decision: 'But look here – that's enough desk work. Before we go to the hospital, or the jail, why don't I take you out to look at the scene? Cassandra – Lady Dedham – is expecting me to pay another visit. We'll take a staff car and go and see whether, in the cold light of day, she's remembered anything more of significance, shall we?'

And time to put the girl at the fourth – and perhaps the hardest – hurdle.

Chapter Eight

The house which had been the scene of murder and mayhem with officers of the law and ambulances coming and going all night was now presenting a quiet and unruffled front. All signs of a police presence had been removed so that the normal life of the street might be resumed and the only reminders of the tragedy were the drawn curtains at all the windows and a recently sluiced area, still damp and smelling of carbolic, stretching from the doorstep out to the pavement.

The door was opened a careful inch only after Joe's second knock. He caught sight of a fearful eye under a maid's bonnet. 'Police, miss,' he said hurriedly before his intimidating features could cause further alarm. 'Commander Sandilands and his assistant.' He passed his card through the narrow gap. 'We're here to see her ladyship.'

Reassured, the girl stuck her head round the door. 'Sorry, sir. Lady Dedham's gone up to her room and isn't seeing anyone.'

'That'll be all, Eva, thank you.' The door was flung open by Cassandra Dedham herself. 'Always in for you, Joe. I'm sorry about the unfriendly greeting. With the master dead, the butler laid low, and the footman helping the police with their inquiries at Vine Street, we females left behind are feeling a bit under siege. Come in, come in. There are two of you? ' She gave a welcoming nod and looked Lily up and down in surprise.

'May I present Woman Police Patrol Officer Lilian Wentworth? Lily, this is Lady Dedham.'

He watched keenly as the two women greeted each other. Clearly, Cassandra Dedham was as surprising to the policewoman as the policewoman was to the lady. Wentworth couldn't fail to be impressed by Lady Dedham, even in her grief-stricken state. Much younger than might have been expected, perhaps in her late thirties, Cassandra had a classical beauty that could not be extinguished by the shock and exhaustion she was suffering. Her oval face was drained of colour, its pallor accentuated by a smear of blood along her left cheekbone. Her earrings were intact, her dark auburn hair was scraped back into a chignon and very nearly immaculate. One strand had escaped to trail unnoticed on to her shoulder. Even as his eye caught it, Cassandra automatically retrieved it and tucked it out of sight under its velvet band.

'Ah! Another of your Scottish cousins flighting south, Joe? The coverts up there must be full of them.'

Joe was just about to fall in with this convenient suggestion and make Lily an honorary relation when she decided to speak for herself. 'I'm a colleague of the commander's cousin Margery, Lady Dedham. A useful pair of hands. In attendance to save him some time. I know how to write shorthand.'

'I say, Lil, do you really?' Joe affected not to know. 'She's modest, you'll find, Cassandra. She's really here to put her sharp wits to our problem. Like you, she's not comfortable with the story that's been hacked together, though she has, as yet, only been able to form a judgement from the notes, of course. I thought you two could put your heads together and sift through the evidence again. Always assuming – and I assume a lot, I know – that you're up to it . . . ?'

A proviso that needed to be made, Joe thought. Under the veneer of calm and normality, he sensed that Cassandra Dedham was very near collapse. An admiral's wife would be made of stern stuff, that was to be expected, but the woman had witnessed and played an active part in a tragedy and was still caught up in it. She was still dressed – though apparently oblivious of it – in the chiffon evening gown she had been wearing when her husband had died in her arms, only feet away from where they were standing. The dark green fabric was blotched with blood, the stains showing up as a black dappling from neck to hem. Her evening gloves were lying where she had dropped them on the hall table the previous night.

This wouldn't do. Should he say something? How far could he presume on their acquaintance? Joe stepped forward, suddenly aware that Cassandra was becoming unsteady. Oh, what the hell! He seized her cold hands and passed an arm under her shoulders. 'You haven't slept. You haven't even changed. Where's the medico I left caring for you?'

'No time. Statements, re-enactments for your people, Joe . . . Endless telephoning to be done. Peterson to arrange for . . . he's doing well, they say . . . Hundreds of people to be informed . . . the press gathering. The king sent round an equerry and you can't deal with one of those smooth young men in five minutes, you know. I sent the doctor away. He was all for giving me laudanum. If ever there was a time when I needed full possession of my faculties, this is it, I think you'd agree.' The tension he felt in her slight form was alarming.

'But who's supporting you? You can't manage without a man in the house. Surely . . . ?'

'Our sons are on their way. They've been at sea on a training ship all summer. Once John and Billy get here I can let go the reins. John's seventeen now . . . man of the house . . . But no, you're right, Joe,' she said, replying to his unspoken thoughts, 'the boys are very young still. I've alerted their older cousin Sebastian – Oliver's nephew. Do you remember meeting him? Royal Flying Corps? He'll rally round.'

Joe nodded, reassured by the mention of the friendly young airman he'd met in the admiral's house the month before. 'I do indeed. He fits the bill. Glad to hear he's invited aboard. Where is he – down in Sussex?'

'Yes. I phoned him as soon as I could. Dreadful thing to throw at the feet of a young fellow but I couldn't think of anyone else. He's completely au fait with Oliver's affairs and that's useful . . . I haven't a clue. He offered at once to set off at the crack of dawn and drive down to Devon to pick up the boys and they'll be here this afternoon. But until they all get here I shall have to manage. And I *can*. Truly, Joe.'

'Nonsense!' The commander glanced around him and squared his shoulders. He suddenly seemed to fill the hallway with his large masculine presence. A decision followed at once. 'I shall stay and take over until the boys arrive.'

He decided he didn't quite like the swift exchange of looks he intercepted between the two women on hearing his pronouncement. Understanding? Amusement even?

'Joe! I knew you would. You're an angel – a godsend.' Cassandra grasped his hands again in her emotion. 'And I battle to stop myself swooning at your feet, whimpering my gratitude. But you know what I'm going to say – yes, I could do with some help, but not from the one man who can bring this foul matter to a conclusion. That's where you're needed – out there running the investigation.' Cassandra's eyes flashed with spirit and she pointed to the door. 'Go out and get them, Joe.'

'And return *with* my shield or *on* it, you're about to add?' he suggested, amused by the deft way she'd deflected his attention.

'Yes. Rout out this noxious growth or other victims will follow,' Cassandra went on, her expression serious. 'Others will suffer as I'm suffering if you fail. Find them and bring them in. That's what Oliver would have wanted. "You're a bloodhound, man, not a lapdog!" Can't you hear him saying it?'

'I can indeed. But I could wish you'd thought of *wolfhound*,' he suggested with a teasing smile.

'For the teeth and the killer instinct.' Cassandra appeared pleased with the image. 'I know you have them.'

'Though I accept your reprimand. I'll get about my business, then. But look, Cassandra, why don't you let me and Miss Wentworth mount guard here for half an hour? We're rather good at that. Give you a chance to go up and . . .' he waved a hand in the direction of her skirt, 'do what you have to do. Mustn't frighten the horses, must we?'

Cassandra looked down at her dress. 'I know – I look like a survivor of the massacre of Cawnpore! And I'm not going to pretend I hadn't noticed. I could have sneaked off and changed. If I'm honest, I've rather been hanging on to the evening, devastating as it was. My last evening with Oliver.' She smoothed down the chiffon folds and touched her cheek. 'Every bit of him was precious to me, even his spilled blood. I've been keeping the last traces of him close about me for as long as I could. But then,' her head went up, 'there's a limit. Oliver couldn't bear slackness. I'm letting him down. I'll disappear upstairs and do something about all this.'

The telephone on the hall table began to ring.

'You'll have to be butler for now, Joe,' Cassandra said. 'It's probably the Prince of Wales. His aide left a message earlier saying His Royal Highness would ring back. But I really don't feel up to a conversation. I can hardly get my words out. And he's so sweet and always says the right thing and I know I shall just dissolve into tears and hiccups. You'll have to think of something.'

As Joe went towards the telephone he heard her whisper to Lily, 'The prince and Oliver were close, you know. "Matloes" both, as they like to call themselves. Oliver was his mentor at one point in his training days at Dartmouth.'

'This could well be for me,' said Sandilands apologetically, picking up the earpiece. 'I asked my super to contact me here.'

'Good. Your Mr Hopkirk. Nice man. Look, while you're busy, may I borrow Miss Wentworth? No time to waste. It occurs to me that she can hear my account while I'm having a bath and struggling out of my cocktail dress and into my mourning clothes.'

The earpiece in his hand, Joe turned to smile his acquiescence. This was going better than he could have expected. He just hoped Wentworth could hold her nerve and make the most of the chances unexpectedly on offer. He was beginning to see the advantages of sending in a woman detective. He was an effective officer himself but there were limits – he conceded that he could never pursue his female witnesses into the bathroom and boudoir. He breathed deeply and censored the image of Cassandra shaking loose her long auburn hair and slipping out of her silken underpinnings.

To distract himself he barked into the telephone: 'Hopkirk? That you? Where've you got to?'

Cassandra set off upstairs, calling over her shoulder to the maid who had lingered on in the hall, waiting for instructions. 'Eva, see that the commander has whatever refreshment he needs, will you? And we'll have a tray of coffee brought up to my room, in about ten minutes.'

'Excellent idea, Lady Dedham,' Wentworth said, picking up the gloves from the hall table and following the widow upstairs.

Lily perched uneasily on the edge of a spindle-legged French chair in Lady Dedham's sumptuous bedroom. The curtains were drawn, a discreet lamp or two lit, and Lily was glad of the concealing gloom as Cassandra began to struggle out of her bloodstained clothes. She averted her eyes as her ladyship, swearing gently, unhooked, unbuttoned, tugged and pulled at her evening dress with hands too weary to obey her satisfactorily. She'd refused the services of her maid. 'Don't worry, Adèle, if I get stuck Miss Wentworth can help.'

The girl had withdrawn, casting an astonished and very unfriendly glare at Lily.

Lady Dedham hadn't asked for help and Lily had to sense when the moment of unbearable frustration came. She moved swiftly forward to undo the hooks and eyes on the back of the French camisole and, as Cassandra stepped out with relief, Lily bent and gathered up the heap of crumpled finery, intending to hand it over to Adèle who, she guessed, would have lingered outside but just in earshot. The ghost of an exotic flower scent still lingered in the peach silk underclothes and it was this final flourish of a vanished age – an Edwardian decadence, carefree and indulgent – that made Lily swallow and blink with emotion. Slipped off in a moment were the silk and gardenias; the widow's weeds waited in readiness. And there they were – the weeds – black garments selected from the wardrobe by the careful maid and laid out, smelling unpleasantly of mothballs, in an uninviting pool of darkness on a chest at the foot of the bed.

Cassandra saw them and looked aside with a shudder. She pulled on a white robe and headed for the adjoining bathroom. Water splashed and gurgled, pots and jars clanged and steam fragrant with lavender began to issue from the room. Lily sat on, wondering whether the ensuing silence was sinister and whether she ought to intervene. Perhaps Cassandra in her exhausted state had fallen asleep in the water? Dangerous. Lily tapped on the door and walked in.

Alarmed at what she saw – a pale face lolling just above the froth, eyes tightly shut – she called Cassandra's name.

'Oh, so sorry, my dear. Didn't mean to startle you. Come in. I wasn't asleep, just thinking. It must be the effect of the lavender, you know – it has a reputation for bracing up the mind.' She smiled. 'This has done me the world of good. Pass me a towel, will you? I think I heard our coffee tray arriving. And now I have something to tell you. A bit of a puzzle to put before you. It's been lurking there at the back of my mind for hours but I haven't had time to think about it. You must hear me and decide whether I've turned overnight into a silly old woman with a silly old woman's groundless fears and fervid imaginings.'

'The men involved have been captured. They'll be coming up before Sir Humphrey Bodkin at the Old Bailey before you know it and they'll be hanged. Take comfort from that, Lady Dedham,' Lily murmured reassuringly. 'They can represent no further danger to you and yours.'

'You're telling me what you think I want to hear, Lily. Come off it. I'm sure that a girl smart enough to be assisting the commander has seen further than the arrest of those two stool-pigeons. Would that be the word?'

Lily was taken aback and replied carefully: 'It will do, but I think, in the trade, we might say "patsies". To describe a pair who were set up – or hired – by some other agency to commit the crime. Is that what's worrying you? I'd be intrigued to hear what gives rise to your suspicion.'

'It concerns me, Lily, that a murderous menace is walking the streets of our capital. There may be other innocent targets going about their daily lives in London, unaware that they're being hunted down by nationalistic madmen at loose in our midst. Who will be next to suffer?' Unable to keep it to herself a moment longer, she sat up and fixed Lily with eager dark eyes. 'Listen. Those two brigands didn't kill Oliver, you know. Oh, I agree that was their intent and they would probably have finished him off, given a little longer . . . who knows? I keep hearing the shots replaying in my head. The first two had the same note – they were fired from the same type of gun and almost simultaneously. But it wasn't those shots that laid him low. Oliver was still on his feet, wielding his sword and setting them to rout, when it happened. Oh, I must be mistaken . . . the street was clear – no one else about, I can swear to that . . . but it was the *third* bullet that did for him. A different sound. I'm no expert but I'd say it was a larger calibre gun. And fired from across the street.'

Chapter Nine

'I have mine with cream and one lump of sugar, my dear,' Cassandra said, slipping a peony-patterned Japanese kimono over her head. She settled on a chair by the coffee table. 'But first, do draw back the curtains and let the light in. Out there in the world it must be lunch time, I'd guess. I prefer to see what the person I'm talking to is thinking and I expect you do too.'

Lily busied herself with the curtains and then with cups, jugs and sugar tongs, hoping she was getting everything right. Presiding over a coffee tray in a sunlit Melton Square boudoir was a new experience for her, rendered surprisingly easy by Cassandra Dedham's friendly, if distracted, acceptance of her. It occurred to Lily that, cousin or not, to be vouched for by Sandilands was no mean accolade. And Cassandra clearly adored him. Whatever Lily's own reservations about the man and his motives, they would have to remain concealed in the present circumstances.

They enjoyed their coffee for a few moments before Lily replied carefully to Lady Dedham's earlier suggestion. 'I don't think you're mad. In fact I think you've come to an accurate conclusion about the shooting. And I'll tell you something else – the commander is of the same opinion. I've seen the notes. He had underlined your account of the third shot and put a question mark in the margin. It would, indeed, seem to have been the work of an organized gang. But no one needs to speculate . . . The moment Dr Spilsbury has made his report, we'll know for certain.

They can take a bullet to the police laboratory and identify the very gun it came from – should they be lucky enough to get their hands on it – by the pattern of striations along the casing. It's the equivalent of a fingerprint for guns.'

'Good Lord! Can they really do that? How clever! And how . . . reassuring. The police grow in my estimation every day. How wonderful for you to be involved with such a fine body as the Metropolitan Police. And it must be such fun working with Joe . . .'

She left a space into which Lily was expected to slide an answer. 'Stimulating is the best I can say, Lady Dedham,' she murmured with honesty. Sensing that her reply was failing to satisfy the commander's admirer, she added: 'He did save me from being stabbed in the bottom by a pimp on Paddington station the other day.'

This was what the lady wanted to hear. Her eyes grew round and a smile lit up her face for a moment as Lily told the story. 'Oh, that's the stuff! I draw the line at a punctured bottom but I should have so enjoyed such stimulation myself when I was young. I should have liked to do something truly useful had there been opportunities in that still-Victorian world. As it was, I only took part in two women's suffrage marches before I became engaged to Oliver. And, of course, pillar of male society that he was hoping to become at that time, he had to call a halt to such activities on the part of his fiancée. Straight from school-room to debutante to future admiral's wife. I had my first child before I was twenty. Not much time for living, you'd say, Lily?'

'I see consolations all around me.' Lily waved a hand at the surrounding opulence and dared to add: 'And you're still young and – forgive me for saying such a thing at this time – full of energy and hope.' This was not an acceptable comment from a stranger on the first day of bereavement and Lily tensed as the widow took her up on it at once.

'Hope? What hope? Oliver and I were looking forward to the next stage in our lives. He was retiring from the

Navy, you know. In the autumn. Coming home to us at last, like his hero Ulysses.' Her smile was forgiving. 'Like Penelope, I'd served my twenty years of loneliness. But, unlike Ulysses' deserted spouse, I shall never have my man back from the sea. Hope gone, you see, Lily.'

'Never!' Lily said defiantly. 'This isn't the time or the place and I'm not the person to sound the trumpet so I'll let the admiral's hero do it himself: *How dull it is to pause, to make an end, To rust unburnish'd, not to shine in use!* Didn't Ulysses say that?'

'Lily! My dear! How could you know . . . ?' Cassandra began to breathe unsteadily, her composure shattered by the words. 'That was Oliver's favourite poem! And now I hear you giving his sentiments back to me. I hear him saying it: "Never grow rusty . . . shine in use . . ." And I don't doubt he would have concluded: *Tho' much is taken, much abides.*' Cassandra seemed to draw comfort from the memory and the verse. She smiled bravely over the rim of her cup and changed the subject. 'Does he terrify you?' she asked.

'He? Me?' Lily stammered.

'Yes. Your commander. You. He can be a bit of a steamroller. He terrifies *me*! So young. So competent. So demanding. One must not be taken in by the handsome exterior, the easy smile, you know. He tried to teach me to shoot. When all this was gathering . . . Oliver was unconcerned, of course. Thought he was indestructible . . . Well, the might of the Kaiser's navy had failed to sink him, after all! Joe offered me a tiny gun – he could see I was worried – to hide in my bag and he showed me how to use it. I didn't catch on very fast, I'm afraid. Hopeless, in fact. After an hour's practice, he shrugged and grumped at me: "Well, the *noise* might scare someone off, I suppose."' She rolled her eyes and pulled a rueful face. 'I felt I'd failed him.'

'You hadn't failed him. Didn't they tell you? Well, I shall. One of your bullets was found lodged in the back of the larger of the two attackers. You got one of the villains, Lady

92

Dedham! A more powerful pistol would have killed him on the spot.'

To Lily's mortification, Cassandra's coffee cup began to rattle on its saucer. She placed it back on the table with trembling hand, gasped and choked. Sniffs announced the breaking of a dam of tears and she reached blindly for the handkerchief Lily quickly took from her pocket and held towards her.

'If only I'd run faster back down the hall . . . if I'd shot straighter . . . with a bigger gun . . . Oliver! Oliver! I'm so sorry!' The words came, haphazard, filtered through the fabric of the handkerchief, bubbling up with the sobs.

What was a woman policeman to do? Most certainly not adopt the course of action Lily took. With her resignation letter crackling reassurance in her pocket, she gave way to instinct and moved round the table to kneel at Cassandra's side. She took the shaking shoulders in a hug, murmuring consoling nonsense into a damp right ear. To her surprise, Cassandra didn't pull away or freeze into immobility or curl her upper lip in disdain. She hugged her back and the volume of hot tears increased. Finally, noting a slight subsiding of the volume and a lengthening interval between gulps of air, Lily drew away and muttered an apology for the contact.

With a final toot into her handkerchief, Cassandra gave a brave smile. 'Rubbish, Lily, my dear! Any time's hugging time . . . And no one else is going to oblige now. My boys are both *useless* huggers! If I try to approach them with a hug in mind they stand like a pair of cold seals with their flippers at their sides and suffer my attentions for two seconds. Is there more coffee left in the pot, do you suppose? Good. Now, I shot one, you say? Well done me! Do you think I may expect to hear Joe's congratulations? I shan't count on it. Tell me – how long have you known him?'

Lily decided on a half-truth. 'The commander? I wouldn't say I know him. We're working on a case together,' she said, holding Cassandra's sharp gaze.

'Ah! Then you'll need no advice from me on handling him. He does have his weaknesses, which can be exploited . . .'

'I wouldn't dream of handling him,' said Lily, taken by surprise. 'But you're right – he does have weaknesses, one of which is, strangely, his sense of honour.' She pursued the thought, hoping to hear more in return for her offering. 'It can be a self-destructive quality. He's resigned his position. Did he tell you that? This morning. Envelope on the Home Secretary's desk and all that.'

'No! How simply dreadful! On account of Oliver's shooting? But why on earth would he consider . . . Well, of course, as I speak I see why, but . . .'

'Completely unjust. It was the Home Secretary himself who insisted on the removal of the protection squads.'

'You can be quite certain of that?'

Lily nodded. 'I am. I've seen his signed instruction.'

Cassandra's eyes grew steely. 'Then he must bear the responsibility.' She thought for a moment. 'I'm going to have a nap in a minute because I sense I'm fading fast, but I shall stay conscious long enough to make a phone call or two. I'll use the telephone in Oliver's bedroom. I wouldn't want anyone to overhear what I have to say. Thank goodness you warned me of this nonsense!' She reached out and patted Lily's hand. 'I can see he's chosen a good girl to watch his back. Promise me that you'll call on me again – soon – and keep me up to date with this miserable business. Between us, my dear, I think we ought to be able to direct his course. I appoint us his guardian angels! Yes, that's how we should think of ourselves. We won't let our man suffer.' She waited for Lily's murmur of agreement. 'We'll finish our coffee and when you go back downstairs to sleuth about with Joe have Eva bring me up the admiral's address book from his study, would you?'

Then Cassandra blurted out words Lily sensed she could never have confided to anyone in her social circle or her family: 'I don't want my life to be over before I've lived it,

Lily. I don't want to be a widow. I shall never settle to it.'
And added, more calmly: 'But, for this one moment, I
intend to use all the moral advantage it gives me.' There
was satisfaction and purpose in her tone. 'Heaven knows
– it's an advantage that doesn't last for long. I shall reckon
on a week at the most before I become tedious. Oliver had
many favours to call in from the most surprising quarters
and who would deny returning them, on her request, to
a hero's grieving widow? I shall make myself an awful
nuisance! I might even feel strong enough to resort to
blackmail, should it become necessary. I could! But I'll tell
you, Lily – I won't stand by and see another injustice done.
From this moment, I consider myself to be at war!'

Chapter Ten

'Two dozen cigarette ends of every kind from Craven "A" to gold-banded special orders. A half-sucked, spat-out, barley sugar sweet. The left leg from a china doll. A stray bullet from Cassandra's gun. A certain amount of disturbance of the turf.'

Joe read out his list. 'Just what you'd expect and all meticulously recorded by Superintendent Hopkirk who had the good sense to wait for daylight before he got his fine-tooth comb out.' He consulted his notes and pointed here and there as they walked the grassed area across the street immediately opposite the admiral's front door. 'Something bothering you, Wentworth?'

'Yes, sir. There is something . . . We've speculated that they must have been waiting here for quite some time . . . several hours . . . in a state of considerable tension. I've looked and I see no trace of the essential bodily functions one associates with males under pressure in a confined space, sir.'

He gave her an amused look. His men would have reported 'No sign of anyone pissing under a tree, sir'. If they'd noticed. This girl took the trouble to phrase her suggestions delicately for a male superior. The least he could do was respond in kind. 'Good Lord! Bladder control! Evidence of lack of it? No sign. You're right.'

He ran each tree and shrub in review again and grinned. 'As you say. Nothing of larger capacity than a pug dog has passed this way. No human had a pee in the night. This was their second staging point. They weren't laid up here for any length of time.'

'Sir, may I?' Lily was already running south towards the next clump of shrubs.

Joe had caught up and was peering over her shoulder when she exclaimed and pointed. 'There – under the large laurel. It didn't rain in the night so the traces are still evident.'

They scanned the murder scene from this new angle. 'Timing, Wentworth! It all depends on split-second timing. Let's test it out, shall we? You'll have to be the two gunmen and do the running about for me. Most of the curtains on the other side of the road are twitching, d'you see? They've probably set their butlers at the windows to watch. If they catch sight of a large man in a black slouch hat racing about in a suspicious manner, they'll call the police. A woman in uniform won't raise an eyebrow . . . You know the script. Ready? Go!'

He watched as his assistant choreographed the incident as she ran, imaginary gun clutched to her side. Bending low, she sought second cover from the trampled patch they had just examined, but only briefly, just allowing time for Lady Dedham to make her way from taxi to front door, then a few more seconds for Lord Dedham to speak to the cabby. Closing in. She counted out a further thirty seconds for distraction time afforded by the appearance of Miss Harriet Hampshire. And how lucky for the assassins that lady's appearance had been! Under cover of this, Lily ran across the road and sidled down the path to take up position in the forward cover of the bushes near the door.

Joe called her back in his precise soldier's voice, breaking the spell. 'That all fits in very well. And I'll tell you something else. I think that girl – Hampshire – could have been lurking about here as well. You have to look hard to see it but there's an indentation here in a bit of earth. It's too narrow to have come from a man's shoe. It's quite distinct and very fresh. What do you make of it?'

Lily knelt and peered. 'The heel of a high-heeled shoe, sir. Evening wear? And why would a girl dressed for a night out be skulking in the shrubbery in this area? Sort of behaviour you expect to come across in Hyde Park after dark but not hereabouts.' She looked at the faint outline again. 'There's a trail.' Lily squinted and pointed. 'She arrived from that direction. The house with the closed shutters on the first floor. Someone giving her shelter?'

'Number thirty-nine.' Sandilands referred to his notes. 'Yes. Here we are. Hopkirk took a statement from the butler, a Mr Jonas Warminster. The owner is a gentleman who goes by the even more fanciful name of Ingleby Mountfitchet. Hardly fits the description of a Sinn Fein sympathizer ... Mr Mountfitchet, who is a bachelor, ex-army, had retired to bed with his cocoa when he was disturbed by the rumpus that broke out in the street below. The butler assured him that the noise was a car backfiring and his master went back to bed. Where, judging by the tightly closed shutters, he still remains ... sleeping something off? Avoiding speaking to us? Yes, Wentworth. I agree. Further and better particulars required, I believe. We should run a check on Mr Mountfitchet. I'll give instructions to that effect.' Joe looked up from his notes and said with emphasis: 'Don't worry, by the way – basic slog-about police work goes on while we're here, dancing about in the shrubbery.'

'Glad to hear it, sir.' Her response was automatic, her mind elsewhere. 'Look, sir – no woman would risk ruining her evening shoes and clothes in this wilderness in normal circumstances. She'd walk around on the path.'

'Meeting someone? Hiding from someone? Lying in wait?' Sandilands suggested.

Lily stood up again, an object clasped carefully between finger and thumb. 'Long enough to smoke a cigarette, anyway. There's lipstick on this. That suggests waiting about. Ambushing? Setting up a diversion?'

Joe produced a paper evidence bag from his pocket and held it open to receive the stub. 'Not an enthusiastic smoker, evidently. Only a few puffs taken before she threw it away. Interrupted by the arrival of the taxi?'

'Who do you know who smokes Balkan Sobranie, Holmes?' Lily asked, laughing at him. She seemed to have been suddenly ambushed by their ridiculous situation.

He answered the question with a grimace: 'Ah! If only it were so simple in real life. Balkan Sobranie, eh? You're right. That would reduce our smoker to a select club of about ten thousand émigré Russians and as many Londoners who think it the smart thing to do. Anyone from a grand duchess who screws one into a six-inch-long Fabergé holder to the girlfriend of a Soho waiter who's decided to have a flirt with the bohemian style.' He sighed. 'Still – worth recording and preserving. Perhaps Miss Hampshire will be able to throw a little light? I must check the plans Hopkirk has for re-interviewing that lady.'

'We're thinking the same thing, sir? On the same lines as Lady Dedham herself? She was convinced it was a third gun that fired the finishing shot from across the road. And we're looking at evidence of a third party present at the scene.'

Joe nodded. 'Yes. Interesting that in all the noise and horror Cassandra picked out a third gun. A killer still at large? I'll tell you – while you two were upstairs, Hopkirk read out to me over the telephone the initial report from the autopsy. Dr Spilsbury had interesting things to say . . .' He took out a notebook and found his place. 'I give you the salient bits . . . Hit, in the first instance, by two bullets fired one from the left and one from the right at a distance of no more than six feet. One narrowly missed the lung and crossed the body to lodge in the muscle under his left arm, the other shot penetrated a lung and would, ultimately, have caused death. The *coup de grâce* was delivered from farther afield and from a higher-calibre gun. Something in the order of a Browning. In the hands of a marksman, I'm inferring from the doc's comments. Clean shot through the heart. He was dead in seconds.

'The first two shots came from guns identified as Webleys. As issued by the British army. Thousands of those about on the quiet in London. Old soldiers sometimes fail to turn their weapons in. Conveniently "lose" them. They get used to having protection to hand and can't bear to give them up. Who am I to blame them – I have an illicit Luger at home myself.'

'Have you any idea of the distance?' Lily asked. 'Of the lethal shot?'

'Spilsbury's estimate from an examination of the wound would place the gunman at the edge of the road, right where the taxi was parked.'

'By someone standing behind and using the motor for cover? Inside it and firing from a window? Or someone at the wheel?'

'As you say. I think we've finished here for the time being, Wentworth. Right – what do you fancy next? Shall I take you to view the wounded at the hospital? I can offer you the butler or the driver, though he was still unconscious when last I heard.'

'No, sir. I'd really like to have a word with the prisoners, if you can arrange it.'

Joe was taken aback by the request. He looked up and down the street to gain time and his gaze returned to hover inches over her head as he replied doubtfully: 'I don't think I can sanction that. No. Not sure it's a good idea. We'll leave the interrogation to those who have the skills. Hard nuts these two boyos, according to Hopkirk. All they would offer at Gerard Street was false names. Sean O'Brian and Sean O'Hara if you can believe!'

'John Smith and John Jones, in other words?'

'Exactly. No address or comment can be wrung out of them. In view of their intransigence, Hopkirk had them carted off to the Vine Street nick where the officers are more used to dealing with such cases.'

He didn't think he could make it clearer. Lily, according to her file, was attached to the Vine Street nick. She could hardly be unaware of their reputation. She appeared to select her next remark carefully, her voice controlled. 'Didn't you say one of them had a bullet – a .22 from Lady Dedham's gun – lodged in his back? Wouldn't one expect him to have been conveyed to hospital for treatment?'

'A doctor was called in to attend, of course,' Joe replied briefly, uneasy with the conversation. 'Anyway, whatever their condition, these are not types a young thing like yourself would want to engage with at any level. I've seen them. Brutal killers. Products of the gutter. You'd hardly understand what they were saying anyhow. They're refusing to speak in English. Leave these things to the experts, Wentworth.'

The constable glowered at him in a silence that rather smacked of contempt. He leaned slightly sideways to look under the brim of her hat. He straightened, snorting and sighing theatrically. 'I had a cat once that could pull exactly the same face. It got its own way once too often and now features at third on the left in my mother's pets' cemetery. Come on then! But on your own head . . .'

As soon as they'd settled into the back of the squad car Joe began to murmur entertaining nonsense about Vine Street: the West End police station located in a side road off Piccadilly. Notorious to some members of the public, celebrated to others, the view of those receiving attention here was coloured by the seriousness of the charges brought. And by the class and attitude of the miscreant. Drunk and disorderly aristocrats hauled in on Boat Race night would relive their adventures for years to come. The carousing in the cells in the company of like-minded toffs, all caught at a hazardous moment in their wild night out in the capital, led to the formation of new friendships. Over fifty years a certain camaraderie had developed among those who could boast they had survived a night in custody at Vine Street. Over the port, moustached old warriors recounted with a glee equal to that with which they told the stories of their conquests the tale of their night in clink . . . 'So there I was, pissed as a newt, caught making mating calls to Landseer's south-easterly lion in Trafalgar Square . . . as one does . . . Thought I was being jolly smart giving my name as the Duke of Wellington, Number One, London, when they chucked me into a cell with – would you believe it? – Field Marshal Haig, Kaiser Bill, Alfred the Great and Jack the Ripper! Of course, next morning Justice Peabody showed his decent side. Let us all off for a fiver each. Except for Kaiser Bill who got charged a tenner for "demonstrating unpatriotic sympathies in his choice of nomenclature".'

And, however deep the hangover, the wise and drily humorous reprimands of the Justice were always remembered and boringly trotted out verbatim after a passage of decades. One of Joe's own uncles, he confided, had worked up a hilarious party piece concerning his own incarceration and release, one Ascot week.

The patient professionalism of the arresting officers as well as the understanding of the magistrate presented a comforting image of an England sadly passing and surely to be admired in these dark days, Joe was suggesting. He wondered at his emphasis. A bleaker version of the Vine Street ethos had reached his ears, though much detail was deliberately filtered out before reports were presented to the upper ranks. Unsure what awaited them, he thought it wise to draw a blind of good-hearted humour and irreverence over it for the moment.

The softening up continued as they sped down Piccadilly. Lily nodded and smiled and maintained a polite silence. Her own judgement of the station and its officers had been coloured by a closer experience and from the inside. She had admitted to no one that, on more than one occasion in her year on patrol, she'd held back from calling her colleague to arrest a suspect, out of pity and concern for the latter's safety in what Sandilands seemed to want to present as a jolly gentlemen's club. The young, the elderly, the feeble, the first time offenders, Lily reckoned had no place in that brutal environment. No one had caught her pulling her punches and releasing suspects with no more than a flea in their ear and now, she realized with a surge of elation, it was too late for her lapses to be discovered. She was resigning after all. At the end of the day.

'Prattle on, Sandilands. Who do you think you're kidding?' Lily said, but she said it to herself.

Their car dropped them on Piccadilly and Lily set off to the station a few steps ahead of Joe, who paused to give instructions to his driver. She was greeted by the constable on duty at the door. PC Hewitt recognized her and hailed her from a distance with the joviality of a man looking forward to relieving his boredom with an exchange of police banter. Lily was known at the station for giving as good as she got and bearing no grudges. She didn't look down on the men the way some of those toffee-nosed women did. She could take a joke.

'Wotcher, Lil! On yer tod today, then? No scrapings from the park to offer us? Just as well. We're a bit busy – it's standing room only in there. Bedlam!'

'Hello, Harry. No, I'm not alone.' She waved a hand to indicate the presence of Sandilands, who was striding up the side road after her. 'Not Halliday – he's gone north. Instead, I bring you the commander. Or he brings me. Not quite sure. But we seem to be together.'

'Gawd! That's all we needed!' PC Hewitt gritted out of the corner of his mouth. 'What's Young Lochinvar doing riding up again? Can't they give him a desk to sit at? And what the 'ell's 'e want with *you*?' Hewitt gave her a look both salacious and speculative.

'Oh, the usual,' Lily said lightly. 'I'm here to provide a little female insight.'

'Lucky devil! I wonder what you can show him that we can't?'

Smiling affably, Lily squared up to him. 'Watch it. How'd you like to greet the boss hopping on one leg? These boots aren't good for much but they're damned good kneecappers.'

Hewitt grinned and, playing the game, jumped back, clutching his crotch. The girl had form. There was a sergeant in C division who had the limp to prove it, and gossip had it that the target zone had been some degrees north of kneecaps. He went into a smart salute as Sandilands approached and with a wink for Lily made a play of opening the heavy door with the panache of a hotel commissionaire.

But before they reached the charge room, the oppressive atmosphere of rage, pain, anger and despair had stopped even Sandilands in his tracks.

Chapter Eleven

The hubbub was punctuated by a top note of banshee screams of female outrage and a bass note of drunken singing. Somewhere a Scotsman was growling out the chorus of 'Loch Lomond'. In the background, cell bells rang every few seconds and the heavy doors to the cell block creaked opened and clanged shut.

Sandilands presented himself to the elderly charge officer, who appeared insulated from the cacophony around him by three feet of shining mahogany counter. He waited for the sergeant to put down his mug of coffee and drop his newspaper to the floor.

'Afternoon, sergeant. I'm surprised you can concentrate on the racing results with this hullabaloo going on. Stop it, will you?'

'Sir! Yes, sir! I'd be only too glad to oblige, but, sorry, sir. I can't, sir.'

There was steel in the commander's tone as he responded to the affected servility. 'You're in charge here, are you not? If you have a superior officer about the place, produce him.'

The sergeant was not easily subdued. He'd seen commanders come and go. 'Sorry, you've got *me*, sir. Best we can do for you this afternoon.' His voice revealed a London man secure on his own patch and resenting the intruder. It was only just sufficiently deferential. 'Nothing I'd like better than a bit o' peace and quiet like what you 'ave at the Yard,' he offered blandly. 'But we've got our hands full today, what with the little bit of extra *you* sent us – those lads requiring a bit of special attention, like. The other prisoners have been backing up. We're using the common space as an extra charge room.' He pointed to a second room where a row of six young men sat disconsolately along the wall awaiting interrogation while a pair of constables filled in their details on forms at a large polished table, barking the occasional question at them.

All this was making an unfortunate impression on the commander. His spine straightened to an alarming degree, his height, already impressive, seeming to increase by a couple of inches. He had taken on a sinister stillness.

At last the sergeant became aware that he was running into danger and adjusted his tone. 'Sorry about the din, sir. That caterwauling's been going on since the constable arrested *her*.' He pointed to a small and dishevelled prostitute who was attempting, between yells, to bite out the throat of the meaty lad holding her stolidly at arm's length. 'She's gone bonkers. Name's Doris. Tart. Has her beat along the Strand. Regular customer. Bit barmy, but this performance is unusual even for her.'

'Sarge,' Lily said, 'give me a minute with her, will you? I've had dealings with Doris before – she knows me. I might be able to sort it out.'

She waited for his nod before making her way over to the wrestling pair. Gently she eased the constable's grip, inserting herself between the two struggling figures. She leaned and whispered in Doris's ear. After a stunned silence, Doris's screams turned to sobs, then sniffles and whimpers. Finally she spoke to Lily in a torrent of words that Sandilands and the sergeant could make neither head nor tail of. It seemed to consist of no more than a list of names: 'Our Alice, little 'erbert, Georgie . . .' Lily nodded, whispered a further question and listened to the outpouring of emotion and fear that followed.

Lily turned to the arresting constable. 'Tom, fetch me a glass of water, would you?' While he went off to fetch one,

Lily spoke again to the dejected figure before her. 'I can see what needs to be done, Doris. And the sooner the better. Look – leave it with me, love. I'll find them, see they're all right and alert Rhoda. She's still living in Bradman's Court, is she? Right you are then. Here, have a drink. Thank you, Tom. Now – you know the routine, Doris. Just go through to the charge room with the constable and do what you have to do. Tom's new around here – you'll have to show him the ropes! It'll be faster in the end. And for Gawd's sake, gel, keep the squawking bottled.'

Sandilands and the sergeant watched in astonishment as Doris nodded, calmly linked arms with the constable and hurried him into the charge room.

Lily returned to the desk, fire in her eyes. 'She has four children under the age of six left at home by themselves. She was out earning some cash for their dinner. Her mother would normally look in on the nippers but she's down with the flu and no one else knows they're there. The smallest is only nine months old and will be screaming with hunger by now. The oldest is only five and can't control the toddlers. I've promised to go round and stir up a neighbour who might be persuaded to lend a hand. It'll take about an hour. Will you excuse me, sir?'

She was turning for the door in her eagerness to be off. Sandilands grabbed her by the shoulder. 'No, I won't excuse you,' he said firmly. He fixed the sergeant with a flinty glare. 'Constable Wentworth is assisting me on a matter of national importance. I will not have her precious time wasted doing social work arising from the incompetence of desk staff.' He produced a ten-shilling note from his pocket and handed it to the sergeant. 'Give the woman this and set her loose. You should have more sense than to allow the premises to be cluttered up by trivial, time-wasting cases at a moment of emergency.'

'Yessir. At once, sir.' The sergeant followed the pair into the charge room, leaving the door open, handed the note over with a flourish and in a few words explained that Doris was to be bailed immediately, orders of the commander.

As Doris ran off with a backward wave and a mouthed 'Ta, love!' for Lily, the sergeant turned again to Sandilands. 'Wonderful, sir. Glad you called by. Now, would the constable like to deal with Rob Roy in the tam-o'-shanter over there? He's been making his way back to Loch Lomond for the last two hours.'

'What's the charge?' Sandilands asked.

'Drunk and disorderly. Could have been grievous bodily harm if we'd been able to make one of the complainants stand and testify. Drunk as a skunk. Caught making lewd gestures with his sporran and assaulting any man he heard talking English in Leicester Square. And *that* takes a bit of doing nowadays but he managed to find and clobber six before we got hold of him. Down here with his mates for a wedding and got left behind. Officer Smithson who's grammar school educated and knows what he's talking about says it's a Celtic custom. All to do with ... stagworship, I believe he said. The horned god ... fecundity ... plenty of drink taken ... that sort of thing.'

'I don't think the Scots need to refer to the calendar before they plan a knees-up. And the many-antlered Cernunnos would hardly recognize our friend as an acolyte,' Joe added since the sergeant seemed to be partial to a bit of northern folklore. 'Lord! Let's hope our chap isn't the bridegroom. What's his name?'

'Doesn't remember his name or his address. Thick accent – we can't work out a word he's saying.'

Sandilands put a hand on Lily's arm. 'My turn, I think, Wentworth. You have his belongings, sarge?'

The officer produced a shoe box from under the counter. 'No calling card, I'm afraid, sir, to give us a clue. Let's see what we have got.' He muddled through the items, listing them one by one. 'Just a small amount of cash, a couple of beer mats, a map of London, a used handkerchief, a ticket stub and a sporranful of confetti.'

Joe held back a flash of impatience as he viewed the contents of the box. These clowns had all they needed to hand and had ignored it. He pounced on the ticket. 'It doesn't exactly have his address on it, but this ticket was issued in Glasgow. He came down on a return ticket and this is the all-important return half. What time is the next train to Scotland from King's Cross?'

'One every hour, on the half-hour, I think.' The response was subdued as the sergeant took account of the lapse. He hung his head, waiting for the inevitable reprimand.

It didn't come. The commander's tone was encouraging. 'Right. Then our problems are over. There's one in twenty minutes. Send one of your blokes with him in a taxi to the station. He's to be sure to put him on the train and watch him disappear.' He took out another ten-shilling note. 'This is for the taxi and any other expenses. Now give him his belongings back and get him out of here.' He looked about him as the sergeant saw to it and commented drily: 'Not sure I can afford to know you lot much longer.'

'Peace and quiet comes at a price around here,' murmured the sergeant.

'I'm already enjoying my quid's worth,' Joe replied as the great door swung closed and everyone listened in relief to nothing but the distant hum of traffic on Piccadilly.

'Now, to business,' he went on. 'Constable Wentworth wishes to cast an eye on the pair arrested in connection with the shooting of Admiral Dedham last night. You still have them here? I left instructions that they were to be handed on to no one else. Come on, man! You have them?'

The sergeant replied with surprise and reluctance. 'Yes. Yes. Of course, sir. In the cells.' He leaned across the counter in a show of confidentiality. 'Not that we haven't had offers from other interested parties to take them off our hands, just like you warned us. I stonewalled 'em, of course. Referred them to you, sir. Seemed to work. But, sir, er ... Not sure the prisoners are fit to be interviewed in the presence of a lady officer. Rough types. They resisted arrest, of course. And they've had an intensive interrogation. They're resting at present. Getting ready for their day in court. Preliminary hearing at the Old Bailey. No one's wasting much time over this, eh, sir? Knotting the rope already, you might say . . .'

Sandilands cut him short. 'We'll go through. Five minutes for each man. No more. You are holding them in separate cells?'

'That's right, sir. Watch out for the big one. He's a nasty piece of work. The little 'un's got no more fight in him. He'll give no trouble.' He summoned up a brute-faced copper with hands like ham shanks. 'PC Kent has established relations of a sort with them. He's got their number. Kent – take them through to see our Irish friends, will you? And watch out for the lady. And, sir, we're saying five minutes, tops, with each. If Constable Wentworth can take as much as five minutes.'

They followed Kent through one of the six doors that gave access to the cells. After a great deal of flourishing with the keys and clanging of bolts, Joe entered a step ahead of Lily into the cell of the larger and more aggressive of the two prisoners.

The stench made him reel back. The small space stank of urine, blood, vomit and a disturbing chemical smell that made him retch. The gloom was disorienting. Somewhere in that fetid darkness a form moved slightly and uttered a groan. Focusing on the sound, Joe eventually made out the shape of a man sitting uncomfortably on a narrow metal bench. He was hunched over, clutching his stomach, and paid no attention to their entrance. Was this the assassin? It could have been anyone. His head was sheathed from chin to scalp in a thick layer of bloodstained surgical bandage. Someone had cut a hole around the nose and mouth to allow him to breathe.

110

With a gesture, Sandilands indicated to Lily that he was allowing her precedence and stood back a pace. Trying to keep her voice level, Lily introduced herself to this nightmare figure and asked: 'Sean, will you show me your back, please?'

The figure growled and shrank further into the wall.

'You'll get no cooperation from him, miss,' said Kent who was standing protectively at her side. 'Bullet's out if that's what you're bothered about. Taken away for evidence. The doc had to put him out cold to extract it. Ether it was, to get him to be still. That's what you can smell. He's been patched up good and proper. They'll take him to the hospital when he's heard his charges.'

The sudden roar from the bandaged head took everyone by surprise. A torrent of abuse in Gaelic poured out. Joe couldn't understand a word but every one was unmistakably a curse.

Kent put a hand on Lily's arm and she started at the touch. 'It's all right, miss. But I'm afraid that's all you're going to get from him. Better come away now.'

The voice came again through the hole in the bandage. Louder. And, alarmingly, it was speaking in English. 'Not quite all. I have something to offer the lady. Where are you, miss? Not seeing too well . . . my eyes have been pounded to a pulp.'

The padded head moved slowly from left to right, seeking her out, until she took a step forward and whispered, 'I'm here.'

Joe's hands clamped round her upper arms and jerked her backwards out of shot, as, with a spitting hiss, a broken tooth in a gobbet of blood landed at her feet.

Lily was still twitching with shock as Kent locked up the cell behind them. 'Sorry, miss. Who'd ever have thought it? He must have been saving that up in his cheek. Little offering for the magistrate is probably what he had in mind.'

Joe, embarrassed and uncomfortable, gave her a moment to pull herself together and then asked, confident of her

111

answer: 'No need to take a look at the other one, I think, Wentworth? Just more of the same.'

'No, sir, I'd like to see Sean number two if you wouldn't mind.'

Kent sighed and shrugged and sought out the key for the second cell.

The same sorry spectacle presented itself in here. The same carefully arranged concealing bandages were in place. Sandilands judged they had been applied by the professional hand of a nurse or doctor following the police interrogation.

Kent performed the introductions.

'Sean – I don't know if you can see me? No? I'm a woman police officer. I've not come to take a statement.' Her carefully prepared questions ran into the sand as she stared with pity at the small, battered body. 'I just wondered if there was anything you'd like me to hear. But it doesn't matter. I'll go away and leave you in peace.'

The voice spoke in English. English with a London twang. 'Peace? If only you could. I'm going to hang, aren't I?'

'It looks very much like that, Sean. You killed a very distinguished man and a London bobby and left a butler and a cab-driver wounded.'

After a pause: 'The butler. I'm sorry about him. And the cabby. Wasn't their business. Just doing their jobs. How are they, miss?'

'They're going to recover. It'll take a week or two but they'll be all right,' Lily said.

'Well that's something. I'm glad of that. It's a crumb of peace you've brought me. Now all I can do is stand up and take my punishment like a man.'

'I must go now,' Lily said and, unbearably moved by his dejection, she evaded Joe's outstretched arm, ignored his shouted reprimand, and went to take hold of the boy's hands. 'God be with you, lad,' she said. 'I'm sorry I can't call you by your given name. But I'm sure you're known to God.'

He called to her as they reached the door. 'Miss? My name. It's Patrick. Can you find my mother and tell her how it is with me? Tell her they used me? Say I'm sorry for the trouble I've caused?' Into their surprised silence he muttered: 'She's in Little James Street, number fifty-seven. Name of Dunne. They'd find out soon enough anyway. And I don't want her waiting and wondering . . .' He turned to the wall, sobbing.

Neither Sandilands nor Kent attempted to stop her when Lily walked back over to the boy, held his hand and waited for the storm of grief to subside. 'My name's Lily. I'll see that your mother hears your message, Patrick.'

The duty staff gathered round the sergeant at the reception desk the moment the door swung to behind Sandilands and his assistant.

'Cor, blast! What do we make of that then? Makes us look bloody fools! Especially you, Kent. How long were you working on that pair with nothing to show for it but an earful of Irish screaming and two false names? Miss waltzes in here and she's got name and whereabouts out of one of 'em in . . .' he looked at his pocket watch with heavy emphasis, 'eight minutes flat. And now they've gone trotting off to pay a call on Mum! Won't be long before they've rolled up the other one as well.'

His shoulders began to shake with laughter and his men took their lead from him, outrage turning to puzzlement and finally hilarity.

'Well, look at it this way, sarge,' offered one, 'at least we got it done in house, so to speak. The lass is one of us if you think about it. This is her home nick. And we didn't give way and hand the buggers over to Special Branch – if that's who they were – when they came calling. We held the line. I reckon we can chalk this one up to the station.'

'Right, Smithson. That's how we'll tell it, if anyone asks.'

'Still – that's a clever operator, sarge. Had you any idea?'

The sergeant looked thoughtful for a moment and said carefully: 'Why is it everybody always coos over the monkey's antics? When it's the sodding organ-grinder they ought to be keeping their eye on?'

Chapter Twelve

The sodding organ-grinder sat thoughtfully at his desk, checked his wristwatch then rang for his secretary.

'One letter, Jameson, before I dash off again. Got your pencil? Internal – and address it to the Commissioner himself, would you? His eyes only or whatever formula you use. Head it ... Vine Street Police Station. Dear Commissioner, I visited today in pursuit of the Dedham case. My experiences there threw up some unsettling observations on the management of the station. I would welcome the opportunity to discuss these face to face as soon as possible.'

When she had left to type up his note he picked up the telephone. 'Pass me Superintendent Hopkirk, will you?'

Superintendent Hopkirk raced into the inspectors' room and peered through the cloud of tobacco smoke. 'Chappel! Put that blasted pipe out. Bloody hell! What a puther. I've breathed fresher air downwind of Grimethorpe Coking Works. Get your team together, fast. We've got the buggers!'

'Vine Street come up with the goods then?' Inspector Chappel asked in some surprise. 'They took their time. We were all betting this pair would take their secrets to the gallows with them. You know what they're like for the rule of silence, these Micks. Worse than the Eyeties. Should have thrown them to the Special boys to have a gnaw at.'

'There's a bit of a turf war going on that's no business of ours, Inspector. Suffice it to say that the powers that be are of the conviction that there's more than an element of *civil* interest in this affair.' He paused to allow this to sink in and, having received the hard stares and splutters of disbelief he was expecting, went on: 'Oh, yes, civil interest.'

The inspector took up the challenge. 'I think I may be missing something here, sir. We've got the chief critic of Sinn Fein done to death by – guess who – two Irishmen still clutching hot guns. Most ordinary folk would be happy to draw the obvious conclusion and hand the whole can o' worms over to an outfit better equipped to deal with an outbreak of politically motivated shootings. But not our boss. Oh, no. CID can have this one, he says. Am I getting this right, or what?'

'To a point. What you seem to have missed, Inspector, is that the hush-hush boys we're all so fond of aren't technically military. Nor are they MI1b, MI1c or any of the rest of the alphabet. They report ultimately to his nibs – to *our* his nibs. Sandilands trumps their director. Whoever *he* may be. But let's not forget that Sandilands isn't the ultimate authority in the Met. And he's saying what quite a few of the upper echelons want to hear. He's sketching out a scenario that pleases the government more than a full-blown military situation. Nobody's of a mind to sound the trumpet and slip the leash on those dogs at the Branch. It would be admitting CID can't handle it – that the bloody Irish terrorists have opened up a front on the streets of London. That the capital's on a war footing.' His audience winced and groaned. 'But cheer up, lads. We seem to have won the latest round. Or at least Sandilands does. He was on the blower just a minute ago to say he wants to see us down the East End.' He waved a piece of paper. 'At this address. Little James Street. Anybody know it? Righto then, get your skates on – he's going to be there waiting for us. Pawing the ground and breathing flames as usual no doubt.'

'On site? Not again,' the inspector growled. 'Here, there

and everywhere. Why can't the man just sit still and stick to signing forms like he's supposed to?'

'Think on, man. One of those forms passing across his desk just might have your dismissal details above his signature. We're being kept up to the mark, Inspector. It's the New Policing. It's why they've put him there – to be the stick of ginger up our arse. Smile and accept. Hope for everybody's sake he's got it right. He's out on a limb and looking to us to prop him up. Now get a bloody move on!'

Joe had stopped the car outside the neat lodging house in Little James Street. He turned to Lily. 'Look, I think it might be politic to leave the inspection of the premises to Superintendent Hopkirk and his men. I've trampled on more than my quota of toes today and it's not yet teatime. We'll sit here on watch until they can get here. I've advised a silent approach, no bells or hooters. Are you aware of our Hopkirk, Miss Wentworth?'

'I don't believe I've ever set eyes on the superintendent, sir.'

'Sound man ... dependable. He's a dour Yorkshireman and a teetotaller to boot. Doesn't smoke either.'

'I wonder what he does for pleasure, sir,' Lily commented unguardedly.

'Plays the trombone, I think. He's risen as far and as fast as is possible from the ranks. A career copper. Destined for the top. He'd have thrived in Cromwell's army. Or Napoleon's. Alexander of Macedon would have promoted him to the General Staff. Good-looking chap, too, in his craggy way.'

'He sounds quite charming, sir. But, sir ... can you ... will you make this piece of millstone grit understand that I must have a few words with Patrick Dunne's mother before I leave?'

'It's not a consideration that would weigh heavily with Hopkirk, I fear, but I'll have a go,' Joe said. The girl was

117

gaining the confidence to make demands of him. Not unreasonable ones, but he must never allow his men to suspect any undue influence. He sighed. A balancing act. Could he keep his feet on this tightrope?

'At last! Good – they've parked a few yards down the road. Who've we got? It looks like Inspector Chappel and a couple of DCs and the superintendent himself. Let's go and shake hands.'

Hopkirk was a good-looking chap certainly, Lily thought, and about the same age as his boss. Joe's brief description had not prepared the constable for the thick brown hair that shrugged off any attempt to control it with Brilliantine, the vivid blue eyes that stabbed once and danced off, or the chiselled features, somewhat marred by a broken nose. If asked, Lily would have advised against the neat moustache which underlined and drew attention to it.

The two men fell at once into an easy and efficient exchange of information and confirmation of tactics. 'Over to you, Hopkirk. I'll await your findings back at the Yard. Oh . . . one other thing. Constable Wentworth – to whom we owe our discovery of the prisoner Dunne's identity . . .' Hopkirk acknowledged this with a nod, 'tells me she is honour-bound to pass a message – entirely approved and authorized by me – to the man's mother. Perhaps when you've finished you can grant them a moment or two alone?'

Lily frowned and Joe could guess the reason for her cross face. He'd rather landed her in the soup. Again. She could now look forward to delivering her message to a furious and grief-stricken woman whose house had just been turned upside down by this crew in an effort to find proof of her son's involvement with terrorism and murder. Not a comfortable interview. The women on the force, he knew, were habitually delegated to carry out the unwelcome task of breaking bad news. 'Females are good at that sort of thing . . . It's why we have you along . . . Don't worry – I'll back you up . . .' He'd heard it frequently from male officers. And the women, bless them, always performed the duty without complaint, largely, he guessed, because they knew the men wouldn't come up to scratch. Men showed no facility for conveying sympathy to the suffering; their blunt, emotionless delivery in no way eased the shock and, if anything, provoked anger. It was the outstretched hands of the women, their soft voices and the pity in their eyes, that the bereaved responded to.

Hopkirk was looking at the policewoman thoughtfully. 'Sir, would you mind? It's just a suggestion . . . Why don't we consider the advantages of sending Miss Wentworth in first? Woman to woman before the old lady's heard the worst, so to speak. She might give something away which she wouldn't otherwise. I have some experience of these Irish women, sir. Leathery as the sole of my shoe but they have their sentimental side if you can locate it before they hit the roof.'

'Excellent notion, Hopkirk. Wentworth – would you be willing to do that? Break the news? Deliver your message? Work your magic again?'

She looked from one to the other, not troubling to hide her scorn for their readiness to exploit a female. 'You want me to break the ground for the superintendent, sir? I'll do what I can to ease his path,' she said with quiet sarcasm.

Hopkirk turned a blazing blue gaze on her and seared her eyeballs for two seconds.

It was Joe who flinched.

The men waited in some discomfort, wincing with each piercing scream of pain and rage that came from the open window of the sitting room. A silence followed, and then they made out an intermittent sobbing. Wentworth's voice was not audible but her questions and comments were interleaved by Mrs Dunne's replies. Vehement, pleading, truculent, and, at the last, despairing, she ran the gamut of noisy emotion.

Lily emerged a quarter of an hour later, pale and shaking. She walked up to the two men and, straight backed, delivered her statement. 'Mrs Dunne is English; her husband, now dead, was Irish. She confirms her son's identity and says she suspected his involvement with a political cause. He is no fire-eating republican – he has a gentle nature – and she insists, as the boy himself indicated, that he must have been led along this path by others. She referred to his best friend, whom she seems to despise, as Ronald O'Connor and gave me his address.' Lily passed a sheet from her notebook to Hopkirk. 'There's a tin trunk under Patrick's bed where you might find further indications concerning the identity of those who were running him. She knows he kept his copies of the official organ of the Irish Volunteers in there.' Lily looked up at Hopkirk. 'I assured her that the forces of law and order would tread lightly in view of her cooperation and not wreck her home.'

Hopkirk shook his head and then said stiffly: 'Then you exceeded your brief, constable.' He turned away from her to hide his flash of anger. Catching the force of Sandilands' dour expression, he added grudgingly: 'I'll have a word with the men.' He called Chappel and the DCs. 'In we go, and we're bidden to "tread lightly". Hear that? No rough stuff, and anything you pick up to examine, you put back in its place. Got it, lads? Pretend it's your granny's house you're turning over.'

'Well done, Wentworth,' Joe said, watching the superintendent bang on the front door. 'I think we can leave them to it. Now – what about a cup of tea somewhere? I'll ask the driver to drop us at the nearest Joe Lyons, shall I? Or would you prefer the Ritz? I think we have a small triumph to celebrate.'

'If you don't mind, sir, I'd like to go straight back to the Yard.'

* * *

120

Lily maintained a stiff silence in the car on the way back, fidgeting with something in her pocket. She plodded up the stairs after him, heard him sing out his arrival into Miss Jameson's office and followed him into his room.

She waited in the at ease position before his desk and watched as he pounced on a large envelope placed centrally and held down by a jade paperweight. *Urgent!* said a handwritten note attached.

'Will you excuse me for a moment?' Joe asked, hardly aware of her presence, his face suddenly strained. He took out a sheet of typed writing paper with a very flamboyant heading and read. He read it again.

He looked at Lily. 'Won't you sit down? You'll excuse me if I do. Rather weakening news at the end of a long and tiring day. As this affects you, I'll summarize the rather surprising contents. It's from the Home Secretary. He refuses to accept my resignation, which he considers precipitate and unjustified. Ah! Tomorrow's papers, he assures me, will sport letters to the editors from various highly placed gents, among them a field marshal, the First Sea Lord, members of Parliament and ministers for Ireland, making it clear that they take personal responsibility for requesting the withdrawal of police protection. No blame can possibly attach to any public servant.' Joe gave her an evil grin and added: 'I should guess he includes himself in that category. We're in the clear, Wentworth. Blue Train to the Riviera postponed. You'll have to put off seeing those palm trees for a bit longer.'

His rush of boyish good humour provoked an answering smile. 'I'm glad justice has been done, sir,' she said. 'Any other outcome would have been a hideous shame. And I congratulate you on having such powerful allies. From what I've seen of the task you have ahead of you, you're going to need them all. I wish you luck with it.'

Joe detected a farewell-and-thanks-for-the-ride flavour to her speech. 'What's this? I don't much care for your tone, Wentworth. What are you trying to say?'

'Earlier in the day I offered you my resignation from the force. I meant it then and the day I've just been through has served to reinforce my decision. I don't care to go to war, sir. I've had enough of bullets and bandages, male mischief-making and female grief. I'm leaving and here's my letter of resignation.' She produced it from her pocket.

He was irritated. 'Don't be rash. What on earth will a bright girl like you do in the world? Do you have other employment in mind? Jobs are scarce, you know. Ah! Hopkirk scared you off, has he? I ought to tell you – he scares everyone.'

'Not at all. I'm going to sell hats, sir.'

'What? Hats? Sell them? Did I hear you correctly?'

'You did. My aunt Phyllis has a millinery business in Bruton Street. I'm going to work for her. When women try on a hat, they smile at themselves in the mirror. I like to see that. I'm going to take up a position that lets me put a smile on women's faces instead of a grimace of pain.'

'Anyone can say "Modom looks wonderful in that". It takes a special kind of girl to tell a mother her son's a murderer and he's about to hang for his crime,' Joe said quietly.

Lily tilted her chin in defiance and handed over the envelope.

Joe took it, stern faced, refusing to open it in her presence. He watched her turn away. She must be aware that no one could treat a senior officer with such lack of respect and get away with it. Not even his equals or superiors would descend to such rudeness. In a building patrolled by his minions, she could expect to find a heavy hand descending on her shoulder before she could make it out into the courtyard.

With a show of unconcern, he didn't rise and come to open the door for her. While she struggled with the knob, he called after her, casual and cheery: 'Off now, are you? Look – don't think of going far, will you?'

As she closed the door behind her, his hand reached out to the electric buzzer on his desk.

Miss Jameson emerged from her room opposite just as Lily prepared to set off down the corridor. 'Constable! A moment!' She ducked back into her room.

Lily started off and then turned to see Miss Jameson stalking after her, carrying an extravagant bouquet of white flowers. They looked each other over in mutual puzzlement.

'I've been keeping these fresh in my room since this morning,' Miss Jameson said accusingly. 'I think they've survived. Glad to be rid of them – they were making my room smell like a funeral parlour. The commander brought them in. He'd like you to have them.'

'Me? Are you sure? But why?' Lily said unguardedly.

Miss Jameson shrugged an elegant shoulder. 'Who can say? If you don't know, I'm sure no one else does. He's a law unto himself. He's known to indulge, on occasion, in . . . whimsicality.' The distaste in her voice suggested whimsicality might well be accounted the eighth deadly sin. 'There's a note in there, you'll find.' She turned on her heel.

Alone in the corridor, Lily fished out a small florist's envelope, opened it and took out a note written in black ink. *Present yourself here at 6 p.m. Saturday week in Mata Hari mode. Something sparkling at the wrist and throat? I have another little problem you can help me with. JS.*

Joe waited until he heard Miss Jameson's door close again and Lily's footsteps retreat down the corridor before he picked up the telephone and requested the internal number he had rung before.

'She's just left.'

Chapter Thirteen

A murmured question at the other end of the line prompted the response: 'Oh, yes, I think so. In any case she'll have to do . . . no time to look further. She's the right age – which is to say a year or two younger than our friend. How old is he these days? Twenty-eight?

'No, she's not out of the top drawer, I'm afraid. The lowest grade for intake recommended by Sir Nevil – what was it? Upper shop-assistant level? Yes, pitch it there. Is that where you'd find millinery? Hats? But her behaviour's acceptable. She'll pass.'

He listened impatiently to a further query and answered briskly: 'Well of course we have. But none of them has the other qualities we require. My cousin Margery might oblige, if I asked her . . . though she runs Girl Guides shindigs on Saturday nights, I believe. And I very much doubt she can do the tango.'

He eased the receiver a little way from his ear. 'Well, there you are then. You'll have to take what's on offer. It's a question of settling for the best balance. I've passed them all in review and you'll have to take my word for it, this is the best we can do. Look – I took the precaution of trailing her before a friend . . . Lady Dedham . . . Cassandra. Knowing nothing to the contrary, she took her for one of our upper-class young ladies. In fact, the girl made a very favourable impression. No awkwardness at all, sympathetic and chatty, was the verdict. Cassandra's asked to see her again – quite unprompted by me. "Someone I can really talk to," she says. And Cassandra Dedham's no one's fool.

'Accent? Do you know, I hadn't noticed one,' Joe lied cheerily. 'They can always talk to each other in cockney, I suppose . . . he's an adept. I've heard him at it. And she *is* a London lass. Though Margery, who seems to have got somewhat fond of the girl, assures me she can, in fact, produce a Mayfair drawl that's indistinguishable from the real thing. Ghastly, but it might be useful.'

The voice at the other end guffawed and exclaimed: 'So that *was* her! Thought it must have been. Did you realize, sir? She rang us up from your office, pretending to be the operator. She got Howard – who's not the sharpest – and pulled the wool over his eyes. It was a beat or two before he caught on. He thinks he got away with it – played the silly ass and burbled a bit. Told her he was the War Office! That must have shaken her.'

'Mmm . . . not so's you'd notice,' Joe murmured. 'I wondered if she'd have the initiative to follow that through. Well, well! I chalk one up to Wentworth. Another one. She seems to be scoring all round the wicket.'

He listened to a further question and replied testily: 'Educated? Gracious, man – does it matter? She's hardly likely to be taking part in a Platonic symposium in the company *we* have in mind. But if you need to know – according to her notes, she matriculated from a boys' grammar school. Odd, that . . .' He consulted his file. 'Is that possible? Should have been followed up at interview . . . Not to be dismissed, those establishments . . . my best super is a product of one such. We'll probably find they've taught her to conjugate a deponent verb and debunk the Phlogiston Theory in a hundred words. Let's pray she's not minded to do either on Saturday week. It would fall a bit flat.

'Appearance? Again, acceptable. No, I'd go so far as to say attractive.' He cleared his throat and admitted: 'In fact, damned attractive. Hard to tell what's under all that serge,

125

of course. I had to use my imagination. Physical type is right – pony rather than the usual shire horse we have on our books. Well coupled up. Moves nicely. A grace that's natural, you'd say, rather than imposed by deportment classes. Fair hair, fashionably cut. I have to say they'll make a lovely pair.'

A further muttered question raised a blustering response. 'Good Lord, man, I didn't ask. I say – there *is* a limit!

'Oh, yes, she has physical courage. Saw her damn nearly get herself knifed at Paddington. Excellent report in her file from her ju-jitsu instructor. And she's resourceful. I'll bear witness to both qualities. And, in Margery's words, she's "forthcoming". By that my cousin meant the girl's ready to speak up for herself.' Joe grinned. 'Some might say impertinent and undisciplined. No idea when to hold her tongue. Still, I keep reminding myself – and I remind you, James – it's not a doormat we're looking for. And perhaps we shall just have to accommodate and learn to *manage* a little female free-thinking. I'm ahead of you there – brought up by a suffragist mother and sister, I've been doing it all my life. But we have one problem, James, old man. When I said a moment ago that she'd left, I meant exactly that.' He gave a shout of laughter. 'So freely does the constable think, she's just buggered off, leaving me with her resignation letter on my desk.

'Yes! Yes! Flounced out! I didn't know whether to have her arrested or give her a round of applause . . .

'No, no need for the heavy hand. Not yet. I had the fore-thought to set a reserve bait. I think I've worked out what makes Miss Wentworth tick. She'll be back in the net before you can say knife. No need for concern. I have our girl in hand. I think we can say with some confidence that it's all on for Saturday week.'

He looked at his watch. 'Now, James, I want you and whoever you've put in charge of next Saturday's jollifica-tion . . . Rupert? Ah, yes – good man . . . to come up here to the ops room for a briefing and exchange of information and to meet your opposite number in the CID, Superintendent Hopkirk. Six suit you? Time we all shook the cards from our sleeves and laid them out on the table. Officers possibly in the line of fire – always a concern whether they're male, doubly so when they're female. And "Carnage at Claridges" is not a headline I want to see splashed across the *Daily Mirror* the next day.'

Chapter Fourteen

'Well, what do you think, Phyl? And please don't tell me he's only after—'

'I wasn't going to. Give me *some* credit. In fact, I was going to say – you seem to have caught the attention of the one man in London who's *not* Only After One Thing!' Auntie Phyl put on the spectacles that dangled on her slim bosom and peered again at the florist's card. 'Hard to say what he *is* after, but whatever it may be, it's not a girl's most precious possession.'

'You sound very certain of that, Phyl. What makes you think so?'

'Hold your horses. What is this – the third degree? I need a Passing Cloud to aid concentration. And a cup of cocoa. Put that pan on the gas ring, love, and I'll tell you. Don't skimp on the sugar.'

The office space and workshop at the back of Auntie Phyl's hat shop was generous and equipped for staff comfort as well as running repairs and the creative flourishes the business demanded. Lily was very much at home here and busied herself with milk pan and mugs.

'Gawd! My feet! I've been on them since six this morning.' Phyllis Wentworth, Modiste to the Gentry, sank grumbling into one of the two armchairs, kicked off her shoes and began to massage her toes. 'Oooh! That's better. Antelope skin – soft as butter and all the go but the heel height's a killer! I'm too young to have bunions! Oh, thanks, love.' She accepted a cigarette from the silver tin

Lily found beside the biscuit barrel, moistened her lips, placed the oval shape delicately between them and sighed. She narrowed her eyes while Lily struck a match and lit it. 'Ah! First puff of the first cigarette of the day! Nothing like it. Have one? No? Suit yourself.' She turned her attention back to the tiny card. 'Give me a minute. And let me get *you* in focus . . . say hello. You haven't been to see me for weeks. I was thinking of going to the police to declare you a missing person. And now you come tearing in here at the end of the day all sparkly eyed, clutching a florist's card like your first love-letter and expect me to do an instant Sherlock on it? And – first things first . . .' She looked about her in an exaggerated way. 'Weren't there supposed to be flowers with this, or have you latched on to the biggest cheapskate in London? A bloke who sends you a card with a picture of a flower on it and a three-line note cuts no ice with *me*.'

'Were there ever flowers! You couldn't see me for flowers as I staggered along the Embankment with them. I left them at the Charing Cross Hospital. What am I supposed to do with a sheaf of lilies in the middle of town? I was attracting comment! If I'd taken them back to the hostel – can you imagine what ideas that would have put into Mrs Turnbull's head?'

'The contents of Mrs Turnbull's head are not something I choose to conjure with, thanks very much. Lilies? Those lovely long-stemmed ones? You should have brought them here. I could have put them in the window. Touch of class.'

'You don't need any more touches. The window looks wonderful.' At last Lily remembered her manners. 'Are you all right, Phyl? Business going well?'

'I'll say! Always the season for hats. And there's no shortage of cash about in the West End. I sold over a dozen models today and took as many orders. The races . . . weddings . . . None under ten guineas.'

'Mum says you're branching out. She's spreading the rumour that you've put in a bid for Harrods.'

'What? Maids' uniforms and off-the-peg celanese frocks? Give me some credit! Still, the old bat's not entirely wrong – I have got something up my sleeve. I've had to take on two more girls this month in the sewing department. You know, Lily love, that there's always a place for you here? And you'll see why it's urgent when I tell you my news. I could do with a manager. And I'd pay you better than the starvation wages you get for pounding the pavements.'

'Perhaps they'd raise my pay if I did some special under-cover work. Work where I can use my brain, Phyl.'

Phyllis looked at her niece with pity and understanding. 'Those upper-class bosses of yours expect you to keep your brains in your boots, love. They don't expect a common or garden girl like you to think or reason, whatever learning she's done. They'd say you were getting above yourself if you started to use all that matriculation stuff you've got in your head. Your mother isn't often right but when she warned your father that it was asking for trouble getting you educated she might, for once in her life, have hit the nail on the head.'

'Well, I'm going to surprise you, Phyl. I've had an offer – a serious offer, I think – of some plain-clothes detective work! This JS was, in fact, quite pleased to discover I could think for myself. Let me tell you why he's really interested in me, shall I?'

Phyllis listened to Lily's account in disapproving silence. 'An unofficial boss? Can't say I'd be happy with that arrangement. When you're dealing with a man you should always agree terms and get things down on paper.' Catching a quizzical glint in Lily's eye she pursed her lips and admitted: 'All right! I'm one to talk. The Awful Warning if your mother's to be believed. Arrangements don't come more informal than my own.'

Lily smiled and hurried to murmur: 'I never know when it's the right moment to ask but I'm always wondering, Phyl . . . the Slip-up? How's he doing?'

Phyl grinned. 'There are times even I'd rather not hear ... but for the moment he's doing well. Going up to university next term. Hardly seems possible, does it? Little Teddy at the London School of Economics? Doesn't seem ten minutes since you were teaching him to count to five, love, with conkers in a jam jar. He was just asking about you before he set off for Florence. We'll have a party when he gets back and you can check him over yourself. I'm more concerned about you at present.'

'And next you'll be telling me never to sign anything until *you've* taken a look at it.'

'Good advice! Did I ever say that? Well, listen now to the voice of experience. I say again – this man's after *something*. It's all here,' she said, tapping the card. 'Choice of flower first. What do we read into that? Lilies for a Lily, eh? Bit bloomin' obvious, isn't it?'

'Well, the lily's my birthday flower – May. He'd have known that from the notes. And it signifies purity. But *that* I'm sure he would not have any information on!'

'Loverish whimsy are we thinking? Can you be sure he chose them? We can't assume that – not of a man with a secretary to do the domestic for him. Still, if she's the supercilious cow you describe, you'd have ended up with a bunch of daisies from the back garden. I'm calculating *he* chose them to flatter and amuse. Now let's read these runes. They look like runes. Black ... chiselled ... bossy. Mmm ... I don't much like what I'm seeing. These message cards are very small. Most men, in their excitement, run over and finish the message on the back, have you noticed?'

Lily smiled. 'Oh, Phyl! I wouldn't know. This is the first shop-bought bouquet I've ever had. A bunch of sticky bluebells and an even stickier kiss from Billy Benson on a charabanc trip to Epping Forest in 1914 is the best I've done so far.'

'Pity your first had to come from a rogue then. Yes – rogue. Look – do you see the writing fills the given space

131

exactly? And he uses a thick-nibbed pen. He's adjusted his normal style and tailored his message. It's calculated to the tenth of an inch. He's given it careful thought. I definitely don't think he's planning to have his wicked way with you, though. Out of the question. A man in his position – in the public eye, two or three more steps more to go on the ladder, would that be? He's not going to risk the scandal of taking advantage of one of the female staff. Too much to lose. No, I reckon you're safe as far as that goes. He's not planning to twang your elastic.' Phyl eyed Lily's outfit with distaste. 'Besides, I don't expect he's noticed there's a pretty girl in there.'

'Well, you may just be wrong, Phyl. I did come in for an inspection of sorts. He checked my height and weight and age. He rather insisted on seeing me without my hat. I thought he might be about to look at my teeth and feel my fetlocks.'

'Dirty devil! And no other female present while he sniffs around, poking under your hat and measuring your hem-line? Well, that's a breach of the rules for a start. Complain to Miss Peto! She'll be down on him like a ton of bricks.' Phyllis shook her head. 'But I still can't see what's in it for him. Where the thrill would be.'

'Never underestimate a man's capacity for perversion, Phyl! There's something about the uniform that sets them off. They love to be dominated, you know.'

'Where on earth do you get all this rubbish from?' Phyl was scandalized but intrigued.

'I learned that from an old jam-tart who trawls the Baze, sitting on a bench in the park. I could have had her arrested but didn't. I usually don't.' Lily laughed. 'In reward for my kindness, she treated me to a lesson in . . . not quite sure what you'd call it . . . um . . . bending gentlemen to one's will, I suppose. Then, once you've got them bending, you give them a good spanking. Whilst wearing a uniform.'

'Which party's meant to be in uniform?' Phyl asked with a grimace of distaste.

132

'Either or both, I expect. Phyl, you'd be surprised to hear the inventive suggestions I've had for bringing my navy serge into disrepute. The offers roll in! I could make a fortune if I were that way inclined. More if I were a nurse, of course.'

Phyllis grunted her disapproval. 'There's probably a word for that sort of thing. Something in Greek that I'd rather not hear. But that's not this man's problem, evidently. He wants to see you in "something sparkling at the wrist and throat". I'm *assuming* something in between . . . yes? I can see you intend to accept this invitation, if that's what it is – it reads rather more like a royal command. So what are you planning? Got any sparklers?'

'He has no idea! I expect he only knows women who visit Asprey the jeweller's twice a week and have wardrobes full of evening clothes.' Lily's voice was bitter. 'He could have asked any of the other recruits. They don't exactly have their tin lockers at the hostel stuffed with ball gowns but they've got silks and satins by the furlong stashed away at the family seat, you can bet. I should think he doesn't even know the price of a pair of evening gloves.'

She gave the cocoa an over-vigorous stir. 'I know. Barmy of me even to think of accepting. I nearly chucked in the towel when I thought about it. But – all too easy to do a Cinderella and stay behind blackleading the grate and sighing with frustration. I can't do that.'

Phyllis looked at her with affection. 'No, love. You were never a Cinders. More of a Little Red Hen – "I can do it myself". God, that can be annoying!'

'I have to find out what this man's up to. Even if I have to kit myself out from a stall in Petticoat Lane. It could be that he really wants me to do a bit of serious detective work and that's a chance I'm not going to pass up. So, I have to work something out. I thought I'd borrow my mother's black silk evening dress – the one she wore to the Mayor's Armistice Day do last year. I could tack up the hem and put a belt round it. You could help me tiddle it up a bit . . . I wouldn't tell her and she'd never notice. I can just afford a pair of new shoes and I wondered . . .' Lily hesitated, hobbled by the task of asking a favour from anyone, even from the woman she was closer to than her own mother.

Phyllis read her thought. '. . . wondered if I'd lend you a little cocktail hat to distract from the God-awful black number you'll be wearing? A little bit of nonsense in silver and pearl trembling over the right eye to hold his attention? Of course I will. You've a dozen to choose from. But look, love, this needs a bit of planning. This sparkling bit is the bloke's way of signalling evening dress. It means he'll be in tails. The Royal Opera House? The Ritz? Either way, your ma's silk is not going to rise to the challenge. And it's summer still – no one under thirty's going to be wearing black. Inconsiderate oaf! Why couldn't he have been more precise? Think back. Did he give you a clue while you were having your chat – express an enthusiasm for Puccini, rave about the *sole normande* at the Caprice?'

Lily shook her head. 'We're not on those terms, Phyl. But I don't somehow see him at the opera. I doubt he could sit still long enough. He's a bit too outdoorsy and twitchy for that. I can more easily imagine him cutting a rug at a jazz club.'

'Gracious! How old is this gent? I'd imagined some old fart with mutton-chop whiskers and gouty knees.'

'No, not at all. He's younger than Uncle David. Not thirty yet, I'd guess. Too young for the position he holds, everybody says. The others of that rank *are* moustached, mouldering old codgers who do nothing more energetic than shift papers from one side of the desk to the other all day, checking staff rotas and sacking people. This one's different. After the Paddington station performance, I asked around a bit. "Know your enemy." He oughtn't to feel like an enemy, but he does. What the men say is that Sandilands is one of the new generation of officers – you know, brought in from outside the force to put a bit of grit in the mix and train on for higher things.'

'My word! Can this be the dear old Yard we all know and hate? I thought you had to wear out fifty pairs of boots plodding the streets before they made you a sergeant.'

'It's the post-war stir-up,' Lily said. 'Talent shanghaied and shoehorned in at the highest level. General Macready, then Brigadier Horwood, made Commissioners ... Horwood's only qualification was three days as a Chief Constable of a county force when he was invited to take over. And what they do is appoint younger men in their own image. They favour ex-military. Though Sandilands predates Macready, they say. He'd already done his regular beat-bashing when he was spotted.'

'Is he good looking?'

Lily considered. 'I'd say so ... if you don't mind the scar.'

'Scar?'

Lily put up a hand and mimed raking it across her brow. 'Tiger claw is what they say in the canteen. Silvery against the tanned skin.'

Phyl stared. 'Oh, I don't think I'd mind the scar. Is he much liked?'

'Oh, yes, he is!' Lily stopped short. Her response had been too ready and too warm. She tempered it with: 'Well – as far as any of the upper echelons are ever popular with the men. Here's your cocoa, Phyl. They like him, first because they actually think they know him – he goes out on the beat with them sometimes and talks to them. Remembers their wife's name next time they meet and all that rot. And then – he's active. Gets things done.'

'You've got to admire that.' Phyl spoke grudgingly. 'What's he stirring up at the moment?'

'Several irons in the fire. He's all in favour of getting the motorized division going and he's running experiments – I'm not kidding – with radio telephone systems to install in the pursuit cars. They think soon they'll be able to direct the drivers from the top floor of the Yard! I talked to one of the sergeants who's training as a driver for the Flying Squad. He was full of information. Sandilands prides himself on what he calls his "hands-on" style. A bit too literally, according to the sergeant, when the hands in question are on the steering wheel of a car doing fifty miles an hour down Oxford Street. "Terrible driver but halfway human" seems to be the verdict.'

'And what do *you* make of him, this half-human Jehu who likes to get his hands on things?'

'Oh, he presents himself well. Good tailoring but nothing flamboyant. Neat haircut, army wrist-watch. Looks like a soldier in civvies.' And, reprimanded by Phyl's arched eyebrow, she added: 'Well, he has a very nice smile.'

'So, they say, did Brides-in-the-bath Smith. Is that it? Could be any of ten thousand men in London. He doesn't seem to have made much of an impression.'

'He does make an impression. He looks crisp and energetic . . . you know . . . fresh out of the shower and looking for trouble.'

'How tiring!'

'He eats three gypsy creams in as many minutes.'

'Well, you've got something in common at least. But you can add to your picture manipulative and up to no good,' Phyl said. 'All things considered, though, I'd say this toff was worth our attention.' Her eyes gleamed with intent. 'But he doesn't know what he's taking on. We'll have him on toast, shall we, Lil? Listen – if he was an officer in the last lot, he's probably got something to hide. I'll ask Albert. Albert's a member of a rather seditious old soldiers' drinking club in Soho. He can ask about. Follow him. See where he goes after dark. If there's anything to know to your boss's discredit, he'll know it within the hour.'

Albert was Phyl's chauffeur and debt-collector. His magnificent physique, combined with his deceptively sweet smile, secured instant cooperation from Phyl's defaulting clients. People seemed to understand at once that, should they demur or cause a moment's distress for

Phyllis Wentworth, his loyalty to his employer would compel him, against all his pacific instincts, to 'take steps'. Albert's 'steps' were known to be earthshaking.

'But first I'll take a quick look through this month's Society and Entertainment pages . . . see if I can't outguess him. Pass it over, will you?' She settled to thumb her way down the columns. 'Now, if I were an energetic gent on mischief bent where would I be planning to spend my Saturday night in evening dress?'

Phyl worked her way patiently through the listed entertainments. 'I see their majesties have opted for the Wagner at Covent Garden. But you say opera's out. Well then, there's early keyboard music at the Royal Institution. No? How about a trip down the Mile End Road to the People's Palace of Delight? They're staging a variety performance for the Excelsior Philanthropic Society in front of the Duke and Duchess of Norfolk. Ouch! Poor dears. Spending their Saturday night down the Mile End – now that's philanthropy for you.'

Lily snatched the pages from her. 'Let's be serious. Theatre – that's my best hope. What have we got on offer? . . . Oh, I say. We could be going to see *The Man in Dress Clothes* at the Garrick or *Partners of Fate* with Louise Lovely. Of course, there's any number of balls on at the moment. One or two charity suppers. Let's pray it's not a charity dinner-dance – how dull. Only one of those promises to be the least bit interesting – the Russian émigrés one. At least it's on at Claridges. Well, where else? Not short of a bob or two, these Russians.'

Phyllis took the listings back again. She fell silent, running her finger along the list of guests expected. 'Sorry, love. Distracted. I was just checking the runners and riders for the Claridges do. At least ten of these are clients of mine and I'm frantically hoping I haven't kitted out two archduchesses in similar confections. Bang would go my reputation overnight!'

At last she looked up with a smile of satisfaction. 'Ouf! I'm in the clear. Right, I think we're ready to take this chap on. Two things we'll need: that bunch of keys I left over there on the draining board and a pair of scissors. Oh, and let's not forget the pumpkin! Not sure whether you're going to the ball or the dogs, love, but your auntie will get you there in style!'

Chapter Fifteen

Phyl hunted about in the kitchen and, suitably equipped, returned to Lily. 'We'll put the shop lights out now. But we're not going far, just next door. I have something special to show you. Come on.'

Lily looked up at the façade of the shop adjoining. It had twice the frontage of the hat shop and was painted in green and gold with a distinctive curlicued script over the window announcing *Madame Cécile. Modes. London and Paris.*

'I say, Phyl, is this all right, what you're doing? Not *breaking* exactly as you have the keys, but definitely *entering* premises without the owner's permission. Whatever's Madame Cécile going to say?'

'*Mais Madame Cécile, c'est moi!*' said Phyl surprisingly. 'The new Madame, anyway. Jacob bought the old one out and installed me in a ready-made business. I liked the name so I thought – might as well keep it. I don't speak French and that's a bit of a problem. Well, not much, as the clients don't have the foggiest either. I've employed a French maid – a real one – and she's teaching me ten useful phrases every day. I've been keeping this very quiet for one reason and another. And I'd rather you didn't mention it to your parents, Lil. Come in. Let me put the lights on. It's getting a bit dark now – we'll be having a thunderstorm next. I'll get Albert to drive you back to your digs. I've got the Buick out back.'

Lily entered a space smelling lightly of freshly laid carpet and expensive perfume and looked about her in awe.

'Crikey, Phyl! I've never been in such a posh shop. Ankle deep in Axminster – shall I take my boots off?' She went to run a hand over the gleaming mahogany surface of the counter, bounced on the tapestried upholstery of a Louis XVI chair and stroked the silken drapery adorning a mannequin. 'Even your wax doll is too jolly stuck-up to notice me.' And, suddenly concerned: 'I say – does Jacob know what he's doing, taking this on? It must be a very expensive place to maintain. Best part of London . . . a hundred square yards of showroom and offices to the rear, no doubt.'

'Fitted out by Heals in the Tottenham Court Road,' added Phyl with satisfaction. 'It works well with my hat shop. I send the dress clients next door and the hat clients round here. And you needn't worry about Jacob. We share the revenues and believe me – he's doing all right!'

'I forgot to ask – how's his wife?'

'Usual. Hanging on to life by her fingertips. Enjoying her bad health.' That was all Phyl would say about her protector's lawful wife. It was all she ever said before changing the subject. 'But look around, Lily – are you seeing the possibilities?'

'What? Are you suggesting I borrow one of these creations to knock the commander's eye out?'

'I think we could manage that. Nothing off the peg, of course – this isn't Marshall and Snelgrove.' Phyl sniffed. 'All made to measure here. And it would take my best seamstress a week to make up a frock for you. But – listen. We mostly sell dresses by showing them off on models. That row of dinky chairs, on a Wednesday, is occupied by rich women and the occasional husband. *They* don't mind being dragged along to a parade because they get a chance to ogle the mannequins without getting ticked off. The flesh and blood ones, I mean. I've got four on the books. Two French, two English. And I have a constantly changing set of dresses for them to show off. I've got a dozen demonstration gowns on hangers in the dressing room at

140

the back. You can have your pick of them. Problem is, my girls are all nearly six foot tall and thin as a whistle.' She eyed Lily critically. 'You're slim enough. You've got the Wentworth figure like me and your pa. Greyhound rather than fat spaniel like your mother. But I'll need to do a bit of shortening. That's where we'll need the scissors.' She took them from her pocket and brandished them. 'Come on! Evening dresses on the left. Let's pick something out!'

Lily was lost for words in front of the rows of dresses. They ranged from pure white satin to darkest mulberry grosgrain, some a daring four inches below the knee for flappers, some ankle-length for dowagers, all intimidating and out of her reach.

'Anything but white,' Lily said, making a start. 'I don't want to look as though I'm being presented at court.'

'And I rule out anything dark. Not for a balmy evening.'

Half the exhibits were whisked aside.

'Some of these are very décolleté,' Lily murmured dubiously, passing the remainder in review. 'And I haven't got the bust for them. Let's remember this isn't a date. I'm going to be working undercover so I ought to have some cover to work under. Something discreet that won't let me down if I have to run or pick a fight or defend my virtue.'

'The shoestring straps are out then,' Phyl said sliding them to the end of the rail. 'Fusspot! Cinderella's fairy godmother never had these problems.'

An apricot georgette and a raspberry crêpe de Chine followed them into the rejected section. 'No bonbons.'

'That leaves us with a choice of two. Well, that was quick. Some women take three hours. Anyway, either of these models will cut down six inches without ruining the proportions and, in their different ways, they're both stunners.'

She held one in front of Lily to assess the effect. 'Heavy silk in eau de Nil: fashionable colour without being outrageous. Green always looks right with coppery hair and a creamy skin. Slim fitting and sleek, but the shoulder straps are built up and embroidered with a Russian motif – very fashionable! And strong – you could go ten rounds with Jack Dempsey and they wouldn't come adrift. I've got the sweetest little headdress to go with it.' Her voice took on the modulated confidentiality of a saleswoman's. 'A cap of green and gold shot tissue with an overlay of oxidized silver thread, pearls, gold beads and bells, madam. Perfect on a heart-shaped face. Just dangle a gold earring on each side and you wouldn't need anything sparkling with this outfit. That would be excessive. This delightful confection tells its own tale.'

'In a mysterious voice carried on the east wind ... It's like a Dulac illustration for *The Corn Spirit*. But you'd need to silence the bells.'

'That's no problem ... a drop of candle wax'll do it. But it's only a dress, love. Don't get carried away. It was, in fact, not made up on spec – it was designed by me and the client herself with a special occasion in mind. She cancelled the order – "held up in Paris", she said. The scandal sheets reveal that she has indeed been detained over the Channel – with a dark-eyed charmer! An Italian tenor, they say. Anyway, I'm left with a work of art on my hands. Now – if we're being fanciful – I'm not sure in what accent this last one will speak.'

'We'll never know. I think probably it wouldn't deign to address a word to us.'

'You're right. This really is *haute couture*. And discretion itself. I nicked the idea from the spring Paris designs. Coco Chanel inspired it though she doesn't know that. It's a bit of a gymslip but then you'd feel comfortable with that – cut and colour.'

Lily looked with approval at the midnight blue silk. A sleeveless bodice ran from the square neck smoothly down to a lowered waist delicately emphasized by a satin sash. The severity of the line was softened by the addition of an overskirt of navy tulle.

142

'Well? What'll it be?' Phyl asked. 'Princess of the Steppes or Saucy Gym Mistress? Want to try them both? Practise a few ju-jitsu moves in front of the mirror?'

'No need. I know what I like and I've made my mind up,' said Lily. 'Get your scissors out, Phyl. I'll take that one, if you're sure that's all right?'

Phyl hesitated for a second. 'If you're quite certain?' she said. 'Will the commander like it, do you think?'

Chapter Sixteen

'Come in, come in. What I imagine the commander would like is to find us all settled down and getting acquainted.' James Bacchus of Special Branch waved a languidly inviting hand across the central table of the operations room. 'I see we've all arrived five minutes early to impress Sir. It's Hopkirk, isn't it? How do you do, Superintendent? Hopkirk, why don't you and your colleague park yourselves over there while we're waiting? And may I introduce my second in command – Captain Rupert Fanshawe, late of the Grenadier Guards?'

'Delighted,' grunted Hopkirk. 'And may I introduce Inspector Charles Chappel, late of the Victoria Vice?'

The four men sat down opposite each other, casting an occasional covert glance across the table. Hopkirk made a show of taking a sheaf of foolscap sheets from his briefcase and arranging them to his satisfaction in front of him. Chappel did the same with a more modest display of documents. Hopkirk placed a fountain pen and a pencil alongside the sheets. He tweaked the lever of his pen to test the ink supply, he tickled the point of his pencil to assess its sharpness. 'I like to be prepared,' he commented. His glance swept unemphatically over the shamingly empty space in front of the two Branch men who were lounging at ease, trying not to catch each other's eye.

They all waited.

'Sandilands is always one minute early and comes in like

a hurricane, you'll find,' Bacchus remarked knowingly to the company.

'Then this would be the moment to bring the washing in and batten down the hatches,' Hopkirk advised. 'If I'm not mistaken, here he—'

Joe came striding into the room. 'No, no, remain seated, will you? Now, Hopkirk is here as officer in charge of the investigation of the admiral's murder. And please note: murder is what we're calling it until further notice, not assassination. Hopkirk, I see you're ready. In a moment you will treat us to an outline of your findings, and we'll follow that with whatever questions the Branch may have.'

He took his place at the head of the table. 'But first, gentlemen . . .' He leaned forward and fixed on the eyes of each man in turn. 'I see you've lined yourselves up for a quadrille, or is it a bout of jousting you have in mind? I'm partial to a bit of cut and thrust myself but I won't have sides taken on this one. We're all in this together and we *succeed* together. I'm not contemplating any other outcome. Don't take me for your scoutmaster or your padré. Think for yourselves. Get it right. Share what you have. Hopkirk, you have five minutes to convince Bacchus and Fanshawe that we are considering a civil misdemeanour in the case of the death of the admiral.'

'Well, thank you for that exposé, Superintendent. I understand you'd have us believe that the nationality of the gunmen is pure coincidence?' Bacchus's voice was gently scathing. 'Now tell me if I'm hopelessly adrift here – two *Irishmen*, both, you are able at last to tell us, with links to Fenian gangs, lay ambush to the most vocal and most respected of British opponents to the notion of Irish self-rule – barring only Winston Churchill perhaps – and you say the motive was not a political one? Moreover, these chancers choose the very moment when protection squads have been stood down . . . and the target steps back on to his home stage in the capital again after a long absence. Well, well! My question is: if we're called on to leave political sensitivities aside, one does rather wonder what Lord Dedham could possibly have done in his last twenty-four hours to upset these fellows to the point of having them turn a pistol on him?'

Hopkirk was not put out. 'A deliberate misinterpretation. I'm just saying we ought to keep an open mind for a bit longer. The victim was other things in his life besides Navy man and politician. He was rich – and that's always something worth bearing in mind. We plan to look with interest at his will when we can get our hands on a copy. And he was an abrasive type . . . even his wife admits he'd made enemies, not all of them in the field of politics.'

'That much is true,' Sandilands said. 'Damned annoying old goat. I nearly throttled him myself once. And his wife Cassandra is a saint. Poor dear! Hopkirk, you would do well to go back and speak to her again when she's had a chance to recover her equilibrium.'

'Oh, I don't think it's me she'd be wanting to open up to, sir,' said Hopkirk with a sly glint in his eye. 'But I'll make a note.'

'Get on with it, Hopkirk.'

'No reason at all to suppose these men we've got banged up in Vine Street held a personal grudge . . . they were easy enough to hire. To recruit to any cause or none. One of them at least drank every night at the same pub – Ye Olde Cocke in Petticoat Lane. The bar round the back's full of ex-soldiers on the lookout for a bit of action that'll bring in cash. They put themselves about for all sorts of strong-arm stuff. Bodyguarding, chucking out and, yes, rumour is: killing. They could just as easily have been home-bred Cockneys, or Italians or Russians or Lascars. They're all on the menu.'

'Could have . . .' Bacchus's voice was dismissive. 'Speculation. We prefer to deal in certainties – established facts. You may not have been aware that the older one of this pair of

146

charmers – whose identity seems at last to have been established – has been in our sights for some weeks now, his activities monitored. We rather regarded him as one of our targets. Two of his drinking cronies report straight back to us – on the books, you might say. Money changes hands occasionally. If we'd gained access to this villain at once we'd have known what to ask him and how to ask it.' He shrugged. 'We could have passed one of the inside blokes off as a prisoner and stuck them in a cell together . . . listened in to the conversations . . . for starters. But here we are, left playing guessing games.' He tapped his neatly trimmed fingernails on the table to underline his irritation.

'Would the super care to indulge in a little more speculation? The provenance of the weapons used?' Rupert Fanshawe took over the polite grilling. 'How did two Irish lads get their hands on service Webleys?'

'No clues about the weapons,' Hopkirk muttered. 'Nothing unexpected from fingerprinting. But, as I'm sure the captain knows, London's awash with Webleys. They could have been provided by whoever commissioned the hit. No reason to suppose the instigator ever laid hand on the guns.'

'No indeed. These deals are arranged anonymously, by telephone. Which brings us to the third shot. The one to the heart that finished him. Browning or the like, you say?'

Hopkirk nodded and passed a copy of Spilsbury's post-mortem report over the table. The Branch men fell on it and spent some minutes absorbing it while the CID maintained an anxious silence.

'At this distance it looks as though we're contemplating a fatal shot fired by the taxi driver, his lady passenger or a third hand hiding in the shrubbery,' Fanshawe commented.

Hopkirk nodded again.

'No mention of such a shot in the evidence given by the passenger?'

'No. She was too hysterical to be able to distinguish one calibre from another. In fact, I couldn't be certain she understood what I meant by "calibre". Pistol, revolver,

Gatling, Big Bertha – all just guns to her. Nasty, noisy things. And she was sensibly cowering down in the back of the cab with her hands over her ears while all this was going on. Poor girl – if she hadn't rolled herself into a ball like a hedgehog, she could have been a third victim. In every respect her statement echoes all that we now know to have happened. The cab driver's actions; the shooting of the police patrolman; the bashing on the head of the cabby when the killers ran out of ammunition. We've now accounted for all the bullets. They each started with a full magazine, it seems, and would indeed have run out by the time they thought of silencing the cabby. Bit of luck for *him*.' He fell silent for a moment, then added, 'Her every statement adds up.'

His tone was a shade too firm.

Bacchus picked up on it at once. 'Tell us more about this passenger, Hopkirk. Unusual, don't you think to come across an unaccompanied young woman out and about at that time? Did you discover what she was doing there?'

'She said she was visiting a friend.'

'A friend who, we presume, backed up her assertion?'

'Um . . . no. We knocked on all doors in the vicinity, in the pursuit of our inquiries. No one claimed to know her. Including the local Lothario at number thirty-nine. His man denied all knowledge.'

'But you have established her bona fides? I'm assuming she has been re-interviewed?' Bacchus said.

Hopkirk hesitated for a moment. 'We sent men to the address in Park Lane next morning . . . the one she gave us for the record and the one to which we returned her after interview at Gerard Street police station. No trace of her. She's disappeared. Done a runner.'

Under the glare of the Branch men he referred to his notes. 'Smart address. Upper-class rooming house. It took us a while to get past the major domo and the maid to the owner. A Mrs Throckmorton eventually deigned to give me her card.' Hopkirk leafed through his notes again and unclipped a small, white, gilt-edged card. He passed it over the table.

Bacchus took it eagerly. 'No idea this place existed,' he said. 'Is it kosher?' He scanned the card again.

Mrs Adela Throckmorton.
Choice accommodation for single ladies visiting the city.
A home from home in Mayfair.
Congenial chaperonage arranged.

'Chaperonage?' he questioned.

'They run a service escorting young ladies to concerts and exhibitions, the theatre, even shopping trips. They do pick-ups and deliveries to railway stations. You know – a sort of "Universal Aunts".'

'Mmm . . . no suggestion of an Uncles Unlimited facility, I suppose?' Bacchus asked.

'You're not the only one with a dirty mind, Bacchus,' said Hopkirk. 'Thought did occur to Inspector Chappel here. This *is* Park Lane we're talking about, within a stride or two of Pinks.'

'And this *is* Inspector Chappel, late of Victoria Vice?' Bacchus acknowledged with a raised eyebrow.

'Sir. Confirm nothing untoward known on this establishment. I personally watched the place for an hour or two,' said Chappel. 'Lady guests coming and going. Some dropped off by Daddy and Mummy – or should I say Papa and Mama? Some being picked up by a succession of old boots in tweed skirts and sensible shoes. The Aunts, doubtless.'

'Chappel, I want you to dig deeper and more energetically in this area. The girl was very keen on returning to Park Lane. You still have contacts?' Sandilands asked.

'How deep should I dig? That's the question, sir. It's posh round there. I could end up revealing cabinet ministers in their socks, military gents out of uniform, police chiefs in considerable embarrassment . . .'

149

'All right, we get the picture, Chappel. Be discreet – but dig! Grease a few palms if you have to. I want this particular trail followed.'

'Well, I'm taking Mrs Throckmorton's for a dead end.' Hopkirk took up the tale again, reddening. 'Nothing known at the address she gave us.'

'My fault.' Joe broke in swiftly to stem his super's embarrassment. 'It was I who authorized her return to what she claimed as home. I was present for the last act of her performance. And what a turn she gave us. We should perhaps be combing the cast lists at the Old Vic to find her.' He gave a rueful smile and admitted: 'I even gave her my handkerchief!'

'She'd already got through mine,' Hopkirk grumbled.

'Yes, I must say – and perhaps the superintendent will agree? – she was the perfect Mayfair gadabout. I still can't picture her in the role of cold-blooded killer who turns up to witness an execution she has organized and paid for. And who coolly proceeds to deliver the *coup de grâce* herself when she sees that her minions have bungled it.'

Bacchus sighed with annoyance. 'Never mind the character assessment. Can we stick to the facts? The gun? Was she searched?'

'No. She could have put it into her bag. She had one of those little velvet dolly bags hanging on her wrist. A Browning's not small but she could have got it in there.' Hopkirk's voice was leaden. 'But – a Browning in a dolly bag? I ask you! Let's be reasonable, shall we? This isn't a woman's crime. They don't like guns. She probably had some perfectly acceptable female reason for being in the vicinity. It might not have been one she chose to share with the Old Bill but reasonable by her lights. Adultery . . . fornication . . . the usual.' His voice was tight with distaste.

'Takes two, Hopkirk, old chap . . . very often one of each sex . . . but in Melton Square?' Joe laughed and pulled a face.

Bacchus and Fanshawe exchanged looks. After a moment, coming to a decision, Bacchus spoke for the Branch. 'You'd be wrong to dismiss a female input,' he said carefully. 'Look here, gentlemen – we know there are Irish *women* heavily involved with the Fenian movement. And they are every bit as fanatical as the men.' With a further glance of consultation with Fanshawe, he added: 'Anyone who reads *The Times* will be aware of that much.' He continued to speak slowly, weighing his words. 'These are women who are adept with gun and bomb and doubtless dolly bag. We've been fortunate enough to extract . . . to come by . . . information from the inside regarding these recruitments.'

No one considered embarrassing the Branch by asking for further elaboration.

'It's what we feared. It begins to look as though we could have got one of those harridans over here,' Captain Fanshawe commented, voicing everyone's worst suspicions. 'Fresh off the ferry? A sleeper recently activated? MI5 got anything useful?'

Joe shook his head. 'Nothing they're confiding to us, at any rate,' he said, sidestepping the question. He was remembering the disturbing report by the head of Irish Intelligence delivered to the assembled group in Devon. Two or three women with links to the IRA had unaccountably gone missing. It was feared that one of them might be bringing her destructive rage to the capital.

'I'm wondering if CID have scared her off. Did she have any idea that you had suspicions of her?' Fanshawe asked.

'How could she? We didn't!' Inspector Chappel voiced his exasperation. 'As far as she knows, she's got clean away. Damn it! All the hankies she could use and a lift out of there!'

'Followed by the sympathies of the crowd.' Bacchus voiced his derision. 'And she will therefore be feeling quite at liberty to take the next step in this escalating series of political murders.' He made an effort not to sound

151

triumphant. 'Well, we are where we are. Snakes and ladders is a mighty good training for this sort of exercise. Welcome back to square one, gents!'

'No. Welcome to the start of a fresh game,' said Joe. 'But this time we play with loaded dice. We look on this as a chance to move forward and up. Before we leave this room we'll have exact plans in place for the next throw.'

Everyone nodded. Spines straightened, not unfriendly glances were exchanged across the table. The Branch men managed an easy smile.

'And the scenario we have in mind? The list of targets we've supplied?' Bacchus's voice took on a chill drawl as he added: 'I wouldn't like to think our information was going to waste. A good deal of trouble – ours – and pain – others' – went into the acquisition of that list. MI5, to whom we handed it, gave it very careful attention. The Home Secretary has commented.'

Joe spoke firmly. 'It's not being ignored by us either. The prime minister has had a copy, of course. But I'm not convinced that it was presented to Lloyd George with the right degree of urgency by our emissary. He was allowed space to dismiss it with a merry quip and a flourish of his usual Welsh panache. Rather preoccupied with the Russian menace, I'm afraid. I shall catch him myself at breakfast first thing tomorrow morning and draw his attention with some emphasis to the three names remaining. This calls for a degree of drama. Perhaps you could supply me with a fresh copy, James? A neat one. With heavy crossings out and asterisks by the last three?'

'A little blood spatter with that, sir?' Bacchus asked. 'We can supply.'

'No need.' Joe didn't hide his amusement. 'One of those three names at least should give him pause. Might even make him choke on his toast and marmalade.'

He turned to the superintendent. 'Hopkirk, I want your squad to continue to handle the admiral's death as a civil case. Revisit the scene. Liaise with the press. Keep them on side. Make frequent mention of the Met's involvement. This may be the moment to adopt the French style of crime reporting. The Branch has to hide itself from the public eye but there's no reason why the CID shouldn't show its face. Everyone loves a hero. Next time the flash bulbs pop, present your handsome features to the camera lens instead of the palm of your hand, Hopkirk.'

Bacchus peered across the table at the superintendent, affecting an interest. 'Full face or side on, sir? In view of the idiosyncratic nose-line, I wonder if you have a preference?'

Joe chose to take the question seriously. 'Full face. And take your hat off, Hopkirk. One look at your leonine head and the country will see a battered Beowulf. And feel itself in safe hands. Didn't he promise to return to his people in their hour of need?'

'That was King Arthur, sir.'

'That was Sir Francis Drake, sir.'

Bacchus and Fanshawe offered simultaneous information.

'Never short of a hero at any rate, this country of ours,' said Joe comfortably. 'Someone always steps forward. And just think, Hopkirk, what one compelling image did for Lord Kitchener!'

'Sir!' Buoyed by Joe's tongue-in-cheek flattery, Hopkirk felt cheerful enough to offer the table his version of the famous Kitchener glare and a parody of the Kitchener gesture. 'And *I'll* remember not to give 'em the finger.'

'Oh – and better to convey the clear impression we are looking no further. Stress that we have the villains under lock and key. We have their confessions. The next man to deliver judgement on the matter will be Sir Archibald Bodkin.'

'Wearing his little black cap,' said Fanshawe with relish.

'James . . . time, I think, to narrow our focus and let the Branch loose to do what the Branch does best – anticipate, protect, save lives. And we'll start by reinstating the security squads we'd set up.'

153

'In the light of events, I don't anticipate any opposition this time round.' Bacchus grinned. His expression grew more sombre as he murmured: 'Even from Winston. Though he'll be a dashed awkward subject. Old soldier that he is, he expects to look after himself. And he can. *I* wouldn't want to try conclusions with him.'

'Are we thinking Winston is the next one on the list then?' Chappel asked.

'No. This organization, if organization it is,' Bacchus added with a concessionary glance at Hopkirk, 'would seem to be going for that moment of weakness, that chink in the armour offered by a person who finds himself – temporarily – both socially and geographically disoriented.'

They all frowned, trying to work out what he meant.

'You mean – General Lansing was just back off the boat from Ireland and making his way home down his own street, whistling "Rule Britannia", when he was accosted and shot at? Admiral Dedham, ditto, and had got as far as his own doorstep . . . I see . . .' Inspector Chappel gave voice to all their fears. 'Oh my Gawd! You know, don't you?' He glowered at Bacchus. 'Who and when. Who's going to cop it next and when it'll happen. You bloody know!'

Joe noted the foreboding that descended suddenly on the four-in-hand as the name of the target burst on them, but in an effort to change the mood and move the meeting on to the next and all-important stage he spoke lightly. 'And I want this operation . . . um . . .' He hesitated then smiled round the table. 'Let's play Boy Scouts for a moment and give it a name! Why not? I think we can allow ourselves a little frivolity, in view of the unpleasantness that would appear to be waiting to bite us in the bum. I'm reaching for a female name . . . Operation *Morrigan* – that'll do. What do you say?' He looked round the table, gathering the assenting nods and smiles. 'I want Operation Morrigan to get under way at once.'

'It's all in hand, I think you'll find, sir,' Bacchus assured him smoothly. 'Fanshawe has the details somewhere. Go and get them, will you, Rupert? We left them on the side table over by the window. *Semper paratus* as we say in the Right Royal Cock-ups. The Scouts don't have all the best sentiments. We'll be delighted to show the CID how to *prevent* a killing. We don't want to leave them with any more "murders" to clear up.' His smile faded. 'And if we get it wrong, we'll all be for the chop. We'll have on our hands the most infamous political assassination on English soil since King Rufus got it in the eye in the New Forest.'

'Lung. I think you'll find it was an arrow to the lung, Bacchus,' Hopkirk corrected. 'I've never been able to decide whether the guilty party was his friend Walter or his brother Henry. Whichever it was, they left an unsolved mystery and a body lying on the forest floor. Fascinating! I'd love to have done the scene of crime stuff on that! But none of us wants to see the next name on that ruddy list of yours lying dead on the streets of London. I'll gladly forgo the chance of solving the crime of the century to preserve the life of any one of the three fine Britons on Bacchus's list,' he concluded, with an unaccustomed show of patriotism that was rewarded with curt nods from the Branch.

Inspector Chappel leaned to Hopkirk under cover of the stir-about that occurred as the detailed planning with its accompanying maps and charts began to be laid out. 'Who the hell's Morrigan, when she's at home?' he hissed in his ear.

Hopkirk snorted and shot a glance at Sandilands. 'Deity in the Celtic pantheon, you'll find, Bert. Seat at the gods' top table. Specializing in mischief and mayhem – she's the flame-haired Irish goddess of terror,' he murmured. 'And she's in our back yard.'

Chapter Seventeen

Applying the handbrake, Albert tipped back the brim of his bowler hat like a visor and squinted a challenge at the mock baronial flourishes of New Scotland Yard. He was not overawed. Any of Cromwell's Ironsides sizing up King Charles's palace would have shown the same derision and loathing. And intent to take by storm, Lily thought, admiring.

Boldly, he'd driven Jacob's Buick in through the Derby Street entrance into the courtyard and pulled up by the grand public entrance.

The duty constable hurried forward at once, impressed and alarmed by the ostentatious motor car. 'May I help you, sir?' he asked stiffly. 'Vehicles belonging to the general public are not authorized to park here,' he added. 'I shall have to ask you to move on.' He eyed Lily, puzzled to see a woman in evening stole and lip rouge in the confines of the Yard.

'We're not general – we're very particular public,' growled Albert in his basso profundo. 'And, yes, you may help us, Sunny Jim. Go inside to reception and tell Commander Sandilands his date for the evening is waiting below.'

The constable reacted at once to the name and hurried inside. He came out a minute later. 'The commander is in his office and would be pleased to receive . . . um . . .' He consulted a notebook, raised an eyebrow and battled on: 'Miss Matty Harry, I believe he said? And requests her to kindly nip upstairs. She knows the way, he says.' He gave Lily a playful but admiring salute before going back inside.

'Cheeky blighter,' Albert commented. 'Can't even get your name right. Are you sure about this, Miss Lily? There's some rum coves work in this building,' he went on, surprising her. Albert's communications were normally restricted to 'yes' and 'no' or, at best, a grudging 'if you say so, Miss Phyl'. 'There's men in there with wide smiles and serpents' tongues. Not to be trusted, any of 'em.' He turned a look on her that might almost have been thought tender. 'I mean not any of 'em. Watch it, Miss Lily. Me, I'd line 'em up and machine-gun the whole boiling.'

'Gracious, Albert! I'm only having dinner with my boss.'

Too late, she realized this information would do nothing to allay the fears of the muscled Puritan by her side.

'Boss, miss? Dinner, miss?'

'It's not *social*, Albert . . . It's more in the nature of an interview. I think he wants to establish that I know how to hold my cutlery correctly.' She fell silent, realizing that she was failing to persuade Albert that the commander was not an evil exploiter.

'Got it. In that case, I'll hang about and wait till you come out and then I'll follow you to the Café Royal or whatever den of iniquity these interviews get done in these days,' he said. 'We wouldn't want to risk a scene and go upsetting Miss Phyllis.'

Albert lived to please Auntie Phyl and Lily understood his anxiety. 'She wouldn't expect you to go so far, Albert. Better do just as she told you and no more. Anyway, I shall be out late – past midnight, I'd say.' With a sudden rush of affection for the obdurate old thug, she turned to him and landed a kiss on his scarred cheek before he was aware the assault was coming. 'Don't fret about me, Albert. I'll remember what you told me to do if he turns nasty – eyes, knees and bumps a daisy!' She mimed vicious stabs on three sensitive parts of the male anatomy. 'And I've got my running shoes on.'

The same young constable was loitering in the vestibule. 'Allow me to conduct you upstairs, miss,' he said, oozing affability. 'It's quite a warren in here and, the commander being on the third floor and you in your finery, I thought you might like me to show you to the lift.'

He spent the awkward few moments in the lift pushing buttons and trying to stare at her under his lashes. Luckily this was an officer she had never met before so she stared confidently back at him. 'Charming weather we're having, don't you think, constable?' she said, enunciating clearly.

'Yes, indeed, madam. Very charming.'

From 'miss' to 'madam' in two sentences. Lily smiled. This was going well. As she stepped out of the lift, she slipped back her cashmere wrap and allowed it to twine negligently down one arm as Phyl had told her. ('Knock him for six, duck. You've got the shoulders for it.')

The constable led her along the corridor and tapped on the commander's door. Responding to a bellow from inside, he opened the door and announced: 'Miss Harry for you, sir.' Greatly daring, he followed added: 'I hope you have a very pleasant evening, sir.'

'Thank you, constable. I'm sure I shall.'

The exchange of male shibboleths was undetectable. The men were too professional to allow a knowing smile or a raised eyebrow to give them away.

She'd arrived exactly on time. Joe was busy with a cigar at an open window, discreetly puffing smoke out in the direction of Horse Guards. Gaze on the middle distance, tails, white tie, severely simple shirt and waistcoat, he caught himself posing and came forward to welcome his guest, then stood and stared at her in astonishment.

He realized he'd been silent for longer than was polite. 'Great heavens, Wentworth! Look at you. Anyone would think you'd just stepped out of a Fabergé Easter egg!'

'Drat! I *knew* I should have worn the gymslip!' he could have sworn she mumbled.

'No, you misunderstand! Oh, please don't droop! Shoulders back, chin up, constable! I meant it as a compliment. You look like something designed by the world's best jeweller. Sleek, precious, unique. A knockout! And that greenery-yallery colour is very ... very ...'

'Fresh and fashionable, sir?'

'Exactly! I couldn't have specified anything better if it had occurred to me to do so.' He fiddled about, extinguishing the cigar he'd just lit and frowning. 'Not in the habit of advising on female attire, unless it happens to be uniform which I'd consider within my province. Forgive me! In fact, I think you look just perfect. But how on earth could you get it so right? Did you know that ...' He gave her a searching look. 'There's no way you could possibly ...'

'Know? I know nothing yet! Are you ever going to tell me what exactly you want me to do this evening, sir? I'm really not at my best being run in blinkers.'

'Of course. Impossible to speak earlier for very good reason. Orders! But now I think I can come clean. That's why I asked you to get here early. And the first thing – you must call me Joe for the duration of the duty ... when we are in company, of course.'

'I'll try to remember that, Commander.'

The telephone on the desk rang and he made a dive for it, realizing he was glad of the diversion. 'No. I went home half an hour ago. You should do the same, Ned. Bring this to me on Monday.' It rang again the moment he replaced the receiver. 'Yes, but I'm engaged. Well, that's a nuisance but it will have to wait until next week.'

He turned back to the Lily. 'Look – as long as I'm here in my office, people will try to get hold of me.' He unhooked the receiver from its stand and put it on the desk. 'That'll do for a start. But we'll find somewhere else for your briefing. Somewhere discreet ... What about the cocktail lounge in Claridges? They have a useful little alcove or two there ... potted plants ... That suit you?'

159

Lily nodded.

'Good. Good. But before we leave – one little thing. Sit down, will you?'

Joe opened the top drawer of his desk and took out a document. Two or three sheets were paper-clipped together. He passed them across to her along with his fountain pen, uncapped and ready. Always an uncomfortable moment. You could never tell how people would react to this ceremony. 'I'd like you to sign at the bottom on the dotted line.'

She put the pen down and began to read.

He interrupted. 'Move it along, Wentworth! It's just a formality. What you have there is a copy of the Official Secrets Act. By signing, you're simply promising to reveal no state secrets . . . cross your heart and hope to die and all that. Breathe a word of what transpires tonight and I'll stick you in the Tower.' He feared his dismissive grin was not reassuring. She ignored him and read on.

'Commander, this is unnecessary,' she announced at last. 'I'm an Englishwoman. My father is a war veteran. My grandfather was wounded in South Africa, fighting in a cavalry regiment for his country. My word – which I'll readily give – should be good enough for anyone. I see no reason to sign such a document. It's pointless anyway. Don't you think I'd be hurrying to sign with an innocent smile and a contemptuous flourish if I were an anarchist . . . or a Communist . . . or a Fenian?'

The three words were delivered slowly. Joe guessed she was testing his reaction to one of these current bugbears of law and order. He recognized a game he'd played himself.

'Instead of which you're digging your heels in, fussing about details and threatening to ruin what could be a perfectly good evening. Champagne, caviar and Cecil Cardew's band complete with crooner are all on the menu. To say nothing of the company of the most eligible bachelor in London.' He allowed time for that to sink in.

'Are you sure you want to sacrifice that spectacular dress for a technicality?'

After a moment he reached over, took up the sheets and put them away in a drawer, sighing. 'Very well. We'll just have to take for granted your loyalty to the State. It makes not a scrap of difference. Step out of line, Miss Wentworth, and someone . . . someone with more clout and bigger boots than mine . . . will settle your account.'

She didn't seem to mind. 'Now that sounds entirely reasonable to me. I'll agree to that,' she said. 'And, in return, you have my word that I'll do and say nothing that could – as far as I understand it – endanger the state. But tell me more about this bachelor. Not, I'm assuming, yourself?'

'You assume correctly – if discourteously. If a list of such things were kept, I believe I'd feature at about number five hundred. And sinking weekly. The gossipmongers have rarely found me of interest and now I'm pleased to say they appear to have given up on me. The last time the hounds of the press noticed me I was billed as "back from India still a bachelor Sandilands". And we all know what that means. It's a degree worse than last season's "confirmed bachelor". It sends a clear message to mothers of marriageable daughters. "This one's survived the Colonial Fishing Fleet – he's clearly a hopeless case!" Not that many would welcome a policeman into the branches of their family tree. It's not only the criminals that the words "Scotland Yard" send rushing for cover.'

He was chattering – still uncomfortable with his briefing task. He battled on. 'No. You're to look on me as no more than your escort – your chaperon for the evening – which, if all goes according to plan, you will spend in the close company of the aforementioned bachelor. Now – let me check – can you dance? Foxtrot? Quickstep? That sort of thing? Not a detail one finds mentioned in the files.'

'Five years of Saturday mornings at the Stretton Academy of Tap Dance and Terpsichore. It didn't seem relevant information for my application form. I dance adequately but I'm no Adele Astaire.'

'Should be good enough. Now – your partner for the evening *is* an exceptionally good dancer. I've seen him performing. He'll steer you around the floor all right. And his name's David. He'll expect you to call him David when you're alone together.'

Lily's voice was chill with suspicion. 'I think I begin to see why you checked my height and weight. Should I be thankful that I chose to wear low-heeled shoes, sir?' She stuck out her right foot for his inspection.

'Ah! You've guessed.' He made a show of examining her foot. 'Not too high, not too low. Good choice. Calfskin, would they be?' This was bluff and bluster, but Joe couldn't help indulging in it to cover his unease. She waited for him to get to the point. 'Well, don't try running off in them before midnight, will you?' His tone was playfully apologetic. He even wagged a finger. 'Your partner is full of youth and vigour and keeps late hours. You're to stay locked in a tango with him for as long into the night as he wishes.'

At last he'd shown his hand.

'They're not calfskin, these shoes. They're antelope. A creature known for its fleet-footedness in escaping from predatory animals,' Lily said sweetly. And added, 'Be they princes or their pimps. Proxenetism is not, it would seem, the exclusive preserve of the lower classes.'

Joe reeled back in his chair as though he'd received a slap in the face. He drew himself together and breathed in deeply. He got to his feet and began to prowl up and down behind her. 'I can see I've gone about this the wrong way,' he muttered. 'I would never have approached a matter of such national importance under an umbrella of obscurity and subterfuge with a male colleague. It was thought – by those who know little of the modern female – that, if approached directly, you might run off squawking with indignation at what we had to propose and scupper the

162

whole thing. Under strict orders to reveal nothing until the very last moment. Had to find out what you were made of before I could entrust you with the knowledge. It's not something a woman can just walk away from. Not used to employing females, you see. That's it. Makes a difference.'

She swivelled round to look at him directly. 'No, sir. You're deceiving yourself. You're not accustomed to dealing with females of my class. Had your cousin Margery been able to tango convincingly and been chosen for this assignment you'd have been easy and forthcoming in your briefing. She'd have been consulted, her opinion sought. I also would be intrigued to hear what you have in mind for me, having gone to quite a lot of bother to prepare myself for it. But I reserve the right to refuse.' She sighed in exasperation. 'Oh, sir! You make me sound off like Goody Two Shoes. I wish you'd just pretend I'm one of your sergeants and set out the proposal in a no-nonsense military manner. It's a style I'm used to.'

This was an invitation Joe couldn't resist and it sounded very like a capitulation. The game might still be on. He broke into a grin. 'Can't say I'm accustomed to shouting the order to go over the top to a princess all kitted out in gold bells and ribbons,' he admitted. 'But here goes. You want the full picture – here it is.'

He returned to his seat and began to brief her for the night's work.

'So there you are. It's a duty, I think you'll agree, that no patriotic Englishwoman can refuse. There is no greater service you can do for your country. And there is no one better placed than yourself to render this service. Indeed, there is no one else. If you refuse to play your part, no understudy will step forward. You were carefully chosen. But what we're proposing is dangerous. Damned dangerous. The best I can say is – I'll be there. I won't take my eyes off you – I'll be watching you every minute.'

'How glad I shall be of that, sir.'

Sarcasm? He'd deserved it.

Sensing her response was feeble, she followed up by putting a sting in the tail. 'And, if nothing else, there'll be a reliable witness of the incident when my bullet-riddled body falls at the feet of the future king of England halfway through the last waltz.'

Chapter Eighteen

He let her talk on in the same vein, allowing her time to get the outrage out of her system.

'Pity you didn't outline your schemes earlier, sir – I could have got my seamstress to add a layer of body armour to the bodice perhaps. Plenty of room in there – as you noticed – for a layer or two of silk padding, after all. I can see the headlines in tomorrow's *Daily Mirror*: "Mysterious maiden of the steppes lays down her life for young prince". I must get together a few last words to deliver as I expire. Or have you already scripted them for me? I do hope Monsieur Diaghilev will be of the party tonight – he may be inspired to have it choreographed for the Ballets Russes.'

'Trench humour is what I'm hearing, Wentworth.' Joe spoke quietly. He understood. He'd have used much the same words himself in the circumstances. 'And *glad* to be hearing it. It's the fellows who make the most savage quips who come staggering back to base. And at last we're talking the same language. I've no time for false heroics.' He spread his capable hands and shook his head. 'I know it's a—' he had been about to say 'bugger', she knew, and she smiled to hear him instantly censor the word and supply 'tremendous nuisance, but Dame Duty calls and I've got tired of trying to shout the old bat down. Her clarion voice always breaks through. She called to you at Paddington. I saw you answer. I watched as you launched yourself at an armed miscreant without hesitation. Don't try to confuse me, Wentworth – you're as much in thrall to Duty as I am. And look at it this way: we're all nothing but cogs in the machinery of State – the State we support and which supports us. Imagine Duty was speaking with the voice of your Boer War grandfather – what would you be hearing?'

A delve into her family history had turned up nothing embarrassing. On the contrary – two or three generations of soldiers, all laden with medals, duty never shirked, had featured in their research.

Lily answered his challenge at once: '"It's a bugger, lass, but pick up thee musket and soldier on!" is what I'd hear from him. "Stand tall and hold the line!" he might have added. But Grandfather lived in a different world. My father no longer accepted such unthinking maxims. He did his duty – as I expect you've discovered. He went over the top when the whistle blew. But his mind and his heart were not what were moving him through the battlefield. His two driving forces were loyalty to his fellow soldiers and the threat of execution for desertion had he obeyed his instincts.'

'An instinct for desertion?' Joe said faintly, trying not to sound as disturbed as he felt.

'Yes. He was not alone. Like many of his fellows, he emerged from the war a pacifist and a – so far undeclared – socialist. An anti-monarchist, what's more, who passed on his views to his daughter.'

'Your father was a schoolmaster by trade, I understand. And he has spoken openly to you – a girl – of such matters?'

'He had no son and has always declared himself glad of that. "No more sacrifices to be offered up to the god of war" is how he puts it. Like most survivors, he's silent on his experiences but he conveys them through painting. And if a child approaches and asks questions about what she sees on the canvas, her father will answer and pass on his philosophy through the painted image. It was my father who taught me to use my head and my judgement.

To question automatic acceptances of patriotism. And loyalty to the crown.'

'You're telling me now that you have no allegiance to the royal family?' Joe was seriously alarmed. He shot to his feet in his agitation and thrust an arm towards her. 'Do you see this right arm, Wentworth? It served King and Country for four years and was jolly nearly shot off at Mons. If revolutionaries were rampaging through the palace I'd slide it through the door latch and they'd have to break my bones before the mob would gain entry to their majesties!' Feeling suddenly foolish, he lowered his arm and sank into his seat again.

The girl was not overawed but at least she didn't giggle, he thought. 'I can admire the depth of your feeling, though I consider it badly targeted,' she said. 'I wonder whether your loyalty is inspired by the office itself or by the people who currently hold and enjoy it?' A question he'd never asked himself. Into his wary silence she plunged on: 'This family has shallow roots in our native soil, being more German than British. They are ordinary mortals who've been fed the notion from an early age that they have a divine right to rule and exploit. They don't. I think the notion of kingship in any modern state is outdated and retrograde. It's the anointed Napoleons, the kings, the Kaisers and the tsars who lead their people to destruction. In their millions. Six, at least, European monarchs have been killed by their own subjects this century – so far – and more dethroned. It seems I'm not alone in wishing for a continent free of autocratic rulers.'

'Great heavens, girl! Hold the speech until I have a soap box fetched, will you? And possibly a set of manacles!' Joe was trying to keep it light but he was aghast. She sat there, looking as innocent as a sugar mouse and uttering views hot enough and red enough to warrant putting her on a charge of subversion. 'I've heard much the same nonsense voiced at Speaker's Corner. Who've you been talking to? Who's stuffed your head with such dangerous ideas? Are you admitting to Bolshevist sympathies? "Off with their heads!" – would that be your war cry?'

'Certainly not. I was as horrified as anyone by the slaughter of the Russian imperial family.'

'Though you do not regret the passing of the institution, evidently. I see. Well, I can only conclude that you must, on your own judgement, ground your musket, pick up your kit bag and take your leave,' he said with finality. He pushed back his chair and got to his feet, the conversation over. 'You have every right. And you have those rights because others in their thousands, your father and grand-father among them, doubtless right back to Agincourt were willing to sacrifice their lives to preserve them.'

'Ouch!' Lily said. 'Steady on, sir! I'm not armoured against such sentiments. The taking of life – whoever is in possession of it – is an abhorrence to me. And if you're saying my presence tonight might help to preserve a life – royal though it be – I shall do my bit. I'd do the same for any poor soul threatened by the murderous forces of anarchy or terrorism that are plaguing us. The Prince of Wales or the conductor on the Clapham omnibus – their lives carry the same weight with me. I just wanted you to be clear about that. Look – wasn't there talk of a drink at Claridges? I think I shall be earning at least a stimulating glass of champagne before the evening gets under way.'

He wondered if he accepted her volte-face too quickly. 'Excellent notion! Let's stop fencing and turn our swords in the same direction, shall we?' He offered his arm and she rose to her feet and placed a hand on it gracefully. 'Only the best, I think, should be offered in the circum-stances. Will a pre-war Bollinger suit?'

'I think I might like that. But wait a moment, sir. I've just thought of something ... someone, rather. If, as you say you fear, it's a case of "hunt the woman", there's a man I know who might be of assistance.' She took a small leather wallet from her bag and selected a calling card from it. 'Can you ring the number you see on there and ask for this person? With a bit of luck he'll be still at his desk. Unless he's headed for Claridges already. And, believe me, with the particular task we have on our hands tonight, he'll be more use to us than a squadron of secret servicemen. He owes me a favour sir. Rather a large one. Just mention my name. He'll come.'

Joe held the card between finger and thumb with mock distaste. 'Oh, him! He'd be there like a shot if invited. But what on earth do you imagine this scoundrel could add to the party? A man of his profession? Jackals! The whole lot of them are banned from the hotel. I remember giving the order myself.'

'He has a very particular skill, sir. The man's a walking Debrett. Duchesses invite him to their shindigs to enjoy his latest gossip. He knows everyone in society. If there's someone at the dance tonight who ought not to be there . . . an infiltrator . . . a *female* infiltrator, as you say your information specifies . . . I can think of no one more likely to spot her. He knows all the usual royal dancing partners. He can list every girl whose waist the prince has ever squeezed in public since he left naval college.'

Joe followed her reasoning and saw the advantages at once. His eyes gleamed as he reached for the telephone. 'Operator, get me an outside line, would you? It's a Fleet Street number.' He read it out and then handed the equipment to Lily. 'Who's he working for now, your chap? The *Daily Dirt*? The *Fortnightly Filth*?'

'Hello. Is Cyril there? Good. Fetch him to the phone, will you? Tell him his woman policeman wants him and it's urgent.'

Joe eyed her with amused speculation while they waited. 'Been moonlighting, have we, Wentworth? Offering special police services to the gentlemen of the press? Sort of thing I'm supposed to be clamping down on.'

'Don't ask, sir. Reputations would suffer. Ah, there you are! Lily here. Lily Wentworth. Yes – too long! Now listen. I'm in a position to do you another favour. How'd you like to be given an exclusive invitation to attend, as a reporter, the Russian knees-up at Claridges tonight?' Lily winced and held the earpiece an inch away until the surge of exclamations and questions receded.

Impatiently, Joe snatched the phone back. 'Calm down, man! Cyril Tate? Is that who I've got? This is Miss Wentworth's commanding officer and I'm the one who issues the invitations. Sandilands ... I believe we've met ... Yes, that Sandilands ... Feeling's mutual ... Your name's been mentioned. I have a proposal to put to you. Got the tools of your trade to hand, have you? Can you climb into an evening suit at a moment's notice?' In an aside to Lily: 'He's already dressed.

'That's convenient. Look, meet me and Miss Wentworth in the snug bar of the Red Lion. Yes, just by the Yard in Scotland Alley. Don't make a fuss! In fifteen minutes.'

He put the phone down.

'You can forget the champagne tête à tête in the Palm Court!' He grinned. 'If we're to be a threesome with that toad it'll be a swift half of shandy-gaff in the Red Lion.'

The newsman eased his way through the crowds to their table in the far corner of the pub, relieving ten minutes of stilted conversation punctuated by sips of warm beer. Sandilands had carried back a half-pint of ginger beer shandy for Lily and two pint tankards of pale ale. He'd downed half of one and left the other foaming gently on the far side of their table. Suddenly, the animated and clever face Joe remembered was there behind the glass and lifting it.

'Cheers!' Tate saluted Joe, drank thirstily and then turned his attention to Lily, staring and blinking. 'Lily, my love! That *is* my lovely Lily? I ride to your rescue! Though how you could possibly expect me to abandon the delights of the Mayor of Clerkenwell's war memorial dedication supper at the drop of a hat for your, er, entertainment I have no idea. How on earth do you come to be all dolled up and in the clutches of this villain?'

Time to deliver a set-down. Joe spoke frostily. 'Not sure whom you think you are addressing. This young lady is one of my many Scottish cousins on my mother's side. Miss Lily Wentworth. What's more, I think she can be the Honourable Lily Wentworth,' he embroidered. 'Second daughter of Viscount Wentworth of Moidart. If anyone asks, that's the information you can pass on. You can add, confidingly, that she's a friend and neighbour of Lady Elizabeth Bowes-Lyon who seems to be all the go at the moment. That's pedigree enough. No one can ever work out the Scottish peerage – some aren't even aware that there is one – and a mixture of Scots and English geography will surely send the hounds the wrong way. I'll give a reward to any keen cove who can find Moidart on the map!'

He noted that Tate followed every step of his intervention, nodding his understanding and, it seemed, approval.

'How very fashionable!' Cyril said. 'Another Scottish girl spreading her wings south of the border? I see your compatriot Lady Elizabeth – ninth offspring of the Earl of Strathmore – is cutting a swathe through the English aristocracy. Three times a bridesmaid this season – the *on dit* is that it can't be long before she's a bride ... a right royal bride, some go so far as to speculate.'

'Save that claptrap for your rags, Tate,' Joe warned. And then, swinging into his role, 'Now, my dear Lily, you may tell this fellow what he needs to know.'

'Very well, Joe,' she responded, according to his instructions. 'Cyril, it's your lucky day. You'll be the only one of your profession there. An exclusive presence. Now, the guest of honour, as I'm sure you will know—'

'I certainly do. We were all wondering if he'd turn up. In the present agitated political climate the odds were against it. Running a bit of a risk, isn't he?'

171

'. . . is thought to be about to come in for a little unwelcome attention this evening. And the signs are – can't tell you more but the authorities seem pretty certain – that the attention will be coming from a woman. A rather pushy female who's determined to get attention for her cause—'

'Cause?' Cyril leapt on the word. 'Ah! No – sorry. Can't get involved with causes. I generally try to avoid political entanglements. Bad for business.'

'Many things are bad for business, Cyril,' Lily told him quietly.

Joe caught her sideways glance, a glance which said, 'I'm silent for the moment but you wouldn't want me to speak out in the commander's company, would you?' She had some hold over the newsman, that much was clear. Joe was intrigued and quietly satisfied to know that someone at least had this hound on a lead.

The hound came to heel at once. Cyril shrugged, grinned and spread his hands in a gesture of compliance. 'As you say. Just tell me *which* cause, will you – a hint will do. Very well – I'll take a shot at it . . . Some enterprising lady from the Emerald Isle? Is that who we're talking about?'

Wentworth nodded. 'Joe's friends – from whom our information comes – will be thick on the ground in support as you might imagine, but it was thought that the close and constant presence of a protective female officer – yours truly – might put the opposition off their stroke.'

'And she might get blown up, shot or stabbed in the process. I don't much like what I'm hearing, Lily.' Tate's debonair grin had vanished and his words were clipped and businesslike. 'Terrorism on the streets of London – that's what we're looking at, isn't it?' He turned a belligerent eye on Joe. 'That's the province of Special Branch. Are you telling me that the Branch are recruiting females now? I find that hard to believe. This is men's work, Sandilands. You should be ashamed to be putting up a woman in the front line. My God, man! You should be risking all – risking anyone – to keep *Lily* safe!' He threw some coins on to the table. 'I don't care to drink with you. I'll be off now and I'm taking Lily with me. Get your hat, love – we're off! Let him try stopping the bullets himself.'

It took all of Joe's strength to check his urge to rise to his feet and seize the fellow by his collar. It was a cool restraining hand on his gathering right fist and a diverting tinkle of laughter from Lily that saved him from making a disastrous move. Five minutes of persuasive chatter was necessary to bring Tate down to earth but she managed. Clever girl, though – Joe was sure she'd detected and not been taken in by the thread of pleasurable vindication in the newsman's voice. He'd caught Sandilands in a less than honourable posture and was making the most of it.

Wentworth was playing down the danger and stressing the more frivolous aspects of her role: the checking of the ladies' powder rooms, the possible need to identify a suspicious bulge under a fold of taffeta – searching females was part of her job, after all. She would keep an ear out for the sound of an Irish accent. And that's where they needed his skills, she added, drawing the net closer around him. He knew all the runners and riders – an interloper would stand out to his eye as to no one else's.

It seemed to work. Tate finally mumbled that they could probably count on his cooperation. 'Tell me more about this comic opera you've got planned and what, precisely, you have it in mind for me to do?'

'You know everyone who's anyone. Home-bred or foreign.' Joe took over. 'The gathering will be very mixed for nationality – most of the European ambassadors will be there in support – but all the guests will have one thing in common: wealth. It's a fundraising do for impecunious émigré Russians. Though none of *them* will be on parade tonight.'

'They'll all be in the kitchens baking the blinis and boiling up the borscht,' said Cyril.

'Kitchens,' Joe muttered. 'Nightmare! Full of instruments, sharp and blunt, and poisons of one sort or another.

The waiting and catering staff have all been thoroughly checked. Four of my department are at this moment ladling out the caviar and pouring the champagne.'

'You only have an invitation to attend if you're rich and influential – or, in your case, Cyril, happen to be a dab hand with a camera. If you catch sight of a stranger or someone who appears to be out of his or her element, someone who doesn't appear in Debrett or the *Almanach de Gotha* – we want you to signal it. If you spot someone who may have Irish roots in the middle of the cosmopolitan mêlée, tell us. That's all. We'd be ... *I'd* be much relieved if you'd agree to do it, Cyril,' Lily concluded.

He'd be a hard man who could resist the unemphatic plea in her soft voice, the shining trust in the straight gaze, Joe thought. 'Behave as you usually do,' he said shortly. 'Any pictures and copy must be passed before me before printing. Are you on?'

Cyril eyed him, unimpressed by his curtness. 'You know, Sandilands old son, you could learn a thing or two about seduction from your little cousin.' He turned to Lily. 'I'll do my best, love. And I promise you absolute discretion. Now – what time's the kick-off and how do we get there?'

Joe had laid on a staff car and chauffeur for the short journey to Park Lane and as they made their way through the West End crowds he unbent sufficiently to repeat his briefing for Tate's benefit.

'The prince has been advised to arrive half an hour after we get there, which is to say at eight o'clock sharp. That'll give us time to get our eye in. He'll be surrounded by a phalanx of gorgeous young equerries, all falling over themselves to take a bullet, naturally. But they have this disadvantage – they can't dance with him. And that's, we believe, where the danger lies. On the dance floor. When he's greeted the hostess she'll bring him over to our table and he'll be introduced to Lily. Their eyes will meet, they'll take to the floor and they'll dance till dawn or however long it takes. Her presence alone – that of a presumed new amour – will be sufficient to keep other females at bay. Anyone attempting to muscle in on the royal attention in such circumstances will immediately announce herself as suspect and will be weeded out. The prince is well aware, of course, of what we expect and will play up to it.'

'Doesn't mean he'll do as you tell him,' commented Tate. 'He's got a streak of cussedness about him. Some call it a sense of fun. It drove his security men mad when he was touring India, they say. Always dashing off into the thick of the crowd at a whim in places where every native has a dagger up his jumper. There were death threats coming in every day but you'd never have known it from his behaviour. Always on show – fair hair shining like a beacon, an easy target for anyone with a Lee-Enfield. Anyone could have cracked his skull on the polo field, pushed him off a rampart, seasoned his curry with something special. The only injury he suffered was a sprained right wrist from all the hand-shaking!'

'We're not expecting it to be easy,' said Joe repressively.

'Still, your assassin – if she exists – ought to stand out a mile. Forgive me for questioning your information, but it sounds a bit barmy to me. I can see your reasoning – Popplewell, Goring, Lansing, Dedham . . . who's next, you must have asked? Probably not Churchill – he's careful and always well armoured against attack.'

Joe acknowledged the accuracy of his calculation with a grin. 'He's the one who guards the guards.'

'Then you had to assume it would be the POW. Our flamboyant, sociable, risk-taking prince. Oh, yes. Prime target. And an easy one. What a coup his death would be! Everybody loves him to bits. It would kick the English right where it hurts. But a woman involved? I'm wondering how reliable your information is . . .' He faltered under Joe's sudden hard stare. 'Just a passing thought . . . And Irish, you say? No. Any flame-haired beauty approaching the prince with a gleam in her eye and a Beretta in her pocket will fall under suspicion and the weight of a pack of hearty Branch men before she gets within range of him. And had it occurred to anyone that, though the Irish and the Russians between them occupy a lot of space in London town, it's not the *same* space? Class, wealth, culture, political ambitions – they have no meeting point. They don't *know* each other. You're barmy! There's going to be no Kathleen O'Shea at *this* party!'

'Another man with a misconception about the Irish. Who said anything about flame-coloured hair?' said Sandilands. 'She's dark. And she doesn't have an Irish accent. It's pure Mayfair.'

In the crossfire of two astonished stares, he smiled sheepishly and added: 'I've seen her eyebrows. And heard her speak.'

He stopped the car short of the hotel and handed Tate a note and signature scrawled on an invitation card. 'Show this at the door and they'll let you in. A moment!' he added, catching Cyril by the shoulder as he prepared to get out. 'Any last-minute advice for Miss Wentworth? You've been trailing our subject for years and must have observed him closely. How should she play her hand? She'll be with him for the whole evening. It might not be easy for her.'

Cyril cut him short with a freezing glance and turned his gaze to Lily. 'He'll be delighted, love. Any man would. Any red- or blue-blooded man, would. I'd say be confident, be direct and keep it light. He's very informal with women. Likes to chatter and laugh, bursts into song on occasions – he knows all the latest tunes.' Cyril turned back to Sandilands, struck by a sudden thought. 'In fact Lily and the prince are two for a pair, you'll find. I don't suppose you had any idea when you set this up, Sandilands. He loves a story, whether he's telling it or listening. He's a good listener. The time will fly in his company, Lily. Oh – I'll pass on something I've noticed . . . something that

176

doesn't seem to have been noted by those of less impure imagination than my own.'

Joe gave a warning gesture but Cyril grinned disarmingly and pressed on. 'He seems to quite enjoy being bossed about. Now, any *bloke* trying that on will receive a right royal set-down and a flash of temper – he's got one! – but he rather plays up to a pretty girl wagging a stern finger at him. Nursemaid with a cockney accent – now that might be the perfect combination to set the royal pulses racing.'

Lily sighed. 'Another one of those? Thanks, Cyril. It's not my style, but if all else fails I'm sure I can play Nanny Whacker.'

Joe grunted in disapproval at the *lèse majesté* he was hearing from this pair and thrust Cyril's camera bag at him. 'Watch out for the Georgian gorillas on the door. They'll probably search you. They've got knuckles like billiard balls,' he added.

Lily waited until the chauffeur had closed the door before she spoke. 'She's dark, sir?'

Joe looked uncomfortable. 'I thought you'd guessed that she pulled the wool over Hopkirk's eyes. Mine too. She had black eyebrows. The taxi girl.'

'Harriet Hampshire?'

'Or not. False name. False address when Hopkirk checked. Embarrassing! She was wearing one of those feathered cloche hats. I didn't get a look at her hair. Very beautiful. A profile like Cleopatra. I think I'd know her again. And, as I rather pathetically noticed, rather emphatic black eyebrows.'

'Sir, have you ever come across mascara?' Lily asked tentatively. 'And hair dye? I've got fair hair and brown eyebrows but leave me for an hour with a bottle of Inecto and I could be a brunette.'

The commander sighed.

They watched the wiry figure of Cyril making its way with a swagger towards the grand entrance and Joe shook his head. 'Are we mad, Wentworth? Entrusting state secrets to the country's greatest blabbermouth? I may have to arrest us for incompetence. We'd better keep our resignations polished and ready to go, I'm thinking.'

'He's clever and wordly. I'll never fully understand him but I like him. Very much. But best of all, Cyril knows how to be discreet. He's been practising discretion his whole life. I trust him.'

Joe analysed his stab of sour feeling as jealousy and rebuked himself. The implication behind her words was, of course, that she didn't trust him. He ought to be pleased with his constable's good judgement.

On an impulse, he reached into her lap, took hold of her right hand and tweaked the middle finger over the first. 'Keep 'em crossed, Wentworth! Time to put your gloves on. Here we go!'

A dazzle of light, a surge of excited laughter, a babble of languages, and a rush of exotic perfume greeted them as they hesitated in the doorway, waiting in the queue to meet their hostess. The Princess Ratziatinsky, a small but impressive figure, was striking in a draped gown of black charmeuse silk with a tall aigrette fixed in place by a headband of gold tissue. She was receiving, a Russian prince at either shoulder.

They listened as she switched from the French she'd been using for the Ambassador and the Comtesse de Saint-Aubain to German for one of the Kaiser's cousins. Catching sight of them, the grande dame deftly ushered the couples who preceded them straight through into the ballroom. She greeted Joe with a kiss on each cheek and a murmured message in English: 'He's here. Early' into the right ear and 'Half an hour ago' into the left.

Alarming news, but Sandilands recovered to say swiftly: 'Then we'll go straight in. Your Highness, may I present

Miss Lily Wentworth ... the Honourable Lily Wentworth, a cousin from Scotland who's visiting the capital.'

'Your Highness. So good of you to ask me, ma'am,' Lily said, dropping a curtsy.

Oh, Lord! He'd forgotten to mention the curtsy. She must have been observing the ladies ahead of her in the queue, he guessed, since the movement was entirely gracious and correct.

'I hear you're an expert dancer, Miss Wentworth. Come. I'll present you to a worthy partner.'

She sailed away before them, headdress bobbing to left and right as she led the way between the dozens of small tables fringing the dance floor. Several couples were already moving enthusiastically in time to a foxtrot. The band was installed at the far end of the room. Rank on rank of green and gold jacketed musicians rose up on an ascending flight of wide stages. And in front of this smart company stood Cecil Cardew, undulating gently. He was famous for the smoothness and quality of his musicians and the strictness of his rhythm. Nothing but the best on offer this evening.

They were accosted just short of the dance floor by a handsome but unsmiling young man who seized Lily's hand and kissed it lingeringly. The ominous words he was murmuring were aimed not at her but sideways at Sandilands.

'There's a problem, sir. It's HRH. He's disappeared. Ten minutes ago. Here one minute, gone the next. Cloakrooms and kitchens negative and secure. Doors and exteriors ditto. Kidnapped? Got bored and buggered off? It's been known. Dunno. I think he's still here somewhere.'

Sandilands' flash of alarm was swiftly controlled. 'Entertain Miss Wentworth, will you, Rupert?'

He strode off, spoke briefly to the princess and then began to quarter the room.

Chapter Nineteen

'Rupert Fanshawe. Would you like to dance, Miss . . . er . . . ?' the officer asked, eyes everywhere but on Lily.

Special Branch, Lily guessed. Bodyguarding royal personages was, after all, their forte. And, as far as anyone knew, their record was one hundred per cent success. They'd escorted British kings and queens throughout Europe and back again in total safety at a time when other monarchs had been falling like ninepins to bomb and bullet. They'd even saved the lives of foreign royalty venturing on to British soil, if the rumours were correct. They'd guarded the Romanov family on their state visit to Britain and all had returned to St Petersburg unscathed. Branch officers had Lily's respect. 'Not sure I'd enjoy it very much, Rupert . . . Cecil seems to have lost the beat, don't you think?'

She glanced in puzzlement at the conductor. Slim and elegant in his evening dress, pink scalp shining through the slicked-back hair, he stood, maintaining his customary half-turn to the dance floor. But his well-known smile was frozen on his face, his eyes fixed uneasily on the middle distance. He waggled his baton with less than his usual enthusiasm. 'Nervous? Look – he can hardly keep the beat going. He seems to have sensed something's wrong. Perhaps he saw something untoward. Up there on the stand, he's more likely than most to have spotted trouble. Have you spoken to him?'

Rupert shook his head angrily, his anxiety increasing.

'Then I think you should try ... No, hang on ...' Lily winced and looked again at the band. She frowned and stared. She grabbed the Branch man's arm and held him back. 'Rupert – all's well. You can stand down. It's the head to the left ... it's a dead give-away. Will you excuse me for a moment?'

She set off for the bandstand.

'Gotcher!' Lily spoke in a parody of a police voice straight into the ear of the Prince of Wales. 'Caught red handed. Clear case of impersonation. Are you going to come quietly?'

He stopped his drumming abruptly, wrong footing several couples on the dance floor. They trailed to a puzzled halt and turned to stare at Cecil, wondering whether the dance was over.

'Oh, I say – it's a fair cop! A moment, please. I'll surrender when I've done the flourish.' He caught the panicking eye of the band leader, nodded and went into a swirling flurry of beats that announced that the dance was indeed over. Moving back into the sides, he peeled off the band uniform coat he was wearing and exchanged it for his evening tails, taking them from the wide-eyed and embarrassed drummer who'd been put to wait in the wings. 'Thank you so much, Tommy,' said the prince. 'I really enjoyed that. Quite got the evening going!'

Edward, pink faced with exertion, turned to Lily and held out a hand. 'I say – you must be my dancing policeman.' He peered closely at her. 'Can I possibly have that right?'

Lily shook his hand, unable to think of any other response. 'Lily Wentworth, sir.'

'You may call me sir if you prefer, Lily, but my close friends call me by my last name which is David,' he said lightly. 'And I think, for this evening, you're meant to be a friend and staying close. How did you spot me?' He laughed. 'I've been watching the heavy brigade tooling about the room searching for me. They never once looked up at the bandstand! And then Sandilands came in and started charging about the place like a bull let loose in Harrods. No attention from him either. You saw me straight away. How come?'

'I have an ear for rhythm – you were half a beat out. And you were the only one of a well-drilled line-up that had his head permanently set like this – to the left. I've noticed it in photographs.' Lily demonstrated, putting her head on one side and staring soulfully into the middle distance. 'When you know what to look for in a group photograph it stands out a mile.'

The prince was entertained by her impersonation. 'I see it! Me and Alexander the Great!' he chortled. 'I always knew we must have something in common. Now that Cecil's recovered his beat ... what's that he's giving us now? Ah – a slow waltz to allow his heart rate a chance to recover ... shall we take the floor?'

The moment they swirled off into the waltz, the whole room seemed to exhale a breath of relief and the floor was invaded by every couple in the room intent on being seen dancing in the company of the heir to the throne. After a few moments, he confided: 'So glad they've sent me a policeman who can really dance – I feared the worst. I've seen your mob on parade. Better equipped for tossing the caber than tripping the light fantastic!'

'Some of us can do both, sir.' Lily smiled and leaned into a reverse turn, relishing Sandilands' astonished face as they swooped by. A discreet and distant flash told her that Cyril was recording the moment.

HRH, as Sandilands called him, had the reputation of being a charming man. Lily had always thought that if she ever met a so-called charming man she'd be sick on his dancing shoes. But after two or three circuits of the floor, she reluctantly had to admit that she was charmed, if by that she meant amused, intrigued and flattered. He had much to say and spoke with feeling and humour. And there was some other quality – a deprecating self-awareness that drew one in. He seemed to have an unending stream of stories, some told against himself, that kept Lily laughing. His relaxed view of events, however, began to alarm her. So unflurried was her partner, he surely could not have been made fully aware of the seriousness of the threat against him.

She raised the matter as tactfully as she could, to be answered by a cheerful: 'Oh, yes. Know what you mean. *En garde* again. What a bore! I wonder what the going rate for me is in England? In India – did you know I'd just got back from India? – it was a thousand pounds a pop. Some over-rich politico – whom I may not name – was brazenly offering a thousand-pound reward to anyone who would lob a bomb at me. Everyone knew who he was. And I had to sit opposite the fiend at a couple of dinner parties. Can you imagine?'

Lily agreed that conversation must have been a little stilted and dared to ask whether he'd been aware of any attempts actually being mounted.

'I'll say! Hard to ignore those quantities of explosive! Not always stable in a hot climate, you know. One or two of the bombers blew themselves up by accident and the security forces raked in the rest. Stout fellows, the Indian police force! Ah! Here comes a quickstep. That's more like it. I say – may I have the honour?'

They'd warned her that he was indefatigable. Lily was glad of the hours she'd put in pounding the pavements of London – any girl less fit would have crumbled after a few dances with the energetic sprite she was teamed with. She was relieved to sit out the slower dances at a table at the edge of the dance floor, a spot carefully chosen, she guessed, to be in full view of the room. There they were joined by an equally carefully chosen succession of the prince's old friends and a scattering of quiet-eyed, handsome young men of military cut. Lily heard a few names: Fruity This, Basher That, Pogo Someone Else, and failed to commit them to memory. She even, for the sake of appearances, took to the floor for a veleta with Pogo Someone Else, leaving her charge between two young Branch heavies for the duration.

The women who danced by their table all tried to catch the prince's eye. Most seemed to be dark though there was a smattering of fair Anglo-Saxon beauties and even one or two redheads. Not one looked remotely threatening. No one tried to get too close to the prince. This was proving to be a wild-goose chase. The ring of security set up around them was surely impenetrable. With pity and a sinking heart Lily wondered whether this was to be the prince's future: a gold-plated, steel-barred cage.

She looked with dawning admiration at the lively man, determined to enjoy his evening come what may. He was preparing to join in the serious business of the evening. Before they went through to supper, the all-important money had to be raised from the well-heeled gathering. And Edward was fully aware, she was sure, of his role in this. On top of the already expensive ticket price, a series of auctions was to raise yet more cash. Everything from a glorious Fabergé ornament to a piece of bloodstained linen allegedly taken from the corpse of a long-dead Russian saint was on offer to the highest bidder. And what a coup – to be able to brag afterwards that one had just pipped the Prince of Wales to the post, outbidding him at the last moment.

Edward pitched his bids neatly, knowing exactly when to whip up interest and when to graciously withdraw. She noticed that he persisted sufficiently to acquire a jewel-encrusted Easter egg and a jade necklace. 'For my mama,' he confided.

The final two items caused a sensation. Neither of the lots had a real monetary value yet they raised approving smiles and nods.

The penultimate offering was – surprisingly – a painting. Two young girls in traditional Russian dress had been delegated to carry it around the tables for closer inspection. They paused for a longer interval by the Prince of Wales and his group and the hostess timed her explanation for this moment.

'The painter, though of supreme talent, is largely unknown in the west. You may view other examples of his work, smuggled out of the motherland, in the Abercrombie gallery. This one is the most accomplished of the collection and is the only one for private sale. As you know, all photographic equipment has been banned from Russia.' She paused to acknowledge the chorus of gasps and wails that ran through the audience. 'The only means of recording the depredation that is occurring in our homeland is the medium of paint. It is at risk of his life that the artist has committed to canvas his view of the dismantling of a once-great land. These works have been brought to us safely here in London by the courage of many. It is impossible to put a price on this piece – the painter is without pedigree but his vision – dark and painful to our eyes – is, I believe, supremely original.'

Rupert, whose half-hourly duty rosta had brought him to Lily's side, leaned to her and drawled: 'Lord! You'll never see that on a chocolate box! Touch of cubism, do I detect? How simply ghastly!'

Lady Katharine Rumbelow, whom he was plying with champagne, overheard, approved and added: 'I'm bidding a month's allowance *not* to have it! What on earth can it be? A gloomy fir forest and a Celtic cross? Is that Russia or Ross-shire? Could be either. Impenetrable forest in the background with – what's that? – a volcano? And what's that meant to be in the foreground . . . ? Oh, gracious! I do believe it's an open grave! And that cross is . . . can I be mistaken? . . . it's made of bones!' Lady Katharine shuddered delicately and the two Russian girls, still smiling sweetly, sensed the time had come to move on to the next table.

The prince turned to Lily. 'Well, I thought it very striking. What d'you say, Lily?'

'I'd say you were right, sir. Gloomy indeed but a brilliant vision, executed with skill and passion.' She heard her father's voice as she said the words. And she'd recognized the scrawled signature in the corner. She dared to add: 'The world will hear more of this young man. A product of the St Petersburg school? Whoever acquires it will not regret his investment.'

The prince grinned and opened the bidding. A few others followed, more out of duty than interest perhaps, though the French ambassador, Lily noted, seemed genuinely keen. As the prince doggedly sent the price higher his competitors faded and retired one by one until Lily was hearing: 'And the lot goes to His Royal Highness, the Prince of Wales. Congratulations, sir!'

Judging the moment, he rose to his feet and nodded affably to left and right.

And the evening moved on towards its climax. The princess herself announced that the last offering before supper would be a song. To the highest bidder was promised the song of his choice to be performed by the finest Russian soprano. Madame Vera Lavrova, who was at present appearing at the Alhambra, Leicester Square, had been released by her producer, Monsieur Diaghilev, for the evening to grace their gathering. Cecil Cardew's drummer gave a roll on his drums and the singer herself emerged from a clump of potted palms to greet the audience, bow and curtsy and stand by, waiting for the winning song to be announced.

The prince leaned close and whispered to Lily, 'Poor dear! She's a baroness, you know, in her real life. Her husband was a cavalry officer in the White Army. Killed in action.'

Small and slender, Madame Lavrova was wearing an outfit that brought a tear to many a sentimental eye in the audience. A slim gown of richly embroidered gold satin reached down to a neat ankle, and a Russian headdress of the same stuff framed a round and girlish face, a face vivid with dark eyes and red lips, open and smiling with anticipation.

The bidding stopped, miraculously, it seemed to Lily, when one of the Russian princes got to his feet and raised it from three hundred pounds to a thousand pounds in one swoop. Beyond that no one would venture. Murmurs of approval ran around the room.

'Then the song goes to His Royal Highness,' the hostess announced. 'And may we all hear your choice of song, Mikhail?'

Lily became conscious that she was witnessing a rehearsed scene and was mortified that she hadn't realized it earlier. These people were elegant professionals, not ones to be caught out by an odd request unknown to singer or orchestra. And yet all were joining in the spirit of the performance, waiting with bated breath and sighing with satisfaction as the Russian prince announced: 'There's a sweet song of these islands where we now shelter. A song of exile. A song sung by men, like us, who wear the white cockade – the Jacobites, in mourning and far from their native land. The sentiment echoes our own: "When shall we see thee again, our homeland?" I wonder if Madame Lavrova has it in her repertoire?'

The exquisite Russian doll inclined her head graciously and confided that yes, indeed, she did know it. It was one of her favourite songs. Cecil Cardew with a twirl of his baton unleashed the string section of his orchestra and they swung into the introduction to a well-rehearsed rendition of the heart-breaking Scottish lament. A delicate compliment to the host country and obviously a favourite with the Russian contingent, who joined in soulfully with the last chorus.

'Gracious!' the prince confided, leaning close. 'The Scots and the Russians caught in mutual lament? Really wrings the withers! Well, I don't know about our hosts but that dirge has quite given me an appetite. Shall we prepare to lead the throng into the dining room? I think it's expected. This, I'm told, may well be the tricky bit. Have your wits about you, Lily! It's to be a sort of indoor picnic, if you can believe! Balancing plates and glasses and chatting to left and right. Always taxing! But it does, they say, enable people to circulate more freely. One is not pinned down with the same neighbours for hours on end. I can see their point. Oh, and someone may be planning, in the help-yourself skirmish they've got planned, to bean me with a ladle or fillet me with an oyster-knife.'

He helped her to her feet with a hand that gave the briefest quiver before being brought under control. His shoulders squared, his chin went up and he surveyed the throng with a merry blue eye. Lily remembered that his formative years had been spent in the tough, no-quarter-given-or-expected world of a Navy training ship. Bombs and bullets seemed not to impress him but the thought of an encounter with a knife at close quarters made him grit his teeth.

'Now, let's stay alert, Lily!'

Chapter Twenty

Charles Honeysett reckoned he had the most demanding job in the world. Steward-in-chief, as he styled himself, was one rung in the hierarchy below the manager (a gentleman whose position Charles had in his sights). He was standing, gold pocket watch in left hand, notes, which he was never observed to consult, in right, an ear ostentatiously cocked towards the double doors that communicated with the Grand Salon.

He listened to the God-awful piece of Scottish misery thrashing itself to a climax – he was glad he'd held out against the bagpipes – and with a flick of a finger dissuaded a flunkey from fiddling nervously with the door handle. The voice of his old sergeant rang in his head: 'Wait for it! Wait for it, laddie!'

Timing. It was everything. He'd learned that much from the army. When to make an appearance and when to disappear. The day after his demob, he'd presented himself at the hotel where he'd worked before the war. And, with his luck, the incumbent steward had been on the point of retiring. It hadn't taken much of an effort to gain the old boy's support with the management. The usual persuasive mix of flattery and discreet financial arrangement. And the job had fallen into his lap.

And now the luck was theirs. With his early background of service in one of the grandest houses in the east of England and four war years' experience at a rarefied level in the catering corps based in Paris, Honeysett offered them the best management in London. The bookings flooded in. London had taken off on an unstoppable wave of jubilation. Party followed party. The lights stayed on all night. 'Brighten up London!' the government had commanded and people leapt to obey. The vineyards of Champagne risked being drunk dry. And there must surely be a limit to the amount of roe you could squeeze from a sturgeon?

Honeysett eyed the gleaming silver tureens filled with caviar. All colours. From the ends of the earth. And obtained at vast expense. It had cost a hundred quid just to fill a small bowl with that special red stuff the princess had demanded. His lip curled at his memory of tasting it when it arrived on the refrigerated truck the day before. He wouldn't offer it to his dog. Honeysett tasted everything in his quest for perfection. But he'd had to call in a second opinion on this one. Young Anna had been working for him for over a month now and had settled well. She claimed to be Russian and claimed to know her caviar when he asked. About 25 per cent of his staff were Russian. And they had a fast turnover. But this girl was different from the usual run of untrained chancers. Her references had been unimpeachable. And she knew her table placements seemingly by instinct. Most girls took a week to learn. And, above all, she was obliging. Didn't object to working extra hours. Perfect English with just a trace of an accent – Scottish, he could have sworn. Was always at his elbow with a whispered suggestion or a sweetly termed correction.

She reminded him of himself at the same age, he thought, and decided she'd bear watching.

When consulted, she'd dipped the tip of a teaspoon into the red slime, delicately licked it with her cat's tongue and closed those big dark eyes of hers. Silence followed. Honeysett was convinced his judgement was right and she was going to be sick until she sighed, opened her eyes again and, to his dismay, burst into tears. Lucky his

190

handkerchief had been clean and crisp. Through the sniffling and gulping he'd managed to learn that the caviar was not only not off – it was wonderful. Supreme. A heavenly taste she'd not experienced for five years. He'd helped her get over her outburst of nostalgia, muttering: 'There, there!' and 'Brace up now, dear.' Emotional lot, these Russians. But five minutes later Anna was polishing the glasses and humming a jazzy tune under her breath, fully recovered from her emotional storm. He appreciated a woman who didn't make an undue fuss. And his handkerchief had been returned this morning washed and ironed.

He'd promoted Anna to joint head of the serving squad for tonight's shindig. Young Antonio, from Italy, would keep an eye on her. This high-stepping matched pair pleased him: Antonio and Anna, handsome and dark and just deferential enough. There they stood, uniform perfect, starched cuffs impeccable, napkin over left arm, at the ready. They'd been told to expect the guest of honour and his partner first in line and to take their time serving up their choice of dishes. After all, the glamour of the presentation was part of the entertainment. The guests should be allowed to feast their eyes on the shining display rising up in artistically arranged ranks on stepped buffets before choosing. Antonio and Anna would place samples of the dishes requested on china plates with a gold rim and heraldic double-headed eagle in the centre.

Some dishes were nestling in wreaths of crushed ice, others were being kept hot in chafing dishes – it seemed to Honeysett a strange and uncomfortable way of serving food and went against all his training and experience but that was what, increasingly, this informal world demanded. Experimentation. Novelty. And Honeysett was nothing if not supple. He rather liked to think that, in the most discreet way, he identified the trends and set the style. And young Anna had come up with some intriguing ideas. She was the right generation, after all. Buffet luncheons, short skirts, fast cars, picture houses – she was becoming a bridge between his Edwardian world and her modern one. He must find a way of retaining her services. By some means or other.

The doors rolled back and the crowd gasped. Several broke with tradition and sacrificed their dignity sufficiently to join the prince in a congratulatory clap of the hands at the sight of the buffet.

The prince leaned over and whispered to Lily, 'Did I say picnic? No. Ali Baba's feast, that's what we've got. What fun! Let's go in, shall we, and inspect it more closely? I don't know whether we're expected to eat it or paint it. Tell you what, where's that photographer chappie? We'll get him to record it for posterity . . . Ah, there he is!'

A murmured word sent Cyril into the dining room where his flash devices were soon adding highlights to the aspic-gleaming mosaic. As he retreated, he managed to speak briefly to Lily. 'All's well. No dark horses in this paddock. Or nameless strawberry roans. More than halfway through the evening, chuck. I'll stay close.'

The prince was still showing a flattering appreciation of the display and shooting a knowledgeable comment or two to the chief steward, who had remained in attendance to collect the compliments. In his easy way, the prince questioned the appearance of oysters in the line-up. Was this an oyster month? Was September quite safe? He seemed satisfied by the answer, which involved a eulogy to the vigorous Whitstable production. He showed a gratifying appreciation of the variety and quantity of caviar. The steward, with a confidential air, recommended that His Royal Highness try the . . . he tactfully suppressed the word 'red' and substituted 'garnet-coloured variety'.

As they made their way towards the two servers, Edward grinned and treated Lily to a line or two from a West End show, the extravagant gastronomic celebration

'Here Be Oysters Stewed in Honey' from *Chu Chin Chow*. His grin widened when Lily joined in, supplying the next two lines of culinary oddities.

A dark-haired steward stepped forward, plate and napkin in hand, to guide Lily's choice. A matching pretty girl offered the same service to the prince. Italians? Lily thought so.

'Oh, Lily, how to choose. Shall we start with fishy things? Caviar? Oysters? Oh, I spot some salmon up there. Mademoiselle, I'll have the salmon. And some soured cream and watercress sauce if you have it.'

The girl smiled and raised the plate she was holding ready for him. She fixed the prince with what Lily, in her state of alertness, recognized as a conspiratorial look and, with a flourish, wiped her napkin across it. A gesture that clearly said, 'Clean plate, no problems.' One of Sandilands' team? How many women did he have on his books? The girl seemed to have the advantage of Lily, apparently knowing exactly who or what she was – there was no mistaking the swift complicitous smile she directed at her. In a gently accented voice she persuaded the prince to sample one or two more of the dishes . . . 'almond-studded fricasseed tails of Persian lamb . . . shellfish tossed with spices . . .'

With smiling good manners, the prince watched as his simple choice of salmon was shouldered aside by piles of highly seasoned exotica. Lily turned to the male server. 'That looks utterly delicious! I'll have exactly the same dishes, please, if you can remember them.'

'But of course, mademoiselle.' Up came the plate and the ladles worked, scooping and spooning, producing a replica of the prince's plate. They followed a footman to a corner table laid for eight and the prince indicated that Lily should sit by his side. They settled to wait for friends of the prince to emerge with their plates from the throng now steadily making inroads into the display.

Edward sniffed appreciatively at his food. 'Ah! The scents of the east! I really grew accustomed to this sort of thing in India. Wonderful cooking! I say – not used to this new style of going on – how long do we have to wait before we can tuck in?'

'Until at least one other couple has settled with us,' Lily said firmly, inventing the etiquette. 'But look, before you start – and you'll think this a bit fussy—'

He interrupted her. 'You're the policeman. Just tell me what to do. I'm your obedient servant this evening.'

Lily took a deep breath. 'I'm going to change plates. I took exactly the same dishes as you.'

'Oh, no,' said the prince with instant disobedience. 'And have you slide under the table stricken with something ghastly? That's just not on. I'll send out for two plates of fish and chips if you like . . . there's a stall over the road in the park that does wondrous haddock . . . but I'm not having a girl act as my food taster. Besides – it's unnecessary. You saw that waitress – the pretty girl who served me? She's one of Sandilands'. He's planted some of his best people in there. She gave me the all-clear. And if any of the dishes were poisoned – well, the whole room's going to be frothing at the mouth in minutes. You can't target a single person with a dish at a buffet. Not possible.' He lifted his knife and fork rebelliously. 'Something else I learned in India!'

In a second, Lily had swept the plate from under his chin and replaced it with her own. 'Orders, sir,' she said firmly. 'It's all right – I'm not intending to eat any of this. I'll just stir it about a bit. I ate before I came,' she lied. 'Ah – here comes someone who knows you, I think . . .'

'It's Tuppy! A chap I was at sea with. Tuppy! Come and join us! Ha! Last seen crossing the bar and swearing allegiance to King Neptune! Two years ago . . . HMS *Renown* . . . Remember, Tuppy? You were sitting in a ducking stool, mouth full of shaving foam! Gracious . . . I wondered if you'd survived that dunking! Good to see you again! And this is . . . ? Your wife! Little Ginny Orde! Of course! I hadn't realized you two knew each other. Well, well! Lily, may I present Thomas Tenby and Virginia, his wife? And I don't believe you know Lily Wentworth who is my guest for the evening . . . Now shall we dive in? I'm faint with hunger!'

The introductions performed and the newcomers settled in their places, the prince picked up his cutlery again and all, apart from Lily, began to eat.

A moment later: 'And here's Connie Beauclerk. And who's this she has in tow? Ah – it's Rupert Fanshawe.'

The prince had this the wrong way round, Lily reckoned. Rupert was towing Miss Beauclerk along with some urgency. He'd cut a swathe through the other diners to reach their table and after a glower directed at Lily he joined them and performed further introductions.

Lily went through the motions of greeting the table guests as correctly as she knew how, liking what she saw. Connie, in pink charmeuse embroidered with silver, was a blonde beauty with large grey eyes that were missing nothing. In particular, they were noting everything that could be noted about Lily. The Navy man's wife was neatly dressed in ivory ondine crêpe with a trimming of antique lace. Intelligent, rather shy but smiling, were Lily's first impressions and she guessed that the couple must be recently married, so often did they exchange soft glances, so often did their hands touch apparently by accident.

Three couples. Lily wondered who had been delegated to occupy the two seats remaining at their table.

The prince looked about him. 'Two more places. Now – for manners' sake, I believe we ought to share our table with a representative of our hostess's homeland. Find me a Russian!' He held up a finger to a passing footman and said: 'The dark gentleman over there. He answers. The gent with the blue star pinned to his bosom – the one ogling us through a monocle – d'you see him? Ask him if he'd like to come and join us.'

195

'Sir, I believe Prince Gustavus to be . . . er . . . Serbian,' said Rupert hurriedly. 'May I advise that—'

'So *that's* him! *The* Gustavus? Well, if he's the sporting gent I've heard tales of, I should rather like to shake his hand and congratulate him!' said Edward. 'Serbian, you say? It'll have to do, for here he comes.'

Enter the assassin, was Lily's first paralysing thought.

The nobleman strode towards their table. Dark clothes, impeccable haircut, fashionably scarred left cheek, neat moustache, the man was a caricature of aristocratic menace. Lily found she was instinctively poised to rise to her feet, clutching a quite useless fish knife and scanning his tight-fitting uniform for concealed weapons. She was relieved to see that Rupert, who had shot to his feet to perform a courtier's duty, was of the same suspicious mind. He was looking repeatedly from the stranger to Lily and she felt, though she could not account for, his concern.

Rupert was skilfully ushering the newcomer to a seat at the far end of the table and indicating that he should settle down on the chair next to himself. The new guest now found that he was seated with his sword arm an inch away from a muscled Special Branch shoulder and at an angle from Prince Edward. Lily admired the adroitness with which the manoeuvre was carried out. Prince Gustavus, whoever he was, had better not reach inside his jacket too abruptly for his cigarette holder, Lily reckoned. Having at once identified his target as a right-handed man, Rupert had, in one move, spoiled his aim and pinned down his gun hand. The smiling young man now drawling out pleasantries in the Serbian's ear would fell him without warning or question. But Rupert had a further test of the newcomer's bona fides in mind. He launched seamlessly into fluent Russian to continue his conversation. Gustavus replied with equal fluency and an eyebrow cocked in mild surprise.

The newcomer changed to German to address the Prince of Wales and a conversation in that language ensued. A pointed courtesy, Lily realized, when Edward broke off politely after a few exchanges and spoke again to the table in English. 'So good to get a chance to air my German. It's the only foreign language I've ever been at ease with. But Gustavus, I know, speaks excellent English so we'll continue with that. Not eating tonight, Your Royal Highness?'

The prince replied that he was too impatient and too old-fashioned to stand about waiting to be served. He rather despised English picnics. And, moreover, he was quite content with the wine. A superb example from Georgia. The princess's choice, he assumed. He took a sip and remarked wickedly that an appreciation of this vintage was the only thing he had shared with Rasputin. 'God rot him!' he added cheerfully.

'Er, yes, quite,' agreed Edward. 'What a good riddance *that* was! The evil peasant priest! We owe a vote of thanks to the band of gallant fellows who finished him off.' He raised his glass. 'To the sportsmen who rid the world of the Mad Monk, God rot 'im! What?'

They sipped and murmured in agreement.

'I had heard, Gustavus, that you yourself were . . . how shall I put it? . . . not unaware of, indeed, not *uninvolved* in the protracted demise of the Russian fiend?'

Edward had voiced the question that all were eager to ask.

The reply was low and curt. 'Several men were involved in the conspiracy – one at least an English secret service-man. I'm sure the details must have reached the ear of Your Royal Highness, concerned as you must have been to see the noxious threat to your dear Russian cousins removed. And, of course, his removal was of deep interest to your country. His death came at a most opportune moment—'

'Long anticipated by many, I'd say,' Rupert interrupted. 'Half Europe and Asia wished the man ill. And there are dozens of stories circulating about his death. I know at least . . .' he put his head on one side and appeared to be counting, 'seven . . . no, eight, chaps who claim to have pulled the trigger. Or wielded the axe. Or pushed him in the river. Depends who's bending your ear and how much he's had to drink.'

'Ah, yes. Well, there are indeed several versions of the events of that night circulating, you know,' said Edward. 'And I too have had my ear bent. But I say it's always interesting to hear from a chap who was on the spot.' His blue eyes sparkled with mischievous invitation.

Gustavus smiled. 'In the end, it took a company of us to dispatch the terrible old ox. He had survived previous assassination attempts, that was well known. The man was indestructible, it was rumoured, and rumour further had it that his strength came from a source beyond the natural. We took no chances. He received and accepted an invitation to a drinking party at the palace of Prince Yussupov on the river in St Petersburg. A merry, unbuttoned evening among like-minded chaps. First we poisoned him – three times – then we shot him – four times – and finally we clubbed him about the head, seized him and threw him into an ice-hole in the freezing river Neva. We watched as he sank under.' He smirked with secret knowledge. 'At least, that's how the story goes.'

This was hardly dinner-table talk, but the audience was eager for more. The death of the Tsarina's sinister influence had taken on a quality of dark farce that made it an acceptable topic of conversation. Rasputin, the much-feared and meddlesome evil genius, had been reduced, in death, to a pantomime villain.

'The pathologist.' Gustavus gave a rumbling laugh. 'You have to feel for the poor chap. He must have been puzzled indeed to come up with a cause of death amongst so many possibilities. Stomach full of poisoned cake and red wine, body riddled with a mixture of Russian and English lead, skull cracked, lungs full of river water and the whole body frozen stiff! I do believe your revered Spilsbury would have been somewhat challenged.'

'English lead?' Connie Beauclerk protested. 'What are you suggesting? The man was shot by a fellow Russian. Prince Yussupov. Everyone knows that. The Tsarina had him put under house arrest. Poor Felix! My brother was up at Oxford with him. A sweetie! Did the world a favour is what my brother says . . .'

Gustavus paused, making a show of filtering the information he could safely allow an English lady to hear. 'Rasputin was, indeed, shot by Prince Yussupov, Miss Beauclerk. Shot, but not mortally wounded. His Highness is not one of nature's assassins. Willing enough but, as you probably know, he has the reputation of being – as you remind us – Oxford educated and something of a fop. And the rumours are true. The revolver he chose for the task proved not to be of a calibre sufficient to fell the monster. When Yussupov approached what he assumed to be a corpse to check on his handiwork, Rasputin reared up, bellowed and seized his would-be murderer by the throat. The prince was extricated from the situation by another gentleman who happened to be at the scene. A gentleman wielding a higher calibre weapon.'

'Ah,' said Rupert, nodding his head sagely, 'the good old Enfield revolver.'

'No. A Webley. Of the kind used by . . . well, you know who uses them, Fanshawe. A .45 unjacketed bullet fired by the steady hand of an Englishman, an Englishman who rid the world of a meddling villain. One bullet in the centre of the forehead.' Gustavus drilled an imaginary hole in his own head with a forefinger. 'One bullet which changed the course of the war—'

'Well, well,' Rupert interrupted loudly. 'A word of advice, Your Highness: ladies present. Not too keen on hearing about the war, you know. We try to avoid any mention. More wine?'

'Oh, don't be a killjoy, Rupert!' Connie complained. 'It's a jolly good story. I love a bit of *Grand Guignol*! Prince Gustavus, I've got one more question. There are those who

199

say' – her voice took on a tentative tone – 'that Rasputin – or his spirit – did in fact survive even those extremes of punishment. There was a hideous scene, I've heard, and one reported by many reliable men who were present at his cremation?'

'You're right, Miss Beauclerk,' the Serbian assured her. 'His funeral pyre was set ablaze in public so that all might see with their own eyes that the beast had at long last been annihilated. I was unfortunate enough to be of the company that witnessed the spectacle. The horror! Many swooned.'

He glanced around the table, gathering the earnest expressions silently urging him to reveal more. Sure of his audience, he lowered his voice and went on: 'In the middle of the flames, the corpse began to sit up. Rasputin drew his knees to his chin and then, slowly, his torso began to rise upright.'

'Golly gosh!' breathed Connie, clutching her bosom. Edward leaned over and patted her shoulder, throwing a concerned and warning look at the Serbian.

'Perfectly understandable,' said Tuppy drily. The Navy man seemed to have taken a dislike to this dark foreigner whose eyes were as wintry and unfathomable as the ice holes he conjured up. 'Clearly some careless funeral parlour operative forgot to cut the tendons. In the heat, they shrink, you know, and pull the limbs about in a disturbingly life-like movement.' He gave a hearty bellow. 'Ha! I've seen corpses get up and dance!' Enjoying the surprise, he added: 'Not just a matloe! I was a medic with the Navy before I inherited my father's London practice. Travelled a lot, saw a lot of strange burial customs. Oh, I say – have I ruined your story, old man?'

Gustavus turned to glower at Tuppy. The sailor's cheery confidence deflected the look, unaffected, but Lily, catching it, had to repress an instinctive shudder. The Serbian's reaction to the set-down was one of anger barely held in check. He had enjoyed the fencing with Rupert but a trip-up by a medical man had fired his wrath. He breathed deeply, chewed his lips and, mastering himself, decided to reclaim the attention of the table. He raised his glass and admired the colour of the red wine against the candlelight. 'It was such a strong wine as this that he was given the night he entered the trap we'd set for him at the palace on the waterfront,' he recollected. 'A wine laced with enough fast-acting poison to kill ten men.'

'What on earth was the poison?' Tuppy asked. 'Rat poison? Digitalis? Arsenic? Strychnine? Forgive my curiosity – a physician is always interested in extending his knowledge.'

The Serbian paused for a tantalizing second, apparently quite aware that Tuppy had offered him a test: a menu of poisons from which to choose the correct one. Finally, he replied: 'None of those. It was potassium cyanide.'

'Makes sense. Not difficult to get hold of, and a minuscule amount will kill a man. Less than a gram would do for a twelve-stone chap. I understand that one gram is standard issue in the glass suicide capsules we dole out to our secret servicemen.' His cheery gaze, which had been taking in the whole company at the table, skipped lightly past Rupert, Lily noticed, at the mention of the service. Another man in the know, she concluded. 'Though for an ox of a man – as you describe him – perhaps you'd need a little more,' Tuppy added sagely. 'And a little research might have told those amateurs that baking it up in a cake is a pretty feeble way of going about things. It's the heat, don't you know. It vaporizes the noxious element. It'd take more than a slice of Victoria sponge to lay low a chap like Rasputin.'

'Well, I've never heard of the stuff, and I read all the whodunits,' said Connie. 'I bet you couldn't just stroll into Boots the Chemist and ask for an ounce, as you can with arsenic.'

'Anything is obtainable. Anywhere. If one has the right connections,' Gustavus told her. Judging, rightly, that his listeners were ready for some relief from the drama, he raised his glass again and proposed a further toast. 'Let us repeat the word that was on every Russian's lips on hearing of his death. In the street, strangers shouted it to each other in their joy and relief that justice had been done. *Ubili! Ubili!* "They have killed!"'

Thoughtfully, all murmured something along those lines, raised their glasses and took a very small sip.

Lily's palms were beginning to sweat with fear. It seemed a cold draught was blowing on the back of her neck. She told herself that the male members of the gathering were not her responsibility. She told herself that a six-foot Serbian sporting a duelling scar and brazenly imposing himself on the company was hardly the elusive Irish woman they were seeking. But the feeling of dread would not leave her. With a surge of relief, she saw the imposing figure of Sandilands passing with a full plate some yards away. She screwed up her courage and called out to him.

'Joe! What ho, Joe!'

He spun around, concerned, alerted by the intimate use of his name.

Almost crushed by the sudden attention she was attracting, she managed an encouraging: 'Won't you come and join us?'

He stood surveying the group until Rupert took over, inviting him to sit next to the Serbian in the remaining place. He introduced Sandilands to his neighbour.

'You've just missed an amazing tale of derring-do,' Edward commented.

'Oh, yes!' Lily added. 'A chapter from John Buchan, you'd swear! Do you realize you're sitting next to an *assassin*, Joe?' Her voice sounded improbably girlish to her own ears but Sandilands' presence was giving her confidence and she knew he was receiving her message. 'A self-confessed assassin! An expert in poisoning, shooting, clubbing and drowning.'

'Great heavens! Your Highness is not, I trust, about to demonstrate any of these skills this evening? Perhaps someone should tell him whom he's sitting next to?' Sandilands said calmly, shaking out his napkin.

'A Scotland Yard detective, I understand?' Gustavus nodded. 'But off duty tonight, I'm presuming? No cause for concern on either side. I perform no lethal tricks where there are ladies present.'

'And, speaking of ladies – where is your own beautiful new wife?'

'You are acquainted with Zinia?'

'No, I haven't yet had the honour, but I read the society pages of the *Tatler*,' Joe said happily. 'May we expect her to join us?' He leaned towards Lily and remarked: 'I think you'd admire her, Lily. I hear she is a dark-haired beauty with a profile to give Cleopatra a run for her money. I've been looking out for her all evening without a single sighting.'

'Zinia has retreated to the powder room to perform some small task – she caught the hem of her dress on a heel, I believe.'

Lily tried not to jump to her feet too eagerly. 'But she's missing the fun! I shall go and find her. Perhaps I can be of assistance. I'm a jolly good needlewoman ... though there's usually a woman in attendance down there with needle and thread.' She tilted her head to the guests and made off before anyone could call her back, glad to escape the demands of her assumed role for a few minutes.

The prince – her prince – was surely safe enough guarded by Sandilands and Rupert. But what of the assassin's wife? Was she another weapon in Gustavus's armoury? Lily reversed her thinking. Was Gustavus a weapon in the armoury of the mysterious dark lady skulking down below away from public view? Lily didn't believe she'd caught sight of any such woman since she'd entered the hotel. Could anyone possibly be hiding in the cloakroom all this time? Ladies' cloakrooms, she remembered from her briefing, were her responsibility. Sandilands would expect her to take action.

Lily found there were two vast and ornate powder rooms in the basement. She was directed away from the farther one by the attendant, who seemed, Lily thought, rather distraught.

'Can you help me?' Lily asked her. 'I'm looking for a friend of mine who came down here some time ago. She's having problems with the hem of her dress.'

The attendant's relief was instant. 'Oh, thank goodness someone's come for her. She's in a right state. I've offered her assistance but she just screams and yells at me to leave her in peace. I didn't know who to call for. She's commandeered a whole room for herself. What am I meant to do, miss, when the after-supper surge comes down? She's in there.'

Lily went through the padded door into a lavender-scented space lit by discreet electric light bulbs. 'Zinia? Are you there?'

Her only answer was a stifled snuffle and 'Didn't I tell you to go away?' from the armchair placed in one corner for swooning ladies who needed to take the weight off their feet. Lily approached, watchful and prepared for action, though the pitiful bundle curled in the depths of the chair seemed to offer no challenge.

'Hello. My name's Lily Wentworth. I hear you could do with some help with your dress.' As there was no reply she added: 'I was just talking to your husband upstairs. He's wondering when you're going to re-join him at the party.'

A howl of anger greeted this offering. A flood of Russian – oaths by the sound of it – and then: 'Never! Swine! Evil, loathsome man! I'm sitting here trying to get up the courage to find a back way out of this place. I shall walk away and never see him again.'

'Seems a bit drastic. Do you have somewhere to flee to? Always a good idea to have an exit strategy.' Lily's tone was exaggeratedly light.

'I'd rather sleep on the streets than next to him. I'd rather sleep in the zoo! In the reptile cage!' The vehemence of the replies was not abating. This display of overheating rage was the last thing Lily wanted to encounter. Any woman with the bad luck to be married to Gustavus deserved her sympathy, but something had to be done to deflate this swelling emotion.

'May I ask you to stand up, madam, put your hands on your head and turn round slowly?' Lily asked abruptly in a police voice.

'I beg your pardon? Why on earth should I? Who are you to ask such a thing?' The girl was sufficiently startled to raise her head and stop sobbing.

'I'll answer both questions when you've done as I ask.'

'Oh, very well! Strange English ways! One is obliged to humour one's hosts, I suppose.' Zinia sighed, stood up, lifted her arms and turned around.

'A beauty,' Sandilands had said. It was difficult to see loveliness in a face that was wrecked by tears that had channelled through her powder and smudged her lip rouge. Mascara was no more than large black smudges under her eyes. And yet the features had the strange attractiveness of a pug dog's squashed face. The eyes were large, dark and lustrous, the nose straight and short above an upper lip that was slightly too long for perfection. The mouth below was well shaped, but over generous in Lily's estimation. Lily was reassured to see that the girl was shorter than herself and very slightly built. And it was clear that, in her clinging silk, Zinia was not concealing a weapon.

'Thank you – just making quite sure you're not carrying a pistol.'

'A pistol?' The astonishment could not have been faked. 'Why would I be carrying a pistol?'

'Wife of a self-confessed assassin – one can't be too careful,' Lily said lightly.

'Assassin!' The word was spat out in disgust. 'He was never closer than a hundred miles to Rasputin, if that's the yarn he's been spinning. And ask yourself this – what sort of man has to brag about being a killer to get the admiration of the crowd?'

'Soldiers sometimes do,' Lily said equably. 'And your husband would appear to be every inch the soldier. The military bearing . . . the scar—'

'Pouf! The scar was incised by a surgeon's scalpel in Vienna. Under anaesthetic. False. Like everything about the man. He is an . . . impostor.'

'That's a very melodramatic word. I beg your pardon. This is all a bit hard for me to understand. Listen, Zinia, and I'll spell out *my* concerns. Your husband was just a few minutes ago introduced to the heir to the British throne, in whose company I find myself this evening . . . Gustavus is even now sitting at the Prince of Wales's table. Surely—'

Zinia cut her short. 'My husband has been tracking him for weeks. Wheedling invitations. Currying favour. So he's managed it at last. The fiend has got within range of his prey.'

Chapter Twenty-One

As the last of the guests trickled through and some began to return to have their plates filled again, Charles Honeysett quivered with the effort of concentration. This was a tricky moment. The dishes had to be replenished and the food kept flowing, but above all the wine glasses had to be continually topped up.

He cast an eye on the table of greatest significance to check that all was well. The pretty girl in the green dress who seemed to have taken the prince's eye had apparently deserted her royal escort for the moment but HRH was in full flow, chattering, laughing with his friends and sinking quite a bit of wine. Egged on by that foreign blighter in the black uniform. That one didn't have the manners to wait for the footman to circulate and pour the wine – he'd commandeered the bottle and called for two more. Where did he think he was – in an officers' mess? Outlandish behaviour! No table manners to speak of either. The steward had never seen a fork wielded like that . . . held in the right hand and used like a spoon . . . kinder to look aside and take no notice. Honeysett thought HRH, who was a stickler for good behaviour, must be deeply offended by this louche way of going on, but he had probably got used to all sorts and conditions of men in his travels.

And, anyway, if a drunken scene were to develop, it would be the fault of that fair-haired man with the big shoulders. Honeysett had marked him down as one of the hush-hush brigade but perhaps he'd read it wrong. Joining in the spirit of the evening, the fellow had reached over and grabbed a bottle himself, strolled round the table and poured out at least two – Honeysett had been distracted and might have missed one – glasses for the foreign blighter. It was no business of the steward's but he couldn't shake off a feeling of foreboding. Something was brewing.

He decided to keep a wary eye on the bloke in black. He didn't like the cut of his jib. He had to remind himself that this class of Russkie was no threat. They were all related to the English aristocracy up at that level. Most of them claimed Queen Victoria for a grandmother. He'd had all this laid out for him by Anna who seemed to know her aristos; he suspected that she was one of them, or had been in a previous life. It was the other bunch, the Reds – the Bolsheviks – you had to watch out for. Murdering scum, according to Anna.

At least now the policeman, the young fellow with the autocratic way with him, had joined the table, and the steward-in-chief felt he could come off watch.

There were undercurrents here tonight. All Honeysett could do was his own job. Thoroughly. 'Just go about your business in your usual manner,' they'd warned him at the briefing. 'Ignore anything that does not concern the provision of hospitality.' Honeysett had no problems with that. He liked a clear mandate. There'd be no cause to lay blame at *his* door if anything went wrong.

'Antonio!' He called the Italian to his side. 'HRH. Check his plate. Top him up if you can. Makes sense to get some food into him to mop up all that wine he's putting away.'

'I just have, sir. He's enjoying his meal and I've helped him to some more shellfish. He's looking forward to the pavlova when his guest gets back to join him for dessert. He sent his compliments to the chef, by the way. I think he really meant it, sir. Oh, will you excuse me, sir? Anna's signalling.'

Honeysett beamed. Away from the royal table, this mad party was going rather well. The sound of merry, excited voices was rising to exactly the pitch he liked to achieve. Yes, there'd be a good write-up in tomorrow's society pages. He looked around for the photographer, tracking him by the flash of popping bulbs. Catching Cyril's eye, he indicated that there was a scene worthy of his lens at the prince's table. The sinister foreigner had slipped Honeysett a large note at the start of the proceedings with a hint as to how he was to earn it. Now seemed to be the right time. The Russkie had insinuated himself into the place the girl in green had vacated next to the prince and the two men were, as far as Honeysett's untrained ears could make out, practising toasts in some outlandish tongue. Getting quite merry, the pair of them. And the blond bloke was still ladling it out. Well, the foreigner was showing some determination to have his photograph taken with HRH. Ten quids' worth of determination. Time for the pay-off. No harm in that, surely?

Honeysett had an understanding with the gentlemen of the press. They did each other favours and made no comment. Only one of the hounds here tonight, but one was all that was needed. Luckily, it seemed the chosen one was Tate of the *Pictorial*. As smooth as they came.

Suddenly Antonio was at his elbow distracting him, whispering in his ear. Honeysett at once accompanied the server back into the kitchens, disturbed by his news. At least the girl had done the sensible thing and come straight off duty, secreting herself out of view in the staffroom. When they found her, sitting on a bench concealed under the rows of coats, Honeysett was alarmed by her pallor and the way she was clutching her stomach. She was leaning over, yelping and panting, seemingly having difficulty in breathing.

Honeysett silenced her attempts to stammer out apologies. In dread, he asked her: 'Something you've eaten, Anna? Have you been tasting any of the dishes out there?'

Emphatically she shook her head. 'No! Only that red caviar you told me to check on before we served it. It was

209

still fine – honest, Mr H. Haven't touched anything else. It's nothing serious. It's just the time of the month.'

'Month? Month? What are you on about? What have *you* got against September? I'm getting a bit fed up with this.'

Catching his blank expression, Anna explained further: 'No, not that. Women's problems, Mr H. Bit early, though . . . must be all the excitement . . .' She bent double again and began to retch.

'Gets my sister the same way,' Antonio supplied. 'Sick as a cow, regular as clockwork.'

'Antonio, get back out there and fill the gap. Pull Alec forward.'

'Sir, I already have, sir.'

Honeysett acted swiftly. 'Home, Anna. At once. Here's half a crown for a taxi. Come back when you're feeling better.'

He sighed as he helped her into her coat and off the premises. Female staff! They came cheaper than men but they had their drawbacks. Honeysett shuddered. Really, there was no place for them working in public view. Better kept behind the scenes. How was a bloke expected to allow for times of the month? Get them to fill in a calendar? Bloody women! More temperamental than the bloody oysters!

Cyril had responded at once to Honeysett's lifted finger. He approached quietly and took his shot without warning before the party at the table was aware of what he was about to do and could begin to strike a fish-eyed pose. He liked to produce a natural effect. He exchanged a glare with Sandilands, who had ruined the photograph by turning away at the last moment.

Something was very wrong.

Cyril went to stand some yards away and stare. He fiddled with his camera, pretending to line up angles to disguise his surveillance of the group.

Lily had vanished, and sitting in her place was a night-marish figure he thought he ought to know. A Danish name came to mind. Or was it Swedish? No – wasn't the man a Balkan of some kind? Serbian? Romanian? Cyril vaguely recollected that there was some scandal associated with the name . . . if only he could remember it.

As he watched, the dark and the fair princely heads bent towards each other in perfect amity. Cyril's alarm increased. Then the stranger looked up. Registering the newsman's attention, he turned his face away from Edward to reveal the scar on his left cheek. He smiled for the camera. Cyril pressed the shutter in automatic reaction to the offered pose, nodded an acknowledgement and scrambled to gather up his equipment.

He dashed off into the fray to find Princess Ratziatinsky.

Chapter Twenty-Two

'His prey, Zinia – what do you mean? Tell me! Quickly! Is he planning to shoot him?' Lily's fingers itched to take the girl by the shoulders and shake her.

The Russian gave a bitter laugh. 'Heavens no! What would he do for a gun? The men were all searched, you know. But it's a shot he's interested in.' She sniggered at the irony. 'He's ambitious. He's attempting to insinuate himself into English society. He wants to appear in photographs in the fashionable journals sitting alongside the prince – his bosom companion to all appearances. He's been planning this coup for some time. Marrying me was part of his grand plan. I . . . in my homeland . . . was connected with the imperial family. I enjoyed the consequence that went with that status. Many doors are still open to me, even here in London, on account of my family name. But when the revolution burst over our heads, like thousands more I had to flee with my parents or face at best imprisonment, at worst execution. Unlike the poor Tsar and his family, I found shelter in this country. *They were not so fortunate,*' she added bitterly. 'But tonight, with so many of my compatriots surrounding me, people who knew me in another life, I could not dissemble. I refused to lend him countenance. I came and hid myself away down here. Though that wasn't my only reason.'

She twirled round again for Lily, hands extended in a parody of a mannequin's pose. 'Just look at me. What do you see?'

Lily could not tell her the sad truth. The girl resembled nothing so much as a sofa doll, one of those slim, silken puppets with huge glass eyes and painted faces whose floppy limbs her mother liked to drape along the couches to startle the unwary visitor. Half alive and wholly sinister.

But Zinia wasn't interested in hearing a response from Lily. 'The princess could hardly believe her eyes when I arrived looking like this.' Her voice took on a tone that managed to be both imperious and petulant. 'Wearing a five-year-old rag cobbled up at the hem. And a single strand of mediocre pearls. She didn't know where to look. I couldn't bear the disgrace. What you see me in now is all I have left. I've sold off and pawned everything of value I had. Since I married the scoundrel six months ago he's got through all I own. He found my last precious gem, a diamond brooch that I had from my mother, and donated it ... *donated* it! ... to Princess Ratziatinsky for her auction tonight. His way of buying access to English royalty.'

'You married him. And yet you can never have loved such a man.'

'In my world one does not marry for love,' Zinia announced. 'My parents died of the influenza soon after we came here. I was alone for months in a foreign country, my wealth eroded, living like a mouse. Someone introduced him to me. He offered to marry me and remake my fortune. Oh, he told me exactly who and what he was before I accepted him. He confessed his roguery with disarming honesty, he promised to involve me in an adventure. "Bury the past," he told me, "it saps the strength. The future is for those who have the wits and the energy to make it theirs." And it seemed an entertaining future. Too late I discovered the chapters in his life he had omitted. The violence, the perversion. The murder.'

Unmoved by the dramatic delivery, the tears, the flashing eyes, Lily came straight to the point. 'If he isn't Prince Gustavus, then who is he?' She was sure Sandilands would expect her to establish an identity.

213

'Oh, when he says he's the son of a Serbian prince, he's telling nothing less than the truth,' said Zinia, annoyingly Sphinx-like. 'In fact he's the spitting image of Gustavus Alexis, they tell me. But he's his illegitimate son. One of many. His mother was a serving maid or something of the kind.' Zinia shrugged a shoulder. 'He was brought up alongside his half-brother, the legitimate heir, in a ramshackle castle in a remote corner of a continent about to burst into flames . . . as his brother's valet.'

'Good Lord! What a very medieval way of going on.'

'On the death of their father, and the ruin of the estate in the war, they harnessed up the one remaining carriage and set off, master and man, to try their luck in Paris.'

'Don't tell me. Only one of them survived the journey?' Lily was eager to cut short a predictable and most probably deceitful story. She was quite certain she'd read something of the kind in a book by Alexandre Dumas. Zinia's wild pronouncements were beginning to irritate her and annoyance sharpened her tongue. 'Another tawdry tale in the annals of Mendacia, my granny would say.'

Zinia was not affronted. She replied to Lily's jibe with a look of knowing superiority. 'Oh, it does happen. Someone has popped up recently in Germany claiming to be the Grand Duchess Anastasia of Russia. The remaining members of the imperial family have been assembled to pass her in review and establish or demolish the young woman's claims.'

'I had heard. Varying opinions given, I believe.'

Zinia's lip curled. 'I can tell you the outcome of *that* claim. Whatever the truth of it, the woman will be rejected and Anastasia Nikolaevna Romanova will be buried a second time.'

'Why so certain?'

'The last thing Europe wants to see is an heir to the Tsar's fortune making an appearance. It has been removed, apportioned and secreted away. And – dare one say it? – even spent. The Tsar was far sighted enough to take out insurance with European banks against his premature death in favour of his children. An enormous amount. No one wants to pay out such sums to a doubtful claimant – or a genuine one! Besides, the young Anastasia was a fiend. Better not resurrected. No, the present custodians of the fortune are not going to surrender it, however compelling the case. The world has outgrown the Romanovs. There is no place for them. If the Tsar himself were to rise from the dead, he'd have to take his chances at the roulette table like the rest of us. Like Gustavus.'

'Murder and impersonation? The behaviour you're describing does not go unpunished in England. This is a civilized country. I have a friend . . .' Lily said hesitantly, 'a friend of some influence who might be able to help you if you were to lodge a complaint with him.'

'An influential friend?' the Russian said, eyes narrow with suspicion. 'You have avoided answering my question. Who *are* you? Who are you to intrude on my unhappiness, offering to pin up my hem and repair my life?'

'An emissary. Lily Wentworth. I'm the guest of the Prince of Wales this evening. We were rather expecting you to join our table. If you come up now, you'll be in time for the last of the caviar. And we're promised a peach pavlova for dessert.'

But her positive tone couldn't penetrate the gloom in which the Russian had cocooned herself. She shook her head, determined to hold fast to her despair. Lily took her by the hand.

'Listen, Zinia, there is only one way out of here and that is up the stairs and through the Grand Salon to the door. Hold on to my hand. I won't let you come to harm.'

Lily suffered a minute or two of exasperation as the girl sniffed and sighed, made her mind up, and changed it, made it up again. Finally, she allowed herself to be led from the room. They climbed the stairs and made their way along the short corridor to the Grand Salon. Lily pushed open the door, still holding tightly to her captive. She was determined not to release her before Sandilands had had a chance to get a look at her face. He would be able with the flick of an eyebrow to let her know whether this was – improbable though Lily thought it – the girl who'd passed herself off as Harriet Hampshire. After that, the lady would either be in handcuffs or free to go wherever she wished.

They reeled back before the happy din of an inebriated crowd underpinned by the strict rhythm of Cecil Cardew, who was well into a post-prandial slow waltz. But the happy sounds were torn apart by a woman's shriek.

As everyone fell silent, the shriek was followed by another, and a female voice babbling incoherently. It was coming from the royal table, Lily was certain. She was almost sure that the voice belonged to Connie Beauclerk.

Tugging Zinia along in her wake, she hurried towards the source of the noise, now pierced by the clatter of falling dishes and the sound of a wine glass shattering.

Into the general silence that follows breaking glass, Connie's voice rang out again: 'I told you he'd had enough, Rupert! You should never have given him that last glass!'

And, from a concerned male voice which might have been Sandilands': 'No, no! He's not drunk. Well, he may be, but that's not the worst of his troubles . . . Oh, good Lord, he's having a heart attack! Tuppy! Help me with this!'

A further howl from Connie startled everyone within earshot. 'Fetch someone! The prince is having a seizure! The prince is dying!'

Chapter Twenty-Three

'Connie! Calm down!' The Prince of Wales's voice was surprisingly firm. 'Fetch someone? We have Scotland Yard and Harley Street here. Who else do you want to conjure up? Florence Nightingale?' He threw an arm round her shaking shoulders and gave her a hug.

'Sorry, David. So sorry! I've never seen anyone die before.'

'Nor have I,' he said gallantly. 'Shock to the system, what? But look here, we might not have . . . yet. Don't give up hope. Prince Gustavus is in the very best hands, you see. If anything can be done, Tuppy will do it.'

Joe had hurled himself round the table at the first splutter. And now, a practised double act to all appearances, he and Tuppy were working on Gustavus, oblivious of the sideshow. As Edward spoke, Sandilands was wrenching off the starched collar from the throat of the man retching and gasping for breath on the carpet by the side of an overturned chair, while Tuppy had a finger on the pulse behind one ear and reaching out his other hand for the stethoscope which, improbably, his wife was handing him from the depths of her evening bag.

'Heart attack? Are we thinking heart attack?' Joe muttered.

Glad of the chance, Joe ran his hands over the contorted body, encountering nothing in the pockets but handkerchief, cloakroom ticket, keys and a cache of folded pound notes. 'Who the hell are you?' Joe wondered silently and

217

angrily. The man had come bounding on stage with all the élan of a pantomime villian. Braggart, liar and avowed assassin, he had himself been struck down in a spectacularly dramatic way. In the tradition of uppity heroes of classical times he had fallen abruptly, foaming at the mouth and clutching his chest.

Gustavus gave one last shudder and his limbs relaxed.

Stethoscope to his ears, Tuppy gave a barely detectable shake of his head.

Joe looked up and saw that Fanshawe had gone swiftly into action, and was directing a pair of footmen rushing forward with screens. Charles Honeysett stood, rock-like, in the middle of the surge, coolly ordering a mopping-up operation.

'No!' Joe snapped at the man who arrived with brush and tray to clear up the fallen crockery. 'Leave everything as it is. We'll have the screens gladly, but leave the rest alone. And have Honeysett move the other diners back into the ballroom.' He exchanged a few words with Tuppy, nodded, and called the steward to his side. 'Inform Princess Ratziatinsky, will you, that Prince Gustavus has had – no, say *is having* a heart attack. He's receiving medical care and is on his way to hospital. The prince apologizes for the disturbance and has asked that the evening continue normally without him. And tell them to wind up the orchestra!'

'Sir, we have a vehicle at the back that you can use for the gentleman,' said Honeysett, as he set off. 'My men know the routine.'

Not the first time a guest had been carried out feet first with the utmost discretion, then. A moment later, after a short announcement in several languages by the princess in the ballroom next door, Cardew's band swooped into the opening bars of the waltz from *The Merry Widow*, the one tune guaranteed to lure everyone back on to the floor.

Becoming aware of the presence of Wentworth, who had squeezed through the closing barricade hand in hand with a second woman – oh, Lord! The man's wife! – Joe beckoned them forward. He rose to his feet and said: 'Heart attack. I'm looking for pills – medication – anyone know if he carries such a thing?'

Zinia had been staring at the recumbent form of her husband with the expression of someone who has almost put a foot on the rotting corpse of some strange wild creature on the forest path, a blend of fear, disgust and fascination. She took a step forward and spoke to Tuppy, who was passing a hand over the staring eyes. 'The man you are attending to is my husband. What on earth's happened to him?'

Tuppy straightened himself and replied, every inch the Harley Street doctor. 'The prince was stricken by convulsions, accompanied by difficulty in breathing. He collapsed, as you see. A massive heart attack. There was nothing anyone could do to prevent his death.'

'His face looks very ... pink.' Zinia voice was almost accusing. She peered again at the body. 'Can you assure me that he's perfectly dead?'

'He is, indeed, madam. You have my commiserations. And my assurance that we did everything we could.'

'His father went in just the same way,' she said calmly. 'No warning. It runs in the family. He fell off his horse in the forest, miles from the nearest doctor. Gustavus was fortunate indeed to have help at his side when his time came.'

'Madam, I am most dreadfully sorry ... Dr Thomas Tenby at your service. My card.'

'Thank you, doctor. I am grateful for your efforts.' Zinia was recovering her haughty demeanour. Still held firmly by Lily, she stared down at the body again.

Joe scrutinized her closely as he murmured his condolences, and then at last he turned his attention to Lily. His eyes said: *No. This isn't the woman.*

He saw the relief with which Lily released Zinia's hand. And was intrigued to note that the Russian instantly seized Lily's back again and held on, her body beginning to tremble.

'Why don't you take a seat, madam?' he said, taking in at

219

last the girl's emotional exhaustion and dishevelled state. 'You've had a frightful shock.' He led her over to a chair away from the table, then whispered in Lily's ear: 'Tate. Leave this and get him in here, will you? He's needed.'

The scene of crime photograph. Lily didn't have to search for Cyril. He was standing, equipment in hand, just outside the folding doors, arguing with a footman. She pulled him inside.

'All's well. I mean, better than you might fear.' Joe told him. 'It could have been worse. Look, I want you to take some . . . er . . . professional shots. For my album. Have you any flash powder left? Can you do this?'

Cyril took in the scene with a few swift glances, muttering, 'Listen, I ought to warn you – they're saying out there in the ballroom that the Prince of Wales has been murdered. Rumour's going round like wildfire. They're talking of storming the barricades to find out. Half the men are ex-soldiers, half the women ex-girlfriends! What I'd call an unstable mix. Concern is at fever pitch. Thought you ought to know. The princess is keeping the lid on it for the moment, but it can't last.'

He went into action, showing all the disciplined anticipation of a police photographer and responding smoothly to Joe's every guiding gesture. When he'd done, he told Joe: 'I'll go straight back and get the night staff on to this. I'll bring the results round to the Yard myself as soon as I have them.'

Joe returned to the table, examining the dishes and glasses. Rupert went to stand at his shoulder.

'I'll get this lot sketched and labelled and then bagged up, sir,' he said doubtfully. 'It won't be easy.'

'The steward will lend a hand.'

Honeysett approached, nodding understanding.

'Honeysett, we need to convey the entire contents of the table back to the laboratory. A formality,' Joe said, holding up a hand to forestall any protests. 'No one is pointing the finger at your food. And your cooperation in the matter

220

would be appreciated, if you understand me? No one, after all, would want to start an unhelpful rumour concerning the quality of the shellfish, now would they? Sure you'll agree.'

'Understood, sir.'

Joe turned his attention to the Prince of Wales. 'Sir, one last thing to ask, and it's a tricky one. Please feel free to—'

'Wouldn't dream of turning you down, Sandilands.' Edward smiled. 'I was just on my way.' He tugged down his tails, adjusted his tie and extended an arm to Lily. 'I think this is one corpse that had better get up and dance. May I have the honour of the last waltz with you, my dear? If you have the knees for it, that is?'

'I'd be delighted, David.'

Joe watched as the pair of them made their way on to the dance floor, where they were greeted by a wave of relief and pleasure from the crowd.

Lily began to feel a rush of something she identified as euphoria. Whatever it was called, it carried her on the lightest of feet around the dance floor.

Edward seemed to be experiencing the same elation. 'I think we can crawl out of the bunker now,' he whispered. 'Danger past. Sandilands thinks he's drawn the venom. Which is what all this is about, you know. Well, for this evening at least. All the same . . . I don't know what your orders are, but I've been advised to make a swift exit if we ever reached this stage. So we must enjoy the last flourish. What an evening! You must let me lay on a motor car to take you home.'

'Thank you, sir, but I think my evening is only half-way through. There was murder done tonight and the commander has no one in handcuffs. The snake has wriggled away.'

Chapter Twenty-Four

Joe was waiting for them when they returned to the table. 'Ah! There you are, Lily my dear. All done here for the moment. Time to say goodnight and thank you for having me to these nice people. I want you to come straight back with me now. You're in for a sleepless night, I'm afraid.' He took her arm and clamped it under his.

'Good Lord!' murmured Connie Beauclerk, watching their hurried departure with sly amusement. 'Commander Sandilands is very direct, isn't he? His Scottish cousin, did I hear someone say that girl was? Mmm . . . a fashionable thing to be, but I do wonder. David, it's my opinion your new girlfriend's just been snatched by the dashing detective from the Met – right from under your nose. She surrendered and went quietly – and, gosh! one quite sees why – but you've lost her.'

Edward looked thoughtfully down at the wreckage of the table. 'But I didn't lose my life, Connie. And I think I was meant to.'

He watched silently as the corpse was taken up in a tablecloth by four strapping young men and carried out of the room.

The commander's car drew up to the rear entrance as they came out and he handed an exhausted Lily into the deep comfort of the back seat, where she dropped off almost at once. She awoke with a start only minutes later as the car came to a halt at a junction. Guiltily she glanced about her, checking that in her unconscious state she hadn't lurched into his iron shoulder but had come to rest against the padded upholstery.

Joe thought he'd better reassure her that nothing indecorous had taken place: 'Lord, Wentworth. You drop off faster than my old Labrador. But you don't slobber and you don't wuffle as loudly as he did.'

'So sorry, sir. How shaming! It's moving vehicles – they put me to sleep. Limousine or old rattletrap – it makes no difference. The conductor of the forty-two bus had to shake me awake once at the terminus. Are we there yet?'

'No, not quite. We've just passed Chelsea Harbour. I thought we'd get out at Westminster and walk along the river for a stretch. Nice night. We'll get a bit of fresh air into our lungs before we start work. Must stay sharp for the meeting.' Moments later, he leaned forward and pulled aside the glass. 'Sergeant – I want you to drop us off here and go home. Call for me at the Yard at six, will you?'

The driver opened the door and helped Lily on to the pavement. A short way downriver, Big Ben boomed half past some hour or other. Taxis sped by full of people in evening dress; ahead of them a knot of shrieking revellers made a dangerous dash across the street to take a closer look at the Thames.

'Half past one o'clock and London's still open for business, lit up and roistering. This is an early night for HRH. Poor chap – he was looking quite done in, I thought, towards the end. Still – he played his part with some skill, don't you agree? Not easy being the mealy worm on the hook at the end of the line.'

'I thought him skilful, brave and – yes – charming, sir.'

A mist was rising from the river and its deliciously chill breath made her shiver. She pulled her cashmere wrap more closely about her shoulders and watched as his car made a daring U-turn and set off in the opposite direction. She turned her head abruptly away from the road, annoyed but amused at what she saw, then looked up surreptitiously to see if he'd noticed the car tailing them.

'I won't offer an arm,' he said easily. 'I've noticed you like to stride out. Tell you what I will offer though ... we've plenty of time before the team starts to assemble. In a hundred yards or so there'll be another comfort available. Tell me when any food last passed your lips, Wentworth.'

She had to think hard before she remembered. 'I had a ham sandwich in the Strand, sir. At midday.'

'Not good enough. I'm sorry for that. You must allow me to make amends.'

She didn't show any pleasure at his suggestion but pattered resentfully after him. He was about to rethink his offer of a supporting arm but decided against it. She wouldn't welcome the gesture and wouldn't quite know how to refuse it.

They marched on in silence, the traffic becoming thicker as they neared Scotland Yard. Joe stopped suddenly when he reached the head of a taxi rank where a long, low building resembling a railway carriage had been constructed. Weatherboarded and painted park-bench green, it had a small black projecting iron stovepipe giving out a blast of coal, smoke and cooking food. A notice over the door declared it to be *Licensed Cabman Shelter No. 402*.

He put his head round the door and shouted a question. Satisfied with the rumbling response from the interior, he opened the door wider. 'It's for cabbies,' he explained. 'A sort of revictualling station. These things are everywhere in London but people hardly notice them. They're not supposed to let just anybody in – they'd lose their licence – but if they get to know you they'll allow you eat here. Let's go on board and see what we can find.'

Joe took off his top hat and ducked through the low doorway. Lily followed, stepping from the chilly street into a welcoming fug.

'Evening, Frank,' Joe said to the whiskered man behind

the counter. 'I'd like something for this young lady to eat. She's ravenous. In fact we both are.'

'Evening, Captain!' Frank looked pleased to see Joe and if he was taken aback by his white tie and tails he showed no sign of it. 'Hungry, are you?'

'I'll say. We've just spent several hours in the restaurant at Claridges, toying with larks' tongues and picking at plovers' eggs.'

Frank's moustache bristled with distaste. 'Ah. Well, you'll be needing a Zeppelin in the clouds with onion gravy, then. That'll stick your ribs together.'

'That's sausage and mash, Wentworth.'

Suddenly the idea of sausage and mash made Lily's eyes gleam. 'Oh, yes please! That would go down a treat.'

'Righto. That'll be two Zeppelins, Frank, and what have you got on for pudding tonight?'

'Figgy duff to follow, sir, with a dollop of custard?'

Lily's eyes lit on a cabby spooning up a richly scented pudding and she nodded.

There were two other solid figures in the shelter, steadily eating their way through a substantial serving of something brown and glutinous. They both greeted Sandilands. 'Evenin', Captain!'

'You're up late,' said one of them through the steam from a white china cup.

'No rest for the wicked,' said Joe, returning the expected reply and enjoying the expected guffaw it produced. And to Lily, 'Shall we sit over there in the corner?'

As soon as they settled, a large freckled hand descended between them and plates of sausage and mash appeared on the table.

'Mustard with that, miss? Ketchup? Cup o' tea?'

'Mustard and a cupper would be grand, Frank,' said Lily. 'Milk, one lump, please.'

'Ah, supper!' Joe exclaimed in anticipation, picking up his knife and fork. 'Supper is one of man's chief pleasures. The other three slip my mind when faced with a banger.'

Lily grinned. She sliced off the crusty end of her sausage first and chewed it with satisfaction, then leaned over to ask, 'You're sure this is all right?'

Joe swallowed his sausage and regretfully put down his knife and fork. 'Well, it is a bit like school dinners, I suppose. But I rather enjoyed school dinners. If you really don't fancy it, I can think of something else.'

'No, it's heavenly. Can't tell you how much I prefer it to caviar. I meant we don't risk ruining Frank's reputation, do we? Look at us. Two refugees from the chorus line of *Florodora*, still in costume. I wouldn't want to scare the customers away. It wouldn't be polite.'

Joe responded to the concern that underlay the light tone. 'Don't worry. They're used to me and my strange ways here, though turning up with a delightful young lady on my arm is not usually one of them. I shall have to put up with a bit of heavy jocularity on that score, I'm afraid. They mostly look on me as a protective presence since I leaned heavily on a street gang that was giving them a bad time. And old Frank's known me for ... oh, it must be going on eight years.'

'The army?'

Joe nodded. 'He was in my regiment.'

'Ah, I understand. You saved his life and he repays you in figgy duffs?'

'No. You couldn't be more wrong. It's to him I owe *my* life. He's no more likely to forget it than I am and – I'll tell you something – you can get rather solicitous and protective of someone whose life you've saved, Wentworth,' he said and added: 'You'll find.'

'*I'll* find, sir?'

'Oh, yes. You'll be for ever involved – at a personal level now – in the continued well-being of HRH. You'll scan the Society pages of the press each day to check up on his health. You'll be concerned by reports that he has a head cold; you'll offer up a prayer when you hear that he's strained a fetlock. It's thanks to you he's on his way home to York House tonight, hale and hearty, instead of the Royal Hospital, toes turned up, under a shroud.'

She stared at him with sudden insight.

'Yes. It wasn't your waltzing feet or protective arms that saved his life – it was your quick thinking and your annoying habit of exceeding your orders that did it.' Joe reached across the table and patted her arm with a sticky hand. 'I'm almost certain I know what happened tonight. I'll say it now because I shan't be able to pick you out for special commendation when we get to our meeting – well done! I'm not sure how gratified you'll be to hear me say it – and probably better not tell your father – but this evening it's my belief you handed the prince his life . . . on a plate!'

Chapter Twenty-Five

Joe spooned up the last of his pudding and eased back his chair, eyeing Lily silently. She'd been the subject of that calculating stare before and responded by pulling her stole higher over her shoulders, a gesture he acknowledged with amusement. 'No need for alarm. I was trying to assess the effect you're going to have on the rest of the male company gathered in the ops room. Yes! I want you to be there!' He answered her look of alarm. 'Your evidence is pivotal – but dolled up as you are ... well, I'm concerned that the officers present may unwittingly consign to you a some-what inconsequential role. You look the part, Wentworth – royal girl-friend – flapperish, fox-trotting gadabout. I don't want to see my men reacting to that image. Most unfair. I'd like you to change.'

'You mean they won't take me seriously if I present myself dressed as I was ordered to dress, sir?'

He ignored the rebuke. 'I know these men. Effective and clever, but women haven't played a significant part in their lives, I fear.'

'Oh, I expect they all had a mother, sir,' Lily said mildly.

'One can never be certain about Bacchus ... Oh, Lord! Bacchus! Give me your impressions when you've met him. He's the handsome dark cove with the heavy mous-tache. Looks like a Sargent portrait of an Italian peasant, I always think – the hooded eyes follow you round the room saying, "I saw what you just did!". You may wish to look away.'

She was trying not to laugh at him. 'Well, I don't know what effect he has on the enemy, but by God, Bacchus terrifies you, sir. Has he any redeeming human features, this man of mystery?'

'What, you are about to ask, does he "do for pleasure"? Well, I'll tell you. Er . . . he translates stories from the Russian . . . Pushkin, I think.'

'Ah.'

'Into Portuguese.'

After a satisfying moment of disbelief, her laughter burst through.

'My other men you already know. I've called in Hopkirk and Chappel, who are still working on the admiral's death, and Rupert Fanshawe whom you danced with this evening.'

'I'd feel easier appearing in uniform.'

'The meeting's called for three a.m. I can send you back to your hostel to change. It's in the Strand, isn't it? Mrs Turnbull's ghastly barracks? I'll put you in a taxi. No – I'd better come with you and face the old dragon myself.'

'No need for all that, sir. I changed at my aunt's apartment.'

'The hat shop lady?'

'Yes. She lives over the shop in Bruton Street. And don't worry about a taxi. I'm quite sure I have my own conveyance close by.'

Sandilands raised an eyebrow. 'Ah! The Pumpkin Express! It's well after midnight. Are you sure it'll still be there – the rather eye-catching Buick that's been following you about all evening? Is that what you have in mind? It was at the Yard. It followed us *to* the hotel. It followed us *from* the hotel. It's been at our heels all along the Embankment.' He enjoyed her surprise for a moment. 'I'm expecting it to be cheekily parked in the taxi rank when we leave. Now, tell me, Wentworth – who do you know who drives a cream-coloured American sedan?'

'My aunt sent me out with her chauffeur, sir. She was concerned for my safety.'

'Prescient lady! Sandilands? Not to be trusted with nieces. Everyone says so.' Joe grinned and looked at his wristwatch. 'You've got just over an hour. Long enough?'

'Ample, sir.'

'Then I'll hand you over to . . . what's his name?'

'Albert, sir. Albert Moore. He was a sergeant in the London Regiment.'

The Buick was loitering conspicuously in the middle of a line of shiny black cabs, an exotically striped chameleon poised to lick up a row of beetles.

With a swirl of his cape, Joe approached the driver. 'Albert Moore? Joe Sandilands . . . how d'ye do? Glad to see you're on hand, sarge! Your Miss Lily's had quite an evening. And so, it would seem, have you.' He leaned forward, elbows on the lowered window, and said confidentially: 'But it's not over yet, I'm afraid. Look – could you take her back to Bruton Street and then on to the Yard? And see our girl doesn't fall asleep on the back seat. We need her fresh, alert and firing on all cylinders. National emergency on our hands tonight!'

Fresh and alert? Lily paused at the door of the ops room at five minutes to three. Was that how she was feeling? Unexpectedly – yes. She'd got her second wind. A strong cup of coffee from the hands of Aunt Phyl, who'd waited up, had sharpened her wits.

She'd been glad of the older woman's understanding comments. And her brevity. 'Back there again? Must be urgent. No – don't tell me yet. Save it for breakfast. It'll be a late one – it's a Sunday. Glad to see the dress has survived the evening intact. I'm assuming the same condition for you, love. I've ironed your skirt and put out a fresh blouse and bloomers. Bacon sandwich? No? A bath, then?

230

You've just got time. Use the Yardley's lavender. That'll spruce you up a treat.'

Smelling sweetly, freshly uniformed, shiny faced, Lily knocked and entered, to find that the men were already in place. All rose politely to their feet. Five pairs of eyes watched her as she came in, some inquisitive, some hostile. Sandilands and Fanshawe were still in evening dress, the outer layers removed, collars discreetly loosened, waistcoats unbuttoned. The other three were in their smart city suits ready for the day.

'Right on time, constable. We've saved you a place over there.' Sandilands greeted her with an expansive gesture. He indicated a seat opposite him at the end of the table.

'Settle down, everyone. Now – Miss Wentworth, I don't believe you've met our James Bacchus, have you?'

Sensing that there was no time for a formal presentation, the Branch man and the constable nodded cordially at each other across the table. Lily registered quiet dark eyes above a large nose and a top lip so exuberantly moustached she had the impression that a small but hairy rodent had climbed aboard his upper lip and gone to sleep there. She found she was smiling at him and receiving a raised eyebrow in return.

'Now then – we all know who we are, I believe? You'll remember Miss Wentworth? And you know why she's here. First I'll update you on the Prince of Wales. He is safely back in his London home, unscathed, and will tomorrow be whisked away to the country – to an as yet undisclosed location – to stay with friends. The press will publish the usual false information concerning his whereabouts.' He cocked an eyebrow at Bacchus, who nodded confirmation. 'And, to go on – it's likely we are contemplating a case of murder. We await the post-mortem report, of course, but according to the medical authority who was present at the scene, the victim died of poisoning. Potassium cyanide.'

The Branch men pursed their lips. A heavy silence fell.

231

Wondering at this sudden paralysis, Lily was struck by a sudden insight and kicked herself for not having made the deduction earlier: she was the only person at the table who was not feeling some measure of doubt and self-recrimination. Her excitement must have dulled her perceptions. Tonight, a man had fallen dead under their very noses and his death would have to be explained. As would the apparently fortuitous escape of the Prince of Wales. Someone would have to tell His Royal Highness how close he had come to a sudden and agonizing end. That the man he had witnessed writhing in agony at his feet was his stand-in.

Not only was there a crime to be solved, there was negligence to be accounted for. Blame to be assigned. And – here it was again – a career to be lost.

Which of these men would end the evening taking the blame? She calculated that whoever emerged as scapegoat would have the doubtful comfort of being accompanied into the wilderness by Sandilands – if the commander stuck to his form of shouldering responsibility. Hopkirk and Chappel, though evidently concerned, were most probably in the clear, she concluded, guided by her scanty knowledge of police politics. This had not been a CID operation. At all events, two of these five officers would not survive the night, Lily reckoned. Sandilands and . . . ? She glanced around the stony faces and came to a sad conclusion.

Her selected candidate looked up at that moment, caught her eye, caught her thought, and scowled.

'The question is – was the Serbian prince, Gustavus, the intended victim or did he barge in and accidentally consume poison meant for our own Prince of Wales? We must consider both possibilities. Either way, this is a task for the Branch. The dead man was a foreigner of doubtful origin and uncertain political leanings – you have a file on him, Bacchus?'

'We have, sir. I'll pass around a few copies for information.'

At this point, Lily, to her embarrassment, found that she'd raised her hand to catch teacher's attention. Someone failed to repress a scoffing grunt.

'Yes, Wentworth?'

'The victim's wife confided to me in the powder room that he is ... was ... "an impostor", sir. That's the exact word she used. I questioned her usage and she confirmed that she meant what she said.'

'Interesting. Possible impersonation. Are we surprised? Lot of that sort of thing about in London town these days. Impostor, eh? We'll take this up again with the Princess Zinia, whoever *she* may be. Takes one to know one, possibly. I'm aware that these jokers tend to work in pairs. Let's admit, gentlemen – it would be greatly to our advantage if we could reveal the so-called Prince Gustavus to be a charlatan.' He smiled round the table. 'Even better if his evening suit should prove to have something interesting in the lining ... like a slender garotting wire or a slim package of some white powder. Yes, Bacchus, a path worth pursuing. See what you can come up with.'

Bacchus gave a wry grimace in response and made a note.

'And we're considering the attempted assassination of a member of our own royal family. This also is in your purview, Bacchus. We'll only get to the bottom of it by establishing just how the poison was administered. We'll trace the events backwards. Rupert – you and I were sitting right there at the table when the Serbian succumbed. Much to our discredit. Miss Wentworth was, at the crucial time, performing her duty down below in the ladies' room, and only surfaced to witness the last moments of the tragedy. Rupert, I want you to give the company an idea of what transpired.'

A knock at the door sent them all silent. A constable entered with a large brown envelope in his hand. 'Sir, a newsman called in at reception. He said you'd be needing these. Top priority, he said.'

'Indeed! Thank you, constable. Leave it on the table, would you?'

Sandilands opened the envelope and spent some moments inspecting the contents. 'As good as police efforts,' he commented. 'No – better. We'll start by reminding ourselves of the evening's work – here's a photograph of the POW at the start of the proceedings, safely in the arms of the Met.' He paused for a moment, studying the print. 'Goodness me! Whatever were you doing with him, Wentworth?'

'A waltz, sir,' Lily confirmed as Cyril's deliberately glamorous photograph circulated to astonished stares from the CID men.

'And he survives to waltz another day – let's keep that in mind. And here's a useful shot of the company at the table before the event.' He paused, absorbed by the next subject. 'Followed by a society pose showing our victim – scarred cheek, shifty grin – in the close and apparently friendly company of the POW.'

Rupert shuddered. 'We should have picked him up and marched him straight out, sir. We sat there and watched.'

'Your anxiety is shared, Fanshawe. But remember Gustavus was there at the Prince of Wales's invitation. Let's not indulge in unwarranted breast-beating; we were reacting to the social demands of the situation. This is not a police state. Our role is to advise and protect. We do not pick up and march out a gentleman who has been invited to seat himself at the prince's table. We had both arrived at the same assessment: that there was no threat to the Prince of Wales's well-being. Gustavus was unarmed. He'd been searched. He was surrounded by security officers – one false move and he'd have been rendered harmless. And he knew that. Rather tormented us with his heavy-footed humour on that score. He was revelling in the attention, you'd say. And enjoying cosying up to the prince.'

'Sir!' Lily spoke swiftly. 'Again, his wife has an explanation. No sinister political motive involved – she claimed that he was seeking proximity for purposes of social aggrandizement. He just wanted his photo in the press . . . posing with the prince, on the front page of the society journals.'

Rupert groaned. 'They *will* do it! I'll make that steward account for the bulge in his back pocket.'

Sandilands nodded and carried on. 'Now here's a view of the table as it was at the moment Prince Gustavus sank gargling from view on the far side. The plates and glasses – I want you to consider them. The contents have been bagged and bottled and are at present at the lab undergoing the usual tests. Rupert – take us through it.'

'The far side, where you see a half-full glass of wine, was the POW's place. Next to him, on his right hand, where you see an empty glass, was the place Miss Wentworth had originally occupied. In her absence, Gustavus, finding the effort of shouting in Serbian from his original place over the table too demanding, had sidled round, taking his glass with him, and plonked himself in Wentworth's vacated seat. He had previously turned down offers to have food fetched but had consumed a quantity of wine.'

Sandilands took over. 'Aided in his consumption by the copious amounts poured out for him by Fanshawe here. What exactly were you hoping to achieve by that, Fanshawe?'

'I thought I'd achieved my end, sir.' Fanshawe's tone was truculent and resentful. 'I was trying to incapacitate the ghastly fellow. He tried several times to reveal secrets he ought never to have been in possession of. You heard him. Miss Wentworth may have branded him an impostor – whatever she means by that *Boy's Own Paper* designation – but he showed a certain depth of knowledge of our services' operations. Showing off for the prince, of course, but there were other receptive ears in the neighbourhood. It seemed the only way of silencing him. No one believes a word uttered by a man in his cups. Rendering the subject harmless, sir, that's what I was doing. As no one else seemed about to take it upon himself,' he added rebelliously. 'It was hardly believable, the gross behaviour the man exhibited, but he caught sight of Miss Wentworth's full plate – she had to my notice not attempted so much as a forkful – and began to dig in. He clearly couldn't resist the red caviar – he started with that.'

Inspector Chappel grimaced. 'Well, they say that Rasputin of theirs had the table manners of a hog and the appetite of a brown bear. Must be the cold winters that do it.'

'Not immediately, but several forkfuls later, in mid-sentence, mouth still full of food, he keeled over.' Rupert pushed on with his account. 'Choking, red in the face, unable to breathe, clutching his heart. All the symptoms of a heart attack or cyanide poisoning.'

'And I can confirm the latter. In attempting to resuscitate him, I'm sure I detected a strong scent of almonds on his breath,' Sandilands said.

'Sir, one of the dishes – the fricassee of Persian lamb – had almonds amongst its ingredients,' Lily offered.

'As well as all the spices of the orient. As good a way as any of disguising the scent of cyanide. I took some of that dish myself. Like many others now snoring peacefully in their beds,' he added thoughtfully. 'So – by mistakenly eating from *Miss Wentworth's* plate, the Serbian signed his death warrant.'

'Er . . . No chance, I suppose, that anyone would be targeting Miss Wentworth herself?' Chappel asked sheepishly. 'I know, I know – it sounds ridiculous, but training makes me bring it forward. Purposes of elimination and all that . . . clear out the underbrush. She was the one who was handed the poisoned plate, after all. Got to consider it!'

'A reasonable thought, Chappel . . .' Rupert Fanshawe allowed, 'if we must plod every tedious inch of the pedestrian way to the truth. But – and this will come as a surprise to you fellows – Miss Wentworth was *not*, in fact, the one who was handed the poisoned plate.'

He waited for the astonished stares then carried on, his voice purring with anticipation: 'And, as long as the spotlight's on the constable, may I suggest we follow up with a further reasonable thought? We should remind ourselves that what we are seeking in all this is a malign female presence. An unknown woman on assassination bent. Our Morrigan.' He turned a sweet smile on Lily. 'Now, Miss Wentworth was the woman closest to the Prince of Wales from beginning to abrupt end and she had continuous access to him. We, gentlemen, had placed our prince in the hands of a stranger for the whole evening. A stranger to him . . . a stranger to *us*. Can any one of us claim to know who she is? Where she comes from? Who precisely stands as her guarantor? Oh, I am much to blame. I should have taken immediate action.' He shook his head to underline his self-recrimination. 'If only I had acted in accordance with my training and arrested Miss Wentworth the moment it became clear that her behaviour at the buffet was suspicious, we could have avoided a murder.'

'Eh? What are you on about?' Lily murmured.

'Suspicious behaviour? Describe it, Fanshawe.' Sandilands was peremptory.

Fanshawe enjoyed the incredulity for a moment. 'I watched as the food was being put out. I watched as Wentworth followed the prince to a table. There she snatched his plate from him and replaced it with her own. Oh, it was neatly done. But the movement was not in the briefing. It exceeded instructions. It was surreptitious and possibly suspect. We were at the ball to prevent a young woman – a young woman with certain social graces – "Mayfair", I believe, was the Assistant Commissioner's judgement – from getting close enough to the prince to kill him. And here was one such sitting by his side and forcing the food *of her choice* on the prince with all the skill of a music-hall card sharp. She could easily have anointed the

237

oysters with something nasty held in her hand. If I'd made a fuss and had both plates taken away at that moment, the poison would have been discovered there and then. And Prince Gustavus would still be alive. You have my unqualified apology, sir.'

Rupert drooped then raised his head in defiance. He swept his floppy blond quiff off his forehead, the better to stun them with his blue eyes ablaze with an emotion which clearly anticipated a coming martyrdom. 'I'm ready to accept whatever proportion of blame you care to assign to me, sir.' And he added coldly into the shocked silence: 'After you've chucked the book at Wentworth.'

Lily shivered, devastated by the implications. The two plates had been exactly alike. If Fanshawe had proceeded with the scheme he'd just outlined there was every chance the plates would have been confused on their way to the laboratory. Intentionally or accidentally. Who would ever know? She wouldn't have been able to distinguish them herself. Both carried her fingerprints and those of the prince. Accusations would have been made. From what they'd stitched together of her background she knew they could make a spectacularly convincing case against her. 'Left-wing, anti-royalist, worms her way into the Royal Presence . . .' Poison was known to be a woman's choice of weapon.

A pit of horror opened up before her. If they were seeking an easy suspect to cover for their incompetence, she would find herself occupying a cell in Vine Street within the hour. She looked instinctively to the commander for support.

Her appeal went unacknowledged. He was watching Fanshawe, head on one side, quizzical, encouraging him to go further. It occurred to her – and the realization hit her like a thump in the stomach – that for these men, all of whom had a position to lose, the career, the life even, of a lowly woman policeman on the point of leaving the service anyway would count for little. She was expendable. They were officers. Ex-military. It was men of their kind who'd sent out Tommies to die in their thousands on the Somme. She too was no more than cannon fodder.

She'd been sitting here playing eeny meeny miney mo, choosing the unlucky victim, never thinking to enter her own name in the draw. If these five men were to behave in concert she was ruined. And there was every sign that, with Sandilands acting as ringmaster, they were coming to an understanding.

Coming to? These were men trained to think and plan weeks and years ahead. The chilling thought came to her that the understanding might have been arrived at some time ago, an undeclared Plan B. If all else fails, look to a scapegoat. Once again she felt the presence of the sacrificial altar and the raised knife.

Lily locked stares with Fanshawe, grasping for words to attempt a defence. Finding none.

But Rupert hadn't finished with her yet. Urged on by Sandilands' attention, he enlarged on his theory. 'And the lady, according to our information, is not exactly a wearer of the white cockade! Oh, she has no overt affiliations with the *red* organizations rampant in the country . . . one would hardly expect it in someone planning a serious coup. But her father is known to be a Bolshevist sympathizer.' He passed a sheet of paper to Sandilands. 'We've been enquiring. Not much time available to us but we have strong sources among the red brothers . . . and sisters. I hand you a list we've got together of meetings attended, associates and acquaintances established.'

Rupert gave an elegant shudder as Sandilands scanned his offering. 'And this is the background of the woman, the stranger, whom we allowed to enter the ballroom unsearched, unchallenged . . . the woman we allowed to juggle with the prince's plate.' His voice expressed disgust and anger in equal measure. 'I'm only surprised we didn't issue her with the latest dinky little pistol to hide in her garter. I'm sure she's an excellent shot too.'

A horrified silence descended on the group.

Sandilands' tone, when he began to speak, was, in contrast, light and controlled: 'You forget to add to your list of notable accomplishments that the constable is also an adept at the dark arts of eastern combat, Fanshawe. I've seen her break a fellow's nose by smashing his head against a station platform. She could have snapped the royal neck at any moment as easily as you or I had she been murderously inclined. But what about an Irish connection? Anything known to Miss Wentworth's detriment on this score?'

'I have to say that we could find no trace of Irish connections,' Rupert admitted resentfully.

'I'm sure you tried your hardest,' Sandilands said. 'I'm wondering why you held off from escorting Miss Wentworth from the premises and throwing her into the deepest dungeon, Rupert. Help us to understand why you didn't react.'

'It was swiftly done and I was on the other side of the room, waiting for Connie Beauclerk to decide between duck and grouse. By the time I got to them, the prince had already made inroads into his food. A difficult moment. I observed that Miss Wentworth was not attempting to eat her own and this she would surely have done – as cover – had she secured for herself an unadulterated sample. Confusing, I think you'll agree?' He looked round the table for support but was met on all sides by the hard stares of men each of whom thought he would have reacted with more panache. 'Well, before I could decide on the action I should take, along comes the wretched, interfering Gustavus, shoving his oar in. So the moment passed. I let it go. But I watched her, and the plates, carefully.'

Around the table air was sucked in through gritted teeth at this admission. Eyes were averted, heads lowered, as they considered the catalogue of negligence. The swift fall of the axe was deserved and awaited.

'Mmm . . . Let's be clear. You sat watching the prince – our prince – eating from a plate you suspected might have been tampered with. I wonder at what point you would have advised him to put down his fork? Before or after the death rattle? I think, as well as indecision, you must have been suffering some puzzlement, Fanshawe.' Sandilands' voice was a tormenting drawl. 'As the evening proceeded His Royal Highness did not fall dead, frothing at the mouth. He continued to chat and called for his pavlova pudding.'

He paused, deep in thought. No one dared interrupt. 'I offer you an alternative scenario. The food may well have been untainted. Heat – as the good doctor told us – vaporizes the poison and renders cooked food containing it harmless. So we would be looking at the uncooked dishes – caviar for example. No other caviar eater succumbed. Is it not possible that the poison – if poison it was – was not administered by plate at all, but by the far less chancy route of the wine glass?

'All those glasses of wine you poured out, Fanshawe? From the bottle? Easy enough for a smart operator like yourself to dispense a noxious substance with which he is very familiar and to which he has easy access through his employment. The death capsules. I'm sure you have been issued with one or two? I must ask you to do a little stock-taking, Bacchus. Account for Fanshawe's hand-out, would you? Your job is largely of a secretive nature and has been known on occasion to require a certain readiness to get one's hands dirty. How dirty is your pouring hand, Fanshawe, after tonight's events? You were holding both glass and bottle. Easy enough to hold a broken capsule at the neck of the bottle and remove it when you've spiked a particular glass. If so, it was, as you'd say, neatly done. And I would expect nothing less of a man of your training. I must say I observed nothing untoward myself and I was watching closely.' His words were unemphatic but Fanshawe's lips tightened. 'Though I wouldn't rule out the possibility . . . not when a clearly inimical and dangerous man is about to spill information the Branch would kill to keep quiet.'

Fanshawe was unable to speak. Bacchus made an offended grunting sound. The CID men maintained a mystified silence.

Only one voice was raised in objection. Lily managed to splutter: 'Sir! That's barmy! It's unfair. How can you say that? Sorry, sir, but Fanshawe wouldn't . . . he couldn't . . .'

'Wentworth, he would and he could if the circumstances demanded it,' Joe explained kindly. 'Now – barmy, you say? Quite agree. Unfair? Completely. So let's all relax and be sensible, shall we? Enough villains out and about to blame for this fiasco – absolutely no need to go looking for anyone nearer home, Rupert old man. I think we need at this stage to consider the prince's plate again. Yes, I think it would enlighten us all if you were to account for the sleight of hand with the plates, Miss Wentworth,' he suggested. 'It worried Fanshawe and it worries me. Clear up our confusion will you?'

'Instinct, sir.' Seeing both Sandilands' eyebrows shoot up, she hurried to add: 'Sorry . . . that's unclear. Say rather I was being over cautious. I know your agent was right there at the scene and she "tipped him the wink", as the prince himself put it, indicating that all was well as she ladled out the food. I saw her do it. Her eyes made contact with mine too. She knew who I was. "One of Sandilands'," the prince told me. But all the same, in spite of the reassurance, I had a feeling that—'

'Wait a minute, Wentworth. Just go back a bit. Agent? What agent?'

'The waitress who was putting out the food. There were two of them, a boy and a girl. Brother and sister, I think. Italian. Or putting on a convincing accent.'

'Anything to do with you, Bacchus?'

'No, sir. You had our list. All four of our operatives were men. We only use English males. You know that.'

'Get them in for interview first thing tomorrow morning. Describe her behaviour, Wentworth.'

'She wasn't behaving surreptitiously, sir. She had rather a flamboyant way with her. Pretty girl as far as I could make out under the frilly headdress. She picked up a plate, one of those special Russian top-table-only-for-the-use-of ones. Those with the double-headed eagle on them. She ran a cloth over it in a marked manner. You know – rather like a conjurer showing the audience there's nothing up his sleeve. She seemed to be declaring that all was well, impeccably clean plate, no need for any concern. I'll show you.' Lily got to her feet and demonstrated. 'She was serving the gentlemen. Didn't you see her yourself, sir?'

'No. She'd disappeared by the time I shuffled to the head of the line. There were several men waiting on by then. No girl. Bacchus, get Honeysett on the telephone. He'll still be up.'

They kept a polite silence while Bacchus went through the procedure of being connected to the hotel. Slim, strong and urgent of voice, the Branch man exuded enough energy to power the London telephone system if you could have wired him in, Lily thought, admiring. Not surprisingly he was put through the channels at speed even at that hour.

'We have the hotel reception . . . They're paging him now . . .

'So that's how they . . . she . . . did it,' Bacchus commented while he waited, one hand carefully over the speaking section of the receiver. 'The prince was handed a plate smeared with cyanide. One gram of the stuff isn't hard to deposit. A broken capsule held in a clean white napkin, dripping poison. We've run tests on our own capsules. In extremis a chap needs to be able to count on his equipment. The scent is strong but would have blended with that of the other exotic spices coming from the food.'

'Sir – the prince asked for plain salmon but the waitress talked him into accepting the more highly spiced dishes,' Lily said.

'And "on instinct" you snatched the poisoned dish from him and sat there with it in front of you for a good part of the evening, Wentworth. While the prince tucked in to a blameless offering. Um ... Some might say your action was inspired by a blend of shrewd calculation, keen awareness and sound defensive play.' Sandilands spoke slowly, his eyes on Fanshawe. 'Rupert, you have something to say?' he asked, in the kindly but reproving tone of a schoolmaster.

It was a moment before Fanshawe could come up with a response. 'Only that it would seem the constable and her instinct saved the life of one prince and killed another, sir. I'm sorry for entertaining any suspicions of your motives, Miss Wentworth.' The supercilious glint in his eye as he sketched a mock bow across the table gave the lie to his sentiments.

'Thank you for the apology, Fanshawe, but, really, no need. We were both doing our job as best we could.' Lily managed to keep her voice unemotional. 'And neither of us killed anyone.'

'No indeed,' said Sandilands. 'You both have a clear conscience. Gustavus was killed accidentally. Let's hang on to that, shall we? His death was triggered by his own greed. The coarser spirits among us might even think he was the author of his own misfortune.'

Chappel grinned. 'As the coarsest spirit here I'll second that! Serve the blighter right!'

'So, while we're awaiting post-mortem reports and evidence from the hotel management and our agents in place, we must look again at this elusive woman. A killer who passes easily in Mayfair society – and now, it would appear, in Mayfair kitchens – as she works her lethal way through the list of IRA targets.'

'Targets. I think in this company' – Bacchus glanced round the table, his eye lingering on Lily for a moment – 'we may say their names out loud, don't you agree?' He voiced everyone's agitation. The Branch man was also, Lily realized, making a gesture of inclusion to her. 'The two names remaining. We assume Miss Morrigan will have her eye on Churchill and Prime Minister Lloyd George next?'

'Seems likely. The prince has gone into such deep cover I don't think even I could find him with a map, a compass and a pack of bloodhounds,' Sandilands said lightly.

His ironic eye skipped swiftly over her as he enjoyed a tension-breaking laugh with the rest of the table and she knew at once that he was lying. Sandilands could have the prince on the telephone in seconds, she guessed. Lily wondered if the men could read him with equal ease and thought, judging by their open and cheerful response, probably not.

'Sir! I've got hold of Honeysett . . . Honeysett, hold the line, will you? I'm passing you to the commander.'

Sandilands strode to the telephone. 'Glad to find you're still up and doing, Honeysett. Now listen. You're to come in to the Yard first thing tomorrow to make a statement. Present yourself at reception. First – a question: can you give me the name and address of the girl who was serving the buffet supper?'

He listened to the answer and called out to the table: 'Anna Peterson.'

Pens scratched on notepads.

'Living at . . . in lodgings at forty-two, Hogsmire Lane, Kensington. Russian immigrant. Working for you for six weeks . . . References, Honeysett? . . . Mmm . . . impressive. I shall need to see them. Bring them with you tomorrow, will you? . . . What was that! Stomach ache? Left the premises at what time? Eleven?' Sandilands rolled his eyes at the assembly. 'One more question for the moment. Where was this lady on the evening of the first of September? . . . Yes, it was a Wednesday . . . Morning shift and she left you at three p.m.? And you've no knowledge of her life outside the hotel?'

He finished the phone call and returned to the table, sombre and puzzled.

'Another woman done a bunk, has she? Irish? Russian? Are we fighting on two fronts now? Who the hell *are* we looking for?' Hopkirk was exasperated.

'Same one? At all events, someone who can pass as a Russian to gain access . . . someone who has inside knowledge of the prince's movements weeks in advance . . .'

'But why would a Russian . . . ?' Chappel spluttered. 'They're relations of the prince, aren't they? The Tsar, God rest his soul, was the spitting image of his cousin, our own King George. People couldn't tell them apart! Best of friends. That posh lot at the ball tonight would never have the Prince of Wales in their sights. White Russians – monarchists to a man. They'd die defending the English cousin's boy. Wouldn't they?'

'You're right, Inspector. A Russian would make no such attempt,' Sandilands said. 'But we're looking for a lady who, as you say, knew well in advance that the prince would attend this do. A lady determined enough to obtain and perform work for weeks in advance in a hotel kitchen.'

'Taking orders from Honeysett,' Lily murmured. 'That shows a certain single-mindedness.'

'What it shows is stamina,' Hopkirk interrupted. 'I've seen hotel kitchens. Not places for the faint hearted and gently bred. She'll be a strong lass, then!'

'Indeed. And she's able to pass as Russian. I think we may be looking for an actress. Someone who can use a variety of convincing accents to approach her prey. A stalker, a hunter. Skilled at blending in with her background.'

'A sower of discord and a spreader of mayhem,' said Hopkirk. 'What's her score to date? From where we started counting, that is,' he added lugubriously. 'And we may be swinging in a little after the beat. Three dead, as far as we know: an admiral, a London bobby and a Serbian prince; and two critically injured: the butler and the cabby. A bloody-handed goddess of death and destruction. She's a Morrigan, all right.'

Lily's voice interrupted the descending gloom. 'Sir. One thing we might try ... I think someone ought to have a word with Princess Ratziatinsky.'

'Would you like to undertake that task yourself, Wentworth? I was going to tell you to take the day off tomorrow ... that is to say – today ... but if you feel like it ... Good. I'll give you the address and ring ahead to make an appointment. It's not far – somewhere in Kensington. I'll try for midday. She won't be receiving before that hour, I should imagine. Not after the night she's had.'

'Will the princess appreciate a police presence on her doorstep, sir?' Bacchus wanted to know. 'In her aristocratic quarter of town? On a Sunday morning?'

'Almost certainly not. Mufti, Wentworth. Put a little frock on. Assume you're front-door calling company. Do you have a calling card? No? I think we can provide. Bacchus? That forger of yours? That idiosyncratic printer over whose dubious production skills we have at times exercised a little influence?'

'Sam? Got out six months ago. And, yes, he's still on the hook.'

'Good. Get him out of bed and give him a rush order. Our own press won't be up and running until nine.' Sandilands scribbled a note and passed it to Bacchus.

'Now, Wentworth. What were you planning to ask the princess?'

'I shall ask her to give me a name, sir. She'll have kept a list of all the people who attended last night.'

Someone sighed in irritation; someone bent to adjust his sock. Joe asked patiently: 'But why, constable? We have such a list ourselves. You can confirm, Bacchus?'

'Yes, sir. We can produce it right here and now. If you think it of interest. All vetted by the Branch. MI1b has gone over it with a magnifying glass ... MI1c raked through it with a fine-tooth comb. The foreign secretary has a copy on his bedside table next to his bible. But if you'd like to pass it before Miss Wentworth, I'll certainly hand it to her. For the purposes of checking it against her instinct, perhaps?'

Joe saw Lily flinch and decided to neutralise the Branch man's sarcasm. 'A quality that served us better than glass and comb and British intelligence this evening, I'm thinking,' he said ruefully. 'You were saying, Miss Wentworth?'

Lily shook her head to clear her thoughts and, having got a hold on them, addressed them to Bacchus. 'No. Listen a minute! It's not the people who were there that we're interested in. We need to see the princess's *original* pencilled-in list of guests. The names she first thought of. And check that against the final attendance list. If this girl *is* Russian and has the confidence to attempt a coup with such swagger, then it's likely that she would be known to this society, isn't it? An insider? One of them. She'd have been invited all right. What it would be intriguing to find is the name of someone who failed to turn up or who refused the invitation. Someone who was not there to be blamed. An unaccountable absence. We're looking for someone who *didn't* make an appearance at the ball.' She realized she was repeating herself, sounding over anxious. She ground to a halt.

'Ah!' said Hopkirk with a rumbling laugh. 'Now I've got it. I was thrashing about in the wrong fairy tale. It's the Bad Fairy we're looking for.'

'Or a Bolshevik aristocrat?' grumbled Chappel. 'No such animal!'

'Like "darkness visible",' agreed Bacchus. 'An oxymoronic and quite ridiculous invention. Looks a teeny bit desperate, I'd say.' He shrugged his shoulders.

'Well, if the constable cares to waste her morning scanning party lists . . . hobnobbing with the princess . . . comparing hemlines and dancing partners . . .' Fanshawe had found his voice again. He oozed on, decorating his theme: '. . . chirruping over a samovar of tea and a dish of Viennese pastries . . . well, that's up to her. Who shall say her nay?'

'You make the occasion sound quite delightful, Fanshawe. Hadn't realized that was your idea of a Sunday morning's entertainment. Are you volunteering?' Joe asked cheerfully. 'No? Then I say Wentworth shall go.'

'Beats pounding the streets, I will allow,' nodded Bacchus. The Branch man turned to Lily and favoured her with one of his rare smiles. Or at least she took the movement in the region of his mouth to be a smile, though the vigorous twitch of the upper lip could as easily have been an attempt to dislodge the sleeping rodent. There was no mistaking the accompanying flash of even white teeth: it held all the challenge of a metal gauntlet thrown at her feet.

Lily thought she had very likely made two implacable enemies before breakfast.

Chapter Twenty-Six

The smell of egg, bacon and black pudding frying and the clatter of a teapot lid brought Lily yawning and sniffing back into the world.

'Seems a shame to wake you up, ducks, after five hours' sleep but you did say ten o'clock sharp.' Auntie Phyl was in her apron and enjoying having someone at home to treat to a lavish breakfast. 'Here – scramble into this dressing gown and come straight through to the kitchen. Bacon's just as you like it – nice and crozzled.'

They ate at the scrubbed deal table. Phyl had domestic help these days but the staff were dismissed at weekends. Never idle, she liked to polish and repair and cook for herself. Lily struggled with her fry-up in silence, hoping Phyl wouldn't expect a full account of her evening until her head cleared.

Phyl was happy to chatter on regardless. 'Well, you didn't quite come clean about your boss, did you, sly-boots? Albert had quite a bit to say – for Albert – when he got back. "Every bit the gent . . . nice man . . . well set up and polite" was his verdict. And Albert's a good judge. Has to be in his line of work. Nothing known to Sandilands' disadvantage from the war years . . . quite the opposite, in fact. I've had him followed. He lives alone in a flat down in Chelsea. No distractions, apparently – works every hour God sends.'

'Sounds too good to be true, are we thinking?'

'Perhaps. Further and better particulars needed, I'd say. No one's *that* innocent. And your bloke's a busy bee too – was he up all night? These came for you – special messenger – an hour ago. I looked. Calling cards. Here you are. I've put them in a case for you because I don't expect you have one.'

Lily had almost forgotten. She took out a card from the silver case she was being offered and examined it.

'There's a dozen, that's all. Not the usual gross, so you're not intended to go scattering them like birdseed . . . or have them for long,' Phyl noted. 'Look at them. Best quality card, embossed, straight edge not deckle and lovely copperplate. Best of taste. And the wording's interesting too. Odd, but interesting. I didn't realize I'd be entertaining an "Honourable" this morning. I'd have swapped the black pudding and tea for kedgeree and Buck's Fizz if I'd known. So this is who you are now: the Honourable Lily Wentworth. No address, but you have a telephone number. And what a number! Whitehall 1212 and an extension number which I assume is . . .'

'Sandilands' office, of course. One of these is meant to get me access to a Russian princess this morning. A passport over the front doorstep. These are my business cards, I suppose you'd say. It's a cheat. Not sure I can go through with all this. It makes me uncomfortable.'

'Go on! It's being a load of fun. Stick with it, if only to entertain your old auntie.'

'Phyl, it's not a barrel of laughs,' Lily muttered. 'I saw someone die last night . . . poisoned. And the corpse could easily have been mine.' She went to put the kettle on again. 'This is going to be a two-pot story.'

The butler was elderly, English and intimidating. His glassy eyes swept her discreetly from head to foot, seeing and assessing while appearing, with the knack only butlers and royalty have, of keeping their subject discreetly out of focus. He allowed himself a well-judged sniff of disdain in response to her yellow print cotton frock. The

251

three-year-old straw hat elicited a twitch of the left corner of his mouth. Without her card, she guessed she would have been instantly sent round to the tradesmen's entrance where an interview for would-be parlour maids might be on offer from the housekeeper. The butler studied the card she gave him and could find no reason to object to it. Nor to the accent in which she spoke the lines Sandilands had prepared her to deliver.

'Good morning, Foxton. I'm here to see Her Highness. I believe Commander Sandilands has made an appointment.'

'Yes, indeed he has, miss. You are expected. If you will follow me? The ladies are still in the morning room.'

She padded after him through a spacious marble-tiled hallway and down a corridor hung with paintings of a quality that risked distracting her. She took a deep breath as he opened a door and announced her. 'Miss Wentworth of White Hall to see you, Your Highness.' With a butler's tongue-in-cheek tact, he had managed in two syllables to turn the formidable police headquarters into a genteel grand house.

'Miss Wentworth! I'm delighted you could come – and so swiftly after the recent events. I'm told you bring news of the prince.' The princess was smiling a welcome. Her voice was a throaty rumble but her English was perfect and, Lily guessed, her first language. She turned to the two young women who were sitting at a table covered in piles of envelopes, notes and cards. They got up eagerly and came forward in age order. They were both in their early twenties and both had dark hair and eyes, but Lily didn't think they were sisters. The older one had a dreamy, rounded face and an easy smile; the other had a quizzical stare and a mouth that seemed ready to laugh.

'Eirene, Sasha, may I present Lily Wentworth who was our guest last night? You may remember seeing her in the company of His Royal Highness. And she is, among many things, the cousin of Sandilands who visited the other day. Miss Wentworth, you will observe, comes to us *under*

252

cover ... Is that the right term?' Her eye lingered mean-
ingfully on Lily's yellow print washing frock and slightly
battered hat, and her two companions laughed nervously.

Lily lowered her voice to a conspiratorial tone and murmured: 'It's a Sunday. Maid's Day Off. I blend in with the
promenaders.' In her imagination she heard her father
splutter his outrage as her grandfather, with a dry rustle of
bones, turned in his grave. With a rebellious flourish, she
took off her hat and shook out her hair.

'Ah! Now I remember! It's the girl in the green dress,'
murmured Eirene. 'The wonderful dancer! We all said ...
didn't we, Sasha?'

The two younger Russians were wearing heavily
embroidered silk kaftans, ankle length and unconstricting.
They seemed to have been dealing with correspondence, so
Lily gathered they were both resident in the house. Family
or friends and clearly going nowhere for the moment.
Their presence in the room was inconvenient.

Formal introductions were completed. The ladies
seemed intrigued and pleasantly scandalized to be in the
presence of a working woman and a woman policeman
at that.

Sasha recovered more quickly than the placid Eirene.
'Lily,' she said, calling her firmly by her first name, 'you're
very convincing. I'm only surprised you got past Foxton!
And I would know about being convincing. When I
escaped from Russia my disguises were every bit as effective. I became quite the expert. You're to come to me if you
need any advice on dissimulation. I've travelled a thousand miles being a peasant, a baker's daughter, a
babushka, a cavalryman ... I've sliced off my hair and
kicked off my heels. But the best part of it all was – no
corsets! Oh, the joy of leaving them off! I haven't put one
on again since!' She wriggled her slim shoulders under the
silk wrapper and sighed with satisfaction.

'And now Mademoiselle Chanel offers us all the same
freedom,' Lily agreed. She didn't believe a word of this

manicured and soignée little butterfly's fairy story but she liked her insouciance.

'But let me warn you.' Sasha's roguish glint faded and her expression became more stern. A finger was raised and she wagged it at Lily. 'As one actress to another. The moment you find the role you are playing more comforting, more alluring, or just more stimulating than the one you were born to – you are lost. Cast adrift for ever on a sea of dissatisfaction.'

'No need to worry about me,' Lily replied as lightly as she could. 'Dancing with a prince was good fun but I shouldn't much care to have to do it every day. Be on my best behaviour every moment? Apologise every time I stepped on the royal toe? No. I'd rather put on corsets again.'

'You choose to mistake my meaning.' Sasha's bright eyes were full of knowledge and Lily tried not to look away. 'Good. I conclude that you are aware of the true danger.'

Only too well aware, Lily decided the moment had come to pull this interview back into line. She caught the eye of the princess and remembered her instructions. 'But I've come, as you say, with news of the prince – that is to say of two princes.' The company became still and attentive. 'The Prince of Wales was in no way harmed, though very distressed, of course, by the events. He's gone into the country to stay with friends for a week or so and has sent his condolences to the widow of Prince Gustavus, who, as you perhaps—'

'Poor Zinia. I have told my friends what happened. You may assume they know as much as I and speak freely in front of them,' the princess intervened.

'It is confirmed that Gustavus died of heart failure.' Lily delivered the lie with all the security of Sandilands' coaching behind her. 'The onset was very sudden. Although an eminent doctor was on hand to render immediate assistance, there was nothing that could be done to save him.'

'Ah. No surprises there. Zinia will have told you, no doubt, my dear, that this is a family weakness.' The princess spoke without emotion. Her words were greeted by understanding nods all round. 'One is sad but not surprised. I was acquainted with the boy's father many years ago. In looks, the son was the image of his father, and, it transpires, he had many of his deficiencies of character. A lying, murdering womanizer,' she said pleasantly. 'The kind the world is better off without. Just as well that the line has a built-in physical flaw . . . they manage to destroy themselves before someone is obliged to do it for them. Ah, here comes our morning coffee. You are able to stay and drink coffee with us?'

A maid entered with a loaded tray, and took in Lily's presence with dismay. Sasha got up and bustled about helping her to find a space on the table. 'Shall I bring another cup, Miss Sasha? I hadn't realized you'd got company.'

Sasha hurried her away with a discreet, 'No, thank you, Katy, that will do. Thank you, my dear. We'll wait on ourselves. You can go now.'

Four delicate cups and saucers of Worcester porcelain, a silver pot, cream and sugar and French madeleines had appeared, Lily noted, pleased that Fanshawe had got it wrong. Though not all his speculations missed their target. Sipping the fragrant coffee and puffing away at Virginia cigarettes, the ladies allowed their affected sadness to give way with surprising speed to gossip and merriment. The hemlines and dancing partners Fanshawe had scathingly conjured up were now, indeed, being trailed before her. Lily was made to tell whether Prince Edward was as good a dancer as was reported. ('As good as my dancing master.' Lily had decided the man had earned a good report.) Was he fun? ('He made me laugh a lot.') Where had Lily come by that wonderful dress? ('Ssh! A secret! Though perhaps I'll leave the address with the princess before I leave.') And who exactly was the fair-haired Adonis to her right . . . sitting at the royal table . . . clean shaven, cleft chin, was he *really* squiring Connie Beauclerk?' ('Rupert

Fanshawe? The most dangerous man in England! You would not want to know him.')

Lily was feeling easy enough in their company to tell them a scandalous story about Rupert Fanshawe that elicited gasps and giggles. A story entirely of her own invention. She hoped it would find its way straight back to the Branch man's ears.

The princess enjoyed the chatter for a while then dismissed the two young women. 'Now, my chickens! You must both go up and change – we're expected at the embassy for lunch, remember. Take your things away with you, will you? I would like a quiet and serious word with Miss Wentworth and I can see I'm not to have the opportunity as long as you pester her for gossip.'

They scuttled off, leaving Lily facing a suddenly shrewd inquisitor.

'Now you can tell me the truth,' the princess said bluntly. 'How did Gustavus die?'

'Cyanide poisoning. Almost indistinguishable from heart—'

'This is understood. And that must be the last mention of the appalling substance. The man died from a congenital heart condition. And largely unmourned. I shall attend the funeral, of course. Thank goodness veils are still in style – I shall find it impossible to squeeze out a tear. As will his wife, the silly girl.'

She took a trinket box from a table, opened it and produced a diamond brooch. 'The fool tried to give this away. To make the correct impression, no doubt. I knew it was Zinia's much-loved jewel that she had from her mother. It would not have been offered for charity with her consent. I arranged for a friend to make a discreet bid and I acquired it. Zinia shall have it back. And the support to start a new life. In Paris perhaps. I think Paris will be good for her. Whether Zinia will be good for Paris is less certain. And now you may tell me why you have come to see me.'

Lily responded with equal succinctness. Her request for

the original guest list was received with no more than the slightest lift of an eyebrow and the princess moved at once to an escritoire. She took a sheet or two of foolscap paper from a drawer, looked over them briefly and brought them to Lily.

'I'll hover at your shoulder,' she said. 'The handwriting is my own and difficult to decipher. Can you tell me for whom you are searching?'

'I'm looking for a name which is here on your first list but not on the lists the Branch men made of arrivals at the ball.' Lily took two sheets from her handbag. 'Here's the cast in order of appearance. And here's another list, with superb efficiency, giving the same names in alphabetical order.'

The princess sighed. 'Two hundred names to consider! But you were right to come to me. I can shorten the task, I believe. The evening was very well attended. It was the society event of the year in the highest circles and there were few indeed who failed to make an appearance. And I am aware of all of them. Two gentlemen, two ladies. Now ... the Duke and Duchess of Sunderland ... here they are, you see, on my list ... did not attend. Elderly couple. He fell off his horse last week and is confined to his estate. Here we have Miss Millicent Gregory (Ludmilla Gregorovich back home in Russia) who found herself unavoidably detained in Paris.' The princess sniffed her disapproval.

'By an Italian tenor?' Lily enquired sympathetically, remembering her aunt's list.

'You have it,' said the princess. 'My word! The Yard is all-knowing.'

'Can you describe Miss Gregory?'

'Pretty as a peony, with half the intelligence. Wet as a worm.' She paused for a moment. 'Ludmilla couldn't brew up a cup of tea let alone administer a dose of cyanide. If it's a poisoner you're looking for in the cracks in these lists, she's not the one.'

A beringed finger pointed to a name near the end of the page. 'And, lastly, here you see the Spanish envoy to the Court of St James. Ah, now there's a handsome villain! He could kill anyone. He's cut a swathe through Europe. Those that don't fall to his charm fall to his knife. I was looking forward to meeting him. But he was envoyed back home last week for bad behaviour more blatant than usual. Can you tell me more precisely what you have in mind?'

'As you suppose, we're looking for the man or woman who poisoned Gustavus, by design or by mistake.'

'But you fear the Prince of Wales was the target? My dear Lily, you've taken leave of your senses. Your prince was never in danger. He was among friends and subjects. He could have raised a squadron of admirers and protectors amongst this company – there was no safer place in England for him to spend the evening. He was as safe as the Pope surrounded by his Swiss Guard! And Edward knew that. That is why, against all advice from your secret services, he felt able to accept the invitation. No – whoever the assassin, I would say he got his man. Though I could wish he hadn't chosen my party as the scene of his crime. Aren't there dark alleys enough in London? So inconsiderate!' The princess gave a grating laugh. '*Mais, quand même* – good luck to him!'

'I think it's in the ancient nature of the assassin to choose a public stage for his coup, isn't it?' Lily suggested. 'And your glittering event would have provided him with an unforgettable backdrop for his effort.'

'Yes, the *hashashin*! You're right. They liked an audience for their dramas. And still do in the modern world. So many men shot and hacked to death in theatres, in arenas, in the course of parades! If one were very naive, one might almost suspect an international conspiracy.'

Lily felt a keen mind at work in the sophisticated woman she was taking into her confidence and decided to press her further. 'Your Highness, we're seeking not a man but a woman, and a woman who may have a connection with the political ambitions, not of your country, but of another.'

'Great heavens! But by whom does she feel threatened – the invincible Britannia? Could you be speaking of the Irish? I've read in the newspapers that ... A Fenian attempt? On poor Edward? Under cover of my party? Oh, I see ... How dare they!' Her outrage swiftly dimmed to foreboding. She shuddered. 'Surely not? Can it have come to this? Such barbarity! France ... Greece ... Russia ... Continents swept by a tide of red, murderous madmen. Incompetent nihilists! Children who break what they do not understand and are incapable of repairing it. Must England suffer the same fate of death and destruction? I had thought it safe from Vandal hands.'

'We have other ways – civilized ways – of managing these things in our country,' was the most neutral comment Lily could come up with.

'Ah, yes. You have Sandilands and his like.' The princess nodded. 'Bastions of law and order. You probably believe that if only there had been a Scotland Yard presence in Sarajevo that day in 1914, a swift arrest would have ensued, the murderer of the archduke would have been instantly popped into the local jail in handcuffs and a convincing and totally consoling cover story put in place. The whole affair dampened down ... war avoided ... millions of lives saved.' Her voice was impatient and pitying. 'I admire your motives but I despair of your naivety. Never! The guns had been manufactured, sold and stockpiled. Armies were standing by, flexing their trigger fingers; commanders were strutting, heads of government were whipping up ancient grievances. The men of Europe were straining for a war. When the will to war is there, one bullet from a madman's gun outweighs years of diplomacy.'

Lily was silent, her heart and her head with the princess as she plunged on with her denunciation: 'And perhaps the will to a further war is gathering already? So soon! Your commander has seen this. I admire him but he is no more than a quixotic boy who has blocked a hole in a crumbling sea-wall with his finger.'

These were Lily's sentiments exactly, so she was surprised to hear herself murmuring: 'Strong finger, though. What would you have him do? See the danger and selfishly run away from it? That is not in his character. That is not in our tradition.'

A cynical bark of laughter greeted this pious but heartfelt assertion.

'My dear Lily! You are too much in awe of your cousin and your country. Sandilands is an admirable man but he serves a selfish mistress. Britannia picks and chooses the causes she espouses and completely without sentimentality. When she meddles in the affairs of a foreign nation, it is always in the pursuit of her own interests.'

'But . . .' Lily was struggling with the need for deference and circumspection which Sandilands had impressed upon her when she would have liked to give her hostess a good earwigging. The princess had gone too far. She had dug deep but she had at last found the vein of patriotism that ran through her English guest. Lily wanted to invoke the generous way Russian refugees had been welcomed into the British capital, the way the British army had stood shoulder to shoulder with the Russians against the Germans, the sacrifices made by young men she had known and still remembered, falling in foreign fields for a cause that was not theirs. She murmured her objections, overawed by the older woman's rank and hobbled by the suspicion that the lady would no doubt be engaged in a telephone conversation with Sandilands the moment Lily had left.

'Russia? A perfect example of Britain's patchy and self-interested involvement! Englishmen were there at the *moment critique* in St Petersburg in their Russian army officers' uniforms and armed with their Webleys to finish off poor, bungling Felix Yussupov's handiwork. Oh, yes, the world was well rid of Rasputin but it was no generous gesture on your part. The British secret service had a very particular reason for silencing him. The maniac was about to succeed in persuading the Tsar that he should order the Russian army to stop fighting on the eastern front and retreat back to Russia. It would have spelled disaster for the Allies. It would have left battalions of Germans suddenly released from action and free to dash over to the western front where they would have finished off the British and French forces. Now that was a pistol shot that saved thousands of lives! I do not criticize. I would have pulled the trigger myself and gladly. But the Tsar? Your King George's own cousin? He asked for asylum in England. His request was refused. Where were your secret service officers when the Tsar needed a passage to safety for himself and his family?'

'It was tried. I'm sure it was tried.' Lily's voice was unconvincing to her own ears.

'It could have been achieved. The imperial family was under house arrest for many weeks. If diplomatic negotiations had failed – and I am not certain that they were even attempted – they could all have been rescued. The British managed after all,' she said with a sly smile, 'to organize a route by which the Tsar's *fortune* could be spirited away. Millions of pounds' worth of gold, jewels and bonds were helped out of banks, strongrooms and palaces on their way out of Russia but it was too much, apparently, to do the same for one small family.'

The princess seemed entertained by Lily's expression of astonishment. 'And you are asking yourself, Lily, why we do not see the Tsar, the Tsaritsa, their four beautiful daughters and the handsome Prince Alexei here in London, living their lives in safety? Well, I'll tell you. It's very simple. The wife of the Tsar is . . . was . . . a German-born woman of difficult character. Alexandra represented the enemy. And she would have been in your midst, this high-handed, manipulative schemer. But, more important, no capital can sustain two royal courts. Especially when the interlopers have a fabulously rich and completely auto-cratic way of going on. Your royal family, bourgeois, hard working, are entirely worthy but, dare I say it, dull – and they would have been eclipsed by the Romanovs.

'Your people look at the Windsors and what do they see? They see themselves reflected. They see an undistinguished family, virtuous and industrious, and, if they don't revere them, at least they honour and accept them. The Romanovs, however, would be a disastrous family to place in exile. They would have attracted their own glittering court about them and expected to go on living lives of decadent splendour. The French saw this clearly. Romanovs were very welcome as high-spending visitors but not as resident royalty. *Non, merci!* The French had long since rid themselves of their own. And someone in England also saw this clearly. So – not a finger was raised to help them and the whole family, all seven of them, and their servants were slaughtered in Ekaterinburg.'

The princess waited for a beat before adding torment-ingly: 'Though there was one survivor of the massacre. A spaniel, belonging to the Tsarevich, I believe, was rescued and made the journey safely to Windsor where he lives out his life in comfort. The English no doubt breathed a sigh of relief. They do so dote on their animals.'

This was dangerous political ground for which Lily had no map. She murmured her regrets and pleaded an ignorance of domestic and foreign politics. Her only source of information, she confessed, was the interior pages of *The Times* of London.

'Who do not interest themselves in the suffering of my country. But why would they when they have their own demons just a short hop across the Irish sea and now a presence in their own capital?' The princess did not consult her wristwatch but, apparently conscious of the passage of time, changed tack. Her voice lost its earnest tone and she was once again the hostess, speaking lightly. 'When you call again, you must talk to my young friend

Sasha. She liked you. I interrupted your conversation. Don't mark her down as a social butterfly. She did not quite tell the truth about her escape from Russia. The true story – of which she still bears the physical scars – is vastly more appalling.' The princess turned her head slightly to hide the quiver of disgust and pain. 'She will confide as much as she thinks right. It will open your eyes, Miss Wentworth, to the sufferings of countries less well *managed* – was that your word? – than your own. Make no mistake – I admire and support the work Sandilands is doing to keep the good ship Britannia on an even keel. And if it comes to plugging up a hole or two in the woodwork to keep the deck firmly under our feet, I will do what I can. As will the young refugees I gather about me. It will do Sasha good to talk to someone her own age . . . someone with understanding who will not run screaming in horror from her revelations. Sandilands tells me you are made of stern stuff, Constable Wentworth.'

Lily responded to the ensuing distancing phrases. The interview was at an end. She was given permission to take away the original handwritten list to check against the Branch's list back at the Yard. As she put both documents away in her bag and started to move towards the door, the princess called after her.

'A moment, Miss Wentworth.' She approached and spoke quietly. It seemed to Lily a prepared speech and one made with regret or some other emotion difficult to place. 'There is a further name. A woman. Though I'm not sure she fills your criteria. In fact, exactly the opposite. You seek someone who was invited and yet did not put in an appearance. The woman I have in mind was *not* invited but was, in fact, present last night at the reception . . . in a manner of speaking . . . a close relation and very dear friend of mine. She is so completely uninvolved with what we have discussed that I am confident I am not suggesting any villainy when I say you will find her name on my first list but crossed out. That was for my secretary's information.

There was no need to send her an invitation, you see. She told me well in advance not to bother to ask her.' The princess gave a dry laugh expressive of disapproval and incredulity. 'She was going to be at the hotel anyway, though not as a guest. Anna Petrovna, her name is. A darling girl, but an eccentric. And a beauty! Wait a moment. You may judge for yourself.'

The princess headed towards a bureau, opened a drawer and took out a photograph. 'Here. You may look at this. I cannot let you take it away – it's the only photograph of Anna that I have left. It's not very clear but it may be of help. You'll see it was taken by an amateur – the grand duchess's French master, I believe.'

Five young girls wearing long white dresses and ropes of pearls were caught, it seemed, informally, standing about holding croquet mallets in a woodland setting. They were clearly on friendly terms with the photographer; unusually, they were smiling into camera, their posture relaxed.

An idyllic moment of leisured innocence from a world so soon to be plunged into horror.

'This was taken, oh, it must be eight years ago – you see all the girls are wearing their hair down. Not yet considered adults ... still in the classroom.' The princess began to pick out the Tsar's daughters with a forefinger. 'Now, let me see. I'll try to get this right but they were peas in a pod, those girls. All very like their mother. And all dressed alike and grinning. Which is which? That one is certainly Anastasia. The shortest. Pretty little rascal. Now ... Olga? Maria? Maria had fairer hair so the one on the right is almost certainly Maria. No mistaking the two arm-in-arm on the left. They are Tatiana and her friend Anna Petrovna. A spectacular pair, and didn't they know it! Both tall, you see. It's hard to tell from a sepia print, which never did Tatiana justice, but she had chestnut hair which contrasted intriguingly with Anna's mop of jet-black hair.' The princess's voice faltered and she looked aside to hide her grief as she said quietly: 'My niece was a handsome girl, was she not? In those days. Sadly, if you ever confront her, you will see that the years of privation and harsh treatment have taken a hideous toll.'

Lily's eyes were drawn straight to the one girl who was not a Romanov. Anna's full-busted figure made her royal friend appear willowy in contrast. A round face – pretty though rather chubby, Lily thought – was being turned away from the photographer in laughing protest but Lily sensed something more in the evasive game. Camera shy? No. The protective sweep of glossy dark hair being teasingly offered to the photographer suggested flirtation and Lily smiled to herself. After all these years, had she guessed Anna's secret?

'The French master? Was he attractive?'

The princess looked at her sharply. 'Many thought so. The girls all adored him.' She took the photograph from Lily and looked at it intently. 'You must understand that, with her birth, wealth and royal connections, my niece was destined to make a good marriage. An English duke . . . a Pomeranian prince . . . something of that order.' She sniffed. 'But today, if you go looking for her, you might well find her working in a hotel kitchen. She is a law unto herself, my Anna. Never will listen to advice. One tries to help – she is one of us, after all, and may count on our loyalty and support to the death.' She shrugged her shoulders to indicate that she had wasted her time. 'Perhaps she will listen to you. If you go at once to her lodgings you will most probably find her there.'

She whispered an address into Lily's ear before ringing for the butler. Her last words to her were murmured: 'I fear she is something of a loose cannon whose movements are unpredictable and dangerous. Mind your toes, Miss Wentworth, should you find yourself treading the deck alongside Anna.'

Chapter Twenty-Seven

Lily headed off to the north-east, guided by the stern bells of the Russian church in Moscow Court booming out on the far side of Hyde Park. They ceased on a dying peal, leaving an unnatural silence flooding down from the rooftops. This was a moment to enjoy – a moment of rare peace when the streets were empty of motor traffic and pedestrians. It would be short lived. Lily caught in the distance the notes of the military band playing for church parade in the middle of the park. Soon the huge crowds the ceremony attracted would be spilling back on to the streets again, spiritually refreshed and heading home or for the pub in search of bodily restoration.

'It's not far,' the princess had said. 'In the middle of that disgusting rookery off the Gloucester Road.' She'd quivered with distaste. 'They keep promising to knock it down and cleanse the area of riff-raff but what happens? Every year another street of houses is repaired and more ruffians move in. Do have a care, Miss Wentworth. Anna could do better for accommodation. Heaven knows, she's not without influential contacts. It's my opinion that she's in the throes of some sort of self-imposed chatisement. Wallowing in degradation. I've offered help but all she will take from me is what I feel least able to give – references to her character when she seeks ever more demeaning posts. She remains in touch with Sasha, though they are no longer as close as they once were, I sense.'

Smells of roasting joints coming from kitchen quarters explained the deserted pavements. After lunch people would flock outside in their hundreds, dressed in their Sunday best. Visiting day in a sprawling capital. Families would be crossing London to see their friends and relations in distant suburbs. Lily wondered how Anna Petrovna – a mentally fragile and lonely Russian woman – was spending her Sabbath. Would she be back in her lair, lashing her tail in fury that her prey had got away? Planning her next assault on the English Establishment? Had Bacchus's men dragged her off already for questioning? If so, Lily rather hoped their first question might be: 'Why on earth are you trying to do harm to the country that offers you shelter?' Or were they somewhere about the place, quietly watching the house?

Lily decided not to confront the woman, even if the opportunity arose. Sandilands wouldn't thank her for muddying the waters. But there were other useful things she could do, if she could come and go unnoticed. She pulled her hat lower on her forehead.

She was entering a very mixed area. What her father would have called 'Queen Anne in front, Mary-Anne behind'. Substantial Victorian facades progressed from family houses of some grandeur and single ownership to well-to-do business premises (Lily noted a firm of solicitors and a car dealer's showroom) to apartment houses with ranks of front door bells and finally to lodging houses.

No vacancies. The signs were strong on the wing. As were *English Gentlemen accommodated*; *No females*; *No foreigners*; *No travellers*. Lily couldn't think how a single migrating Russian girl had ever managed to find a toehold on this cliff face of forbidding respectability.

A left turn into Hogsmire Lane answered her question.

Hogsmire Lane didn't live up to its bucolic name. It conjured up muddy fields and wild hedgerows a-froth with may blossom but here there was not a sign of foliage, flower or farm animal, though this must, at one time in the last hundred years, have defined the western outskirts of the city, its ragged line marking the place where the built-up town ran straight into the fields and hedges. Nor was it a 'lane', but a short and run-down street linking two grander ones, a left-over, left-behind, rotting backwater. It was not a thoroughfare in which the princess would ever have set foot and, modestly dressed though she was, Lily hesitated to walk down it herself. A narrow, heat-cracked road separated York stone flagged pavements that abutted the front walls of the narrow terraced houses. One or two of the houses were boarded up with plywood planks at door and window but, for the most part, panes of glass gleamed, a tribute to the elbow grease, newspaper and vinegar of the housewives. Front doorsteps, all nine inches of them, were recently donkey-stoned, proclaiming to who-ever was passing that here resided a decent God- and neighbour-fearing family.

Lily thought she knew what to look out for. Bacchus's men were too professional to be discovered loitering in the street re-tying their shoelaces or propped against a lamp post with their heads in the *Racing Times*. She decided to watch out for fit-looking men dressed a little too well for the area; encyclopedia salesmen with heavy briefcases; Jehovah's witnesses in dark-suited pairs. She decided there was no sign of a Branch presence.

Lily crossed the road to avoid a swaggering youth being tugged along by a bulldog puppy on a chain and paused to get her bearings. Honeysett had reported that the address he had for Miss Peterson was 'care of number 42'. And yet the princess had told Lily number 67. What was going on? A quick glance along the street told her that number 42, on her left, the one that would have come in for a certain amount of attention from the Branch, had a brown front door, recently painted and it was still on its hinges. The house had discreet net curtains at its ground-floor window. In front of it, on the pavement, was a group of children out at play. Lily was pleased to see them. In any street the behaviour of the children was the best indicator of unrest or aberration, and these children were playing normally.

They were already dressed for the day in their smartest clothes. Probably expecting a visit from Grandma or due any minute to set off with the family across town themselves. They'd clearly been got ready and sent out of the house with a warning to keep themselves clean and tidy. They had on white collars, pulled-up socks and shiny boots, Lily noted. One boy, the smallest, was even wearing a Little Lord Fauntleroy suit, years old and passed down the family. He appeared ill at ease in it and was sitting cross-legged a few feet away, excluded from the game, Lily guessed, on account of having to keep his frills clean while his three brothers and one sister played hopscotch. They bobbed with subdued energy up and down the number grid chalked on the flagstones.

Number 67 was opposite but not directly opposite. In a confusing old London way the numbers on this street ran consecutively and started back on themselves to complete the tour. Number 67 had a green front door, as did several others in the street, and like number 42 it passed Lily's clean window test.

With a confident smile, she approached the children. She grabbed Little Lord Fauntleroy from behind and, carrying his slight weight in front of her, she began to hop the chalked grid, bouncing his feet on each of the squares and chanting the rhyme as she went.

'Five, six, seven, this way to heaven. Eight, nine, ten, turn round again.' She reached the top and hopped back. 'Three, two, one, you've had your fun!' She deposited the giggling child on his feet at the start.

'Again! Again!' he shouted, holding up his arms.

Lily obliged.

Fighting for breath she addressed the oldest boy, distinguished by his sailor collar. 'I wonder if you can help me?'

They stared at her with surprise and suspicion. No one replied. Instead they gathered together in a huddle and the big boy appeared to be laying down the law. His sister defied him. 'Naw! Gerraway, Jim! She's never! Look at 'er! Seccetary or somefin' – that's what she is. An' anyway – rozzers i'n't *women*. An' if they woz they'd never play hopscotch.'

Emboldened, Jim looked her up and down and asked: 'You the law, miss? You with the rozzers? We don't talk to them . . . Dad'd tan our arses.'

Lily was affronted. 'Crikey, no! I'm looking for digs. Secretary as you guessed, miss!' Lily beamed at the little girl. 'I've just got a position in a solicitor's office . . . Crabtree and Bingham at the end of the road. A friend of mine lives hereabouts . . . she's going to help me find a respectable place to stay. I've just got in to Paddington this morning. Only I've lost the number she gave me. I'm sure this is the right street and she said it had a green front door.'

The children relaxed. 'Oh, that'll be Mrs Royston's at number sixty-seven.' They all pointed. 'She takes gels in.'

'And she'll have a room spare. She'll be looking for someone to fill the upstairs front now,' the girl added knowingly. Head on one side contemplating the stranger, she came to a decision, grinned and confided: 'Don't offer her a penny more than five bob a week, all in. She's a mean old bat. She'll screw more out of you if you don't stand up for yourself.'

'Well, thanks for the advice!' Lily said cheerfully. She lowered her bottom to perch casually on the window ledge of number 42 and took off her hat as a gesture of ease. The children gathered round, intrigued. 'I wonder if you know my friend? She's called Anna and she's got dark hair and she's very pretty. She works up west in a big hotel.'

Their faces fell and they looked at each other again. Finally, the girl offered: 'Well, you're out of luck. Annie's gone. Legged it. Right after the rozzers was 'ere.'

'No! You must have got that wrong. Annie's never in any trouble . . . she's a good girl, Annie. Hard worker. Honest as the day is long. I'd go bail for her any day.'

'Oh, she's in trouble all right,' the boy said portentously. 'Five of them there were. Four uniform and one in plain clothes. Knocked us up before six. Ma and Pa were having their breakfast. Ethel and me – we listened on the stairs. Wanted to know where a certain Anna Peterson was, they said. Come over real nasty when Pa told 'em where to get off.'

'Pa don't like the law,' the girl explained. 'No one round here does. Always on the take. Bent as a hairpin, my ma says. They banged Pa up in the nick once. Fitted him up for receiving. He never deserved it. It were only a dish o' tripe as no one else wanted. He don't forget! Sent 'em off with a flea in their ears.'

'Good old Pa,' said Lily. 'That's the stuff to give 'em. And they had no idea where Annie was?'

'Naw! They banged on a few doors . . .' Jim indicated the houses on either side and immediately opposite, exactly the houses Lily would have tried herself if she'd been on police duty, 'but nobody in this street'd split. "Don't know nuffin'! No idea what you're on about!" that's what they all said. Even crabby old 'erbert at number sixty-five told 'em to sling their 'ook. They never tried Mrs Royston's. Annie got clean away. She must have heard the ruckus. Waited an hour and ten minutes, she did, before she done a runner.'

'But how do you know she was leaving, Jim?'

It was Ethel who answered. 'We were here in the street. She came to her window. Up there, miss. And she waved to us. And blew us a kiss. She had her hat and coat on.'

'And did she say anything as she passed you?'

Looks of scorn greeted this question. 'Naw! She never passed down here,' said Jim. 'More sense. She'll have gone out the back way. Over the yard and across the allotments, turn left and you're in the Church Street.'

Lily began to see a further advantage of a roost in Hogsmire Lane.

'We waved back. We wished her good luck,' Ethel said with a touch of defiance. 'She was a nice girl, miss, your friend. Gave us all a lollipop every Saturday. I've still got mine that she gave me yesterday.' The little girl rubbed her eyes with the hem of her pinny and began to sniff.

'She may come back when the bother – whatever it is – has blown over,' Lily said. 'She'll be glad you stuck up for her. And look – I think my friend would like you to have this.' She took a sixpenny bit from her pocket and handed it to the girl. 'You can be quartermaster, Ethel. Next Saturday's lollipops. In case she's not back in time.'

As the small silver coin disappeared with coos and muttered thanks into the depths of Ethel's pocket, Lily put her hat back on and stood up. 'Well – I can see I shall have to go back to Paddington and pick up my suitcase before I knock on Mrs Royston's door. Landladies don't take kindly to females who appear with no luggage on their doorsteps and I see this is a very respectable part of town. A good five bob's worth! Keep your eyes peeled for the rozzers, kids! Especially the ones with the moustaches. They're the nastiest.'

Chapter Twenty-Eight

Joe was uneasy. He prowled about his office closing drawers and straightening pictures. He tapped the wall clock and checked it against his wristwatch. They agreed that it was now two o'clock. Where'd she got to? He'd quite forgotten to tell her they were expected at Cassandra Dedham's house for tea. Would she make an appearance back at the Yard in time to accompany him?

A phone call had come from Princess Ratziatinsky at noon to say that Wentworth had left. He wanted to finish up at the Yard, close his files and get something to eat. He'd had time for a shower and a cup of tea and a change of clothes back at his flat just before dawn but since then had been chained to his desk, listening to reports and moving his men around. He'd told her to take a taxi back. A ten-minute drive.

Common sense reasserted itself. She'd probably nipped off to visit her parents and tell them all her adventures. Sunday. It was her day off. She'd completed her self-imposed task and was clearly at liberty to spend the rest of the day as she wished. Yes, that's what London girls did on the Sabbath, after all – they went back home for luncheon with Ma and Pa. The traditional slice of roast beef, no doubt. Apple pie to follow? A pang of hunger hit him and he dealt with it.

Hunger and lack of sleep he'd learned to accommodate in his war years. He hadn't expected he'd need those skills working at a desk job. He allowed himself a momentary tight grin. He would never accept an easy existence. Too many mischief-makers to be brought to account; too many scores to settle. This blasted Morrigan, for one. The woman should have been under lock and key by now. She was running rings round him. A slight but unmistakable feeling of dry-mouthed giddiness disturbed him. He recognized it for the moment of controlled terror before the whistle blew. A warning he should heed?

Joe reviewed his plans. The prime minister and Mr Churchill? Aware, alert and doubly guarded. The prince? Hidden away. The rest of the royal family? Not on Bacchus's list but, after much thought, Joe had taken the precaution of advising a week at Sandringham. On their remote estate in Norfolk they were easier to isolate but close enough to the capital to protect. Distance, the local plod and a selection of Branch men were covering the situation.

He grimaced. This was turning out to be an expensive operation in policing terms. And it would get worse.

Still no Constable Wentworth. There had been no problems with the interview. The princess had been impressed with the constable's discretion and had been able to supply her with what she wanted, which seemed to be the names of five people who had ducked her event. No harm there . . . and she might even come up with one of her 'insights'. And the girl was merely running errands, not running into danger. The pavements of London were her territory, its low life her confidants, by all appearances. She was probably safer in their company than his.

Joe grimaced as he reminded himself of the close shave Lily had had the previous evening, sitting, fork in hand, messing about with a plateful of poisoned food. The lab tests had, indeed, traced the cyanide to the lower stratum. She'd taken it well – no squeaks or recrimination. No, not one. But he'd rather not get a reputation for sending girls in to do a man's job. And his chaps had certainly not been impressed – disharmony and disruption had been mentioned. *Threatened*, he'd say, if he were honest. Better take her out of the equation, all things considered, he decided. She'd done her bit and he wasn't prepared to put unnecessary strains on morale.

He slid the photographs of the ball from their envelope and studied them, pausing for rather longer than he ought over the one where she'd been waltzing with the prince. He wondered if the arsehole Tate would sell it to one of his society rags. Joe doubted that he had the power to prevent him and he could see it would be hard to resist the temptation of publishing a shot as glamorous as this one. Please God the girl's identity wouldn't become the subject of national speculation! Embarrassment bound to follow for all concerned. Perhaps the undeclared hold Lily clearly had on Cyril Tate and the respect – even affection – he seemed to have for her would be strong enough to stay his hand? Puzzle, that. With her modest origins and his rackety, disgraced aristo background, any common ground between the constable and the newsman was a mystery to Sandilands.

He stared, disturbed by the print. He ran a speculative thumb around the face he rather thought Botticelli would have admired. With women about the place, he'd have to watch his language more carefully. Was it right to impose this extra discipline on his men? It had been fascinating to observe the reactions around the table. And informative. Joe liked to collect these impressions; he liked to be aware of weaknesses as well as strengths. He'd noted interest varying from lascivious appreciation (Chappel) to exaggerated distaste (Fanshawe). Hopkirk, he would have judged, was unmoved. Bacchus, like Sandilands himself, he would have sworn was intrigued in a professional way by the possibilities. Until she got up his nose and seriously challenged him. The girl was a chameleon. And, as such, she might have proved of some use to them. Shame no one else was prepared to acknowledge this.

But perhaps there *was* someone who would appreciate her qualities?

Sandilands came to a regretful decision. She'd fizzed like shaken-up ginger beer at the idea of redeployment but had been quite seduced, he was sure, by the group photograph of Philip Lane surrounded by his harem of bright young girls. He'd ring his friend in Lancashire and start paving the way for a transfer. Now she'd had a taste of the detective's life which Sandilands had, from their first meeting, deduced was an unusual but overriding ambition with this girl, she might welcome the chance to train on for the real thing with Philip.

He snatched at the telephone at the first warning burble. 'Send her straight up, will you.'

'Ah. Do come in, Miss Wentworth. Sit yourself down. Glad you could spare me the time. Sunday. Your day off, of course. Lots to fit in, I expect. Father and mother both well, I trust?' The tone was understanding, the smile devastating.

Lily showed no sign that she was deceived by this show of affability. She looked at the clock in consternation. 'Oh, I see. Gosh, I *am* late! Oh, sir, I hope you weren't worried . . .'

'Worried? I shot myself in a mood of black despair an hour ago,' he said drily.

'Terrible aim, sir! Glad you missed.'

He felt himself responding to her shy grin with a surge of good humour. He controlled it and cleared his throat. Straight to business.

'Now – I'll bring you up to date. Here, back at base, we've been very busy. The Branch have been gathering everything they had on these Russian women who seem to be blighting our lives at the moment.' He pointed to a thick file on his desk. 'This has just come up. It's all the Branch could scrape together on Miss Peterson. Bacchus and his chaps went round with cat-like tread and cutlass between teeth to the address we'd had under surveillance since the

276

early hours. They mounted a raid on the premises. With no result, I'm afraid. No one at home.'

'No one, sir?' She was looking at him in astonishment. 'Not even a little family having breakfast?'

'What? As a matter of fact, if I must dot the i's and cross the t's, yes, there *was* a family in residence. A perfectly innocent family – man, wife and five children apparently in various stages of readiness for the day, taking an early breakfast. No lodgers kept. The father's a porter at Smithfield meat market. Husky sort of bloke. He made objection to Bacchus's invasion and ranted on about Englishmen, homes and castles. Sent Bacchus off, tail between his legs.' Joe couldn't hide his satisfaction. 'The men made further inquiries in the street and hung about observing for an hour then gave it up as a bad job and came back to HQ. Another false trail, I'm afraid.'

'Did you see Honeysett? Was he of any help?'

'Yes. He tried his best. But his female employee gave away little about herself. Did her job well. Went home at the end of the day. She never socialized with the rest of the staff. We checked on her three referees. Princess Ratziatinsky – conveniently or sinisterly, depending on your point of view – was one of them. Conspiracy are we suspecting? She was the only one who gave a telephone number so, naturally, it was to her that Honeysett approached initially. Satisfied by all he heard from that establishment and being unable to make swift contact with the others – one was a lady at present travelling in Europe and the other a military gentleman posted to the North West Frontier province a year ago ...'

'False, sir?'

'I don't doubt it. Honeysett was devastated. Angry to have been taken for a ride. There was no intention on the steward's part to deceive, of course. He told us what he knew. But what he knew was a load of codswallop. No such girl ever at that address. And where have we heard this sorry tale before? Bells ringing, are they? So there we are. Again. Now – I've spoken to the princess. You made a good impression. And tell me, did she come up with anything that interested you?'

The girl seemed amused. Worse than that, she was grinning at him. She took off her hat and began to fan herself with it. Her straw-coloured hair stuck out round her face and he realized that she was, in fact, a bit breathless but shining with excitement. His mother's cat, the ghastly old tiger-striped killer – what was his name? Tippoo – came to mind. Electrified by triumph. Hair on end, Lily had come to tell him she'd killed a rat and he might expect to put his foot on the squishy corpse the moment he stepped outside.

'Oh yes, she did, sir! She gave me the name of the woman who tried to poison the prince and told me where she was living. I went straight round there – oh, I know, disobeying orders, and I expect you'll be angry with me, but it was on my way back . . .'

'Get on, constable!'

'Well, she made fools of Bacchus and his Keystone Kops, but I've got her, sir!'

Joe looked anxiously at the door. 'Got her? Lord! You've not left a body down at reception, Wentworth? What on earth have you done?'

'Oh, nothing like that! No fisticuffs. But I did some detecting. I know what she looks like, I know who she is and I can guess *where* she is but I can't for the life of me work out *why* this woman would want the prince dead. Or Admiral Lord Dedham or Churchill or Lloyd George. Perhaps you'll be able to tell me?'

'Wentworth, start at the beginning. You got there . . .'

Joe listened patiently to Lily's account, making occasional notes of names and other details that caught his attention.

'And you'd describe the princess's manner as – helpful – on the whole?'

'On the whole, sir. And on the surface. No more than that. I wouldn't trust her as far as the garden gate.'

'Aha! Let's think of her as "Princess Rat"! Go on, Wentworth.'

'She doesn't like us much. She has strong views on the political situation and, though grateful to this country for the shelter she's receiving, doesn't scruple to voice her criticisms. But she would never, I think, condone the assassination of the prince or cover for any would-be assassin. Her community of refugees has too much to lose. It would be a suicidal idiot who stove a hole in the lifeboat he was travelling in. And she has much loyalty to the notion of *kingship*, which seems in that company to trump nationality. Or even friendship.' Lily paused for a moment and then added: 'She's a politician. She weighed her options and in the end she decided to give her up. Your Morrigan. But on her terms. Not ours. Oh, no, not ours.'

'In what way did she "give her up"?'

'She handed me the name of a woman who might well have been at the ball as a guest but was, in fact, working in the kitchens. No surprises! It's the girl I saw smearing the prince's plate. She's Anna Petrovna, and she's related to the princess. She was living just a short distance away, but in a much less grand district. In fact just across the road from the address Bacchus raided. She was watching his antics from behind the net curtain of her upstairs front. I thought I'd just check on it on my way back here . . . I hadn't at that time realized I too was being deliberately sent off on a wild goose chase. These Russian women are making monkeys of us, sir.'

'It's how they pass their time, Wentworth. I wish they'd take up needlepoint but they find espionage more stimulating. So, you're reporting that Miss Petrovna is gadding about London, free as the wind. You haven't got her at all, any more than Bacchus had. Or Hopkirk. A stroll across the allotments and the whole of the West End is at her feet.'

'No, sir! I know exactly where she is. I must have been within a few yards of her this morning. She was listening to what I was saying through a keyhole for all I know.' Lily shivered.

'Keyhole? Whose keyhole?' he asked with suspicion. And then with sudden alarm: 'Oh, my God! She was there? Within a few feet of you? What makes you think so?'

'The coffee cups. A tray arrived moments after I did. It was laid for four. The maid who brought it was surprised to see me and asked if she should bring another cup. Which would have made it five. One too many. She was hurried out of the room. There had been four women there when I arrived, not the three who greeted me. Anna must have skipped out when I rang the doorbell. The coffee cups had no significance for me at that moment but it hit me later. The princess was pleased and relieved to be able to get me off the premises by sending me along to Hogsmire Lane. The gesture made her appear cooperative to the police but she was giving nothing away as she knew perfectly well that the address had already been abandoned. She – and possibly the whole of the Russian establishment – is sheltering this woman. You're going to find that a hard nut to crack, I think.'

'Wentworth, we are not unaware of this. The princess and her entourage have been the subject of close surveillance ever since she moved to London. She knows it, of course. Clandestine manoeuvring is meat and drink to her. She's at the heart of a network that has tentacles covering the world and she works tirelessly for her own kind: émigré Russian aristocrats. She has a finger in every ambassadorial pie from here to Hong Kong and back again the other way.'

'I've just remembered – they were about to set off for lunch at the embassy. They could have taken Anna along with them and . . .'

'And left her there. On what is technically foreign territory. If she stays holed up in the embassy, we can't touch her. They could spirit her out of the country in a bag in no time. But I think she was pulling the wool over your eyes. Which embassy, for a start? Did she say? That part of town is an international diplomatic enclave. You can't throw a stone without knocking off an ambassador's silk hat. And with the political situation as it is at the moment in that benighted country Miss Petrovna would be the very last person the present Russian mob would want to see come grinning round the door. We're not contemplating the usual diplomatic protocol – these are bloodletting rogues and scoundrels we have to deal with. No idea how to behave on a world stage. They might approach our government and ask to have her removed.' Joe sighed. 'With the usual vociferous complaints about Scotland Yard intimidation and mismanagement. Whatever happens, I think we could be looking at diplomatic involvement. The quickest way to wreck a career. Damn!'

'Sorry, sir. If I'd caught on straight away I could have rung you from the princess's house . . .' Her voice trailed away and she hung her head, waiting for a rebuke.

He smiled. '. . . and requested a snatch squad? "Come quickly! She's hiding in the butler's pantry!" I can't quite see how that would have worked.'

'No. They'd never have got past Foxton, sir.'

'Well, cheer up. You've done wonders. I'm very pleased, Miss Wentworth.' He sat back, eyeing her with satisfaction. 'Would you like to hear me ruin someone's lunch?' He picked up the telephone and asked for a London number. 'Have I got Bacchus? James! Listen. You may wish to reschedule your surveillance in the light of certain information which comes to hand. Your girl was watching your storming of forty-two, Hogsmire Lane from her outpost in the upstairs front room of number sixty-seven . . . yes, I said sixty-seven . . . which was her actual address. No . . . not there any longer. Clean pair of heels over the allotments at the rear . . . She's taken shelter with her countrymen. She was playing cards with the Princess

Ratziatinsky when Wentworth called this morning. Yes. Wentworth has been entrusted with the girl's details ... things like real name, character, possible motive, that sort of thing ... By all means. I'm sure she'll be glad to update your information.'

Joe held the earpiece at an exaggerated distance from his ear and grimaced. 'That's got him going. He'll burst a blood vessel trying to keep up now. I wouldn't want to be one of his chaps.'

'And you've just killed off any chance of my ever gaining Bacchus's confidence, sir,' she murmured.

'No harm done. That was dead in the water anyway. You're never going to be soulmates. In any case, I doubt the chap has a soul.'

'Poor Bacchus! No mother and now no soul? I can begin to feel sorry for him.'

'Waste of time. I'll try to keep you off his back. Best I can offer.'

He watched as the girl shrugged and conceded a bleak smile. He thought he'd try for a warmer one. He'd been a bit hard on her, perhaps. 'And now ... reward for a jolly good morning's work! I'm going to say a few words that may produce a reaction. Are you ready?' He gave her the benefit of his most seductive tone. 'What about roast beef ... Yorkshire pudding ... horseradish sauce ... apple charlotte ...'

He sat back, alarmed, as the girl went off like a pistol, jumping to her feet and laughing. 'Gawd, sir! You know how to make a girl wet her knickers! ... Oh, Lord! Oh!'

Her face turned crimson at her indiscretion. She put a hand over her mouth, eyes wide with horror, burbled something and started for the door.

Joe leapt up, dashed over and grabbed her by the arm. 'Steady on! Don't bolt! I'm not insulted. I've heard worse in the trenches.'

'Sorry, sir. It's just a common saying ... where I come from it means nothing, not a ...'

'Shh. Don't go and spoil it. I've never had a compliment of the kind before. I'm rather relishing it. The nearest I've come to such a pinnacle of approval is from Amalthea Jameson who declared once, in a fit of heightened emotion – occasioned by a bunch of violets, I remember – that I certainly knew how to make a lady's heart flutter. I think I prefer the earthier tribute! But look – before you lose complete control of your tongue and any other dicky bits of your anatomy, why don't we get someone to drive us to Simpson's-in-the-Strand? Lunch goes on there until supper time. And their gravy is wonderful. They make it with red wine, you know.'

Joe burbled on, calm and amused, until he felt her muscles begin to relax again. He released her arm. Though still avoiding his eye, Lily managed to get her voice in gear. 'I'd like that, sir. And perhaps while we're about it, you can tell me about Anna Petrovna's *motive*. I don't think I mentioned one?'

She was putting on her gloves when the phone rang.

In his urgent quest for roast beef and suitable accompaniments, he very nearly ignored it. Grumpily he picked up the earpiece and announced himself. He looked questioningly at Lily.

'A package, you say? For Miss Lily Wentworth, care of this office? How big is this package? Three feet by two? That big? And heavy? I say – have you checked it for . . . Of course. Can't be too careful these days. Then get two strapping fellers to haul it upstairs, will you? Use the lift. I'm just off to lunch but I can wait a few more minutes, I suppose. Tell them to get a move on, will you?'

The commander waited until the two uniformed coppers left before he approached the brown-paper wrappings of the carefully boxed parcel with a penknife. He first examined the label. 'They made no mistake, Wentworth. It is indeed addressed to you care of my office. Were you

283

expecting anything of this nature? Bagatelle board from Hamleys? Travelling guillotine? The missing *Mona Lisa*?'

She shook her head, perplexed. He clicked out the blade of his knife and began to strip away the wrapper.

After five minutes of combined effort, they stood speechless, absorbing the contents.

Sandilands was the first to regain his voice. 'Congratulations, constable! You seem to have made a very favourable impression. A most gracious gesture – I'm sure even you will agree.'

He bent and picked up an envelope that had fallen from the wrappings. He waited while she opened it and read the message on the single sheet it contained. When she coloured and put it away he asked no question.

They continued to stare. Joe approached the painting of the Russian forest, now reset in a heavy gilt frame, and peered at it more closely. He shook his head and looked again. His fingers reached out to touch it but left off before they contacted the oil surface. He began to speak hesitantly, as though talking to himself and feeling his way through hostile territory in the dark: 'I wonder – and you'll tell me if you think this a fanciful idea – are we . . . could we possibly be . . . looking at a motive? Of sorts? A motive for murder? Anna Petrovna's reason, if you can call it that – most would say "unreason" – for wanting the Prince of Wales dead? Is it staring us in the face? Am I making an unwarranted and utterly crazy assumption? If not, it's worse than we thought.'

He turned to Lily, full of foreboding. 'We're staring into a depth of madness that makes anarchy and revolution look like cool common sense.'

Chapter Twenty-Nine

In the bustle of Simpson's, Joe sat wrapped in thoughtful silence, paralysed by his insight. Disturbing though this clearly was, it showed no sign of affecting his appetite. He settled to his rib of beef and was halfway through it before he remembered his manners and engaged again in conversation with his equally preoccupied companion.

'Lamb suit you, Wentworth? Mint sauce not too fierce?'

'It's all perfect, sir.'

After a pause: 'You can't send it back, you know . . . The painting, I mean.'

'That's exactly what my mind was turning on. I'm not used to receiving such lavish presents. I was trying to find the right phrases for a note to the prince.'

'Well, you can forget about returning it with a few polite words. Out of the question. No one returns a royal gift. Ever. You must admit that it was a thoughtful gesture – and well deserved. Altogether, highly appropriate.' He caught his bossy tone and added, more mildly: 'I say, you weren't really minded to return it, were you?'

'Not on your nelly! I'm keeping it. I'm not such an ingrate as to spurn a gracious offering. And besides, I like it. My admiration was genuine. I encouraged the prince to bid for it. I can't wait to show it to my father. It has an uneasy and depressing presence but it's wonderfully done.'

'Know what you mean. One wouldn't hang it in one's drawing room, perhaps . . .' Joe agreed. 'Tell me what you see in—' He stopped talking, seeing the wine waiter approach to pour more burgundy into his glass.

Lily waited until they were left alone. A table discreetly placed in a corner, behind a small tropical forest of broad-leafed plants, had been put at Sandilands' disposal. And not for the first time, judging by the warm greeting and the swift accommodation from the maître d'hôtel. The rest of the diners who crowded the room had already embarked on their sponge puddings and custard; some were as far advanced as brandy and cigars. All were loudly talkative, cheery and unbuttoned. No one was paying the slightest attention to the quiet couple in the corner.

'It's a frightening vision,' Lily said. 'Deliberately so. The princess told us all – do you remember – that no photographic equipment is allowed any longer in Russia. The country's being laid waste, people are fleeing their homes or starving to death, massacres are going on, and what do the rest of us see of this? Nothing! The painting is an allegory. It's a scream of protest, a warning, a cry to the world for assistance from whoever sees it. It shows the trackless wastes of the artist's homeland but in the forefront there's a deep, freshly dug grave. Reminiscent of a plague pit. It's standing ready to receive its cargo of corpses. We know this from the crosses lining up in the background. Crosses made of human bones. Russian bones.'

'Is that what you see, Wentworth? An allegory? Is that all?'

Lily looked at him in puzzlement. 'Isn't that enough? A foreshadowing of disaster for the Russian people? The death of a great empire?'

'No. You haven't looked closely enough. Look – we'll finish up here and go back. We'll pass a magnifying glass over the paintwork. And I'll fill you in on our goddess. I called her the "Morrigan" after the Irish deity but I see I may have been poking about in the wrong pantheon.'

Joe talked on while Lily concentrated on her lamb and mint sauce. 'She's really Morana. In Russian and Slavic pagan religion, Morana was the goddess of death and winter. A beautiful girl with black hair and light skin but endowed also with wolf's teeth and clawed hands. And she has form – she's known to have killed her own husband, the god of fertility. She's a dangerous goddess of darkness, frost and death.'

'I begin to think you see one of these charmers around every corner, sir. Herr Freud might suppose you were frightened at an impressionable age by an odd-looking nursemaid!'

Joe reflected that Miss Jameson would never have dared to tease him so blatantly and wondered why he allowed it.

'And is there any remedy against this recurrent nightmare?' she wanted to know. 'Or is Morana invincible?'

'Apparently not. No. It's her only useful attribute: she *can* be overcome – if only temporarily. She's the spirit of winter, after all, and winter passes into spring. Even on the Russian steppes. Just to be quite certain they were rid of her, the country people used to make a straw puppet representing Morana and throw it into the river.'

Lily grunted. 'And we know what *that* signifies. It's just another way of celebrating the destruction of the matriarchal society and its replacement with a patriarchal one.'

Joe shot a warning glare across the table. 'Stop right there. I must ask you, Wentworth, not to bend my ear with all that suffragist talk. You're preaching to the converted. The Pankhurst ladies are good friends of my mother's and therefore – of mine.'

'Well, I've never heard of your Morana – I think you're making her up – but it wouldn't surprise me if she existed. She's probably Celtic in origin like the Morrigan . . . similar names. Same root? All these stories come with a warning – women are nasty, dangerous creatures. Chuck 'em off the nearest bridge.'

The flippant comment provoked a dry response. 'No use. They'd bob to the surface in that annoying way they have and float, then we medieval-minded men would have

287

the bother of fishing them out and burning them. Look here, I think we can manage without pudding, don't you? In all the excitement I forgot to warn you that we're expected for tea at Cassandra's. Better leave room for the tea cakes.' He signalled to the waiter that he'd like his bill. 'She's got her two boys back home and I think she rather wants to introduce us to the new head of the family. We've just got time to go back to my office and take a proper look at that painting.'

'I see a Russian landscape. Desolate place, miles from anywhere ... probably Siberia. Summer time – there's no snow. Thick forest,' Lily offered in return to his challenge.

'You're not looking carefully enough. Stand closer.' Joe put a hand on her shoulders and steered her towards the canvas. Surely this bright girl could see what he was seeing? 'It's all in the detail. It's summer time, yes. Forest – yes. And I think the trees: birch, larch, pine ... and the soggy terrain ... would indicate a scene in the Ural mountains. But miles from anywhere? No. I think we can tie this spot down very precisely. In fact I can point it out to you on a map.'

He produced a map of Asia from a drawer of his desk and, after a moment's search, found the place he was looking for. Lily's eyes widened as she read off the name and she went back to stare at the painting.

He followed her. 'There, what do you see on the horizon?'

'I think I see the gates of hell,' Lily murmured. 'Hieronymus Bosch would have admired this.'

'Many would agree with that interpretation. A hellish place. And it's not imaginary. It's very real. What seems to be the entrance to the underworld or a town on fire is the heat and smoke of dozens of factories, smelting works, and mineral processing plants. The biggest iron works in Europe is what you see belching away there, Wentworth. And the whole hot nastiness is emanating from a mineral-rich earth.

There's a saying that "If you haven't found gold within twenty miles of Ekaterinburg, it's because you haven't looked for it." Precious stones and metals – they've been dug out of the soil here and fashioned into the jewels and precious objects that decorated the Tsar's palaces for years.'

'Ekaterinburg! I had no idea. That's the city? It's just a name . . . a rather terrifying name . . . the place where the royal family was murdered.'

'It's terrifying for the poor souls who work there and for those who make their way through it – in shackles. It's in the Ural mountains – the division between Europe and Asia. Ekaterinburg is the gateway to the prison camps of Siberia. Thousands of the Tsar's prisoners were sent from jails in Moscow and Petrograd to walk with shackled feet and bound hands on their way across Russia to a miserable death. Men, women and children tramped through. And still do. But now they tramp in greater numbers and these prisoners have the benefit of no legal process. They're condemned for no good reason by the Bolshevist butchers who rule the empire now. It's enough to be intelligent, skilled, outspoken, unpopular with a neighbour – any of those qualities or none will have you arrested and obliterated.' Joe gave a sharp grunt of laughter. 'You and your father wouldn't last two minutes in the new Russia, Wentworth. But in Ekaterinburg in 1918, the Tsar and his secret police force were hated. The "Crowned Executioner" they called him . . . or "Nicholas the Bloody". This was the last place on earth he would have wished to be sent himself as a prisoner. He knew that he and his family could expect no mercy at the hands of the Ural Regional Soviet.'

'But who sent them there? They were doing no harm where they were held in detention in . . . Tobolsk, was it? Siberia?'

'As long as they were alive, they were always going to be a focus for the royalist party. In 1918 the White Army was still active and making progress. They'd joined forces with a rather effective Czech contingent and were fighting their way towards the city. In the last days, you could hear the guns getting closer. It was undoubtedly Lenin, back in Moscow, who gave the order – by telegraph – for the guard to carry out the assassination of the whole family before they could be rescued. He was wily enough not to sign his name on any incriminating documents.'

'Lenin? It was reported that the local Ural Soviet took matters into its own hands.'

'A cover story! The whole affair has his fingerprints – if not his signature – all over it. Never forget who sent them to the Urals in the first place. And to whom did the executioners dash to report success? To Lenin in Moscow. All part of a larger plot. Many other Romanovs were executed in various unpleasant ways at about the same time. The Bolsheviks were making certain that Russia would never be in thrall to the imperial family again.'

'And this is where they shot them? In the forest?

'No. They were executed in the cellar of the house in which they'd been imprisoned. A villa requisitioned from a local industrialist called Ipatiev. The bodies were transported by lorry into the countryside some miles away, we're told. To just the place you see here,' he added thoughtfully.

'And this pit isn't a broad allegorical reference to the death of Russia at all? It's very specific? To one family?'

'Yes. Highly specific. It's the Romanov grave. And geographically specific, too. Do you see the light in the sky?'

'Ah, yes. Yellowish – white. Too pale to be sunset. Dawn? The light's breaking on the left of the picture, so that must be the east.'

'So where does that place the city in relation to the artist's viewpoint?'

Lily thought for a bit, moving her hands about, and then she said: 'It would be to the south-east. So this grave is . . . um . . . ten miles or so north-west of Ekaterinburg.'

'Well done! It is – to be exact – a particularly depressing corner of the Koptyaki Forest, a place called the Four

Brothers, after four tall pine trees that grow hereabouts. That could be one of them, there, on the right. It's a quagmire underfoot and riddled with old mine workings. Just the place to lose eleven bodies.'

'Eleven, sir?'

'The Tsar and his wife, their five children and four of the household. Maid, valet, footman and the loyal family doctor – Botkin – all went to their deaths with the imperial family. But there's something else we can glean from the picture. Take this magnifying glass. Go and see what you can find carved on the surface of the crosses. I'm sure I noticed something.'

'There's an A, an N, and smaller – an O, another A, an M and a T and a third A. You could easily miss them. These are crosses for the Tsar Nicholas and his wife, Alexandra, and their five children, aren't they? Olga, Tatiana, Maria and Anastasia. And this smallest cross here is for the youngest, the boy Alexei, the heir to the throne.'

'Aged only thirteen when he died.'

'Are you thinking, sir, that this was done by an eye-witness? Now I see the precision . . .'

'Yes. Or by someone who was given a detailed description by an eyewitness.'

'Sir? May I ask you how you come by all this knowledge? You seem to know more than I've managed to glean from the news reports. I'd expect that, but . . . well, this is a remote place we're talking about. It's thought that no one really can be sure what happened to the Romanovs. Their death was announced on three different occasions by the British press in the months *before* that July. By the time they really died, people were shrugging their shoulders – it sounded like old news. But I was the same age as one of the girls and my nephew was thirteen at the time like little Alexei – I felt for them. I read and was convinced by each account of their massacre. Like the rest of the nation. But, then, I found myself equally convinced by the stories that it was all a smokescreen and that the family had been taken to safety. Who's to say this isn't all a pack of lies? That this grave in the forest story isn't false? A bumbling amateurish set-up. Who could possibly have witnessed this scene? Lived to record it? And got it out of the country?'

'Witnesses?' Joe gave a sarcastic grunt. 'This apparently godforsaken spot was crawling with 'em. One behind every bush. Local villagers, fishermen, White Army officers reconnoitring ahead of their advance on the city, and even the odd British secret service officer. All watching in disbelief as a cut-throat crew of drunken, power-crazed incompetents crashed about noisily in the forest in trucks and bulldozers, trying to bury the evidence of their butchery. And the murdering thugs – can you credit the indiscipline? – met up with their mates in the city afterwards and spent a jolly drunken evening at the smelting works social club bragging and singing about their exploits. Paying for their beer with jewels snatched from the pockets and the underwear of the imperial family. Not much of a secret!'

'Deliberately, showily incompetent are you saying, sir? A set-up?'

'One does rather wonder.' Joe was silent for a moment. 'I've weighed the evidence. A workmanlike investigation was undertaken – is still being pursued, by a man who seems to know his trade – into what they're calling the "Romanov Murder Case". We were graciously sent a copy. I rather think it was aimed at foreign consumption, to put an end to speculation. It ended up on my desk. It's a good report. Credible and professional. I dutifully ploughed my way through it. I have to say, though, they've turned up a pitifully small amount in the way of human remains. Not enough to satisfy a British coroner. And all burned and broken beyond recognition. Our man Spilsbury would have laughed them out of court. But what they *have* dredged up is a truly impressive quantity of Romanov possessions – jewellery, icons, buttons . . . everything from the Empress's huge diamond pendant to the Tsarevich's belt buckle.'

'I saw pictures of those in the papers.'

'And again, one wonders. What sort of execution squad in a starving country leaves the contents of an Aladdin's cave littering the forest floor? But, as so often in a murder inquiry, it was one small detail that trumped all others. One detail that confirms for me that executioners did indeed perform their grisly task in Ekaterinburg . . . The doctor's false teeth.'

He smiled to see her puzzlement. 'Dr Botkin's upper plate. It was found at the edge of the pit in which they initially stashed the bodies overnight. Yes,' Joe sighed. 'My Russian confrères have three crime scenes to work on. Nightmare.'

'If you were laying a false trail, it would be easy enough to scatter pearls and buttons about, but what kind of mind would think of asking a man to relinquish his false teeth?'

'Exactly. You have a pretty devious mind yourself, constable, but would it have occurred to *you*? No. Nor to me. In the quest for verisimilitude, Wentworth, this would be a step too far. And I'll tell you something else. The last telling detail was the caking of mud between the front teeth, consistent with a grisly scenario where the doctor's body was dragged by the heels, face down, towards the pit. The teeth scraped along the ground and became detached.'

'Now there's a subtlety. A convincing detail, as you say. So – unless some overarching malign intelligence was running this show . . .'

'Bacchus was engaged elsewhere at the time. I checked.'

'. . . the massacre must be a true bill. They died there and were buried in the forest. Poor creatures! But you mentioned a British presence. How on earth did his majesty's agents fetch up here in the wilderness?'

'Ekaterinburg may be a far-off outlandish sort of place, but where there's money about, and in enormous quantities, there you'll find international interest also. There's a whole boulevard taken up by embassies of one sort or another. The British have an outpost there. And we have in our consul, Thomas Preston, and vice-consul, Arthur Thomas, two active, intelligent, Russian-speaking officials of the highest calibre. Bold too, I may add. The vice-consul went along to bang on the table and make demands of the local soviet concerning the security of the Romanov family once too often. He was almost shot on the spot by a gun-toting official. They did what they could and kept the villa where the Romanovs were held under very close surveillance, remaining in touch, telegraph permitting, for as long as possible. And then, of course, we have our man Lockhart out and about and up to mischief. I can say no more. Just accept that we know far more than ever appears in the pages of the London *Times*.'

'I'm thinking this is a puzzle of a painting I've been handed.'

'Yes. Intriguing possibilities here . . . A potentially dangerous work, though. It could cause difficulties for you if it got about.' Joe began to pad about the room. 'You see – it's empty, the grave. It's been dug but there are no bodies. Not a sign of one. Do you think the artist would have been able to restrain himself from adding a symbolic smear of blood-red staining the oily puddles of the taiga floor if . . .' He was muttering almost to himself as he stared again at the painting. 'I wonder if I could use this to our advantage? The uncertainty?' He took a few more steps about the room and then: 'Look here – I think you should leave the picture with me. It was addressed to you, care of Commander Sandilands after all. I'll put it away in my cupboard.' He watched as her expression changed. 'Oh, all right. Let's agree to wrangle about that later. Come and sit down. I need to hear your female opinion. Let me move your chair round here; you'll want to take a look at this file with me. Bacchus managed to come up with something he thought we might find useful. It's all we have on Anna Petrovna. Now, come on, constable! She's in here . . . the woman and her motives. We have to get into her skull. We have to understand what she's up to and why on earth she's turned assassin. And, most importantly, how much further does she intend to go?' He opened the file with a flourish. 'First let's take a look at her. Not much in the way of photographs but here's what we have.'

He found two sepia prints and laid them out on the desk. 'First, a line-up of nurses. Hair concealed under those white headdresses they wear. The imperial ladies, led by the Empress, rolled up their sleeves and did some pretty basic nursing work in military hospitals during the war. The older girls, Olga and Tatiana, worked like Trojans apparently. Tatiana, the sprightlier of the two, inevitably, having led such a sheltered life, fell hopelessly in love with a White Army officer under her care. Her first and only love,' he added. 'Bacchus's gossip . . . not sure that'll be in the notes.'

'Oh, dear! I can't imagine much good would have come of that,' Lily said sadly.

'No indeed. He must have been a spectacular young man, however. Even the Empress – the fussiest and most snobbish woman on earth – liked him and was reported to admit he'd have made a wonderful son-in-law, if only . . .'

'An imperial archduchess would be destined for one of the European *royal* heirs. Our own Edward? Oh, goodness – now, there's a thought. Well, I'm glad to hear the girls had a taste of real life before . . .'

'We think this girl here, the tall, full-bosomed one, is our Anna. Hard to be certain. Some of their friends did join them on the wards. And then there's this snapshot, in different mode. A rather distant and blurred shot of five girls on a summer's day – the imperial daughters plus Anna and, honestly, she could be any one of them. They all look alike to me. A froth of white lace, a glimmer of jewels and a gallery of sulky faces. Has a Romanov ever been observed to *smile*?'

'That one's our girl, sir,' said Lily, pointing without hesitation.

'Now how do you know that?'

'The princess showed me a photograph. She wouldn't part with it. But I can remember her features well enough to be able to identify her from this. She'd be the one standing next to Tatiana. Beauties, both.'

Sandilands peered. 'We can't use this for identification. Not clear enough and five years out of date. They all look alike to me though I think I can spot Tatiana! What a girl.' He looked again. 'Her raven-haired friend is spectacular too. The face is similar but she looks . . . heavier . . . than the taxi girl, Miss Hampshire.'

'Puppy fat, sir? Some girls are blessed with it and lose it with age. And after all, there was a war on over there in Russia too.'

'As you say. But then . . . Anything to reveal about her character before I open these pages and find out what she's really been up to?'

'Quite mad, the princess would have us believe. "A loose cannon" she called her. Utterly devoted to the imperial family. A Royalist to the core. But there are other things we can work out for ourselves, sir.'

'Go on.'

'She's clever. She got the better of Bacchus, after all. She doesn't act on instinct – she plans ahead. Six weeks ahead in the matter of her preparation for the Prince of Wales's assassination. She's ready to get her hands dirty in the pursuit of her aim – as Hopkirk, was it, said, she must be a strapping lass to survive the kitchens of a London hotel. And the address she gave . . . it was carefully chosen. She was always going to have early warning of interest from the Special Branch. Any strangers coming calling would receive a hostile and probably noisy reception where she sent them. The children would act as her guard dogs. She knew she'd have time for a quick exit round the back.'

'So – resourceful and tough.'

'But there's another side to Anna. I sense her people are genuinely fond of her and would go to some lengths to protect her. Even to the extent of sending the forces of law and order on a fruitless chase around London while she goes into hiding. And the children – the street kids in Hogsmire Lane . . . I know she bribed them with lollipops but there was something more. Kids aren't easy to deceive. And these ones really truly liked her and were concerned for her welfare. If they'd known I was a policewoman on her trail, I do believe they'd have turned their father on me!'

'So what are you saying?'

'That we're looking for a girl of good character who's been diverted – cut loose from her moorings like a ton of bronze cannon to crash about the decks – by some apparently overwhelmingly strong force that's turned her mad. She now has a mind to murder and nothing's going to stop her trying. Again and again.'

Joe's nod said that he had already reached this point. 'Let's see if we can identify the force that turned her loose on us, shall we, Wentworth?'

Chapter Thirty

'Born 1897. Which makes her twenty-five these days. High class family. Mother a lady-in-waiting to the Tsarina. I expect the little Anna was considered a suitable companion for the royal children. They had few enough of those. English is her first language, with French, German and Russian, of course.'

'Who compiled these notes, sir?'

'None of this is from the lady herself, you understand. It's a résumé of snippets of information from various Russian sources put together by the Branch, with additions from other interested parties. She's known to have arrived in London and signed her entry papers under her real name of Anna Petrovna with the joint sponsorship of the Princess Ratziatinsky and the captain of an English naval cruiser who seems to have been ready to vouch for her.' He paused for a moment, deep in thought. 'All too ready, perhaps. He was the naval gent who welcomed her aboard his vessel in Murmansk and brought her over here to England. The girl was in a poor state – reduced to skin and bone apparently – when the British consul enlisted Captain Swinburne's help. He dropped her off with her friends, then she promptly went to ground in the capital. She had no intention of becoming better known to the authorities, it seems.'

Joe gave Lily time to absorb the brief notes on the first page before turning over.

'This is interesting, sir, wouldn't you say? It's only an aside scribbled between the lines but it may be significant.'

'A close and tender relationship appears to have been established between Miss Petrovna and the crown prince Alexei. The heir to all the Russias, poor little boy.' Joe's voice had softened. 'What a weight to place on those thin shoulders.'

'Are all the stories true, sir?'

'Yes. I can confirm that the press and rumour had it right all those years – he was indeed very ill. Terminally ill. Haemophilia. Inherited from his mother's line and untreatable. The only relief from debilitating pain and the constant threat of death from uncontrolled bleeding seems to have been administered by the foul Rasputin. The Tsarina firmly believed so. The prince led a sheltered life, his every movement monitored by family members and servants.'

'And friends. It says here that Anna was frequently with him, telling him stories, carrying him about, making him laugh. How does Bacchus *know* all this?'

'None of your business, Wentworth. I can just say that the Branch and MI1b and c have done intensive research into the expatriate Russian community . . . compiled dossiers, listened intelligently to people only too happy to tell their tale.' He smiled. 'Articulate lot, Russian émigrés and they all have a blood-curdling story to tell.'

'May I speak from personal experience, sir?'

'One of the reasons you're sitting here with me now, Wentworth. Fire at will.'

'I know what it is to get fond of a . . . disadvantaged . . . younger boy. It can be a strong feeling. One combining the best impulses of sister, mother, nurse and friend. I think it's a girl's natural urge to care for something or someone smaller and weaker. A doll or a pet animal often has to substitute. Combine that love with an overriding belief in the divine right of the Romanovs to rule . . . It's something a girl would sacrifice her life for.'

'Would she sacrifice someone else's life?'

'To take vengeance of some sort? Yes. Possibly. Oh, some-one ordinary like me would rage and fume and curse and plan all sorts of retribution but wouldn't necessarily arm herself and put it into practice, but . . .'

'But you feel you could do it? If you were pushed?'

Lily swallowed and hesitated. 'Yes,' she said. 'I could. Women do. It's not unknown. But it would take a frightful force to push me over the edge.'

'We'll press on and find the origin of this impulse to slaughter, shall we? I don't think we've got there yet.'

'And here it comes, in all its disturbing detail,' Joe said some time later, turning the page they had just read. 'I should tell you that no woman has been allowed a sight of these documents. Bacchus gave clear warning that the con-tents are not fit for a girl's eyes.'

A different hand had written notes in the margins of the typed text. Watching Lily, Joe was aware that her breathing was increasing in speed as she read. He listened to her sighs and the small noise of pity that caught in her throat.

'Are we beginning to see it, Wentworth – the motive for the wholesale slaughter of a section of the British Establishment?'

'Oh, yes.' Lily scanned quickly through the text again. 'Am I to gather that her whole family was killed off? Anna is the last remaining?'

Keeping his voice level, Joe replied briefly. 'It seems so. Apparently the family behaved with great courage. Father, mother, the girl Anna and two younger brothers followed the Romanovs into detention in Tobolsk in Siberia. Many – about fifty – of their devoted courtiers made the move with them. They tried to follow when the royal family were suddenly entrained and sent off south and east to Ekaterinburg. Fearing the worst, Anna's father made a fuss and the local soviet, with the loss of temper and discipline that characterizes these people, had the whole family arrested – with others – and taken off by their guards. Seems to have been a favourite trick of the Bolsheviks – throwing families down mine shafts . . . alive . . .'

'And dropping grenades on top of them? Until the screaming stopped?' Lily's voice was tight with horror.

'The investigators report that some managed to crawl away down side shafts where they lived on for hours, perhaps even days, before succumbing to their wounds. Or starvation. When the bodies were recovered by a contingent of the White Army that swept through the region, Anna's was missing.'

'And all this happened in the dead of night. I can't begin to imagine . . .'

'That's the way they do things. In the confusion and struggling . . . the father had armed himself and defended his family with some spirit . . . no one noticed that Anna was being bundled offstage by one of the guards. A young and impressionable lad.' Joe sighed. 'Had he fallen for Anna, are we to suppose? Some of the Bolshevik guards were anything but the sadistic fiends they have been portrayed as . . . One of the Romanov guards, in Ekaterinburg, with starvation stalking the streets, got hold of the wherewithal to bake a birthday cake for the archduchess Maria's nineteenth birthday. She was a bonny lass, Maria, flirtatious and friendly. The guard was discovered being given a kiss of thanks and the poor lad was sent off to the front. To certain death.'

'Our Anna may well now wish she had gone to certain death with her family in the pit,' was Lily's comment as she turned the page and read on. 'I don't much like the sequel to this tale.'

'It gets worse. Hardly a romance, is it? A lost year spent hiding in a village somewhere in Siberia in the family of this young ruffian. He claimed to have married her, but she denies this and says she was raped, kept as a slave, overworked and beaten by the members of the family. Finding

301

herself with child, she chose to stay until the baby was born and then escaped and somehow made her way north to Murmansk on the coast. The consul secured her a passage aboard Captain Swinburne's gunboat – we keep a snarling presence in those waters – and fetched up in London. Where she rejoined her compatriots, nursing her hatred to her bosom.'

'Not her baby. Left behind? Perished?'

He flipped through the notes again, checking. 'We don't know. And Anna's not saying, apparently. This stage of her life seems to have been reconstructed from accounts of her friends who have chosen to follow a less secretive way of life in their adopted country. Two or more accounts, all telling the same tale.'

'And after her harrowing time she learns that not only is her own family dead, but Alexei too and her friend Tatiana. But, perhaps most shocking of all for a Russian of her class, the Tsar – "the anointed of God"! He was more than a man, more than a king. By the grace of God, he personified the Russian people. All things considered, this was a crime of heinous proportions.'

'Proportions big enough to unseat you from your moorings, would you say, Wentworth?'

Lily nodded, her face glacial. 'I'd go looking for my gun,' she said quietly. 'And a target for my rage.'

They were both silent for a moment, Joe turning back instinctively to look once again at the photograph of the five lovely girls in their white silks and satins.

'She must have asked what the British monarchy did to help their cousins,' Lily said. 'I've heard the question asked – were the forces of the British Empire not equal to the task of rescuing one small family? They had over a year to plan and effect their removal. They can send in gunboats to save nations – surely a horse and cart to fetch out seven people could have been managed?'

Joe resented her implied criticism but replied mildly enough. 'King George had his hands full at the time, you might remember, fighting the Germans to a standstill in the last stages of the war.'

'I don't think that would have weighed heavily with a Russian aristocrat. She would have focused her bitterness very precisely on the ones who had washed their hands of the Romanovs in their hour of need. Shall I speak their name? On the Windsors, I mean. Is this what's staring us in the face? Vengeance? An eye for an eye. A prince for a prince? Her own prince was lying dead in an unmarked grave in a Russian forest. Ours is alive and well and being fêted wherever he goes. On a polo field, in a night club, down a coal mine – wherever he finds himself, the reaction is the same: unthinking adulation. He was engaged in a triumphal tour of India soon after she arrived here. Sporting and popular. Everyone's blue-eyed boy. It must have rubbed salt in the wound. She was going to make him atone with his life.'

'I fear you may be right, Wentworth. And will she stop at one? More royal figures may follow if we don't lay hands on her. They're safely up in Norfolk for the moment but they won't stay there for ever. They work hard, they travel around the country. They have their seasonal movements, their social demands. And I'm quite sure they feel themselves inviolable. They'll soon break out of my protective ring. It can only be a matter of time and patience on an assassin's part.'

'But I have to ask because I don't understand – why the admiral, sir? What's the link? *Is* there a link?'

'Where, indeed, does poor old Dedham feature in all this? An opportunistic coup? I don't think so. I fear there may be a link to chill the blood, Wentworth. There had been a series of crimes by the IRA ... Scotland Yard itself had survived an attempted bombing. It was expected in the press that national figures were in line for assassination. What better cover for our Anna than the admiral dying spectacularly on his own doorstep at the hands of a pair of Irishmen only too happy to confess their patriotic motives to the waiting press? We all had Dedham marked down as number four in a series of IRA attacks. Clearly, the next attempt was going to be politically motivated also. And the one after that. And everyone knew the Prince of Wales was an Irish target.'

'She's not intent on martyrdom, then, sir? She hasn't shot and surrendered. Or topped herself.'

'Which can only mean, if I read her desperate mental state aright, that she wants to stay at liberty long enough to slay others. Covering her killings with the blanket of Irish nationalism. My God! We can expect more of the same. She's going for the whole family!'

'Sir? We're thinking that this woman sacrificed Admiral Dedham as no more than a smokescreen for her further activities? A murder to conceal the motive for further murders? It's insane . . .' There was horror in Lily's voice.

'Quite.' Joe hoped he could trust her to toe the line he was about to draw. 'Listen, Wentworth – Cassandra must never find out. A hero's widow should not be burdened with the knowledge that her husband's death was no more than a distraction, a diversion from the main business . . . a cover for a thrust of mad, venomous spite directed at a completely different target.'

'And those other poor dupes – the Irish lads?' There was pity as well as a question in Lily's voice. 'Young Patrick told me he'd been used. He didn't know the half of it!'

He was being offered a bargain he was glad to accept. Joe replied at once: 'They also should be left in ignorance. They think they are dying a patriot's death. We can let them go to the gallows with that last comfort at least.'

He closed the file. 'We must dash if we're not to be unpardonably late in Melton Square. I'll fill you in on the Dedham scenario as we go. One last thing to do here. I won't let this show go on a moment longer. I have the glimmerings of a scheme to neutralize this woman. I shall need your help. Tomorrow morning. Nine o'clock suit you?

Here? Rather a lot to think about . . . Excuse me while I set this up.'

He grabbed his phone and asked again for Bacchus. 'James. That article in the Californian newspaper that caused you such amusement . . . *San Francisco Advertiser*, was it? Still got the cutting, have you? Bring it with you tomorrow. Here, at nine. Two more requests. Can you lay hands on the box of Romanov bits and bobs we have in stock somewhere? . . . No. Not the box that was delivered to the palace last year. That was just body parts and I've no wish to inspect those bogus offerings . . . charred jaw-bones . . . severed fingers and the like . . . I'm sure they've been sent out of the country anyway. Hasn't the Pope taken delivery? No, I'm talking about the other one . . . You know very well . . . Shall we call it the Ekaterinburg hoard? . . . Oh, I make it my business to know these things. Never you mind! Just get hold of it! I don't care how we came by it or how many arms you have to twist to get it . . . do what you have to do. And lastly, our forger-printer chap – roust him out again and tell him to start flexing his fingers. Oh, one more thing.' He glanced speculatively at the painting. 'A camera? Can you operate one? Bring it along, will you?'

Chapter Thirty-One

'On your feet, Wentworth.' Joe handed Lily her hat. 'We have something to announce to the admiral's family. And it's rather surprising. I've spent the morning on the telephone to the Home Secretary and the Commissioner, planning and scheming. And, to a certain extent, it is their perceptions that must guide our actions.' He ignored her look of surprised objection and cantered on. 'Now, as we go, I'll put you in the picture. You will hear me making a few assertions and I don't want to be let down by any ill-timed reactions from my own corner.'

He began to deliver his briefing as they walked down to the taxi rank.

'This Sebastian you're about to meet – he's Dedham's nephew. His older sister's boy, name of Marland. Amateur pilot before the war, he joined the Royal Flying Corps at the outbreak. Something of a wartime hero. Not many of those chaps survived. Sebastian was wounded early on. You'll see he has a limp. He spent the subsequent years training others to go up and get themselves killed. And he proved to be that valuable resource – a survivor who could draw on his experience to devise devilish tactics for aerial combat. In fact, he was one of the hard-nosed brigade who turned the war in the air from the chivalrous gallop across the skies it was at the outset into a deadly three-dimensional pheasant shoot.'

'And is he still a flyer, sir?'

'No. In 1918 when the Corps became the Royal Air Force, there was no room for a now elderly – by their standards – chap with a game leg. Into his late twenties by then, he found himself surplus to requirements. After that he rather annoyed his family by getting his hands dirty. He threw himself – and his slender resources – into motor engineering. He set up a workshop and a test track on the family land in Sussex. Seems to be doing well. Decisive . . . abrasive even . . . he's not to everyone's taste. But . . .' Joe gave her a long, speculative look. 'Yes. I have to say, I think you'll like him, Wentworth. In fact he may be just your cup of tea!'

He was pleased with the startled look he'd provoked. He enjoyed startling the constable.

'Joe! At last. We'd almost given up on you. And you bring us your colleague. Boys! Come and meet the young lady I've been telling you about, the one who's helping Joe with our problems.'

Sandilands walked into the sitting room, tugging Lily along with him. He released her in order to go and have his hands squeezed by Cassandra Dedham, who rustled over in pearl grey silk, clinking jet and a waft of Mitsouko to kiss him on each cheek in the continental fashion. An anxious appraisal told him that the widow was looking surprisingly bobbish.

The two boys looked on for a moment, tender and amused. Then, the older one in the lead, they advanced on Lily.

'We'll introduce ourselves, miss,' he said. 'Once Mama gets Commander Sandilands in her sights she loses track of mere mortals like us! We shall have to entertain ourselves. I'm John and may I present my brother William, though we call him Billy.'

'No, we jolly well don't! Not now I'm fourteen!' came the mock rebuke.

Joe listened until he heard Lily making sociable noises and beginning to chatter with the boys and he decided it was safe to come off watch. His assistant had been struck by a fit of unaccustomed shyness as they entered the room and had nearly bolted. But, now, smiling with these two, she appeared calm again. And she was in safe hands. They had impeccable manners, the pair of them. And, in their different ways, they were thoroughly nice chaps. A credit to Cassandra's upbringing. The admiral seemed never to have quite managed to ruin their lives, thanks largely to his prolonged absences at sea, Joe reckoned. Out of the corner of his eye, he was pleased to see them reacting in a coltish way to the easy laugh and big eyes of a pretty girl.

And why not? With her yellow frock and shock of yellow hair, Lily looked like a sunflower in the gloomy room, he thought. She raised the spirits. John, serious and competent at seventeen, was a good head taller than Lily, Billy on eye level. Joe checked covertly for signs of distress in the sons and saw none. In fact Billy, he would have said, was a little over-excited for a Sunday teatime, and so soon after his father's death. He was talking loudly, even laughing with Lily.

Cassandra caught his concern. 'Goodness. The little ones will be asking permission to play with their marbles on the carpet next,' she said indulgently. 'I've just sent Sebastian to organize a pot of fresh tea. On Sundays we mostly do our own fetching and carrying. There's only Eva left scurrying around. Darjeeling suit?' Cassandra broke off to perform her duties. 'There are still lots of sandwiches left and we haven't set about the cake yet. I sent out for your favourite, Joe – a Fuller's walnut. Ah, here's the tea.'

The door was opened by a flustered Eva who stepped aside to make way for a gentleman dressed in mourning and carrying a heavy tray.

'Company,' the stranger said cheerily. 'Thank you, Eva. Now do stand clear and don't fuss me. That'll be all, my dear. We'll wait on ourselves now – you and Cook can put your feet up,' he said.

Eva smiled, cast him a shy glance and bobbed her way out.

Joe froze as Sebastian Marland ran an assessing eye over the distance to the nearest table, made his calculation, and set off across the Afghan rug. Always a tricky decision: whether to dash forward and snatch the tray from his hands or studiously ignore the disability. Taking his cue from Cassandra, who was nonchalantly busying herself clearing a space, Joe stayed put.

Sebastian Marland touched down safely and turned to greet Sandilands. 'Commander. Good to see you again. Though I could wish it were in different circumstances.'

Joe nodded and smiled with equal pleasure. 'Captain. Gloomy time for you all . . . May I—'

'No need for all that. Commiserations taken as understood.'

Sandilands began to relax into the familiar exchange of military brevity. You knew where you were with Marland.

Open and brisk, the young host came straight to the point. 'And thank you for all you've done, Commander. Cassandra's a lucky woman to have you in her corner – and I've said as much. But I see you bring an accomplice?' An enquiring eye sought out Lily.

'You've found exactly the right word.' Joe smiled. 'Miss Wentworth is, indeed, my partner in crime. Let me introduce you to her. Lily, this is Sebastian Marland, Admiral Dedham's nephew.'

Marland shook Lily's hand and murmured a welcome. Joe was intrigued to witness the instant effect of warm eyes and a sincere voice. He observed flirtatious smiles and batting of eyelashes. And Wentworth didn't appear unmoved either. Joe grinned. But Marland's attention was quickly drawn back to Cassandra, who was beginning to fuss and call everyone to the table. 'No, no. Sit down, my dear, and I'll pour out. That full pot's a sight too heavy,' he said. 'John, come and make yourself useful. Grab a cutlass and section up this cake, will you? And don't mangle the walnuts.'

'Sebastian is rather more than nephew now, Joe,' Cassandra began quietly, watching the steady hands at work with the tea things. 'When Oliver's will was read, we discovered that—'

'Oh, come now, Cassandra, Sandilands knows the contents. If he's any good at his job, he'll have known before we did!' A disarming grin was directed at the commander. 'But Miss Wentworth may be unaware? The thing is, Lily . . . I may call you Lily? . . . I was appointed joint guardian of the boys until their majority, along with their mother, of course. With immediate effect.'

Joe nodded his understanding and approval of the situation. Sebastian was far too young to exert paternal authority but he was a man any boy could look up to and he had a sound head on his shoulders.

'And, being a working man – a businessman of sorts – I shall interest myself in the family's affairs in an active way,' Marland went on. 'A few changes to be made—'

'And one of them made already!' Billy sang out happily. 'I'm going to tell the commander my good news. Sir! Cousin Seb says I needn't go back to that frightful hole when term starts. He's sending in my papers or whatever nonsense you have to do to break out of there. He can do it! He just has to sign something. I've served my last day at naval college!'

Cassandra exclaimed and pressed a handkerchief over her mouth. Huge eyes appealed to Joe for understanding.

'I say, steady on, old man! It's surely a bit premature to be thinking about unpicking the admiral's arrangements . . .' Joe began to murmur, but was firmly interrupted by Marland.

'*Au contraire!* Not a moment too soon. One more term of bullying and beatings and they risk breaking the boy's spirit. They've already broken his hide. The lad's cut raw by the last effort to make him like the Navy. It won't do. He has his mother's sensitive nature. And he's not a born sailor like his brother.'

Everyone in the room turned to look at the born sailor. John, blushing at the attention, defiantly put an arm along his brother's shoulder. 'We can't all be a Nelson. *I'm* not, never will be. But I love the Navy.' He spoke in sharp phrases, clearly embarrassed by William's outburst and directing his remarks to Joe. 'It's a tough system, sir, but I agree with Cousin Seb – I must survive it and try to change the things I don't like. And I can survive because I love the life. Billy can't because he doesn't. Could never . . . I mean . . .'

Cassandra, sniffing and exclaiming, hurried across the room to clasp both of her boys to her bosom. They stood, arms at their sides, enduring the show of affection for a count of ten.

Cousin Seb lit a cigarette and looked on, narrowing his eyes against the smoke. Joe had waved away the offer to join Marland in a cigarette and helped himself to a slice of cake. He knew he ought to be relieved that Cassandra and the boys were being cared for and, it seemed, cared about. This was one self-imposed burden he could now slip from his shoulders. Yes, it was all turning out well. He couldn't account for the feeling of foreboding he was experiencing.

With everyone finally herded back to the tea tables, the conversation began to flow on more conventional topics. Eventually Cassandra broached the question of the admiral's funeral and, at a suitable moment, Joe inserted the information he'd come to deliver. Everyone fell silent to hear his announcement.

The Yard had completed its investigation of the murder, he told them, and the trial of the two perpetrators was to be held at the earliest possible date. He left a space for their reaction and unobtrusively watched for any sign of dissent.

Marland interrupted Cassandra's whispered thanks. 'Hang on a minute, Commander. You've skipped a paragraph. Wasn't there a question of a third assassin? The girl in the taxi? The high-calibre bullet that finished off my uncle? Cassandra tells me she voiced her suspicions to the police.' He shot a glance at Lily, who nodded back.

Sandilands looked a warning and spoke crisply. 'We are indeed aware, but this is not perhaps the place, Marland, or the time—'

'Nonsense! If it's the boys you're concerned for, forget it. They know how their father died. They're au fait with the case. Cassandra and I see no reason to hold back the details from them.'

The boys nodded. Cassandra nodded. Joe realized that he was addressing a unified family and refocused his delivery.

'Very well. The pathologists's report upheld Cassandra's assertion. She was not mistaken. However, the girl in the taxi has been exonerated by the cabby, who has had a lucid interval or two in his hospital bed and has made a statement saying that it was not she who pulled the trigger.'

'Glad to hear it. Common sense – and science of course – have prevailed, then. Not a woman's crime, shooting in the street. Sure you'd agree. But if not her, nor the cabby, then who *did* pull the trigger?' Sebastian persisted. He was clearly not going to let Sandilands off until he'd revealed all he knew.

'The solution, as it often is, was staring us in the face,' Joe admitted with a shamefaced grin. 'The killers have been questioned at length and have made full confessions. The tougher one of the pair, in the end, admitted that he was issued with two guns, just in case one jammed. Sensible precaution.'

Marland gave an understanding nod. 'Makes sense.'

'Fleeing to the taxi, the gunman noted that the admiral was still on his feet, selected his more powerful weapon and shot again. Unnecessary, as Dr Spilsbury is of the opinion that the two Webley bullets would have done for him in minutes anyway. But, in the heat of the moment, the

312

villain must have seen it as a wise precaution. We haven't recovered the gun. We assume it was thrown out of the window somewhere between here and the police station where they were arrested.' He noted that Lily looked aside as he told his fluent lies.

'Mmm ... probably picked up and kept or sold on. There's a market for such things,' Marland said. 'I see. Sounds reasonable to me.' He looked questioningly at each boy in turn, silently gathering their views before continuing. 'As you say then, all done and dusted. Case closed. And now that your chaps have finally released the old bird, we'll be able to move on and finalize our plans for the funeral. Cassandra didn't want the State ceremony that was on offer. I have that right? Do correct me if I assume too much.'

'Oh, yes. I couldn't bear it. And I don't believe Oliver would have expected it. He was, at heart, a plain sailor, a modest man, you know.'

Sandilands and Marland exchanged astonished looks and indulgent grins over her head.

'All the same, it was *so* kind of the prime minister and Their Majesties to offer. But, in the end, we've decided on a small service for family and friends to be held in the church at his family seat in the country, next Saturday. We're so hoping you'll be able to come, Joe.'

'You won't be the grandest guest there, sir,' said William. 'Not by a long chalk! Tell him, Mama!'

'Shh! Don't brag, William. Anyway, it was a charming gesture. The king and queen have made it understood that if we were to send them an invitation they would be pleased to attend the ceremony.'

'The king and queen?'

'Yes. And such of their offspring as are staying with them. It's only just down the road from them after all ... a mile or two.'

'Cassandra, where exactly are you planning to hold the funeral?' Joe asked carefully. 'I had imagined Westminster. Or St Martin's ...'

'I've just told you, Joe. Weren't you listening? At St Mary's, Upper Dedham. Had you forgotten that Oliver was, like his hero Nelson, a Norfolk man? And – isn't it surprising how these things turn out? – the royal family has gathered together for the next few weeks in Sandringham. Not their usual annual progress – one might have expected them to be up at Balmoral by now, surely? Odd, that ... but conveniently for us, that's where they are – in Norfolk.'

'Surprising, indeed,' said Joe. 'But – convenient? Not so sure about that.' He caught the flare of alarm in Wentworth's eyes and began to get to his feet.

Chapter Thirty-Two

He clamped Lily's arm under his and set off at a fast lick up the boulevard towards the taxi rank in Grosvenor Place. The scene he'd just witnessed had disturbed him and he wondered how much of the undercurrent had been picked up by the sharp young woman trotting at his side. He decided to find out. He'd come at it crabwise.

'Well, what did you make of Cousin Seb, then?'

'A dangerous man, sir.'

'Really? In what way?'

'In the way a sixteen-point stag is dangerous to any rival. He's marking out his territory, bellowing about the place and making sure of his hind.'

'Great heavens! You make that genteel drawing room sound like a Scottish moor in the rutting season.'

'A good analogy, sir. And if I were you, I'd pause for a moment to count up my own points. Because it's *your* eye he's planning to poke out.'

So it was out in the open. She'd seen that much at least.

Joe stopped and turned her to face him. 'I'm not sure I understand your implications,' he began, 'but I am quite certain I don't like the sound of them. The chap's no more romantically interested in Cassandra than am I. If that's what you're suggesting. Good Lord! Attractive woman, of course, and not short of a bob or two, but the man's totally unsuitable. A good five years younger than she is for a start. No money to speak of. And somewhat of an assertive character. Men with a high kill rate in their fighting years

rarely settle down to peaceful domesticity, you know. No –
too much of a daredevil for comfort.'

'Exactly, sir. A modern man. A nice change for
Cassandra. You forgot to add good looking – if you can
accept the Ramon Novarro moustache. But with those
heart-melting hazel eyes who's going to quibble about a
'tache? He's a bit bashed about but he's energetic, and I'd
say exciting. I bet he's got the tickets for Venice booked
already. Yes, Venice . . . that's where he'd take her. Lucky
woman. I envy her.'

'Good Lord!' Joe said again faintly. 'Perhaps you should
register an interest? Join the hinds? But – seriously – ought
I to warn Cassandra of her danger?'

'I'm sure that's not necessary. She knows what's what.
And the boys seem very happy with the new arrangements. I'd put quite some store by that. William's a
romantic but John is surprisingly mature for his years. He's
made his calculations and read the small print in the will,
I'll bet. The only point on which the boys are confused is
what they perceive to be their mother's warm attentions to
you, sir.'

Joe started to walk on. 'None of your business,
Wentworth, but since you brazenly choose to air it, I'll tell
you – she's a demonstrative woman who's been married
for donkey's years to a chap who was mostly absent and
when present was not the best at expressing emotion.
When a sensitive and concerned fellow – that's me – shows
a little regard she responds with a shade too much warmth,
perhaps. Stop sneering! I think I have enough experience
of life to know the difference between genuine affection
and a show of it.'

He left a pause to allow her to absorb the suggestion of
his worldliness, angry with himself that he had even
embarked on self-justification.

'All that hand-clasping, sir?'

'Yes, that. And the slightly calculated and over-long
embraces . . . the pretence of intimate knowledge . . .' Joe

shook his head. 'As a matter of fact, I prefer *chocolate* cake ... No, all a sham ... I regret to say,' he added, to be tormenting.

'Have you asked yourself why she would bother, sir?'

'Can't say I've given it much thought with all the other things screaming for my attention. Assassination trumps a languishing look any day.' He sighed and gave her arm an encouraging squeeze. 'And, at all events, you can put all this *Milady's Boudoir* nonsense out of your head – we have more serious matters to mull over. Cassandra's news was a bit of a facer, don't you think?'

'Glory be, yes! Norfolk! A selection of the royal family gathered together under one doubtless rickety church roof.'

'And, before you ask – I had no idea. If our Morrigan gets to hear of this – and on the rambling grapevine that is English society, she's probably had word already – she'll be forging her invitation, hiding herself behind the arras or planning to blow up the church. Next Saturday. It's tight, but she must be accounted for well before next Saturday.'

'Morrigan! Entertaining load of cobblers you were dishing out for the Dedhams! The cabby ruled her out? Oh, yes? And have you investigated a connection between the possible Sinn Fein lady and the possible gent at number thirty-nine?'

'Mountfitchet? He's not as white as the driven snow. Bacchus managed to gain access to the gentleman in one of his more wakeful moments. Kicked out of his regiment for naughtiness of various kinds. But he hasn't two working brain cells to rub together, nor a political bone in his body, which is English to the core. No Irish connections whatsoever. Dead end I'm afraid, Wentworth.'

Taxis seemed to be few and far between on a Sunday afternoon. And, annoyingly, the moment Joe had attracted the attention of one, Wentworth unhooked her arm from his and turned a stricken face to him. 'Oh, my Gawd!' she gabbled. 'Sir! Ever so sorry. I've left my shoulder bag by

317

the sofa back at the admiral's.' She looked to left and right, calculating distances. 'I'll nip back and get it. Straight in and out. Don't you come – they'd haul you in again and offer us drinks and we'd lose another hour. Look, that taxi's drawing up . . . don't let it go. Hop in and I'll see you back at the Yard. I can just stay on the doorstep and ask Eva to fetch it out for me.'

She was six steps down the road by the time he called after her. 'I know what you're up to, constable! Stay clear of the hazel eyes – and the antlers!'

The taxi was turning in to Victoria Street when he began to curse himself for all kinds of a fool. He'd seen her hang her battered old satchel on the hatstand in his office before they left. Too shabby to take out to tea in Mayfair?

'Cabby! Back to Melton Square! Fast!'

Lily walked past the Dedhams' house and went to tug on the door bell of the residence of Mr Ingleby Mountfitchet.

She didn't much like the look of the manservant who answered. Untidy, unwashed she suspected, and displaying all the cold cunning of a polecat. She told him she'd been sent to meet Mr Mountfitchet. His master would be expecting her, she added, dropping her voice to a confidential purr and putting a foot over the threshold.

'Don't be daft,' was the rude response. 'He's said nothing to me. It's six o'clock on a Sunday. He's in his room. Recovering. And he's not asked for one of your kind as far as I know. You've got the wrong day. It's Fridays he's frisky.' He began to swing the door shut.

This was exactly what Lily wanted to hear. Her calculations and wild theories had been on the right lines. She wasn't withdrawing now. She decided to make a scene. In her loudest cockney screech and waving her arms about, she pretended to lose her temper. 'What the 'ell's going on 'ere? I've come halfway across town for an encounter with Mr Mountfitchet . . . This is number thirty-nine, isn't it?

318

Well then, muttonhead, I'm the replacement for that last little disappointment. Besides, he owes us and I'm here to collect. Let me in or I'll have to stand in the street an' shout fire an' rape an'—'

'For God's sake get her in off the doorstep, Warminster!' The voice from the shadows at the end of the hall was lazy and amused.

The manservant stood aside, slammed the door behind her and grumpily moved off down the hallway.

Lily looked around to get her bearings. She was remembering a conversation with the ageing tart patrolling the Baze. 'Before yer takes yer 'at off, dearie, yer checks yer exit. In case 'e turns nasty.' Lily located the door knob and noted that the door was not locked.

The space in which she found herself hadn't changed since Victorian times. She had an impression of tiled floor, mahogany furnishings, drooping drapery and dust-filmed plants struggling for survival in ornate pots. A grandfather clock whirred and clunked and began to strike six. There was about everything a sweet smell of rotting foliage.

The source of it moved quietly forward.

'Well, well, let's take a look at *you*, shall we?'

Ingleby Mountfitchet proceeded in accordance with his own suggestion. He stared long and critically at Lily. She stared back. He was in his forties and what Lily thought of as 'going to seed'. Stooped shoulders, long unkempt hair, a pot belly and a dingy skin marred what might once have been a good-looking man. The impression of neglect was offset by the splendid Chinese lounging coat he was wearing. In brightly patterned silk and of loose cut, it was the perfect choice of garment for a Mayfair gentleman recovering from something unspecified on a quiet Sunday afternoon. Lily refused to speculate on what he might or might not have on beneath it. His breath stank fruitily of alcohol. Lord! Could that smell be cherry brandy? But he was by no means incoherent. She was relieved to see, as she gave him a professional evaluation, that his eyes,

319

though rheumy, were perfectly focused. They swept her from head to foot and his lip curled.

This was the moment when Lily's plan might very well falter. She stood tall and, aware that she had very little to tempt a man in the bosom department, stuck out her chin instead. She peeled off her gloves and placed them on the hall table; a hatstand received her hat. She shook out her hair. That at least always seemed to get attention. She took a few nonchalant strides down the hall towards him.

'Two out of ten,' he sneered. 'Blonde and young. But the rest . . . a bit of a disaster, wouldn't you say? The upholstery? Oh, my dear! Someone's rather skimped on the filling. They field the reserves on a Sunday, I take it? Or is Mrs Braithwaite running out of full-bodied recruits?'

Lily raised her eyebrows in scorn. 'Mrs Braithwaite knows her business. She knows her clients. You should trust her. I've been specially selected for this visit. She thought you might be in need of a good whacking after your disgraceful conduct the other night. And I'm rather good at punishing wayward young gentlemen.' Lily advanced on him aggressively, reached out, and grasped the loose collar of his robe in one hand. She tugged his face close to hers and snarled, 'You upset one of our girls. One of our top-drawer first eleven. Can't have that, can we? I think I'm going to have to send you up to your room and deal with you.'

While she spoke she passed her other hand round his back and slipped the sash of his gown from its moorings at his waist. Trying for a lascivious leer, she looped the length of silk playfully round his neck, encountering a bobbing Adam's apple but no resistance.

'Good boy,' she breathed. 'I usually use a warm silk stocking. This is what's called a *collier de soie*. Tight enough for you?' She pulled harder until he gasped and nodded. Gratified to hear his breathing growing faster, she put a hand in his oiled hair and pushed him roughly down on to his knees. 'And this is the position I like my naughty boys to adopt. Stay down! Now, before I drag you off upstairs to administer your punishment' – she nodded towards the sweeping staircase – 'I need an apology to take back to the boss. I want to know what you did to make our girl run off in the night. You're about to be blackballed, you know. You'd better make your side of the story convincing if you're to do business with us again. We're very particular who we deal with.'

His voice took on a little boy's whine as he replied. 'Not my fault, honestly. How was I to know her husband was in the same regiment? It's your fault. Should have done your homework. "Confidentiality assured" my arse! "Companionship of the first quality provided" – at least they got that right. She's married to snotty old Buster Belton, and they don't come more top drawer than that. Never could stand the fellow! Colonel now, they tell me . . . swanning about in bloody Burma, leaving his wife alone for years. Deserves all he's getting. I recognized her at once, of course. Good-looking woman, if you like 'em raven haired. We'd met at two or three regimental dos. I was willing enough, but she wouldn't have it. Oh, no. Put her completely off her stroke.'

'You threw her out without paying is what we heard.'

'Not true! It was her decision to beat the retreat. Too prim and proper despite the tawdry trade she's involved in. A telephone tart! I wonder if it's got to old Buster's ears yet? Perhaps someone ought to tell him the memsahib's spending her evenings doing war relief of a kind he wouldn't approve of?' He made the mistake of turning a waspish face to Lily. 'Perhaps I'll ask Warminster to bring me a sheet or two of regimental writing paper . . . that'll get his attention. I'm sure I still have some about the place . . . Anyhow, upshot is, she screamed and ran. Stupid cow!'

An evil twist of the sash round his neck reminded him he was supposed to be abject and he whined again: 'All her fault . . . do agree . . . but I'm ready to take my punishment if you think I've deserved it.'

Lily had all she wanted and was eager to leave. She released her grip on his neck and hair, and wiped her sticky hand on the Chinese silk at his shoulder. 'Thank you for that. Tempted though I am by your offer of a fat bum to thrash, I think I'll be off now. You can get up, you disgusting old toad. I'll let myself out.' She made for the door.

He was fitter and less drunk than she had reckoned. And much more angry.

With a snarl he was on his feet, gown flapping open, and coming after her. Lily turned, reached for and grabbed the loose sleeve of his outstretched arm. As his dash along the corridor carried him forward she pivoted, stuck out a foot, twisted and heaved. He landed full length on his back with a thud and an ominous crack as his skull hit the tiled floor. A plant stand, knocked out of kilter by his flying right elbow, wobbled. Its cargo of aspidistra in heavy pot fell to the ground and exploded like a howitzer in a shower of earth and shards by his ear. He howled. He began to raise himself, hugging his elbow, dazed but vowing retribution. 'Who the hell *are* you? Just you wait, madam . . . I'll see you in jail. No, I'll get Jonas to help me drag you upstairs and teach you a lesson . . . Jonas!' Filth began to flow from his lips as he embroidered on the punishment he intended to inflict.

The manservant, drawn by the yells and the crash, appeared at the end of the hallway in time to see the tart he'd just let in, one knee on his master's chest, doing something unspeakable but clearly painful to Mountfitchet's recumbent and semi-naked body. He stood, uncertain, unable to react. To intervene or make himself scarce? What in hell was going on? Some kind of game? He'd seen some rum scenes under this roof – participated in some, too – but this one looked a bit too real for comfort. Mountfitchet screamed again. Warminster drew his conclusions: this wasn't playtime. The girl was making him suffer all right.

He decided to let 'er rip.

Aware of his presence, she called out to him. 'Warminster – if that's really your name – come closer. I need a witness. In a moment you must fetch a bucket of water and chuck it over your master. He's not harmed. He's just had a dizzy spell and tripped over an aspidistra. Oh, and bring a mop for the floor. It's covered with filth of one kind or another. Now, Mountfitchet, I'll say this clearly, and if you should later find you're a little hazy on the details you can refer to Warminster here who is listening with commendable attention: your regiment has severed ties with you, and I for one trust their judgement. Leave those ties cut. Make no attempt to contact the officer you've just mentioned to me. Mrs Braithwaite has her connections – she'd set the law on you. And I'd come back and separate you from your crown jewels. Such as they are. My hat and gloves, please, Warminster.'

She paused in the shrubbery, as Mrs Colonel Belton apparently had, to hitch up her stockings and straighten her hat. If Lily had had a Balkan Sobranie available in a dolly bag, she'd have lit it. And taken a couple of nerve-calming puffs while considering her options.

Mountfitchet apparently was not a man to risk an appearance on the streets of Mayfair in his underpinnings. With no sign then, as now, of pursuit, the entirely innocent woman who'd used up so much police time and so many police handkerchiefs had made the mistake of trying to jump into the admiral's cab. Out of the frying pan and into the line of fire. Poor woman. An encounter with Mountfitchet followed seconds later by one with Fenian gunmen? No wonder she'd been emotional. No wonder she'd stuffed her fingers in her ears, shut her eyes and screamed. And then gone underground.

Sandilands, in his lies, seemed, in fact, to have stumbled on the truth.

Mrs Belton was no more than a neglected army wife seeking cash and excitement. One of the hundreds of lonely and desperate women stepping out under the bright lights of the streets of London. Lily, out on her beat, had shared a park bench and an intimate conversation with many such. She'd heard confidences so raw, so devastating, they could only have been whispered into the receptive ear of a stranger who would listen and not condemn. The dangerous life of a London prostitute was no mystery to Lily.

Mrs Belton was clearly leading a dubious life that could only end in disaster, but she was no Morrigan.

And yet Morrigan had been here.

Someone had fired the last decisive bullet from the pavement a few feet from where she was standing now. Lily retraced Mrs Colonel Belton's steps through the shrubbery and on to the pavement edge.

With unnerving coincidence, a taxicab screeched and swayed to a halt in front of her.

Chapter Thirty-Three

The door opened. Joe got out, bowing and smiling.

'Still searching for your bag, Wentworth? Let me help. I think I may have a clue. Do get in.' He called to the driver. 'Change of plan, cabby . . . another one. Take us to St George's Hospital, will you?' He was trying for unconcern but feared he betrayed his tension as he asked: 'Successful raid mounted, I take it, Wentworth . . . judging by the jaunty angle of your hat?'

'Very successful, sir.'

'And now you're going to reassure me that you came into no direct contact with the dubious owner of the premises in front of which I find you skulking? That nothing . . . untoward occurred?'

'Oh, plenty of untoward, sir. Lashings of it. Threats of a deviant sexual nature, blackmail and violence amounting to actual bodily harm all occurred. I'm afraid the gentleman has grounds for complaint against the forces of law and order, but somehow I don't think he'll fancy standing up in court to tell exactly how his privacy was invaded.'

She was smiling as she spoke but Joe was horrified. 'Tell me you're all right, for goodness' sake, Wentworth!' he croaked.

'Tickety boo, sir. I came out as intact as ever I was when I went in.'

Joe sighed. 'Here we go again! Very well – you got there . . . ?'

* * *

'So, you see, she's not your Morrigan, sir.' Wentworth gave him a sideways look, uneasy with Joe's silence. 'But I think you already knew that. You weren't lying to the Dedhams, were you? And why are we coming to the hospital? The cabby really has regained consciousness – is that it?'

'Notes of some of his communications with members of his family have started to come through. We're in the neighbourhood . . . I thought we might check on him ourselves. If we should be lucky enough to find him compos mentis I should like to shake his hand. Ah, here we are.'

The matron welcomed them herself and had them conducted to the private room that had been allocated to Percy Jenner. 'There's a constable on duty and his daughter's sitting with him,' she'd told them.

'But he's asleep! How can he possibly be taking notes? This amounts to dereliction of duty,' Joe hissed. He prepared to poke the gently snoring constable in the ribs, but found his arm being restrained by the young girl at the cabby's bedside.

'Please don't bother him, sir. He's done double time. His relief didn't turn up and I was here anyway so I says just you have a quiet kip in that chair over there and I'll stand watch. I'm Percy's daughter, sir. The eldest. Clara. I've been taking notes. Sent 'em on to the super . . . what's 'is name . . . Hopkirk. Didn't they get them?'

Percy Jenner's daughter was a pretty girl of about sixteen and if she had her father's presence of mind she would be a good girl to leave in charge, Joe thought. He calmed himself.

'Thank you, Clara. Well done. Commander Sandilands. And this is my assistant, Constable Wentworth. We did indeed receive your messages. Glad to hear your pa is doing better. Anything more to report?'

'Same as ever. "Lucid intervals" is what the doctor says he's having. Good sign, they think. But his brain's swollen,

326

or something . . . can brains swell, sir? Anyhow, they don't want him using it for a bit. He needs to be asleep most of the time. I think they're giving him something to keep him under. Not natural to be unconscious all this time, is it?'

'Has he spoken? Does he remember what happened to him?'

'Oh, yes, sir. It's all down here in my notebook. Constable Mills copied it in his own hand to present to the super.' She offered up her notepad. 'Shall I read it out? It's in shorthand. Not very good shorthand, but I can read it back all right. I'm taking a secretarial training. It's all here with dates and times. He came to the first time yesterday when Ma was with him and started muttering. Family stuff you wouldn't want to be bothered with. Said he was sorry for the trouble. Now – this morning with just me here, he asked: "Is she okay – the girl? Did they shoot her too?" He was out of his skin with worry. Twitching with it. Memory coming back . . . I said as no, she was all right and not to fret . . .'

'Just the right thing to say, Clara, and quite true. Carry on.'

'He said who'd done it. Irish. He went on about Fenians. I couldn't spell the words he used even in shorthand, but I had a go. Those two blokes, sir, he said they'd shot the admiral and the policeman and the butler but he didn't know what they'd done to the lady passenger.' She consulted her notes and went on more hesitantly: 'And then he said . . . um . . . maybe he was rambling a bit . . . he said: had they got the third man?'

'Look again, Clara. Are you sure he said "man"?'

'Yes. And *third*. As though there were three villains. But it only mentioned two in the papers. So I thought he must be confused. I asked him, "Dad, who else was shooting?" "Dunno, Clara," he says. And then he says: "Bigger gun – Browning." Dad would know about guns. "Who was it shooting, Dad?" I asked him again. "Burlington Bertie from Bow," he says. Then he laughs and starts singing the song. Rambling a bit, I thought. Next he grunts out a few more words that don't make much sense but I took 'em down straight . . . just as he said. Then Dad coughs and sinks from sight again. What shall I do now?'

'More of the same, Clara. That's excellent work! Look, stay on watch, will you? I'll go and telephone for the constable's replacement. You might like to stir him up a bit in a few minutes. Give him time to straighten his collar. He'll want to look a bit sharper when the super comes roaring in. Just one more thing . . .' He took his own notebook and a pencil from his pocket and passed them to Lily. 'The constable is an adept at shorthand too,' he said genially. 'Just get your heads together, will you, and work out word for word that bit about the third gunman. It's important.'

Lily scribbled as Clara showed and read out her shorthand. Suddenly she exclaimed and raised her pencil from the page, staring at the words she'd just written down.

'You all right, miss? Aw, you've gone and broken your point! Here, borrow mine.'

Chapter Thirty-Four

The telephone was ringing on Joe's desk as they entered his office. He hurried to answer.

'Sir! Yes, sir. Just got back. All as we supposed. Message delivered just as we discussed. By the way – I was invited to attend the admiral's funeral . . . I wondered if you . . . of course. Yes. Norfolk . . . Just inside a week . . . It will have to be . . . I've got this in hand, sir.' He made polite retreating noises and put down the telephone.

'Well, that was quite an afternoon, Wentworth. One way or another. Bit of a facer. Clears up questions I had, confirms some outrageous suspicions and presents us with a diplomatic minefield to tiptoe through.' Joe pointed to the telephone. 'My every move monitored, you see. Actions guided. Outcome decided by committee. Now, Wentworth, the words we have to exchange are to stay within these walls and between us. Do you understand?'

'No, I don't. All you want to know is who shot the admiral. Hopkirk will want to know. Bacchus has probably worked it out already.'

'Your faith in Bacchus is beginning to make me uneasy, Wentworth. Leave the men to me to brief. They will hear what I want them to hear.'

The girl's puzzlement was turning into truculence. 'But what I found out in Mountfitchet's lair throws light on the Russian aspect of this case. It shows us that it's simply not there. It severs the connection. Hopkirk will—'

'Listen. We had already eliminated the taxi girl.' Joe steeled himself to deliver the disappointment. 'Routine police work. Chappel called in a few favours on his old patch – excellent stuff – and we came up with Mrs Braithwaite. Not her real name. She keeps an annexe next to the Pinks Hotel with a useful rear entrance. High-class operation. Never one to give trouble. The calibre of the customers seems to render it immune to the prying eyes of the law. Indeed, some of their number *are* the prying eyes of the law. The lady was persuaded by someone more influential than Hopkirk to look in her books and verify the existence of Mr Mountfitchet's visitor on the night in question. All is as you supposed, Wentworth. As, indeed, you have actually demonstrated by your intervention. You heard me tell the admiral's family that she had been eliminated from our inquiries. You also heard me say the inquiry was concluded. No need for further investigation. I thought I'd made that clear.'

Joe was trying to be discouraging; he feared he was being bombastic and annoying.

To his surprise, she smiled at him and the smile was broad and free from any trace of irony. 'Good old Inspector Chappel! Well done, that copper! Routine police work, as you say, sir. Glad to hear bread and butter bobbying is getting results!'

'But you're thinking – I know *I* am – that it would have been even better to have heard it before you opened negotiations with Mr Mountfitchet.'

'Oh, I quite enjoyed it, sir. Stimulating. But I'm still puzzled. I thought you were looking for a *civil* motive for the killing. Are you now saying you're happy to accept a political one? When it's obvious that at the bottom of all this there's a possibility that someone hired the Irishmen to do the killing for quite other reasons? That someone hired known Fenians deliberately, following the previous attacks on military men, to send everybody down the wrong trail? Well, it worked. And our villain stayed at the

330

scene long enough to fire the decisive bullet when it looked as though his schemes were going wrong. It wasn't an exotic goddess of terror we should have been looking for.' She looked him in the eye as she delivered her thunderbolt. 'It was a home-grown family member.'

Joe flinched and slowly nodded. He looked at the notebook she produced and passed across the desk to him. He looked at the last page. 'Burlington Bertie? What are we to infer from that?'

'I think you've already done your inferring, sir. And you're as unhappy with it as I am. We're each waiting for the other to go first.'

'Yes. Well, it's a concise image – for someone hanging on to consciousness. The cabby did well. Again! It's a clear picture in two words of the man we're looking for. A swaggering figure in top hat and tails. Everyone knows the music hall act. Everyone can sing the song. A man a little the worse for wear after a boozy night out. A toper staggering home down the street would be just part of the scenery in that area. You wouldn't look at him twice.'

Lily took the book from him and began to read. 'The cabby's exact words were: ". . . pissed as a newt, he was. Couldn't walk straight. But he could shoot straight all right." And Dr Spilsbury confirms that. Single shot, right through the heart. So, a man, not drunk but unsteady on his feet.' Her voice faltered. 'I couldn't help it, sir . . . the image of Sebastian Marland came to mind.' She fell silent, colouring with embarrassment. 'Oh, sorry, sir. When I say it out loud I can hear how ridiculous it sounds. I've gone and done it now, haven't I? I must look a complete idiot. Um . . . I think I'd better make myself scarce. It's been a long day. Sorry . . . I really will remove myself from the premises now.'

'Stay!' Joe spoke automatically. He got up, went to the door, locked it, and put the key in his pocket. Apologetically, he smiled and said: 'I've seen you move, Wentworth. You could outrun me as well as out-think me, so I take no chances. You won't leave this room until you've signed the forms I put before you last evening. You're into something way above your head ... my fault entirely ... but you must trust me to do the right thing as far as your career is concerned! I was just speaking to the Home Secretary ... or being spoken to ... for the umpteenth time today. I suppose you'd better hear what transpired this morning while you were out playing hopscotch!'

Chapter Thirty-Five

It was uncomfortable. It was demeaning. He was a high-ranking officer, for God's sake! He could have this girl shorn of her epaulettes and buttons and stuck away in the Tower or somewhere quiet in five minutes, no questions asked. He owed her nothing. She was eminently dispensable. Why was he sitting behind his desk, at bay, hesitating to meet her eye?

Because, for a start, the wretched girl had – foolishly but bravely – put herself in bodily danger to single-handedly unearth evidence it had taken a squad of men days to piece together. Sandilands didn't shoot sitting ducks, carrier pigeons or game out of season. And he didn't undermine effective officers. Fair was fair. And besides, although, for old-fashioned reasons, he'd advised against the involvement of a woman at the outset, it had become very clear that this one, at any rate, had considerable talents. Talents they still had need of. They hadn't finished with her yet, he told himself firmly. One last job to do. He thought hard and decided there was no risk involved for her. No risk at all.

And those damned eyes were hard to meet when you weren't entirely sure that what you were telling them was the truth. Too big. And too grey. You might just as well try fibbing to the goddess Minerva. Or your nanny.

Joe fidgeted with his blotter and launched into his account. Always give the good news first. He tried for a positive tone, picking out the first favourable aspect of this whole murky affair that came to mind. 'Well, it seems that Hopkirk and I had it right all along. A common domestic murder, not an assassination, is what we had to deal with. And what has triumphed in the end is – as you noted – good old regular police work. The superintendent has done some ferreting around in Sussex and reported back to me. He's banged on doors and interviewed bank managers in the time-honoured way.'

He pulled a page of notes from under the telephone and glanced at them briefly. 'Frog's Green, that's the village. Sebastian Marland's motor business is not as healthy as we had been led to believe ... managers sacked, disappointing trials ... though banking records reveal no evidence that he is actually in debt yet. And he has an alibi for the night of the killing, if not a watertight one. His housekeeper, who appears devoted to the chap, declares he went to bed early and was still abed when she took him his early morning cup of tea. She's the kind of lady whose evidence would stand up wonderfully in court ... you can imagine?'

'No mention of a phone call in the night?'

Joe smiled at her perception. 'No. She reports that, after a hasty breakfast, the young master made two phone calls and screeched off in his car, claiming he was responding to an emergency.'

'But didn't Cassandra imply that she'd spoken to him in Sussex straight after the murder? I'm sure she told us she had.'

'It was vaguely phrased to lead us astray. I don't believe Cassandra has any idea that records of trunk calls are available to us. I checked. Many calls were made from her telephone that night, but none to Sussex. I don't think we could make an accusation stick. He could certainly have sneaked off up to London. He could have loitered in evening dress in Melton Square or anywhere in Mayfair and not raised an eyebrow. He certainly wouldn't have been bothered by the beat bobbies. As you say, upper-class drunks are ten a penny on a Saturday night. And, as the cabby observed, steady gun hand, unsteady on his pins. He could have done it. Hired the Irishmen and hung around to make sure they did the job. But we run into another factor that would get me a clip round the ear if I approached the Director of Public Prosecutions with a request for arraignment. There's no kind of motive – financial, I mean – that would stand up and convince. He inherits a modest lump sum from his uncle and a yearly retainer for supervising the boys, and he had foreknowledge of that, but it's a long way short of a fortune. No judge in the land would accept it as an incitement to murder.'

'But if he were to marry Cassandra, sir?'

'Ah. Then we have a different scenario entirely. The widow has money of her own and a good slice of the admiral's wealth comes to her too. But it would be assuming quite a lot, wouldn't you say?'

'Yes. And to take the risk, he'd have had to be able to count on gaining her affection?'

'Exactly. Quite a gamble.'

Lily frowned and took a deep breath. 'What I'm thinking is – there *was* no gamble. He already had it, sir. Her affection, I mean.'

'Explain yourself, Wentworth.'

'I didn't have the impression that he was the kind of man who would kill a close family member for an *uncertain* source of cash. We know that he's a man hardened and made ruthless by his wartime experience – he's used to shooting people, to put it bluntly. But I think it would take a much stronger reason than financial gain to make the man I saw this afternoon pull a trigger in cold blood.'

'What have you in mind?'

'The strongest motive of all. Love, sir. For Cassandra, yes. But more than that. He has affection for those boys too. Neglected by their father, they must have felt he filled a certain gap in their lives. They clearly love and trust him. An older man, a war hero but not one on a pedestal. A man who looks them in the eye and understands their needs in a way their father was not able to do. Didn't you get a feeling of ... unity ... common purpose ... *understanding* which we weren't invited to share in when we were there this afternoon, sir?'

Joe nodded. 'I was happy to see the family closing ranks. Quite proper.'

'The admiral was on the point of retiring, wasn't he? The whole family must have had mixed feelings about that. His return to the family hearth after years away striding the bridge might not have been entirely welcome in some quarters. Autocratic, authoritarian and no longer five hundred sea miles distant . . .'

Joe grunted. 'Silly, bone-headed old twit. Dedham, I mean. It was young William who precipitated the whole thing, I shouldn't wonder. The first time he ran away from school his father, who was at sea, had him sent back – by telegraph. Last winter he ran off again, apparently. This second time the admiral happened to be at home. He gave him a talk about disgracing the family by behaving like a weed, administered a good thrashing and sent him straight back to school, where he was thrashed again. Cassandra was distraught and, I think, angry.'

'You're never going to say it, sir, so I will: it's a conspiracy we're looking at, isn't it? Penelope got tired of waiting for Odysseus. She got fed up with unpicking that wretched weaving of hers and fell for one of the suitors.'

Joe sighed and spoke reluctantly. 'It was Sebastian who pulled the trigger but it was with Cassandra's knowledge and perhaps more ... she might have devised the whole scheme. Under the layers of scented chiffon, she's as tough as old boots, I'd say. And I'd guess, Wentworth, they've been lovers for quite some time. They have that trick of reading each other's mind – finishing sentences, speaking for each other – did you notice? And on a practical note – Cassandra knew in advance exactly where the admiral would be and when on that evening.'

'So her affectionate attentions to you were nothing more than a blind. If she's embarrassing *you* with suggestions of interest . . .'

'Say rather *intriguing*, Wentworth. I was not embarrassed.'

'Very well, sir. Drawing you in, luring you with kisses and cake . . . you're not going to suspect her of an amorous connection with anyone else, are you?'

'I didn't. Not at all sure I do now,' he added rebelliously.

Lily noticed his gathering unease and changed tack. 'And then there's her shooting. She tells me you taught her and that she was a very poor pupil? You despaired of her ever hitting a target?'

Joe looked up sharply and frowned. 'That's not right, no. As a matter of fact, she was rather good. I've known one or two women who were adept with firearms.' He smiled briefly. 'I owe my life to their skill and readiness to use them. Cassandra fussed and pretended to be hopeless but she could hit a target all right. Well she did, didn't she? She was pleased and surprised.'

'Exactly. And if she'd hit and killed *both* Irishmen she'd have been even happier. It was probably always her intent to eliminate them. Just in case. It was pure bad luck for her and Sebastian when Mrs Colonel Belton hove into view and commandeered the getaway taxi. She rather fouled things up.'

Joe had no time for protective self-deception. 'We were taken in, Wentworth. By a skilled actress.' This was the moment to rip off the bandage and assess the damage underneath. 'You were rather less taken in than I, I have to say.'

'Oh, I swallowed it whole – the flattery and the flannel. Faithful Penelope! Ha! The tears, the confidences, the "brave little widow" stuff. And all the time she was using me as an unsuspecting source of inside information on the inquiry.'

'Inside information? What did she wring out of you? You'd better tell me.'

'I'm afraid I confirmed the existence of the third shooter, sir.'

'Mmm ... and she managed that with some skill. By raising the matter herself she diverted suspicion. An old trick ... and we fell for it. Anything else?'

'I mentioned your resignation, sir. She declared her intention of calling in a few favours to keep you in post.'

'Ah! So that's how it happened. I could wonder why she should bother.'

Lily looked away.

Joe's grimace of a smile showed his discomfort. 'Better the fool you know, I suppose. Keep in place the gullible young idiot you already hold in the palm of your hand ...'

'No! Loyal and gallant friend! She exploited you, sir, but the blame is entirely hers. Who wouldn't want you in their corner? I would.'

Her innocent support surprised him. 'Shall we agree, then, not to be too hard on ourselves? They're both considerable performers.'

'I can't wait to see the act they put on for Sir Archibald at the Old Bailey. He'll see through them. And there's one thing you got right, isn't there?'

'Oh, yes?'

'Your Morrigan. At least Cassandra has red hair.'

'Indeed she has.' He fell silent, waiting for her next inevitable challenge.

'Who are you going to detail to arrest them?' she asked carefully. 'Not an enviable duty. Have you decided what you're going to do?'

'It's been decided for me. And it's absolutely nothing, Wentworth. Abso—'

'Absolutely bugger all, sir?'

He smiled and glanced again at the telephone. 'I had a conversation with the Commissioner. I told you I'd had a rough morning. I apprised him of my suspicions; I told him where the investigation was leading. Ten minutes later I find I have the Home Secretary himself on the telephone.

I've – we've – been well and truly gagged, Wentworth. As you remind me, no one wanted to stomach a political assassination, but since the two miscreants had been arrested and a confession extracted before their guns were cold, it was thought that at least this redounded to the credit of the forces of law and order. It was neat, Wentworth. The papers went to town in a froth of support for two English heroes – an admiral fighting, sword against bullet, on his doorstep, a brave London cabby fighting for his life in hospital – they liked it. It rallied the troops. They were pleased to hear a much-needed patriotic hurrah from the nation's throat.'

'And with an election imminent,' Lily said grumpily, 'and the men of the country rushing to the polling booth to support a strong party . . .'

'And the certainty of swift retribution. A good hanging is always appreciated by the British rabble, let's not forget that.'

'A double hanging being irresistible.'

They were doing a lot of agreeing, echoing each other's thoughts. Joe paused. He knew he was about to shatter the appearance of concord.

'But the second scenario I was putting before them – one English war hero gunning down another, Royal Air Force and Royal Navy at each other's throat, the threat of famous names splashed across the front pages, a grieving widow to be paraded before the courts, two fine Navy sons and their careers dragged into the mire by the whole thing . . . Well, you can imagine how the blue pencil came out for that lot. And to top it all – we now discover that the royal family is about to attend the victim's funeral . . . be photographed lavishing condolences on the man's killers. It's all too much for the public to be burdened with at this politically sensitive time. The National Character would be called into question, apparently. Englishness put in the pillory. Lloyd George himself has made his views clear.'

'So a Welshman, in the interests of preserving the English reputation, is prepared to make a pair of Irish lads take the rap for the whole nasty business?'

He looked at her sharply, skewering her to her chair with a stare as focused as a thrown lance.

'Sorry, sir. That must have sounded prissy.'

'Prissy? I'd have said hectoring and indisciplined.'

Having delivered his shot, Joe lapsed into uneasy silence. He'd asked for this. Lily was doing no more than putting a sharp point on views he held himself. If he'd been sitting over there on the other side of the desk, he'd have been making much the same noises of protest. Throughout this business he'd encouraged her to speak her mind, invited her to share her thoughts with him as an equal. In his self-critical mood, Joe feared his motives were less honourable. He'd made use of the girl. He'd required her, in her bright independence of mind, to question, evaluate but ultimately endorse his actions. It was with a belated clarity that he saw again the relationship that had existed between himself and his mentor in India. Sir George, in his deviousness, his unshakeable belief in the rightness of the country he served, had been exasperating. His smoothly engineered solutions to moral problems had left Joe open mouthed and spluttering objections.

And yet, Joe remembered the verdict of an American girl he'd grown close to in a frontier fort: 'Joe is more like Sir George than he would ever want to admit. Give him a few more years and you won't be able to distinguish the one from the other . . .' He'd snorted and denied it but, only months later, here he was, sitting on the powerful side of the desk, delivering a second-rate imitation of Sir George.

What the hell! At the most inconvenient of moments, the rebel in Joe rose up and yelled a challenge. The rebel was yelling now.

'Get up, Wentworth!' He dashed round the desk and grabbed her by the arm. 'Sit there!' He pushed her without ceremony into his own chair and went to perch himself in

340

the seat she had occupied. 'Now then, instead of bombarding me with bolshy disapproval, just try for a minute or two to pretend you're representing the State and its interests. The people who employ you to preserve the peace and see justice done. The sword and the scales, Wentworth – they're in your hands. What are you going to do for the best?'

White with alarm, she was, for once, speechless.

He began to regret his impulsiveness and looked for common ground. 'From either side of this desk, I'm not at all averse to preserving England's reputation, but like you I'm unhappy about the role of those Irish lads in all this. They pulled the triggers. They shot two men dead and wounded two more. They will die whatever you or I do or say. And they will have deserved it. But they were paid? incited? persuaded? to commit murder by a third party. A third party who traded on the men's nationality to achieve a smokescreen of terrorist aggression to hide his own narrow, personal motivation. I will add the two deaths on the gallows to his tally. The Irishmen, the admiral, the beat bobby . . . Constable Swithins his name was. He leaves a widow and three children. Four men dead.'

'I'm glad to hear you've been keeping count, sir. But this bill – nicely tallied though it is – will never be presented, will it? As you say – the State interest will never allow it.'

'Presenting and payment – not the same thing, Wentworth, as any tradesman will tell you.' He came to a decision. 'It will never be *paid* for the reasons I've given. But I see no harm in confronting the man ultimately responsible. It sounds pretty feeble to your ears, perhaps, but it's the best I can do. And no one else, believe me, Wentworth, is going to bother.

'I'm invited to the funeral on Saturday. I shall make time and space for a heart-to-heart chat with the admiral's killer. There's an Indian poet I've got fond of – Rabindranath Tagore. He has something to say on the subject of punishment. "He only may chastise who loves." Well, I can't claim to love the bloke but I think he sensed he had my friendship and respect before all this. And at least, I don't think he'll fail to notice the warmth of my concern! I shall name his victims one by one – I may go so far as to write out their names and head it *Butcher's Bill*. I'll note that it is, for the moment, unpaid.'

'And leave him wriggling in excruciating suspense?'

'Something like that. I agree, it sounds a bit feeble. He may not care. May just take me for a pompous fool and laugh in my face.'

Lily considered for a moment. 'Then *he* would be the fool, sir. But we know that he's not a foolish man. He is, though, hardened. It would take more than a gentlemanly ticking off from you to penetrate his armour. You'll have to pierce him in his soft part . . .'

'I beg your pardon, Wentworth?'

'One short sharp stab is all it will take.'

Joe swallowed. 'What exactly are you proposing?'

'I'd say the thing that mattered most to him in the world is the ready-made family he coveted, the respect and affection the boys have for him. I'm glad they're able to give it and it pains me to say it but sitting over here makes it possible – he's usurped the place of their father. Snatched it without a by-your-leave, killed four men and ruined many lives to achieve his end. If he puts a foot wrong from this moment, or fails in the domestic duties he's taken upon himself, he should be quite certain that the boys will be given the true facts of their father's death. *They* love him all right – they'd be in a position to chastise him. You might have had your hands tied but you can always do a little fancy footwork. Put the boot in, sir.' She looked at him quizzically. 'Not sure you're tough enough. I could do it. I will if you like.'

'Good Lord! What a scurrilous suggestion. A decision worthy of Sir George Jardine,' Joe said faintly. 'Come back over this side at once.'

'I'm out of my depth, sir,' she said, reclaiming her place with relief. 'Does this sort of thing happen . . . Has this happened . . . ?'

'Oh, yes. The ship of State is a cumbersome but sometimes skittish vessel. It takes many skilled hands to keep her on course. And, in stormy weather, the crew have to work together and obey the single voice of the captain.'

He watched her roll her eyes at his histrionics and grin.

'Something amusing you, Wentworth?'

'I was just trying to decide where my position was on this ship of yours – rolling about in the bilges or getting sick in the crow's nest.'

'I think I see you in the brig, Wentworth. Yes . . . alongside Long John Silver in manacles in the brig. And that reminds me . . .' He dug about in his desk drawer. 'Got a pen, have you? We have some pretty filthy business to conduct here tomorrow morning and you're going to be up to your ears in it. We've accounted for the Morrigan but the Morana – goddess of ice and death – is still out and about and seeking a victim. And there'll be half a dozen assorted royal lives on the line next Saturday. I need to know you're on side.'

Chapter Thirty-Six

Bacchus and Fanshawe arrived at the ops room at eight thirty on Monday morning to find Sandilands already installed. The Commander's face lit up at the sight of the large cardboard box Fanshawe was carrying. He didn't try to hide his relief.

'You've got it! I won't embarrass you by asking how on earth you managed to get your hands on it, but well done!'

Bacchus grimaced. 'Had to take a hostage for it, sir. The Home Secretary gets his granny back at noon today if she behaves herself.'

'I expect you've already had a rummage around?'

'Who could resist? Fascinating stuff. I think, with a touch of imagination, we can make something of it.' Bacchus seemed unusually positive.

'And my other request? Did you manage to get the tickets?'

He put an envelope down on the table. 'No problem there. Except for the cost of course which made my eyes water. But then I thought you were most probably expecting it to be accounted for by your department. I've sent in the usual chit. And I have the news item you asked for.' He took a sheet from his inside pocket and put it next to the envelope. 'We have our forger standing by. Name of Sam Scrivener. All we need is the text of the letter and we're off.'

'And the postman,' said Fanshawe. 'Is everyone quite happy about this aspect of the scheme? I mean – couldn't I or Bacchus or even the post office delivery man take care of that? I can't see why we have to involve Wentworth again.'

'I wonder whom you prefer for this duty, Fanshawe? We could send you but they'd just drag you in, subject you to heavy flirting and tell you nothing. The menace of Bacchus's moustache would silence them. These are women who have narrowly escaped summary execution at the hands of the Bolshevik not-so-secret police. They know what it is to have a price on their heads. They know they are still, in a foreign land, pursued. They're jittery. The princess – quite rightly – trusts no one. Especially the people's police force – that's you and your minions, Bacchus. I do believe she regards you as a sort of Cheka-on-a-leash. But she has declared herself ready to accept Wentworth as go-between . . . ambassador if you will. We're not the only shadowy organization to keep this house under surveillance. A young girl paying a visit here is not in the least remarkable – there's a constant stream of them passing through as you are aware. Miss Wentworth has established a relationship of sorts with them and she is, after all – and this cuts some ice with these people – the girl who danced with the Prince of Wales in such amity the other night. She would appear to be in his confidence.'

'They'll know by now that it was Wentworth's interference that saved his life, sir. And thwarted them.'

'Not *them*, Fanshawe. I don't believe we're dealing with a conspiracy. These are people who define themselves by their reverence for monarchy. The British strand may be in bad odour with one of them at the moment but they are and always will be impressed by royal favour. They accept Wentworth as a sort of *chargée d'affaires*, the effective and unthreatening mouthpiece of our establishment. And so, gentlemen, like it or not, she is!'

Bacchus produced the camera bag he'd slung from one shoulder. 'Not sure what you want me to do with this?'

Joe walked over to the easel he'd installed by the window and flung back the covering sheet.

345

'Lord!' Fanshawe exclaimed, recognizing it. 'Not that again! It's the God-awful Russian painting. What are you doing with that daub, sir?'

'It has its part to play in the little show I'm putting on. Hocus pocus, Fanshawe. Never disregard it. The picture belongs to Wentworth. A thoughtful gift from HRH for services rendered. I've examined it closely – more closely, I'd guess, than the Russian contingent have. It's sending us a message. One that I think we can interpret in our own way and call to the attention of the princess and her coterie. Can you take a snap of it in this light with your equipment, Bacchus?'

The Branch man appeared delighted to be challenged and set about putting his camera pieces together, muttering happily of lenses and focal lengths and distances as he worked.

The preliminaries complete, the men looked at each other in satisfaction.

'Do we have to wait for the constable or shall we set about it now and present her with a fait accompli? She is, after all, just delivering the package,' Fanshawe wanted to know.

Joe appeared to be choosing his words. 'The princess will interrogate her – in the most civilized way, of course. And our would-be assassin will most likely be listening in. One would hope so. I would like Wentworth to be familiar with the facts and sufficiently in command of the strategy to be able to improvise if necessary. She has to understand the importance of the offer she is about to extend to the Russians. I want her to be listening when we put it together. Wentworth is not to be regarded as cannon fodder – she's a well-aimed bullet.' He looked at the clock. 'I asked her for nine . . . though her time-keeping seems to be a bit erratic. So . . .'

One minute later they heard the tap on the door.

* * *

'It's a confidence trick, sir!'

'You have it, Wentworth. I put my hands up to it. A deceitful piece of chicanery! A dirty bit of business!'

'The end justifies the means, then, you'd say?'

'Don't be tedious!' Joe responded to her cross face with a flash of impatience. 'This is not a debating society. This is a police force. And a national protection unit. It will take considerable nerve and a degree of low cunning to pull it off. You, I observe, are not short of either, so stay with the stroke I set, will you? We're anticipating no less than the removal – the *permanent* removal, one hopes – of this menace to the lives of the prince and the rest of the royal family. When it's removed, gone abroad, they'll be able to go about their daily business once more without the constant fear of assassination.'

'You say "it", sir.' Lily spoke hesitantly. 'We're talking about "she" – a strong-minded woman who will object to being manipulated. She may refuse to accept a suggestion that she simply leave the country.'

'I would expect so. And that's why we have to make her an offer that is irresistible to her. One that will give more satisfaction than sticking a knife in HRH or whatever she has planned for him next time. We have to thank some ancient Greek for an old military proverb: If you wish to get rid of your enemy, build him a golden bridge to flee across.

'Aristides' advice to Themistocles, I believe, sir,' Bacchus chipped in. 'Concerning the Persian retreat back across the Dardanelles.'

'Thank you, Bacchus. I believe you're right. And we're going to take it again. It's exactly what we're going to do. With the utmost politesse we're going to show our enemy to the border and offer a passage out. The golden bridge in question is a first-class berth on a luxury liner – the *Hirondelle* did you say, Bacchus?'

'Yes, sir. The pride of the French fleet,' he announced. 'She starts on Friday from Cherbourg where she takes on

347

board a few chefs de cuisine and a chanteuse or two. Then she nips across to Southampton where she picks up the English contingent and goes in one hop to New York. Dancing and dining and entertainment all the way. From there, first class again on the transcontinental railway . . . Chicago and the sunset route west to San Francisco.'

They all fell silent, imagining the luxury, the adventure, the wide horizons. Someone sighed.

'May I ask what Anna Petrovna is supposed to do with herself once she gets to California, sir?' Lily asked.

'Ah, yes! The whole point of the exercise! Now – what would constitute an impulse strong enough to counter the urge to kill? I'll tell you: friendship, a reunion, the promise of a fresh start and a wonderful climate, they tell me, in California. And a thriving Russian colony to welcome her. Got your cutting, Bacchus?'

The Branch man showed it around the table and began to read out salient details. 'This appeared a week ago so it's very fresh. There's a good chance that she's not seen it. It's an eye-witness report. A woman recognized as the arch-duchess Tatiana has been sighted in the city of San Francisco. Several times. Climbing aboard a cable-car . . . dancing at Governor Stephens's fund-raising event for Asiatic orphans . . . sipping champagne in a night club . . . You can imagine.'

'Well, you know how it is,' Joe said with a smile. 'An odd thing, but anyone who disappears is reported to have been sighted in San Francisco.'

'Your hero, Oscar, responsible for that little insight, I believe?' Bacchus commented.

With an impatient sigh, Lily burst in: 'San Francisco? But that's halfway round the world! What would a Russian princess be doing in San Francisco? What would *any* Russians be doing there? It's a nonsense!' Her voice was amused and disbelieving.

Fanshawe, for once, concurred. 'Another one. For dead girls, the Tsar's daughters don't half get about the globe.

The last sighting was in Rome. Another one in Japan. And then there was that novice who turned up in a Greek nunnery last year . . . That was supposed to be the religious one – Olga. There's an Anastasia or two doing the rounds in Germany . . . that one they fished out of a canal in Berlin last winter seems to be putting on a convincing act. They're all over the show. Anywhere but in the Koptyaki forest buried under a ton of railway sleepers. They're dead. The whole lot of them. And we don't have to guess – the Bolshies have held up their bloodstained hands for this one.'

'Many would think twice before accepting evidence or even a confession from those duplicitous thugs,' Sandilands reprimanded. 'This identification is not so easily dismissed, Fanshawe. And it's one we really could wish had not surfaced. I have to tell you . . . it is supported by other evidence of survival.' He pursed his lips and fidgeted with his tie.

Oblivious of the exchange of scathing glances and a snort of disbelief, Joe went to stare at the painting, absorbed by dark thoughts. 'I agree – there *are* bodies buried under the taiga. That much I accept. Unfortunately, in spite of our best efforts, no one has been able to establish exactly whose bodies they are. Burned, rotted by acid, crushed by bulldozer and scattered, they could be remains filched from the refuse bins of the local hospital for all we know. Or corpses simply swept up from the streets – heaven knows there was no shortage at the time – starvation and disease were rife. Impossible ever to be sure. I'll tell you now and the story is not to be mentioned outside this room.'

He caught a nervous glance from Bacchus and responded to it: 'We can speak freely. No listening equipment, Bacchus. I haven't authorized it in the ops room.'

Unusually serious, even hesitant, he caught and held everyone's eye, each in turn.

'There are indeed Romanovs buried in the forest near Ekaterinburg. But not all. The Tsar and his son, the heir, were shot and bayoneted to death along with their doctor who tried to intervene. Poor old Botkin. Loyal to the last. The Empress? It's less clear at this point – we really don't know – but it's thought she succumbed and died of natural causes. She had been very ill for some months. Her body may lie there also. It's possible.' He was weighing his words, not wishing to say more than he could verify.

'Uncouth and dangerous though they were, the guards appointed by the Ural Soviet could not bring themselves to shoot the girls, of whom they had got quite fond during their three-month incarceration. They'd appreciated the way they put on no airs and graces but rolled their sleeves up and cooked and cleaned for the household. And kept the peace. In a cramped space with a sick little brother, an increasingly deranged mother and an ineffectual father, the girls were up against it but they made the best of their imprisonment, remaining good natured and friendly with the young lads who were guarding them.

'These were only too pleased to look the other way when a diesel truck turned up one night at the Ipatiev villa with papers granting permission to separate the women from the men and take them away. The family had travelled this way before, as a matter of convenience, and made nothing of it. But this time the Empress – with foresight perhaps? – refused to leave her husband and son. And that's where we lose track of her. The four girls were bundled off. They were driven to the relative safety of the estate of an old marshal of the Tsar's at Lysva which was by then in the hands of the advancing White Army. We have a touching confirmation of this from the villa itself. Our eagle-eyed man in Ekaterinburg during his inspection of the premises after the murders noticed a word scrawled backwards in haste across a mirror ... the letters spelled out *LYSVA*.

'It cannot have been until much later that the girls heard of the deaths of the Tsar and Tsarevich. By then, they had been split up. A quartet of pretty girls with aristocratic ways travelling about Russia would not have got far. They were moved about singly with escorts, dressed in nun's clothes or as nurses. Now, from our geographical perspective we see Russia as Moscow and St Petersburg – a sort of exotic but civilized offshoot of Europe. We forget that thousands more miles of it run east, right over to Japan. And Ekaterinburg is in the middle of this land mass. With access to the Trans-Siberian railway ... The Romanovs didn't go west to the capital – they went *east*, further into the wilderness.

'There was a British frigate – yes, we did *not* abandon the family' – he flicked a quick glance at Lily – 'patrolling on the China station – you will know the one, Bacchus – and it made a pick-up later that year at Vladivostok on the east coast. Thirty-nine packing cases of Romanov goods and a few passengers. It sailed away. To Hong Kong? Possibly. I've not been able to track it. Its log is mysteriously under wraps even to men with more clout than I have. But you can probably see that if you plot a straightish course across the Pacific ocean, you fetch up in California. San Francisco. The shipping port for the armaments that were being sent by the Americans to Russia in support of the Czech contingent and the White Army. Having unloaded their guns, the ships often returned to the home port with a human cargo – refugees. The Vladisvostok–California route has been a very busy one.'

'Good Lord!' Bacchus breathed. 'So that accounts for ... But how the devil ... ?' Frowning, he turned a mutinous face on Sandilands, incredulity, resentment and deference doing battle for his tongue. Joe well understood his officer's dilemma. Bacchus was aware that Sandilands, with his Military Intelligence background, had access to sources he would never reveal. The information he came by was as likely to be acquired over dinner at the Vineyard or lunch at Buck's as garnered from official files.

Resentment won. 'You can't possibly know this!' Bacchus spluttered. 'That's the log of HMS *Kent* you're on about . . . How did *you* get access to it? Sir, you exceed your . . . Who've you been talking to?'

The challenge amounted to indiscipline and he fell silent, seething with indignation and awaiting the commander's set-down.

Joe grinned and playfully poked a finger at his lieutenant. 'Gotcha! You walked right into it, Bacchus. Well, what do the rest of you make of my story? Easy enough to get a pair of old romantics like Bacchus and Fanshawe worked up, but will the Russian ladies be deceived? What I've just handed you is a load of cobbled-together nonsense. A thumping great lie! Full of holes, I confess. But I find the best way of getting someone to swallow a lie is to season it well and stick it between two thick slices of truth. Worth a try?'

There followed a ruminative silence. Joe followed his audience's reactions through from sharp anger at being deceived to disgruntlement, puzzlement and finally a cynical acceptance. He pressed on. 'There you are then – I've given you the imaginary skeleton so to speak, now help me put some real flesh on it.'

'Oh, no. Another corpse that's going to get up and dance,' Lily muttered.

'Exactly that. We're going to resurrect a princess of the blood royal. Tatiana lives! We've got to make them believe that. Get your box out, Bacchus, and let's see what we can use. Unless I've been misinformed, there's a very particular relic of the second daughter in there.'

Mumbling and mistrustful, Bacchus pulled the box into the centre of the table and opened it up.

Inside was a perfectly ordinary Gladstone bag, its leather stamped with the emblem of the United Kingdom. Bacchus took it out and opened it up. 'Our man – one of our men – in Ekaterinburg owned this bag. He had it with him when he made a consular call on the villa in the aftermath of the shootings. In the chaos that reigned – there was a squad still mopping up the pools of blood, retrieving shell cases and looting – he quietly helped himself to some Romanov goods. Not the obvious valuables of which there were plenty lying about the place. He went for the more interesting stuff – letters and diaries. He found things hidden behind water cisterns and under the bath – places the guards hadn't thought to ransack. The outside world had managed to keep in touch with the Romanovs for many a month. Better that such incriminating documents did not fall into the hands of the Bolsheviks, of course.'

He began to take objects from the bag, laying them out with care on the mahogany surface of the table. Lily noticed that he was beginning to sort them as he picked them out. Medals, rings, icons and lockets were put in one corner, small leather-bound diaries and notebooks in another, photographs and letters in the centre. Lily could not hold back a gasp of emotion as she saw a white lace-edged handkerchief embroidered by a child's hand in red silk at the corner. The wobbly letter A – Anastasia? Lily reached for it and held it, breathing in the trace of a spicy cologne lurking in its folds. No, this A was for Alexandra – a gift from a child to its mother.

'It's Tatiana we're hunting for, remember,' Joe reminded them, seeing his small group distracted and sinking fast into fascinated absorption. 'Anything of her in here? We have to reconstitute her from these bits and pieces. We have to breathe life into her . . . conjure up an image so real that her best friend will be convinced she's alive and well and calling her to her side.'

Fanshawe found a sheet of paper. 'Got something, sir! Here's her writing. That's a start. Letter to a friend. In English. Thank God they all seem to have used English, or German. It was never sent, apparently.'

'There was a clamp-down on their correspondence once they were at the Ipatiev house,' said Bacchus. 'It must have been suppressed and kept. Here's a notecase full of letters received.' He handed it to Lily. 'See what you can find.'

Lily was instantly absorbed by the task. After a few moments, her voice trembling slightly, she said: 'I've found a letter from our girl – Anna Petrovna. And it's addressed to Tatiana. 1917. Before all the nastiness burst over them. Oh, she's put . . . there's a hank of hair in here.'

'Hair? Yuck!' said Fanshawe. 'Well, I suppose they were very young things in 1917.'

'It's dark hair,' said Lily, holding it to the light. 'Blue-black, you'd say. Your Morana, sir? I think we've found her.' She skimmed the letter quickly. 'Not much of note. Grumbles and complaints and – oh, talk of patients. A handsome officer she's fallen for . . . they were all at it . . . leg amputations . . . disease . . . She was nursing, of course, following the imperial example of devotion to patriotic duty. The hair is mentioned at the end . . . "By my hair shall you know me!" Strange thing to say?'

'From the Bible. Matthew's gospel. "By their fruits shall ye know them . . ." something like that. Religious lot, the Romanovs. And their correspondence was probably even at that time being monitored by the Red factions,' said Bacchus. 'They found ways of getting round the surveillance. Cocking a childish snook at the enemy. They didn't know then how serious it was all going to get.'

'Prepare to yuck again, Fanshawe,' Joe said with satisfaction. He'd been passing a hand around the bottom of the bag following its turn-out. 'Here it is. Yes! This is what I'd heard mentioned.'

He brought out, wrapped in brown paper, a wild flower album. When he opened it, no collection of dusty stalks and petals fell crumbling from the stiff pages. On each was glued a specimen, but not a botanical specimen. One after another, thick hanks of hair appeared, five in all, ranging in colour from fair to dark brown. Sandilands looked at the date in the front of the book. 'Gathered up and stuck in the day all the children had their hair cut off. They caught some disease or other – measles, I believe – which necessitated a shaven head. But – this is it. This is something we can use. Wentworth – pick out Tatiana's hair, will you?'

Lily took the book from him and leafed through it. 'Here's a fine, brownish-blond that must have been the Tsarevich's hair . . . and . . . Ah! Here it is, sir. It's a wonderful rich red. Dark red. Titian, would you say?'

'That's the one.' Joe reached for it and began to smooth a forefinger along the still-gleaming tress. 'Celtic ancestry. This lady could trace her line back to Ivan the Terrible, let's not forget. And a selected lock of this is about to make its way from California in a letter, written in Tatiana's hand, and it will say at the end, what was it? – "By my hair shall you know me!" Can we arrange for an envelope from the States, Bacchus? Stamps and suchlike? Evidence of diplomatic clearance?'

'Nothing easier,' Bacchus told him. 'I'll get straight on to it. Not sure I can compose the text of the letter though, the phrasing. I mean, I'm a thirty-five-year-old bloke. This is a twenty-five-year-old woman who's meant to be speaking. Hand me a written version of what you want said and I'll get our forger to do it.'

The men glanced at each other in dismay. 'Um . . . yes . . . ah . . .'

'Don't look at me!' said Fanshawe.

'I'll do it,' Lily said. 'Just give me time to read through these letters of Tatiana's and get the flavour and an ear for the phrasing. Can anyone tell me what sort of girl she was? I suppose I ought to know that if I'm going to pretend to be her.'

It was Bacchus who replied. 'We hear plenty about the others but not a great deal about this one. Mother's favourite . . . reserved . . . stand-offish and squashing. Her pekinese dog was shot dead in the bloodbath. Sorry, I'm not being very helpful. Now if you wanted Maria we could supply – people are only too pleased to talk about her and they smile when they speak. A true Russian beauty, open and friendly. It was the little one no one could stand – Anastasia. Even her mother called her a devil. Mischievous little troublemaker seems to be the general opinion. Sorry, Wentworth, this isn't of much use, is it?'

'Just tell me how long I've got.'

Bacchus smiled. 'That's what I like to hear. I've got Sam standing by, pen in hand, but a job of this complexity is going to take him a while . . . An hour? That long enough for you to turn yourself into Her Imperial Highness?'

Chapter Thirty-Seven

The Branch men went off, muttering of arrangements to make, plates to develop and arms to twist and promising to return at eleven to pick up the text of the letter. Joe was left behind to supervise Lily. He occupied himself with agitatedly sifting through the Romanov relics, glancing every thirty seconds at the constable who was calmly reading her way through a pile of correspondence. Had she any idea how infuriating she was being?

Finally, she looked up at him. 'Sir? Am I allowed to use my own knowledge? I mean, if Tatiana really were alive, she'd make some mention of the place she's been living in for the last few years, wouldn't she? She might even say something to tempt our Anna ... *her* Anna ... to pack up and go over to find her.'

'Sounds reasonable. What do you know of San Francisco, Wentworth?'

'Not much. But probably more than Anna Petrovna knows. At least I read the popular magazines, sir.'

'Go to it, Wentworth. But keep it brief. You can say too much, you know. We don't want to gild the lily.'

'Then I'm ready to have a shot at it. Will you pass me a sheet of writing paper? And Sam might be instructed to set it out on his page as closely as he can to my effort.'

'He'll be using some American writing paper we've supplied him with.' Sandilands took a sheet from his briefcase. 'Here's one. Use this for practice. The heading should be ... let's call her ... um ... Miss Theresa Robinson, care of the British Consul-General, One Sansome Street, San Francisco. Off you go!'

He knew he was being annoying but he couldn't restrain himself from prowling about the room as she wrote, passing behind her and making her flinch when he tried to sneak a look at her production.

My dearest, darling Anna! he read before she put an arm over it like an embarrassed schoolgirl. A further patrol revealed: *I may not sign my name but – you said it! – 'by my hair shall you know me!' Less lustrous than it once was – the sunshine out here is unkind to complexion and hair!*

After a bit of pen-chewing she followed with: *I had thought you dead. And now word comes to me that you live! And are safe among friends. I have news of my brother and sisters, though I know you will be sad to hear that my parents have succumbed to old age and disease. At least they died together.*

After a few sighs: *I have before me as I write a photograph that has travelled half the world with me. I look at it every day. Taken in the shade of a tree in the summer time. Yalta? 1916? You will remember! You are beside me, gazing with commendable attention at our handsome French master who, I think I remember, is trying to drum the subjunctive into our skulls. Attention? I think there is something more in your look, Anna! I have news of Pierre also.*

'Wentworth, how do you know . . . ?'

'It says so on the back. In pencil in an English clerkly hand. Bacchus? The girls are identified, along with "Pierre Gilliard, Fr. Master".'

'Keep it short, Wentworth. Every single letter is a work of art for our chap, remember.'

She finished with a rush. *If I thought a command would influence you, I would say: 'Come! At once!' But I now beg you, dearest Anna, to come to me and complete my happiness. And here in this delightful place I know I have the means to make yours. Leave that drab and violent continent to its death-throes and sail into the sunshine! We are waiting with our arms outstretched! Silent, upon a peak – in Darien! Your devoted friend, T.*

Joe snatched it from her the moment she had blotted it. 'Good!' he said. 'That would get *me* rushing for the boat!' And, thoughtfully, 'That's a neat bit about her brother. It wasn't in my briefing. Is this a case of "Miss thinks she knows best"? I believe it is. But does it add up? You don't say that he's alive or that he's dead. Just enough to sow doubt. There *are* rumours about – strong ones, especially in Romanov circles – that the whole family was spirited away. And the promise of a warm welcome over the ocean may well be ultimately persuasive when our girl considers the alternative we have on offer for her here in London.'

He took a deep breath and came to a decision. 'Yes! Wentworth, we'll go along with your scenario. If she's convinced by this, Anna Petrovna's reason to stay on plotting mischief over here is removed at a stroke. If only . . . What do you say to appropriating one of those lockets? There's one containing a wisp of the Tsarevich's hair.'

'No, sir. That would be overplaying it. She wouldn't send something so precious across in the post or even the diplomatic bag. Wouldn't feel she needed to. This is Her Imperial Highness writing. Enough for anyone to be told, in her handwriting of course, that she survives. She wouldn't expect to have to supply proof or answer questions. I think you're right – it should be understated . . . no one's impressed by a gilded lily. We should keep it . . . tantalizing.'

'This reference to the French master . . . Assuming too much, do you think?'

'Take a look at the photograph again. Our dark-haired beauty is casting what I'd interpret as a decidedly languishing look at the tutor. Whatever she has on her mind, it's not French grammar. And it's a pretty safe bet anyway. There weren't many men under forty and over fourteen in the lives of these girls at this point and Pierre Gilliard was

359

a well-set-up fellow. Every girl falls in love with her French master. Done it myself.'

'It's a bit of a risk. We'll have to see what Bacchus thinks of it. I think we have time for a little rehearsal.'

Bacchus read the sheet and then read it again. He opened his mouth to comment and closed it. Finally, he said, 'This will do. I note the change of plan. In the Wentworth version the Tsarevich very likely survives also. Another prince saved. That's two in a week. Well done, miss! But what's this here about Darien? Will she be familiar with Keats?'

'I think everyone knows this line . . . the poet's vision of the conquistadors standing on a height above the bay, rendered speechless by their first sight of the Pacific Ocean. I noticed that the girls liked to scatter literary references about.'

'Now, can we get through the final briefing for Miss Wentworth's performance tomorrow morning?' Joe suggested, and without waiting for a response he launched himself into the task. 'The constable presents herself at St Katharine's Square at nine sharp. The princess, fully briefed by then, receives her. With a bit of luck, Anna Petrovna will be lurking behind a door listening in. Now, all Russians like a mystery, I observe. So we offer one. The photograph of the painting, Bacchus? Ah, thank you. Still damp? I'll be careful. You know what you are to say about this first offering, Wentworth?'

'Yes, sir. I suggest that there is a hidden message in it. The grave is empty. There is no attempt to convey butchery, none at all. There are simply – no corpses. The inference the observer is meant to draw is that the family has escaped this burial pit. And gone . . . where?'

'Right. You plant the question and then supply an answer. This is our first slice of realia.'

'Ah. Well, next comes the bully-beef filling. I offer the letter purportedly from Tatiana. The princess remarks that it has been opened. I say – of course! All communications from our consulates are screened and the interesting ones examined. I say that she will realize, as did our secret service, that this is a letter of some importance. It contains a shattering piece of information that the British government is honour-bound to keep from being broadcast. The first thought was to suppress the letter but wiser counsel prevailed in the present circumstances. I say that with heavy emphasis. I hand the letter over and she reads it, exclaiming the while.'

'Yes, remember to leave plenty of reaction time for the princess. Remember that she is Anna Petrovna's anchor in an unsafe world. Our girl will place much faith in her advice.'

'When she's taken this in, I hand over the second envelope containing the tickets to heaven and a British passport in the name of Anna Peterson and say they come with the compliments of the British government who are finding Anna and her activities a bit of a nuisance and would be glad to see the back of her. It's that or a spell in Holloway jail. Finally, I present the second slice of something verifiable: the newspaper report.'

'And bring yourself straight back here. That's a clear order.' He thought for a moment and added: 'Make no attempt to deal face to face with Anna Petrovna. It's our opinion and that of an alienist I've consulted that the woman could be dangerously deranged. Suffering a condition not unlike shell shock. She's primed and ready to explode. She's failed once and that may well have increased the pressure. We know her targets and I, for one, recognize that she may already have begun to associate *you* with the forces that gather protectively about them. Do not put yourself into her path.'

'Sir?' Fanshawe had a question. 'If we're giving this deranged criminal a British passport, what's to stop her turning round and coming straight back into the country when she finds she's been duped?'

'Our border force, Fanshawe. You know their qualities. Her passport will be flagged and she'll be arrested at the port.'

'And that's it. I make my farewells and walk back here,' Lily finished.

'Then we go on watch,' said Bacchus with satisfaction. 'She'll do her packing, and leave. Either she'll go north to Norfolk or south to Southampton. To jail or to freedom. It's her choice.'

Joe raised his eyes to the ceiling. 'No it's not! No more than you would have any choice over the card you picked out of a greasy pack offered to you by a conjurer at the Palace of Varieties, Bacchus.'

'That's it then, sir?' Lily asked.

'Yes. We can all go home and get some rest while Bacchus goes to work with his forger. Seven o'clock start from here tomorrow. Best of luck, chaps! If there's really nothing more you want to check . . . ? No? Then you may dismiss now. Oh, Bacchus! Just a quick word if you wouldn't mind?' He waited until he heard the others' footsteps going down the stairs then closed the door and turned to Bacchus, resting a congratulatory hand briefly on his shoulder. 'I think that went well.'

Bacchus murmured something which might have been agreement.

'What do you think of our chances?'

'Not much. They'd have been better if we hadn't been required to pussyfoot about. In fact, I've got a bad feeling about the whole thing . . . I just hope we can get through the preliminary pantomime without loss of life and reputation. Never underestimate the Russians, sir. We ought to remember: "Russian grain will not grow in foreign ways." We think they've acclimatized, adjusted to western methods, but they haven't.'

'Mmm . . . I'll remember that about the alien corn. Your friend Pushkin, Bacchus?'

362

'No, sir. His friend Shakhovskoy.'

'Ah! I haven't yet had the pleasure. Just one thing – or three. The moustache, James. In view of what's to come, perhaps ... ?'

Bacchus put a finger to the moustache as though surprised to find it still on his upper lip. 'Oh ... Sorry, sir. Left over from the last job. I suppose it does attract attention. I'll get rid of it.'

'And you mention *feeling*, James? Not a recommended activity in your line of work. You are perfectly clear ... ?'

'My orders are precise and either have been executed or are about to be carried out. Commander.'

Joe smiled. The Branch seemed at last to be responding to a firm hand. And there was nothing better than a cry of 'View halloo! Fox in sight!' to get them racing off in the right direction.

'Our target? Our "loose cannon" as the princess calls her?'

'You know as well as I do, sir, there's only one sure method of dealing with those rolling disasters at sea.' He extended a hand and mimed a downwards diving motion. 'Open a gun port and let gravity take care of the rest.'

'Heaven forbid!'

The exclamation drew a hard glance from Bacchus. 'We're in the business of saving lives, sir. The right lives. Sometimes you have to make a trade. We've had our orders from above. And if we refuse them the matter will be ... er ... taken out of our hands and passed to others. The type who don't ask questions. At least this way we still have room for manoeuvre.'

'Yes. We've wangled ourselves one more throw of the dice. It might just come off ... Bacchus, I want one of your men on board that liner to monitor – or if the worst should come to the worst manage – the outcome.'

'I'd thought of that. I've got a ticket. Second class. Cherbourg to New York and back. That should be far enough to know what's what. And I'll go myself. Always wanted to see New York.' He began to take an interest in his well-kept finger nails. 'The constable, sir? Would you like me to manage her outcome as well?'

'You've enough on your plate, man, getting yourself off to the liner. I've made other arrangements for Wentworth.'

Chapter Thirty-Eight

Foxton was all smiles. The princess was all smiles. She even leaned forward and pecked at each of Lily's cheeks in welcome while she held her hands.

'How simply delightful to see you again, my dear Lily! This is not too late – or too early – to join me in a pot of chocolate? I was just about to indulge . . . Good.' She turned to the maid. 'And we'll have French macaroons with that, Katy.'

There was a trace of something . . . roses, Lily thought . . . in the air. The princess had smelled of nothing more than Pear's soap when she approached. So, Lily guessed, it was reasonable to suppose that Anna Petrovna had until a moment ago been in the morning room conferring with Princess Ratziatinsky. Her hostess was in receiving mode but at leisure in a purple Circassian kaftan. Lily's own white linen dress, borrowed at the last minute from her aunt Phyl, would pass muster, she thought. Restrained, unlikely to attract attention.

They chatted of this and that as the maid poured out the chocolate and handed macaroons and shortcake biscuits. When she bobbed and left, the princess's tone became brisk.

'So. You come, the commander tells me, equipped with olive branch, white flag . . . something of that nature?'

Lily laughed. 'It's more of a message in a cleft stick.' She was determined to keep the business light. She had chosen to bring her documents with her in a battered old military messenger's pouch she had been given by her soldier grandfather. 'This bag,' she said with an air of mystery, 'was once the property of the Royal West Surrey Regiment. It carried the news of the relief of the siege of Ladysmith. It is still doing its bit.'

The princess smiled. 'Coming to the relief of besieged ladies?'

'Yes, that. But its main purpose is, as it always was, to serve its country. I know you understand that.'

The princess raised an eyebrow and smiled again. 'Produce your rabbits,' she said.

Lily was pleased to have raised both pencilled eyebrows when she handed over the photograph of the Koptyaki grave.

'But this is . . .'

'Given to me by His Royal Highness. And I am delighted to have it. If there's anything our secret service is good at, it's spotting secrets and decoding messages. One look at this and the interpretation was clear.'

The princess peered more closely at the picture. On the hook, Lily judged. She launched, in a confiding, excited but carrying voice, into Sandilands' invention of Romanov survival. She noted that, by the end of her account, the princess was looking pale and disturbed, thin fingers twisting in the pearls at her throat. 'And all escaped? Is this what your government is thinking?' she murmured. 'The painting had not spoken to me.' She placed the picture on the table at her side, not offering to return it.

Lily dived into the bag again and took out the Californian letter.

'For Anna? But this has been opened,' the princess objected, before correcting herself. 'Ah. Yes, of course . . . it would have been opened.'

She listened carefully to Lily's prepared explanation and nodded her understanding. Unfolding the letter itself, she gasped as the lock of hair became visible. Mastering her emotion, she read the letter and read it again. She held it to the light and examined the watermark. With a quivering hand she extracted a slender skein of hairs from the thick lock and wound it round a finger, tears gathering in her eyes. Then she replaced the letter in its envelope. This also came in for scrutiny.

'We haven't finished yet,' said Lily. 'Here's a news cutting explaining the letter. Perhaps you saw this? Tatiana has been indiscreet, clearly. Distance from the centre of things leads to lack of concentration. Our consul is aware and taking steps. But in San Francisco she remains for the foreseeable future. Last exhibit: a passage to San Francisco for Anna Petrovna.'

Lily talked on, delivering her rehearsed speeches, reacting to the princess's sharp questions when they came. She gave information when she could, admitted ignorance where an answer was outside her brief or her invention. And the moment came for her departure.

'You may keep all these items. Except for the bag I brought them in. My grandfather was badly wounded carrying it between General Buller and Spion Kop,' she said. 'I like to think those are his bloodstains. I would not want to lose it.'

The princess shuddered delicately and gestured to Lily to take it back.

Coming to the end of the exchange, the princess walked to the bell-pull to summon Foxton. Lily was puzzled to see that she did not actually tug hard enough to make contact. A few moments later: 'Foxton? Curse the man! Where can he be? I'll show you out myself.'

At the front door and out of earshot of any listener, the princess grasped Lily's hand and spoke urgently. 'You have done your best. And now it's up to me to do mine. You must understand that our loyalties are like railway lines . . . they are going in the same direction but they never actually converge. Disaster if they did!' She smiled. 'I have many irons in the fire – you know that. I trade with this side and that, trying to keep a balance, but my loyalties are always with my people. And Anna is very dear to me. I would move heaven and earth to protect her and achieve her happiness . . . if that is still possible. I have been making my own quiet arrangements to resolve our problem. But I see I must put on a burst of speed to keep up with Sandilands. He is moving faster than I would have wished.'

Her voice became more sombre. 'I cannot promise I shall succeed. Great hatred runs deep and, once under way, gathers momentum and powers itself. It is not easily diverted from its course. In fact, I know of only one thing strong enough to counter it. An equally great love!' Her face lit up with youthful mischief as she added: 'What was the date of the sailing? So soon! I must make a telephone call to Paris without delay!'

Lily knew she was walking unsteadily, and put it down to euphoria. She took a deep breath of fresh morning air, hitched the leather bag more firmly on to her shoulder, set her eyes on the end of the elegant row of houses and made for the Thames.

It had gone better than she had expected. And faster – hastened by the princess's understanding and anticipation. Passing the conversation anxiously in review, she couldn't recollect a slip. She prepared to entertain Sandilands with her account. There were no taxis about to speed her journey but there was really no hurry and it was only a mile or so from Kensington to Westminster. She had time enough to stroll along down Birdcage Walk on her way back to the Yard. There was nothing more she could do. It was out of her hands and into Bacchus's. The thought brought relief.

She passed Buckingham Palace, and wasted several minutes mingling with the crowd watching the guard change. She was skirting St James's Park when the hairs on the back of her neck gave her warning. By the time she entered Great George Street with the Thames sparkling ahead of her, she was sure she was being followed. One of Bacchus's men? With an unprofessional rush of mischief, Lily decided to flush him out. No shoelace business – these men would scorn such a ploy. The street was relatively empty. He should be easy to spot. She stopped abruptly and looked behind her.

A young woman in a cream linen walking suit was striding out in the opposite direction. Across the road, a nursemaid was pushing a baby in a pram into the park to visit the duck pond. A vicar in a black homburg hat had stopped to shake a rattle and coo to entertain this youngest member of his flock. Two men, walking purposefully, bowler hatted both of them and practically invisible on the London streets, caught her eye. One of these? Lily waited until they were within yards of her and she was sure of receiving an unprepared reaction, then stood in the middle of the pavement and nonchalantly lifted her skirt. She bent over and proceeded to straighten her stocking and adjust her garter. Whichever man she caught staring at her leg she reckoned would be an innocent city gent, the one looking hastily aside at the architecture would be Bacchus's man.

To her confusion, both men stared and hurried by. One uttered a 'Faugh!' of disgust, the other turned and objected: 'I say, miss! This *is* Westminster! The Wellington Barracks are a hundred yards back down the road. You've missed it.' He pointed helpfully.

Lily was still shaking with silent laughter when her arm was seized from behind and clamped tightly to the side of a tall woman striding out towards the Thames. Lily had to scamper along to avoid being swept off her feet, such was the onward rush, the iron grip on her arm.

Cream-coloured linen, no gloves, no handbag. She'd left home in a hurry. But she'd snatched the time to pull on a cloche hat in natural straw. A waft of Attar of Roses confirmed Lily's identification.

'Anna?' she murmured. 'Anna Petrovna, is this you?'

369

Chapter Thirty-Nine

'No. I'm Anna Peterson, my dear, according to my new passport. Thank you for that. And you, I take it, are Lily Wentworth. Constable in the British police force?'

Lily nodded, alarmed but puzzled. The voice was low and well modulated. It had, surprisingly, what Lily could have sworn was a reassuring trace of a Scottish accent. Every time she raised her head to look at her companion the wretched woman looked aside, hiding her profile with the brim of her cloche. The first swift glimpse Lily had had of the stranger's face revealed familiar features and she tried in her mind's eye to link them with the face she'd so fleetingly seen under a frilly lace cap at the Claridges reception.

Could she be sure this was Anna? Lily decided to be certain. 'Before I forget,' she said, 'I have to pass on regards and good wishes from Ethel and Jack.'

'I think you mean Ethel and *Jim*,' the stranger corrected wearily. 'If you mean my young friends in Hogsmire Lane. Do let's stop all this secret service rubbish, shall we? We're not overgrown Boy Scouts. And we haven't much time to set the world to rights. I've been longing to talk to you – I feel I know you, having listened in to your chats with my guardian. Now, thanks to you, I have some exciting shopping and packing to do. You may have advice to offer me on that ... And I'm sure you're looking forward to spending some time with the handsome commander, drinking a celebratory glass of champagne and toasting an absent friend.'

They walked on for a while, Anna relaxing the grip on Lily's arm and slowing her pace. And then: 'Ah! There's Westminster Bridge straight ahead. One of my favourite places in London. Your Wordsworth seems to have liked it. *Earth hath not anything to show more fair* and all that. But then he'd never seen the river Neva flowing in majesty. He'd never seen St Petersburg. In fact he hadn't seen much, your national wordsmith – I cannot call him "poet" – nor had much experience of places or people. To his naive eye, the French Revolution was a wonderful thing along with daisies, peasants and this view of a polluted river lined with grey buildings. Still, it is the best you have to offer so we'll go on to the bridge and watch the Thames flow for a while, shall we?'

To all appearances the best of friends, Lily strolled with Anna Petrovna, self-appointed Nemesis of the royal family and possibly mentally deranged killer, on to the bridge.

'On no account should you confront Anna Petrovna,' Sandilands had told her. But how did you break off a discussion with a friendly girl on the relative merits of Lillywhites and Harrods when it came to buying hot-weather clothes? How did you leave in the middle of a laughing disagreement over the comparative virtues of cotton and celanese knickers? How did you make your excuses when your arm was being clutched in apparent friendship?

They leaned companionably over the waist-high parapet and decided that the current was flowing east.

'There's a tide running and it's going out fast,' remarked Anna, staring into the black water swirling fiercely around the piers. 'It's racing along with the current, you see. Anything falling into the water from here – if it survived being sucked down into that whirlpool – would be swept up and come ashore . . . um . . . round about there.' She pointed. 'The Savoy's back garden. Let's test our theory, shall we?'

Catching Lily completely by surprise, she tore the bag

371

from Lily's shoulder and threw it into the river. Lily squealed and turned on the taller girl, who had reapplied her hold on her right arm, squeezing until it was painful. The only way to attempt to break it was to smash upwards with the left fist at her face and stamp down on her instep at the same moment. Not a difficult manoeuvre. Lily had practised it on bigger and stronger targets. But it would be a desperate move and possibly a noisy one which she'd rather not attempt in a public place with people passing by. A punch in the face would get her out of trouble but she knew that the London bridges were patrolled by beat coppers. Sandilands would not be amused by a report that his plainclothes woman policeman had been arrested for an attack on a Russian aristocrat on Westminster Bridge.

'Why did you do that? It was my grandfather's bag. And very precious to me,' she said, hoping to elicit a response she could understand.

'Inherited goods mean nothing. They weigh one down. There it goes – the sweat, the screams, the bloodstains. The memories. It's not popped back up again . . . it's settling to rot on the river bed. Gone.'

'I haven't much of a past to let go,' said Lily. 'I can't afford to be so cavalier with the little I have.'

'Poor creature.' There was no sympathy in the voice. 'You are upset by the loss of a dirty old bag? I have lost the world. A country. A family. A fortune. A name. All I have left is my life and what is that to anyone? An embarrassment. An anachronism. Even a threat. I've become a danger to Aunt Tizzi and my own people. Time to move on.' Her eyes were drawn in fascination again to the water. 'They tell me this is the most popular spot in London for suicide. One sees why. How those dark depths call one to oblivion!'

She dropped Lily's arm and edged a few paces further on to the bridge. She put her hands on the parapet, leaning dangerously forward to stare into the river.

Lily sidled after her. She recognized suicidal despair in the girl's voice and at last realized why she'd been brought

372

here. Many people killed themselves quietly, dying alone in holes and corners all over London, hugging their unbearable sorrows to their breast. But some – those who seemed to bear a grudge against society – preferred to go with a flourish, screaming out their hatred . . . or their guilt. Lily knew with a chilling certainty that she'd been chosen, lured on to the bridge, to hear the last words, to witness such a death.

'I've stood here before, you know. Many times. Never quite having the courage . . . and always stopped by the same thought. Do you suppose, Lily, that if one were to jump, and . . . natural impulses changed one's mind at the last moment, one could swim to the bank from here?'

Lily prepared to share her suffering and her speculation. She looked down into the water and shuddered. 'It's possible,' she lied. 'You might survive. But of course it would depend on the strength of the undertow and the swimming skill of the jumper. Only a strong swimmer would make it. You'd have to be very certain that you really wanted to die and weren't just calling attention to your own sorrow.' She remembered with a stab of pity that the moody girl at her side was the survivor of rape, slavery and goodness only knew what other horrors. Horrors which, if Sandilands and his psychiatrist had it right, had affected her mind with the destructive force of unremitting shelling.

Alert to the slightest hint of a suicidal move, Lily closed in on Anna. She assessed her chances of preventing a determined dive off the bridge as poor. The girl was taller and stronger; her arms appeared well muscled from weeks of hotel work. And she was as tense as a bowstring.

Lily scanned the bridge. She needed help. This would be a good moment to catch sight of the police patrolman approaching. Not a sign of him. A few tourists wandered from side to side at the far end, chirruping and pointing. Too slow to react . . . useless.

Talk. Calm reason. Understanding. That was her best – her only – tool.

'You've been *half in love with easeful Death*? I can under-stand that. Very well. Let the past go then, Anna,' Lily said. 'But I'm wondering whether you have the same disregard for the future. You have a future. Have you had a chance to consider the offer I left with the princess? Is that what you're doing here? You've chased after me to thank me for handing you a new life and an old friendship?' She was trying for a lighter note in a conversation whose sense she could barely grasp.

'Nonsense! You haven't seen it at all, have you? This let-ter, purportedly from a friend in California, is an elaborate charade! You want to be rid of me.' Her laughter was sharp and scathing. 'Who but the English, sensing a threat to their Establishment, would hold back their secret police killers and send in a single girl armed with a few sheets of paper? This is a parlour game – an entertaining piece of whimsy!'

She took Sam Scrivener's page of meticulous work from her pocket, tore it in two and threw it after the bag into the river. She leaned far over to watch the pieces swirl and dance on the dark surface, drawing a cry of concern from Lily.

'May I expect to see the tickets for the *Hirondelle* fol-low?' she asked, reaching out to take Anna's arm. She was beginning to lose patience with this haughty girl but she would never allow her to jump. She persevered. 'It would be a pity not to see the western ocean. We have a poet I think you must like – a man who died young . . . no older than we are, Anna. Keats had never set eyes on the Pacific . . . was never likely to have the chance . . . but he wrote four lines which would make anyone yearn to do that.'

She murmured them, careful not to allow emotion to take over.

> '. . . *like stout Cortez when with eagle eyes*
> *He star'd at the Pacific – and all his men*

374

Look'd at each other with a wild surmise –
Silent, upon a peak in Darien.

'It's all about eagerness to seize the next experience, to watch the next horizon come into view ... the elation of discovery.'

'Ah, that was you, the line of verse? You have strange skills for a policewoman. The tickets? Entirely appropriate and welcome. Those I shall keep and use. But not for the reason you ascribe to me. Do you think I could be deceived by a clumsy lie? Fools! What an irony. There will be no wild surmise for me on the heights ... no Russian welcoming committee on the quay.'

She turned at last to face Lily directly and spoke with emphasis. 'In San Francisco there are no Romanovs. No Tatiana, no Tsar, no Tsarina, no Tsarevich.'

'How can you be so certain?' Lily's voice was scarcely audible as she at last made sense of the familiar features and the appalling answer struck her. 'Who are you, Anna?'

With a wide gesture, the woman swept off her hat and ruffled her hair with a hand. Hair cut short as a boy's. And not the black hair Lily was expecting. It gleamed and glinted like a cap of bronze around a lovely face in the morning sunshine. Dark eyes looked down at her with the bitter mischief of a Peter Pan.

'I wish I knew! I have been so many people in the last five years I can't be certain. I do know there is one man who will tell me who I am. But I'll remember the manners I used once to have and introduce myself properly, shall I?' The Russian tilted her head in an old-fashioned gesture of greeting. 'You have the honour of addressing the Grand Duchess Tatiana Nikolaevna of the House of Romanov. How do—'

In mid-sentence two rough hands caught Lily off guard. They encircled her wrists and jerked her forward on to a raised knee that knocked the breath from her body. She felt herself being pushed towards and rolled over the broad

375

rim of the parapet as though she were no more substantial than a doll. Thrashing and scrabbling uselessly at the stonework, Lily was held dangling yards above the filthy water that swirled between the arches. One by one, her shoes fell and were sucked down into the whirlpool. Her feet tried for a toehold on the smooth stone facing and found none. Her only link with the world above was the capricious grip of a woman who hated her and all she stood for.

'Nothing to say? Your eyes are begging to know why. Well, listen! It's short. I won't keep you in suspense.' The jibe was accompanied by a burst of laughter which told Lily she could expect no mercy. 'Your prince should have paid with his life for my brother: your king for my father: your queen for my mother. A modest demand; I would have been satisfied with three lives, though the debt is much greater. But you put yourself in my way. Poor, silly creature. They've abandoned you, your handlers. Had you guessed? A sacrificial sop! They'd be relieved if I worked through what they assume to be my murderous rage by killing *you*. They don't care to leave witnesses of their bad behaviour lying about.'

She broke off, and with a disturbing change of mood directed a dazzling smile down into Lily's terrified eyes. 'But I'm not quite that unhinged. And besides, you're lucky, Miss Wentworth. For the best of reasons – the *very* best of reasons – you catch me in a frame of mind which is neither suicidal nor murderous. I'm going to let you off with no more than a cold swim to teach you a lesson . . . you and your meddlesome handler Sandilands.'

She let go Lily's left hand and enjoyed the squeal the abrupt imbalance jerked from her victim's lips. She lunged over and grasped Lily's right arm in a two-handed grip. Lily responded by reaching up and clamping her free left hand about her attacker's wrist. When she dropped, she would at least take this mad girl with her.

'If the master is impregnable, one can always thrash his horse. Believe me, this little punishment will annoy Sandilands almost as much as it annoys you. Take a deep breath! It's quite possible, you say? To swim to the Savoy? Were you telling me the truth? Let's see.'

Lily had heard the blast of a police whistle coming from the southern end of the bridge. A voice called out and the whistle blasted again. Nearer. A second later, a concerned voice called from the north end. This voice was close. Very close.

'Hang on, miss! I'm coming. Hold tight!'

The girl above looked from one side to the other, assessing her situation. With interference approaching fast on each side and her victim like a limpet to her arm, the instinct for self-preservation that had served her so well came again to her aid. She made a swift decision. 'Help! Suicide!' she yelled. 'She's trying to jump! I can't hold on to her any longer! Help me!'

A pounding of feet and two large male hands reached down and grabbed Lily firmly under the armpits. The Russian released her grip with a loud sigh. 'Ouf! Thank you, sir. She *would* do it. Wouldn't listen to *me*! Perhaps you could speak to her?' And then: 'Well, I never! You look like just the fellow to make her account for her sinful behaviour!' Her whoop of amusement was completely spontaneous.

Lily was hauled upwards to the sound of a patter of applause and a few ragged hurrahs from a small crowd hurrying now from all sides to see the drama. She took in the sober black suit, homburg hat and ecclesiastical dog collar of her rescuer. She thought the face above the collar was the finest sight she had ever seen. He looked down at her in concern. Strong arms hoisted her over the parapet, carried her to a nearby bench and set her down. The clergyman sat down alongside, trapping her body against the side of the bench, and put round her shoulders a comforting yet restraining arm.

He launched with clerical confidence into a soothing address to the crowd. 'Officer ... everyone ... no harm done, as you see. A touch of the hysterics but sound in wind and limb, I think we can say. But the mind? Ah, the mind! And the soul?' He shook his handsome head in sorrow.

'She's lucky you were passing, Padré,' someone commented.

'Indeed! I thank God for the guidance He has given me. I *had* intended to take the Tube this morning. But now I shall need to have a quiet word with this poor young thing and explain to her the Almighty's views on her impulse to self-destruction. Do feel free to stay and hear His words . . .'

An invitation guaranteed to start the crowd moving off. But the beat bobby knew his job. Suicide was more than a sin in the Metropolitan district – it was a crime. He advanced officiously on Lily, notebook in hand.

The vicar produced a small bible from his pocket. He took a card from it and passed it to the officer. At the sight of it, the custodian of law and order began energetically to move the remaining spectators on and then, after a certain amount of huffing and puffing and saluting, marched off himself, back down the bridge to the southern bank.

The crowd had gone, leaving Lily eyeing her saviour with suspicion. 'Cor blimey, sir! In that suit and dog collar, you're almost unrecognizable. If you were following me, why did it take you so long to step in?'

'I *was* following you. You seemed to be on such good terms with our friend I thought I'd let you finish your conversation. And, at the *moment critique*, I was mobbed by a crowd of tourists wanting to know how to get to St Paul's. Quite took me by surprise – you were there one second and gone the next! It's some time since I did basic training in shadowing . . . I clearly need a refresher. Should have sent Fanshawe . . . No – perhaps not. I say – you didn't really try to jump, did you?'

'I was going to be her next victim. Murdering, vindictive cow!'

'Mind your language, constable, and stop fussing. All's well, isn't it? I don't think I see you swimming for shore exactly.'

'You were never likely to. Sir, I can't swim!'

The confession was the trigger. Lily could not suppress her body's reaction any longer. She began to shake. After an injudicious exclamation of dismay, Joe tightened his hold on her and began to mutter encouraging formulae into her ear. Lily thought she heard: 'Brace up! Worse things happen at sea. You're quite all right, you know.'

'You saw who she was?' Lily mumbled when she could stop her teeth from rattling together.

He nodded. 'Hard to believe what I saw. Red hair . . . face of an imp . . . Not the girl either of us was expecting. When you've calmed down, perhaps you'll confirm my awful suspicions.' He looked about him swiftly and murmured, 'A corpse dancing? Did we conjure it up? We weren't both hallucinating, I suppose?'

'No. That was the second daughter. But you let her get away.'

He rolled his eyes in disbelief. 'Next time, then, I'll chase after Her Imperious Haughtiness and let you drop,' he said pleasantly. 'Now, if that's enough excitement for one day, *I* could do with a cup of tea. Joe Lyons Corner House suit you? Come on. I think we'd better get our story straight before we report back to the Commissioner.'

Lily stuck out her legs and wiggled her shoeless toes.

Joe groaned. 'Piggy back, then. I'll have to carry you. And just hope the man from the *Mirror* isn't rushing here, camera in hand, attracted by a telephone call from the police box at the other end of the bridge. *Botched suicide plunge. Young woman flees scene in arms of knight-errant vicar.* It wouldn't do either of us any good.'

'No need for heroics, sir. Strong feet. I can get as far as the nearest taxi stand.'

Chapter Forty

Cherbourg, the Hirondelle, *Friday*

He had his introductory speech off pat but he nervously rehearsed it again as he unpacked his luggage. He could hardly present himself at the door of her state room – no, that wouldn't do at all. It would never be his plan to impose himself on her. He thought it best to come across her by chance, standing at the rail staring out to sea perhaps. Yes, that's how it would happen. He wouldn't rush it. He'd time his appearance for dawn on the first morning out from Southampton. Always glad to come through the dark hours, she loved to watch the sun rise, he remembered. She'd be there at the stern. 'I say, miss, for a moment I thought I knew you. Great heavens! I *do* know you!' he'd say in surprise. If she didn't instantly deny it he'd carry on: 'We met quite some time ago, I believe . . . What would you say to taking a turn around the deck and remembering old times?' Or some such rubbish. He acknowledged that he was not honey tongued with women.

He hunted frantically for a razor amongst his things. Must get rid of the beard. She didn't like beards. He'd hastily crammed a selection of necessities into a bag when the telegram from the princess had reached him at his digs in Paris. Could one cross the Atlantic in three shirts? If things went his way, he could always restock in New York. The old girl had thoughtfully sent word that she'd wired a large sum of money to an account in his name at the

Fifth Avenue Bank so he would at least be able to cover emergencies. But how the hell had the old girl known he was in Paris? Had she been tracking him about Europe for the last year? He'd hardly known where he was himself most of the time. And how could she have been aware of the dubious state of his bank balance? None of her business and he resented the interference. All the same . . . and despising himself for sentimentality . . . he'd kept the telegram. It was in the breast pocket of his jacket.

Only a Russian would pay no heed to the conventions of telegraphic communication. No short phrases here and hardly even a stop. It ran on like a conversation. A one-sided conversation. It had been two years since he'd exchanged a word with the princess and here she was ordering him to drop his wandering life and get himself to Cherbourg to board a liner with one day's notice. He wasn't offended – he was amazed and delighted to obey.

With funds running low, he'd only been able to afford a second-class cabin so there might be difficulties. But his cabin was spacious, the fittings elegantly French, and he had a porthole. And at least the clientèle in second seemed to be of a good sort and rather his style. The chap in the cabin next to him . . . quiet, hooded eyes, military bearing, had impressed him with his undemanding overtures. He'd be glad to meet him for a lunchtime drink in the bar later. Calm his nerves and pass the time agreeably until they picked up passengers at Southampton.

Bacchus watched as the passengers came aboard at Southampton, spotting her willowy frame moving lithely up the gangplank. Both targets safely aboard. So far, so good. He stayed at the rail, lazily watching the comings and goings in the port, and sighed with relief and antici-pation when the liner finally upped anchor and began to ease its way out into the Solent, setting its bow to the westering sun. He'd managed to get off a last report for Sandilands, ship to shore, and he could come off watch.

They were in his pocket now. Both of them.

His new friend had confided over a gin or two, after some pretty skilful probing on his part, that he was contemplating reviving an old friendship and was planning a romantic dawn encounter with a young lady in first class. It hadn't been difficult to get him talking. Men always confided more than was wise to a congenial fellow passenger. Particularly men head over ears in love. Bacchus had offered a sympathetic smile, worldly advice and encouragement.

A considerable man. Bacchus liked him. They'd agreed to have dinner together tonight. Poor bloke, though. Had he any idea what a hell-cat ... Bacchus caught himself. If any man was equal to the task of handling the appalling young woman, this was surely the one. He wondered briefly what the attraction was for him. Apart, of course, from the stunning good looks, and the fortune tucked away in an American bank. Bacchus allowed himself a moment's speculation and decided he wasn't, himself, man enough to take her on even with such tempting assets. But he could sense a depth of common sense and a firmness of purpose under this man's charming exterior. He probably had no illusions. And Bacchus had established that, as well as being used to command, the fellow was highly intelligent, fit and active, free of all ties of family and career and spoke several European languages.

Far too good for her.

Bacchus resolved to chuck the girl overboard and recruit the fellow.

At least that's how he'd tell it for Wentworth ... just for the pleasure of seeing her shocked reaction. Bacchus was disconcerted to find that it was the face of the constable his imagination had conjured up for the rehearsal of his tale. He shrugged. If she was still haunting the Yard when he returned, that is. But he wouldn't get involved with this

382

pair of firecrackers unless something quite untoward happened. Sandilands hadn't needed to remind him – no feelings! He'd made his plans.

Bacchus was still lounging at the rail outside his cabin, toying with the idea of a sherry before dinner, when she arrived. He checked his watch. On the move already? She ought to be just getting round to unpacking and having a shower. He noted that she was still wearing the blue linen dress she'd had on when she came aboard. No hat, no gloves, no bag, sandals on her feet. Hardly decent, really. She'd left her stateroom in a hurry and came, not striding with confidence for once, but walking tentatively, looking about her like a wild creature. He realized she was checking the numbers on the cabin doors. Her eyes were wide with . . . could that be fear? Nervousness, at least. Bacchus thought he'd have been looking at her a long time before the word assassin came to mind. Nevertheless, his professional eyes skimmed her slender figure, seeing no evidence of a hidden gun or knife to precipitate his instant intervention. Better stay on watch, though. A killer out on business, as a last gesture, checked his weapon, the hand going towards the pocket or holster a dead giveaway. The very best, and Bacchus counted himself among these, knew they didn't need to. Her hands performed no such manoeuvre – they were twisting together in anxiety.

She found the door she wanted, stared at it for an age, then knocked.

A bad moment. She'd caught her man dressing for dinner and he appeared at the door flustered, a tiny blood-stained patch on his cheek and in his shirtsleeves.

A series of unintelligible exclamations followed. Gasps and snorts and giggles. And then, at last, a few words that Bacchus, by straining his ears, could just make out. Nothing out of the ordinary. Boring stuff.

'You're looking well, Anna.'

'You too. Oh, you've cut your face again!'

'And you've cut your hair . . .'

383

'Oh, it'll grow . . . At least I've managed to get rid of the hair dye.'

'Glad about that. We never did say goodbye, did we?'

'. . . in the middle of a conversation as far as I remember . . .'

'I say, are you sure this is all right?' Bacchus heard him murmur gallantly.

At last Miss Peterson found her courage. She put her hands on his shoulders, pushed him back into the cabin and stepped inside after him. Bacchus heard the door click shut.

Grinning with relief, the Branch man went to dress and prepare himself for a lonely dinner.

Chapter Forty-One

'Well, that's it. For better or worse, they're afloat. The love-birds are out of our reach on the high seas,' Joe announced happily, waving a message sheet at Lily. 'And Bacchus is safely aboard to ensure a good outcome. The admiral's funeral went as well as you could expect and no one else dropped down dead, though a certain young airman made a hasty departure, looking, I'm pleased to say, rather green about the gills. I took your advice. The boot was firmly put in. Well, thank you for coming in on a Sunday morning. Charge it to overtime, won't you? I thought the least I could do was to invite you to come along with me for a final confrontation with the princess. She owes us a maca-roon or two.' He looked at his watch. 'Might even get a sherry.'

'The princess! Do I have to? Honestly, sir, I've seen enough of that double-dealing old fiend for a lifetime. The acting! I still can't believe how she pulled the wool over my eyes. She knew what was going on right from the beginning. She'd always known who Anna was. She sat there and listened to the guff you made me spout without cracking a smile. She actually twisted a lock of dear dead Tatiana's hair around her finger, sighing with emotion.'

Joe grinned. 'And the dear, un-dead girl was hiding in the woodwork at the time. She's awfully good, isn't she, the Princess Rat? I sometimes wonder what she'd get up to if we didn't have Foxton keeping a close eye on her. Oh, yes, she's well aware,' he added in response to a lifted eyebrow. 'We both pretend his presence in the house is for her own safety . . . as indeed it is, of course. Damn dangerous place, London. And she was right to conceal Tatiana's identity. The girl wouldn't have lasted five minutes if it had become known.'

'But wait a minute, sir. What was that you said about lovebirds? *They*, sir? Are you saying Bacchus is watching two people?'

'Yes. What did the princess tell you? About countering a great force of hatred?'

'She spoke of an equally great love, sir.'

'Well there you are, then. A great love. She performed in accordance . . . provided same.'

'But where do you come by such a thing at a moment's notice? They don't have that on the shelves at the Co-op. What's she been up to? Are you saying she's got a bloke lined up and given him marching orders to get aboard ship with that killer? Sir! This can't be right!'

'Oh, I don't know . . . seems to be working. Get your hat on, Wentworth. We'll go together to put the screws on the old girl. Find out what she's stirring up and who it is she's cajoled or bribed to cosy up to our Anna. I shall go on referring to her as Anna. And I want you to do the same. Remember I've got your signature where it counts!'

Foxton was expecting them. 'Her Highness is up in the drawing room where she hopes you will join her in a glass of champagne,' he said, smiling a conspirator's smile.

The champagne was chilling in an ice bucket and a manservant was on hand to uncork, pour and offer dry French biscuits to accompany it. The princess, Joe noted, was looking very chipper. She'd chattered non-stop since they entered the room and seemed to have had a load lifted from her shoulders.

386

When they were all equipped with flutes of Dom Perignon she dismissed the manservant and waited for a moment, examining the bubbles. 'A toast, Commander?'

'Certainly. Let's drink to Stout Cortez! And may our absent friend be struck with the same paralysing wonder when she claps eyes on the Pacific.'

'Ah! Cortez! Now tell me – wasn't he the Spanish gentleman who set the fashion for burning one's boats?' The princess dimpled and twinkled and sipped her champagne in a high good humour.

'Indeed. I understand he set fire to his whole fleet to prevent any retreat from the New World to Europe,' Joe confirmed with relish. 'And a further toast to the equally stout-hearted gentleman who is at present accompanying our adventurer. I'm thinking he too deserves our good wishes. Are you ever going to tell us, Your Highness, who it was who drew the short straw?'

'Villain!' The princess smiled flirtatiously. If she'd had a fan she would have tapped him with it, Joe thought. 'I'm only surprised you haven't worked it out, Commander. He's the best of men and now has what he's long wanted. He would expect our congratulations. It was difficult to decide and I cannot be certain even now that I made the right choice. If I've got it wrong, you're not to tell me!'

Sandilands poured out more champagne and waited.

'Choice?' Lily filled the silence. 'You mean there was more than one candidate for this position?'

'You are surprised? She is rich (I have seen to it that her affairs are in order) and lovely. There are many men in her past who would have died for her. But there was one special man, an officer in the White Army, with whom she fell in love when she was nursing. He is alive. I have kept him in focus all these years, never quite knowing whether I might need to call on him. He lives in France now ... something of a wastrel it has to be said, but free. I do not enjoy playing God and I might well have done the wrong thing. I shall try to think of myself as God's instrument,' she said with a slight smile. 'But I rejected him. A gambler I'm told. I take no risks with the Romanov fortune.'

Sandilands and Wentworth exchanged anxious glances and waited.

'When Tatiana fetched up on that doorstep in Murmansk, your consul identified her correctly – indeed she made no secret of her identity to him. She declared herself and demanded protection. He knew there was a price on all Romanov heads – they were being purged all over Europe. A discreet man who had the good sense to trust no one, not even the secret services available to him, he gave her an alternative identity that she could fit into easily. That of her own dearest friend Anna Petrovna. She had heard of Anna's death with that of her family. It was the consul who whispered in the right ears the story that the body had never been recovered – indeed, it hasn't, but in the chaos that reigns over there, who will ever know? The consul's wife had a bottle of black hair dye and used it to good effect to turn out a convincing Anna. The three of us – the consul, his wife and I – were the only ones who were aware of her identity. From that moment she had become in all our minds, and in her own, Anna Petrovna. And, of course, when she arrived, she slipped easily enough into English life since she spoke English as her first language, albeit with a strong Scottish accent.'

'I think I might have noticed that,' said Lily, drily. 'The last words you hear before you die tend to make an impression.'

'The children all spoke thus. When young they conversed solely with their nannies and the upper servants – all of whom were brought in by the Empress from Edinburgh where, she'd been told, the best English was spoken.' The princess smiled. 'Elocution lessons in later years failed to eradicate it.'

'There was more to her disguise than hair dye and a

Scottish accent,' said Lily. 'The appalling story about the baby and the sufferings in the Siberian village – was that also a deceit?'

The princess shook her head sadly. 'No. That was her own experience. She merely told the truth, but as if it had happened to Anna. She related her hideous tale bit by bit to the captain of the frigate that brought her back to England. Told him everything. She trusted this officer, grew very close to him, I believe. He is the one man who knows the depths of her degradation, is aware of the violence and anger she clutches to her and understands it. The one man who can love her.'

'Except that he can't,' Sandilands objected, remembering. 'Swinburne. Navy man. Married, I understand.'

'Was. No longer, Commander. His wife died of the influenza last year. He immediately took advantage of the reduction in the naval service to resign his commission, to everyone's surprise, and set off into Europe. To travel about and lose himself, no doubt. As men of a certain age with certain concerns do. *I* didn't let him go. I have always taken an interest in the good captain, though he was becoming ever more difficult to track. Luckily he was in France latterly, where they know how to keep a record of visiting foreigners. And if you know the right man at the top of the right department – and I do – you can find someone without much difficulty.'

'And he came when you whistled? He's there with her now, out on the Atlantic? Swinburne?' Sandilands could not disguise his concern.

'Ah! You do not like to think that a fellow English officer has been sacrificed in this way?' The princess's good humour was wearing thin. 'No sacrifice involved, believe me. I say again: he loves her. Now, let's finish the champagne and congratulate ourselves on lives saved and a love affair rekindled.'

* * *

'Just as well we put off that trip to the Riviera, sir. She'd have us tracked every inch of the way,' Lily grumbled as they left.

'Probably. Formidable organization she's running, right in my bailiwick. I sometimes think she regards me as a not entirely to be trusted Steward to the Household. Useful in his way but better kept under close supervision. Not the sort of policing I was offered.'

'Not the kind of policing I'm used to either. And not the kind the Chief Constable exposes his girls to in Lancashire, I bet,' was Lily Wentworth's summary as they entered Sandilands' office.

'I quite agree,' was his easy response. 'You've every right to feel tetchy. Life-threatening situations experienced twice in a week . . . consorting with murderers, spies, fornicators and bogus clergymen – enough to try any girl's nerve. I quite understand. Well, just write up your notes, will you, sign your forms and you can be off. It is the weekend after all. So good of you to agree to stay on. Remember to charge your hours at the overtime rate. Look – I've had a campaign desk put over there for you to use.' He pointed to a small, spindly piece of furniture. 'It's very much in your style, Wentworth. Light and manoeuvrable. And it folds, you see. When you've done with it, you can just leave it out of sight behind the door.'

He whisked off to the ops room without saying goodbye, leaving her alone.

She'd been busy for an hour, recording the last of her comings and goings and filling in claim forms. She lingered for a while, checking her work, expecting him to dash back in at any moment. But he didn't appear.

When she could find nothing further to do, she folded up her desk and propped it against the wall behind the door. Lightly manoeuvred out of sight. Out of mind. She took her papers to his desk and left them in a neat pile. As an afterthought, she found her unopened resignation envelope still under its paperweight and placed it on top of the pile. She waited a little longer, hands shaking, eyes staring but seeing nothing, recognizing this paralysis for what her father had described as the bleak emptiness that follows the high tumult of action. He'd tried once to express it in a painting and at last she understood the emotion behind the leaden greys of his canvas. And this numbness was the forerunner of the moment when feeling returned – the moment when you realized you'd taken a hit. And it hurt like hell.

She went off back down the deserted stairs.

The duty sergeant in the vestibule saw her and called her back just as she reached the door.

'Constable Wentworth? Is that you? Hard to tell when you're not in uniform. Cor! Nearly missed you, sneaking off like that. Got something 'ere for you. Left at the desk.'

He reached under the counter, clanged a foot on a bucket and produced with an amused flourish a lavish and violently coloured bunch of flowers, their dripping wet stalks wrapped in brown paper.

'Lovely, i'n't they? Hope you like orange, miss? Not to everybody's taste, p'raps. My grandfather grows these on his allotment. 'E were pleased to spare them for a lovely lady. Oh, an' the guv said as I was to draw your attention to the card what's in there.'

Lily hurried down to the Embankment before she took the card from its small envelope. In runic script, the words were very clear: *These are called Tiger Lilies, I believe, on account of their striped boldness. I have a good deal of respect for tigers, miss. The most formidable ones I encountered in India hunted as a pair.*

The words ran over on to the back: *Sharpen your claws and present yourself here at 9 on Monday. There's something else you can help me with. JS.*